David Lea_____ *Family Dancing*,
was a finali_____ itics Circle Award
and PEN/F_____ ___ _____ author of *The Lost
Language* _____ n by the BBC;
*Equal Aff_____ hile England
Sleeps*, w_____ ageles Times
Fiction Pr_____ hailed as 'a
literary tr_____ ark Mitchell
he is co-ed_____ *t Stories* and
*Pages Pass_____ Tradition of
Homosex_____ to 1914*, and
co-author _____

A recipient_____ nheim Foundation
fellowship and a fellow_____ National Endowment
from the Arts, Da___ Le____ ives in Italy.

MARTIN BAUMAN

David Leavitt

An *Abacus* Book

Published by Abacus 2001
First published in Great Britain by Little, Brown 2000

Copyright © David Leavitt, 2000

The moral right of the author has been asserted.

A CIP catalogue record for this book
is available from the British Library.

ISBN 0 349 11463 3

Extract from 'The Victor Dog' is reproduced
by kind permission of the James Merrill estate.

Typeset in Sabon by M Rules
Printed and bound in Great Britain by
Clays Ltd, St Ives plc

Abacus
A Division of
Little, Brown and Company (UK)
Brettenham House
Lancaster Place
London WC2E 7EN

For Mark and Tolo

Contents

A little dog revolving round a spindle

Gives rise to harmonies beyond belief,
A cast of stars . . . Is there in Victor's heart
No honey for the vanquished? Art is art.
The life it asks of us is a dog's life.

James Merrill, 'The Victor Dog'

1

Flint's First Principle

I FIRST MET Stanley Flint in the winter of 1980, when I was nineteen. He was between editorial greatnesses then, just fired by the famous magazine but not yet hired by the famous publisher. To earn his keep he traveled from university to university, offering his famous Seminar on the Writing of Fiction, which took place one night a week and lasted for four hours. Wild rumors circulated about this seminar. It was said that at the beginning of the term he made his students write down their deepest, darkest, dirtiest secrets and then read them aloud one by one. It was said that he asked if they would be willing to give up a limb in order to write a line as good as the opening of *A Portrait of the Artist as a Young Man*. It was said that he carried a pistol and shot it off every time a student read what he considered to be a formidable sentence.

As the former fiction editor of *Broadway* magazine, Flint was already notorious in those days, though his notoriety was of an oddly secondary variety, the result of his having published, during his tenure there, the first stories of some writers who had gone on to become great – so great, in fact, that their blazing aureoles shone backwards, as it were, illuminating the face of Flint the Discoverer, Flint the Seer, who had had the acumen not only to recognize genius in its rawest form, but to pluck it from the heap, nurture it, refine it. Soon he had such a reputation that it was claimed he needed only to make a phone call and a writer would have a publishing contract, just like that – until the editor in chief of *Broadway*, either from jealousy or because Flint had had an affair with his secretary (it depended who you asked), fired him. Much media uproar followed but no job offers, and Flint went to work as a teacher, in which role he cultivated an aura of mystic authority; for instance, he was supposed to have gotten one of his students a six-figure advance on the basis of a single paragraph, which was probably the real reason why three hundred people had applied for the fifteen places in his class.

I remember vividly the room in which that seminar took place. Located just off the informal library of one of the dormitories, it was oblong and narrow, with wheezing radiators and shelves full of books too obscure or valueless even to bother cataloguing. On the chalkboard – left over from an Italian class that had met earlier in the day – the conjugation of the verb *mangiare* was written in a tidy hand. Because I had arrived twenty minutes early the first evening, only one other person was seated at the battered oak table, a girl with circular glasses and tight blond braids, her attention scowlingly focused on some German worksheets. Not wanting to appear idle in the presence of such industry, I busied myself arranging my coat and scarves over the back of a chair (it was January), then, pulling a book at random from one of the shelves, sat down and started to read it. The book was called *Dawn to Sunset*, and it had been published in 1904. On the title page its author had written the following inscription: '*Con molto affetto*, from one who spent his formative years 'neath thy Ivied walls, James Egbert Hillman, '89. Sorrento.'

'*Florence!*' the first chapter began.

Flinging open the curtains, Dick Dandridge stared wonderingly at the piazza in morning light. Such a buzz of activity! It was market day, and at little stalls old women in black dresses were selling apples and potatoes. Two horses with caps on their ears pulled a wine cart past the picturesque medieval church. *Italy,* Dick thought, remembering, for a moment, his mother weeping as his ship set sail from New York, and then his adventures in London, in Paris, at the customs house in Chiasso. He could not wait to get out into it, and pulling his nightshirt over his head, he called out to his friend Thornley, 'Get up, slug-a-bed! We've Florence to see!'

A Hispanic girl with bangs and acne on her forehead now came in and took a seat; then a pair of boys, in avid conversation; then a boy with a withered arm whom I recognized from a class on modern poetry the semester before. We saluted each other vaguely. The girl with the braids and the big glasses put away her worksheets.

A conversation started. Over the voices of Dick Dandridge and his friend Thornley, one of the pair of boys said, 'I wasn't on the list, but I'm hoping he'll let me in anyway.' (At this last remark I smiled privately. Though only a sophomore, I *was* on the list.) The boy who had said this, I observed, was handsome, older than I, with wire-rimmed spectacles and a two-day's growth of beard; it pleased me to think that Stanley Flint had preferred my submission to his. And meanwhile every seat but one had been taken; students were sitting on the floor, sitting on their backpacks, leaning against the shelves.

Then Stanley Flint himself strode through the door, and all conversation ceased. There was no mistaking him. Tall and limping, with wild dark hair and a careful, gray-edged beard, he carried a whiff of New York into the room, a scent of steam rising through subway grates which made me shudder with longing. Bearing a wine-colored leather briefcase with brass locks, dressed in a gray suit, striped tie, and fawn trenchcoat that, as he sat down, he took off and flung dramatically over the back of his chair, he seemed the embodiment of all things remote and glamorous, an urban adulthood to which I aspired but had not the slightest idea how to reach. Even his polished cane, even his limp – like everything about Flint, its origins were a source of speculation and wild stories – spoke to me of worldliness and glamour and the illicit.

He did not greet us. Instead, opening his briefcase, he took out a yellow legal pad, a red pencil, and a copy of the list of students he had accepted for the seminar. 'Which one of you is Lopez?' he asked, scanning the list. 'You?' (He was looking at the girl with bangs and bad skin.)

'No, I'm Joyce Mittman,' the girl said.

'Then *you* must be Lopez.' (This time he addressed her neighbor, another Hispanic girl, her hair cut short like a swimmer's.)

'No, I'm Acosta,' the neighbor said.

A low murmur of laughter now circulated – one in which Flint's raspy baritone did not take part. Looking up, he settled his gaze on a tall, elegant young woman in a cowl-neck sweater who was standing in the corner. She was the only other Hispanic in the room.

'Then *you* must be Lopez,' he said triumphantly.

The girl did not smile. 'Did you get my note?' she asked.

'Did you bring the story?' he answered.

She nodded.

'Over here, over here.' Flint tapped the table.

Extracting some pages from her backpack, Lopez walked to the front of the room and handed them over. Flint put on a pair of tortoiseshell half-glasses. He read.

After less than half a minute, he put the pages down.

'No, no, I'm sorry,' he said, giving them back to her. 'This is crap. You will never be a writer. Please leave.'

'But you've only—'

'Please leave.'

Lopez wheezed. A sort of rictus seemed to have seized her – and not only her, but me, the other students, the room itself. In the high tension of the moment, no one moved or made a sound, except for Flint, who scribbled blithely on his legal pad. 'Is something wrong?' he asked.

The question broke the spell, unpalsied poor Lopez, who stuffed the crumpled pages into her backpack and made for the door, slamming it behind her as she left.

'In case you were wondering what happened,' Flint said, continuing to scribble, 'Miss Lopez sent me a note requesting that I look at her story tonight, as she had missed the submission deadline. I agreed to do so. Unfortunately I did not think the story to be worthy.' Gazing up from his pad, he counted with his index finger. 'And now I see that there are twenty – twenty-two people in this room. As I recall I selected only fifteen students for the class. I would appreciate it if those of you whose names were not on the list would please leave now, quietly, and without creating a spectacle of the sort that we have just witnessed from Miss Lopez.'

Several people bolted. Again Flint counted. Nineteen of us remained.

'I should tell you now,' Flint said, 'that the stories you submitted, to a one, were shit, though those written by the fifteen of you whom I selected at least showed conviction – a wisp of truth here or there. As for the rest, you are courageous to have stuck it out, I'll give you that, and as courage is the one virtue every fiction writer must possess in spades, I shall let you stay – that is, if you still feel inclined after I tell you what I expect of you.'

Then he stood and began to speak. He spoke for two hours.

So began life with Stanley Flint. I'm sorry to say I don't remember much of what he said that evening, though I do retain a general impression of being stirred, even awed; he was a marvelous raconteur, and could keep us rapt all evening with his monologues, which often ranged far afield from the topic at hand. Indeed, today I regret that unlike the girl with the braids – her name, I soon learned, was Baylor – I never took notes during class. Otherwise I'd have before me a detailed record of what Flint had to tell us those nights, rather than merely the memory of a vague effulgence out of the haze of which an aphorism occasionally emerges, fresh and entire. For instance: 'The greatest sin you can commit as a writer is to put yourself in a position of moral superiority to your characters.' (Though I have never ceased to trumpet this rule, I have often broken it.) Or: 'People forgive genius everything except success.' Or: 'Remember that when you ask someone to read a story you've written, you're asking that person to give you a piece of his life. Minutes – hours – of his life.' (The gist of this idea was expressed by 'Flint's first principle,' of which Flint's first principle was exemplary: 'Get on with it!')

It was all a great change from the only other writing class I'd ever taken, a summer poetry workshop sponsored by the Seattle junior college – a remnant of sixties idealism, all pine trees and octagons – where my mother had once gone to hear lectures on Proust. Of this workshop (the word in itself is revealing) I was the only male member. Our teacher, a young woman whose watery blond hair reached nearly to her knees, imparted to the proceedings the mildewy perfume of group therapy, at once confessional and pious. Often class was held outdoors, on a lawn spattered with pine needles, which is perhaps why my memory has subsequently condensed that entire series of afternoons into the singular image of one of my classmates, a heavy girl with red spectacle-welts on her nose, standing before us in the sunlight and reading a poem of which only one line – 'the yellow flows from me, a river' – remains, the words themselves flowing from her sad mouth in a repetitive drone, like a river without source or end.

Flint's seminar, to say the least, had a different rhythm. It worked like this: at the beginning of each session a student would be asked to read aloud from his or her work. The student would then read one sentence. If Flint liked the sentence, the students would be allowed to continue; if he did not, however – and this was much more common – the student would be cut off, shut up, sent to the corner. A torrent of eloquence would follow, the ineffectuality of this slight undergraduate effort providing an occasion for Flint to hold forth dazzlingly, and about anything at all. His most common complaint was that the sentence amounted to 'baby talk' or 'throat-clearing' – this latter accusation almost invariably followed by the invocation 'Remember Flint's first principle!' and from us, the responsorial chant, 'Get on with it!'

Soon we understood that Flint loathed 'boyfriend stories,' stories in which the protagonist was a writer, stories set in restaurants or cocktail lounges. To cocktail lounges he showed a particular aversion: any story set in a cocktail lounge would provoke from him a wail of lamentation, delivered in a voice both stentorian and grave, a sermonizer's voice, for the truth was, there was something deeply ministerial about Flint. Meanwhile the student whose timid words had provoked this outpouring would have no choice but to sit and percolate, humiliated, occasionally letting out little gasps of self-defense, which Flint would immediately quash. An atmosphere of hyperventilation ensued. The windows steamed. Those Flint had maligned stared at him, choking on the sentences in which, a moment earlier, they had taken such pride, and which he was now shoving back down their throats.

Yet when, on occasion, he did like a sentence – or even more rarely, when he allowed a student to move from the first sentence to the second, or from the second to the third – it was as if a window had been thrown open, admitting a breath of air into the churning humidity of that room, and yet a breath that would cool the face of the chosen student only, bathing him or her in the delightful breeze of laudation, while outside its influence the rest of us sweltered, wiping our noses, mopping our brows. Sometimes he even let his favorites – of whom Baylor, the girl with the braids, soon became the exemplar – read a story all the way to the end. On these occasions the extravagance of Flint's praise more than matched the barbarity of his deprecation. Not content merely to pay homage, he would seem actually to bow down before the author, assuming the humble posture of a supplicant. 'I'm honored,' he'd say, 'I'm moved,' while the student in question glanced away, embarrassed. We all knew that his adulation, at such moments, was over the top – a reflection, perhaps, of the depth to which his passions ran, or else part of a strategy intended to make us feel as if his approval were something on which our very lives depended.

Still, he was nothing if not consistent. Whether delivering tirade or paean, he never wavered from his literary ethos, at the core of which lay the belief that all human experiences, no matter how different they might seem on the surface, shared a common grounding. This theme ('Flint's second principle') he trumpeted at every opportunity. To perceive something one had gone through as particular or special, he kept telling us, was to commit not merely an error, but a sin against art. On the other hand, by admitting the commonality that binds us all, not only might we win from readers the precious tremor of empathy that precedes faith, we might also near, as we could from no other direction, that mercurial yet unwavering goal: the truth.

In retrospect, I wonder at my ability not only to survive, but to thrive under such circumstances. Twenty years later I'm more sensitive rather than less, more cowardly, less likely to consider the ordeal of Flint's criticism worth enduring. I feel sympathetic toward poor Lopez in a way that I didn't then. Also, so many people have studied with Flint since 1980 that by now his detractors far outnumber his supporters, among whom – with some reservations – I count myself. According to these detractors, Flint was nothing but a bully, a petty dictator, his classes the ritual induction ceremonies of the cult over which he presided, like a fat little demigod. For what, after all, was this alternation of upbraiding with intemperate homage that he practiced, if not the very essence of brainwashing? Yes, to his detractors Flint would never be more than a mountebank, a literary equivalent of Werner Erhard, the self-help guru who in the late seventies stripped his would-be disciples of their wristwatches and forbade them to go to the bathroom. Nor can I deny the legitimacy of their complaints, for he did all the things of which they accuse him. And yet – how else to say it? – he was great. And if greatness, these days, arouses suspicion, if not outright hostility, simply by making itself felt, perhaps this is because great men and women are rarely nice, and often capricious; or because something in the very nature of democracy chafes at the idea of too much greatness residing within a single human frame, instead of being placed at the center of the arena to be fought over; or because greatness demands of us that we reconsider, and possibly revise, the very terms according to which we define our humanity – a task from which mediocrity, by its very nature, cowers. His detractors are right to describe Stanley Flint as the leader of a cult. They are wrong in assuming that it was a cult of personality. If Flint was a missionary, then literature was his deity. 'You'll never meet anyone who takes writing more seriously than I do,' he told me once. He was right. I never have. Of himself, on the other hand, I am convinced that he thought very little.

This became more and more obvious as the semester proceeded. The third week, for instance, he arrived in class red-faced and winded, wearing black boots and a Heathcliffish cape. 'Children,' he said, limping to the table and opening his briefcase, 'I have a special treat for you tonight,' then went on to explain that he had just received some pages from the novel on which Leonard Trask – the great writer he had discovered a decade ago, when Trask was still a mineworker in Montana – had been at work for the past ten years. And these pages, for our delight as well as our edification, he was now going to read aloud to us; a rare privilege, as even Trask's publisher had not yet seen them.

I remember wondering, that night, at Flint's cape. Certainly it contributed to the element of theatricality that underlay his performance, a quality of spectacle with which Flint invested all his readings, but particularly those of the writers he had discovered, or whose work he revered. Diction precise, voice rapturous, he offered us Trask's finely tuned sentences as if each were a delicacy, a slice of white truffle, or a toast point spread with caviar. Indeed, so sumptuous was his delivery that today I recall nothing of the reading itself. Instead it is only the voice of the caped orator that resonates, a voice so charismatic that it seemed to eclipse everything around it: our faces, the snow outside the window, even the novel-forever-in-progress that had occasioned it.

Another recollection: one particularly cold, blizzardy night, Flint brought in a copy of some literary quarterly – I forget which one – and thrust it in front of our faces. 'Do you know this magazine?' he asked, pointing at the matte white cover, which was already smudged with fingerprint-shaped patches of *New York Times* ink.

We did not.

'I'm going to read you a story I've had occasion to see here recently,' Flint went on, 'because I want to know, honestly, what you think of it.' And he began to read. One sentence, two sentences. He stopped. 'No, no,' he said, shaking his head. 'All wrong. No life. Take this as a lesson, children. The language is being mangled, not caressed. And this sort of thing appears all the time in our better literary journals.'

We stayed silent. Clearing his throat, he read another sentence – and stopped again. 'You see?' he said. 'It is in your eyes. The story has failed to captivate. It has failed to seduce. I wrote this,' he added casually, slipping the magazine back into his briefcase as a rattle of surprise passed through the room. For up until that moment, we had not known that Flint himself was a writer.

The next morning, I looked up his name in the periodicals index at the library. It turned out that he had published a dozen stories over the past decade, all of them in obscure journals with tiny print runs, none in the great organs of culture in which the work of his disciples regularly appeared. Of the stories themselves – all of which I dug out and read – I remember few details. Most of them were not even stories, so much as brief bits of language torture, congested, constipated even, and redolent of some long and futile labor – as if the sentences had been subjected to such anguished revision, worked over so many times, that they had finally expired from the effort. Then, for the first time, I felt that I understood Stanley Flint. Far from some disinterested nurturer, he was a literary Tantalus, from whose dry and reaching lips that flow of eloquence, a single taste of which would have satiated him, forever bent away. Yes, his was the cruel position of the high priest who finds himself envying the very God it is his sacred duty to cultivate; and yet who can say whether this envy is not itself intended to be the ultimate test of his faith?

Although in memory those hours I spent under Flint's tutelage have now bloated to the point that they seem to obliterate everything else I did and thought that semester, the truth is that every day except Wednesday (when the seminar met) I was leading the typically desultory life of the undergraduate, in which Flint played no part; that is to say, I went to class, I studied, I brooded over futile crushes, I ate my dinners and breakfasts in the dining hall, I had friends. Never in my life have I had so many friends. Lately I've come to believe that the process of growing older is essentially one of ruthless and continual editing, so that the novel of one's experience – at nineteen a huge and undisciplined mess, heavily annotated, the pages out of sequence – will by forty have resolved itself into a fairly conventional tale of provincial life, and by sixty be reduced to one of those incisive, 'minimalist' works in which irony and wordplay displace 'plot' (a word I put in quotation marks because Flint loathed it). Thus at thirty-eight I travel in a comparatively restricted circle. At nineteen, on the other hand, I had dozens of friends, and more than that, I looked upon every one of them as a potential intimate.

Occasionally, during those abundant days, I would run into my classmates from Flint's seminar. Mittman was one of the servers in my dining hall – she'd barely nod at me as she spooned eggs Florentine (hard-boiled eggs with spinach, and not Florentine at all) onto my plate. Baylor and I were taking the same big lecture course on the art of the Italian Renaissance. We used to encounter each other in the dimly lit gallery wherein were hung reproductions of the paintings and sculptures the titles and locations of which we were supposed to memorize for our midterm. In the gloomy silence she'd sometimes cast me a conspiratorial glance, as if we were members of one of the secret societies that flourished on the campus.

Once, at an informational meeting about an internship at a New York publishing house for which I wanted to apply, I ran into Lopez. Legs crossed, dressed as before in a sleek cowlneck sweater, she sat across the table from me and took notes, her face a study of elegant composure. Yet when I smiled at her, she turned away, refusing so much as to meet my glance.

Still, despite all this activity, Wednesday nights remained the epicenter of my life that semester, the black hole into which all the other days and nights collapsed. In part this was due to anxiety. The term was nearly half over, and I still hadn't managed to get past the first sentence with Flint. 'Bauman, Bauman, Bauman,' he'd wail whenever I started to read, and cover his head with his hands. It seemed I was making the same mistake over and over: I kept trying to write about my mother, who was at that time undergoing radiation therapy treatments for cancer, and I couldn't get it right. Every sentence had to do with lumps: '"Feel my lumps," my mother says to my father' is one example.

'You're playing for sympathy,' Flint would tell me whenever I read these sentences. 'You want us to feel sorry for you. See? *We don't.*'

Finally I decided to change my tactics. I'd recently read an article about a couple called Bo and Peep, who would later become the founders of the notorious Heaven's Gate cult. At the time, however, they were just another pair of late-seventies lunatics, wandering through the Midwest and soliciting disciples to go with them to some spot in the desert where a spaceship was supposed to pick them up. In their rather pathetic (and surprisingly successful) efforts to enlist followers, I sensed the possibility of a story, the heroine of which would be my oldest aunt, Lily, who shocks her family by deciding to run off with Bo and Peep, whom I renamed FeeFi and FoFum. Lily, already in her eighties by this time, and living in a Florida retirement community, I called Bessie, and repatriated to the Brooklyn of her youth.

That Wednesday I hoped Flint wouldn't call on me. I didn't think I was ready yet. Also, I had a good feeling about the story and wanted to wait until it was finished before I shared it. As it turned out, however, I had nothing to worry about, for when Flint stormed into class – late, for the first time all semester, and clutching a mass of documents in his fist – it was obvious that something momentous (and probably terrible) had occurred. 'I'm sorry to have kept you waiting,' he said, throwing off his coat. 'I don't know if you've heard what's happened . . .'

We said nothing. Clearly no one had.

'Children, I arrived this evening on the campus of your great university, full of beans, eager to see every one of you,' he continued. 'Little did I imagine that upon stepping into my office I would be confronted with this' – he indicated the documents – 'a situation the likes of which, in my wildest dreams, I could never have imagined. I'm deeply bereaved. I'm also outraged. Especially after last week, when Baylor delighted us so much with her marvelous story . . .'

Again, silence. Sitting down, he thrust a heavy hand through his dark hair. 'And to think that just a few hours ago . . . And now this *horror*, this sickening *slander* . . .'

'What happened?' Mittman asked meekly.

It turned out that Lopez – the same Lopez whose work he had so efficiently decimated the first night of class, and whom I had only a few days ago encountered at the internship meeting – had lodged a formal complaint against him, of which he had been apprised only that evening. Her affidavit, phrased in the acid, impersonal language of lawsuits, he now read aloud, holding it away from his face as if it were literally noxious. My impression was that more than anything else, the writing itself wounded him, for what was this affidavit but that story that most offended his delicate sensibilities, the story that lied, that put itself in a position of moral superiority to its characters, that failed to recognize the commonality of the human condition: in short, the very story Lopez had handed him our first evening, and that he was now finding himself obliged – bullied, even – to read through to the end?

Alas, the bullying worked. For the moment, at least, Lopez triumphed. According to her affidavit, Flint had glanced first at Mittman, then at Acosta, then at her, and said, 'You wet-backs all look alike to me.'

'A gross libel!' he shouted now, throwing down the pages. 'I never said such a thing!' Mittman affirmed that he had not. Acosta seconded. 'How can literature survive in such an atmosphere? Ah, children, how numerous are the enemies of the imagination – and in what guises of piety they clothe themselves! The literal is never the truth. Take this down. The literal blinds us. The facts *do not speak.*'

He wiped his eyes. He looked – this man who craved only the purest water – as if he had just been forced to swallow a gallon of bile. 'To make such an accusation against me – *me,* of all people,' he went on, 'I, who have always been the great-est advocate of tolerance, who has suffered himself bigotry the likes of which, children, I pray you shall never know! Anyone could tell you that. I was in Selma, for God's sake. I was *arrested* in Selma. The record proves it. I published the first story by a black woman ever to appear in *Broadway*, and it was a hell of a struggle to get it through. And that woman was Nancy Coleridge. She was on welfare. In Cincinnati, on wel-fare. And now look at her – they say she may get the Nobel Prize, for Christ's sake! This complaint of Miss Lopez's, this is not a crime against me personally, this is not about me personally, this is a crime against art. For what has she done but use language – our most precious asset – to level a blow at freedom?'

Someone lit a cigarette. The boy with the spectacles offered to fetch Flint a cocktail from his room. He refused.

Needless to say, no one read that night. Instead Flint talked. He talked and talked. First he said he was going to resign. Then he swore he would never again set foot on the campus of our university. We pleaded with him to reconsider. We offered to write letters, to start a petition. He kept shaking his head. I think he rather enjoyed being the object of our entreaties. Finally he thanked and dismissed us, promising to mull the situation over before making a final decision. For the first and last time all term, the seminar let out early.

The process by which all of this was resolved – of which I learned the details only several months later – was as follows: after class that evening, Mittman and Acosta paid an unannounced visit to Lopez in her dormitory, dismissing her roommate peremptorily. Behind locked doors, the three of them then spoke heatedly for several hours, emerging, according to a witness, only around sunrise, arm in arm, tears in their eyes: a photo op for sisterhood. That morning, accompanied by her new friends, Lopez officially withdrew her complaint against Stanley Flint.

The next week he was back, as volatile and jubilant as ever. No allusion was made to the black events of the previous Wednesday. For several sessions he oscillated in his usual way between approbation and decimation, while I, uncalled upon, labored privately at my story about Aunt Lily. Progress was slow; by spring break I still hadn't finished. Instead of going home to California I decided to stay on campus, where every afternoon I holed up in the rear smoking section of the undergraduate library. Most of my companions there were lesbians, some with rings in their noses, all followers of one or another of the fashionable theorists of the moment, and at work on long essays or theses. To my left Gretchen, a deconstruction-ist, wrote about Jane Austen; to my right Schuyler, a Lacanian feminist, toiled away on Melanie Klein. I ground out my story.

Spring break ended. Classmates I didn't like returned, bronzed and fit after vacations in Florida, while the lesbians, their skin library-pallid, smoked and wrote and ignored them. I finished my story, then stayed up most of Tuesday night typing, so that I could bring it to class the next evening.

It was now April – the sort of April we see less and less these days, during which winter, like an obstinate old tenant, refuses to leave, even as spring tries over and over again to evict her. No sooner would tiny buds have appeared on the trees than a biting wind would have whipped up, shriveling these nubs of life before they could flower. Or I'd be sunning one day with my friends on the lawn in front of the library, when suddenly rain would start to fall, and within a few hours a blizzard would blanket the fresh grass with snow. A perpetual sludge of muddy ice made the flagstones treacher-ous. The night I read aloud for the seminar, because I had on the wrong shoes, I slipped on the way, tearing a hole in the knee of my jeans. My eastern classmates, all of whom owned more appropriate footwear, laughed at me when I entered the seminar room. Every sign for success seemed inauspicious.

Then Flint limped into class with his briefcase, his smell of subways. 'Good to see you all again,' he said gruffly, unwind-ing his long cashmere scarf in a way that meant business. No preludes, no reading from newly received galleys. 'Well, who are we going to hear from tonight?'

I raised my hand.

'All right, Bauman. Wow us.'

He sat back. Baylor crossed her arms and stared at me.

'Aunt Bessie was thirty when my father was born,' I read, 'the first son at last after nine daughters.'

I paused, taking it for granted, after so many failed efforts, that Flint would now interrupt me, shake his head, mutter, 'Bauman, Bauman, Bauman.'

Instead he said, 'Go on.'

I looked up. My heart began to race.

'His birth was a relief to my grandparents,' I read, 'who could finally stop conceiving.'

He smiled. 'Go on.'

I went on. I read the entire story – all thirty-five pages. It took almost an hour. By the time I'd finished rain had started outside, and Flint was still smiling.

'Who'd have ever thought,' he said, 'that something like this would come from Bauman?'

I think I almost fainted. It was as if, with a single gesture, Flint had swept away winter. Suddenly I danced in a spring glade. His words flowed around and over and through me. I caught nothing of their meaning. Instead (as I am told is the case with dogs) it was the *cadences* of his approval, the *intonations* of his praise, that warmed and restored me.

From that evening on, I was his favorite; and not merely *a* favorite, but the favorite among favorites. Like the snow itself, my anxiety melted and was gone. It was as if, having written such a story, I'd been absolved (at least by myself) of that necessity to win Flint over that had driven me since the beginning of the term. Freed from pressure, I came to class laughing, and took always took the seat directly to his left.

Now, I think, is the moment to make certain confessions regarding my character, then and now. For all my awkwardness as a young man, my timidity, that tendency to feel ill at ease among strangers which had made me so shy the first night of Flint's seminar, I was (and am) both ambitious and competitive. What I craved, more than anything else, was success, a word that in my mind I took to be synonymous with 'approval.' The origins of this misapprehension I shall explore in greater detail later on. Suffice it to say, for now, that as early as my freshman year, I had a reputation among my peers for being both arrogant and opportunistic: a reputation, moreover, which, though the natural result of my loud and occasionally obnoxious comportment, could not have been more at odds with the image that I cultivated of myself, as sincere, generous, and above all guileless. I didn't recognize, in other words, the degree to which my desire to please dictated not only my conduct, but the very approach I took to writing, which even then I considered my métier. Thus you may recall that earlier, when describing the process by which I came to write the story with which I eventually won Stanley Flint's heart, I said, without even being conscious of it, that at a certain point I decided to 'change my tactics.' Tactics, more than I care to admit today, dictated my decision to write that particular story. Above all else, I wanted to please my teacher. I was a revolting example of the 'teacher's pet.'

I must have been unbearable. For instance, a few weeks after my triumph with Flint, I was reading aloud from a new story, a slapdash thing that I considered to be extremely funny – so funny that halfway through I broke into a fit of debilitating laughter. 'I'm sorry,' I spluttered, putting down my pages.

No one else was laughing. 'It's all right,' Flint said coolly. 'I always enjoy the spectacle of a writer amusing himself.' (It is a testament to my denseness that I took this remark as a compliment.)

Shortly after this episode he assigned us one of his rare in-class exercises: each of us was to write a one-sentence description of someone else in the room, then read it aloud, after which the rest of us would try to guess who it was that was being described. I have no memory of what I wrote myself that night. What I do recall is that Mittman described a very beautiful girl named Thompson (with Flint we were all on a last-name basis) as 'silvery'; also, that the boy with the wire-rimmed spectacles, when his turn came, described someone as being 'ready to pounce on a sure thing.' At first I couldn't imagine to whom he was referring, until Baylor said, 'That's Bauman.' A murmur of concurrence followed. 'Bauman,' the choristers repeated. And Flint agreed: 'No doubt about it. Bauman.'

Ready to pounce on a sure thing. When I was a child the boys at my bus stop used to call out 'Faggot!' as I approached in the morning with my lunch box. Just as they intuited from my behavior – in particular, from the ways I interacted with them – a facet of my identity of which I myself was still unconscious, so the boy with the spectacles, with that uncanny prescience of peers, had detected a strain of ruthlessness in my character that would later blossom into fanatical professionalism, but remained for the moment, as it were, latent, unbudded. For I had a lot invested, in those years, in an idea of myself as innocent and goodhearted; nor was I far off the mark, since the truth is, ruthlessness of the sort I displayed can *derive* from innocence and goodheartedness; specifically, the innocent, goodhearted craving of the child for adult approval.

The boy with the spectacles attracted and scared me. I'm sorry to say that today I don't remember his name, even though I often thought about him then, in particular about the way his chest hair – the color of champagne – seemed literally to bubble out of the collar of his sweater. A few years later I ran into him in New York, and he told me almost boastfully that after class that first night Flint had approached him to find out where on campus he might go to get some 'pussy.' That was the word he used: 'pussy.' Our conversation left me with the impression that between him and Flint there had developed one of those buddyish intimacies to which the joint pursuit of women lends an erotic edge. I pictured them prowling the campus like male dogs who have picked up the scent of a female in heat, an image the contemplation of which left me feeling emasculated, excluded, and faintly aroused.

I suppose now that I was a little in love with Flint. And why shouldn't I have been? He was a good-looking man, lean and surly, with hands like broken-in leather gloves. Nor did his reputation as a womanizer in any way detract from the effect he had on me. On the contrary, it served only to intensify my idea of him as an avatar of masculine virility. For what I wanted from Flint, I told myself, wasn't so much sex as permission – to write, to think of myself as a writer. Today I recognize the degree to which this need for his approbation encoded a desire I had heretofore never admitted: the desire for men – and more specifically, for older, fatherly men who *didn't desire me*. (About this desire I felt a sense of shame that persisted even after I had come out, leading me to pretend that I was attracted to 'nice' boys my own age, instead of the burly men in their thirties and forties who figured in my daydreams.) A long time later, when I was living with Eli Aronson, and having always to come up with new sexual fantasies by means of which I could maintain the façade of mutual lust upon which our relationship depended, I started for the first time to have explicitly sexual thoughts about my former teacher. Giving Eli a blowjob in his loft on Elizabeth Street, I'd find myself back in my college dorm room. It would be late at night – Wednesday night – and someone would be knocking at the door. I'd answer. 'Bauman, Bauman,' Flint would say, 'I'm desperate. I can't find any pussy.' And I would invite him in, sit him down on the bed (he would require help with his bad leg), undo his pants and take his penis – long, I imagined, and not terribly hard, though ruddy – into my mouth . . .

What was exciting to me about this fantasy (and what made it one of the ones, in those years, on which I could count even when all else failed to carry me through the bouts of fretful lovemaking on which Eli and I so perversely staked our happiness) was the fact that in it, Flint showed no sexual interest whatsoever in me. Instead I was only a last-ditch alternative, a cavity into which he might pour his overarching need for that realm of feminine receptivity to which the boy with the spectacles had alluded when he'd used the word 'pussy.' 'Help me out, Bauman,' Flint would say in this fantasy: never 'I want you' or 'I love you.' That would have spoiled everything. Indeed, if someone had told me that Flint was secretly homosexual, or that he was in love with one of the boys in the class, I think I would have lost all respect (not to mention desire) for him, instead of living, as I did, for the day when he might let me call him mentor.

As for his real life – his life in New York – I knew almost nothing. That he was married and had several children, one a sophomore at my university, I had divined from casual references he'd made during class. The names of these children, however, he never shared, just as he refused to give us (or anyone) his home address and phone number. Like many great and neurotic men, he had a persecution complex, and feared lest some madman – probably a writer whose stories he had refused to publish in *Broadway* – should track him down and shoot him in his bed.

Even murkier were the details of his early years. For example, though it was assumed from a certain lilt in his accent that he was Southern, no one I asked seemed to have any idea where exactly he'd grown up, where (or whether) he'd gone to college. Baylor said she'd heard that 'Stanley Flint' was not his real name, while Thompson, who had connections in the magazine world, claimed to have it on authority that he'd done time in prison. I wasn't sure whether I believed any of this; nor, if truth be told, did the details of his youth interest me nearly as much as the mystery of how he spent all the days of the week that weren't Wednesday, those days when he tarried in realms of sophistication to which, I felt certain, he was habituated, and which I longed to know. Unfortunately, about these points he was equally unforthcoming – not only, I suspect, because he wanted to protect his privacy, but because his enthusiasm for writing itself rendered all other aspects of the literary life, in his mind, superfluous. Thus he might casually mention having run into Susan Sontag 'at a party,' but only as a way of introducing some trenchant observation about Sontag's work – an observation the most basic rudiments of which I would fail to take in, so awed was I by the very idea of a party at which Susan Sontag would be a guest. Or he might tell us that he'd been at dinner with a young writer named Liza Perlman, the daughter of the literary agent Sada Perlman, who seemed to represent all his favorites. Though only twenty, she had just published her first novel, *Midnight Snacks*. 'Look at this,' Flint would taunt, thrusting in our faces the book's backside, from which Liza's benign, oddly asymmetrical face, framed by red hair, stared out. 'A junior in college, and already she has a book out. It makes you jealous, doesn't it? But could *you* do better?'

The fact was, I had no idea if I could do better. Indeed, so dazzled was I by Liza Perlman's public image (and what was that photo on the back of the book but a literal public image?) that I barely registered her reality as a human being with whom I might someday compete. Though later she would become an intimate fixture of my life, Liza existed for me in those days less as a person than as a sort of fleshly emanation of that city in which she had gone to dinner with Stanley Flint, and in which I, too, hoped someday to live; indeed, had hoped to live ever since the summer my mother had taken my sister and me to spend two days at the St Moritz Hotel, two days during which we did only the usual tourist things – shopped, and went to Broadway shows, and ate lunch at

Rumpelmayer's, where a waitress, when I asked for more water, snapped, 'You've had your quota.' And yet even this glimpse of New York had been enough to provoke in me a hunger for the city that lasted the next twenty years.

'And another hundred people just got off of the train,' Marta (in the guise of my sister) sang in a community theater production of *Company* to which I went that autumn. It was curious: watching her from the audience, I wanted to *be* one of those hundred people, for even then the city's famed and pitiless indifference to new arrivals appealed to me at least as much as the array of beguilements, sexual and cultural, with which it enticed – movies and plays, lovers and restaurants, that whole landscape of anonymous distraction through which I saw myself wandering, not so much invisible as unrecognized, a hurtling atom in some charged and fluid field of possibility.

That night I began nurturing a dream of the adulthood I would have in New York, a dream in which I lived on a high floor of a new skyscraper, in a perfectly round apartment the entirety of which was taken up by a circular mattress covered with pillows, and from the cushioned heights of which I might look out, each evening, at the brilliant light show that somehow I possessed even as it possessed me, along with Stanley Flint and Liza Perlman and all its other denizens. Denizens, not citizens: already I was thinking of New York as a place to which I was doomed. And as it turned out, I wasn't far off the mark. 'It's ruined me for anyplace else,' I used to tell people in those years when I really did live in a high-rise (albeit not in a round room), the years when I hardly stepped off the island of Manhattan, and felt sorry for anyone who had the misfortune to live anywhere else (especially – because the most vivid horror is always that nearest to home – in Brooklyn or Queens). I couldn't imagine that a day would come when I'd view the city as being at least as narrow and provincial as that landscape of my adolescence which, like the protagonists of certain stories by Willa Cather, I'd thrown over, thinking myself too good for it. And yet how could I have recognized this, when I insisted so stubbornly on endowing New York with the power to authorize my very selfhood?

One advantage of my university, for me, was its relative proximity to 'the city,' which was only an hour east by bus. Already I went fairly often, usually with my roommate, Jim Sterling, whose parents lived in a vast apartment on Central Park West. These weekends we devoted almost exclusively to the consumption of culture: museums and movies, and on Saturday nights, the theater, usually serious plays, the latest works by Marsha Norman or David Hare, instead of the 'shows' – things like *Cats* and *Evita* – to which my mother had taken my sister and me, and which I now disdained. Jim's ambition was to write for the culture section of the *New York Times*, and so in the mornings, over Sunday brunch, he would amuse his parents and me with disquisitions on whatever we had seen the night before – long monologues the thread of which I would gradually lose as I stared over the platter of bagels at Central Park, thinking about my own adolescence, how meager and colorless it seemed when compared to Jim's, which had been crowded with activity: visits to the Temple of Dendor, and Radio City Music Hall, and the Museum of Natural History. Not that I had grown up in Willa Cather's Nebraska; indeed, our pleasant Seattle neighborhood was by any standard other than my own a utopia. I exaggerated horribly – as if the future I longed for required as its prerequisite a lonely and impoverished past.

Toward the end of that semester I entered my story about Aunt Bessie in a fiction contest that had been initiated a decade earlier by a famous television reporter in memory of his son, who had died in a mountain climbing accident. The story won – the first time the prize had ever been given to a sophomore. Not surprisingly, everyone else in Flint's seminar had entered the contest too. My classmates greeted me, when I arrived for our last meeting, with a sort of low snarl of congratulations: good wishes beneath which I could detect the distinct and scary purr of feline rancor.

The weather was unseasonably warm that May. Outside tulips, undeterred by the late snowstorms, bloomed with a fretful vigor. The air through the open window of the seminar room smelled sweet, while on the blackboard the subjunctive conjugation of the verb *piacere* – last remnant of that Italian class on which I had eavesdropped through the semester – testified to the human capacity, mysterious only when you think about it, to learn. Even Flint, dressed in a pink shirt and a jacket of greenish tweed, seemed to be in a sweet mood, at least to judge from the warmth with which he saluted us. Indeed, so kind was his welcome that for the first time I wondered whether the savage aspect he had shown that first January night might have derived not from some streak of sadism in his character, not even from an idea he had about teaching, but from simple shyness.

I remember that in keeping with an old tradition at the school, everyone had brought food or drink to this last class: bags of potato chips and bottles of Coke and Sprite and plates of cookies, which we spread out over the seminar table like goods at a bake sale. Only Flint did not eat. Instead he talked. 'Children, children,' he intoned, his plaintive voice betraying a nostalgia to which I would not, at first, have thought him susceptible. 'How quickly things end. It's hard to imagine that only a few months have passed since our first evening together . . . yet this is the nature of things. You have been a blessing to me, every one of you. Of course you shall all receive A's, and if there were a higher grade in the universe I would bestow it upon each of you. I wish I could give you more than A's. But I can't – only this little letter that may be of some use one day, along with a few parting words, a last assessment, some advice to take or ignore as you see fit.'

All sounds of consumption ceased. I think that what surprised us wasn't so much this announcement itself as the fact that he was planning to give these final evaluations in class. Yet such, apparently, was his typically unorthodox plan, for now he began to make his way around the table, from student to student, granting each of us – even those who, having never gotten past sentence one, had given up trying – an appraisal at once judicious and generous, a liberal dollop of that balm he had previously dispensed only in tiny quantities, on the rare occasions when one of us wrote something that pleased him.

As for me, I waited. Because – teacher's pet that I was – I was seated immediately to his left, I knew I would be the last to be addressed.

My turn came around ten. 'Bauman,' he began, turning his chair toward mine and stretching out his legs. 'Bauman, Bauman, Bauman. What can we say about you? You have won the prize.'

Silence. Was this meant as congratulations?

'You have pulled the brass ring, and now you get to ride the merry-go-round again. In fact, I don't doubt but that you'll be riding the merry-go-round the rest of your life.' (Laughter.) 'At first I wasn't sure what to make of you. You seemed so eager, and so incompetent.' (More laughter.) 'But then you got ahold of something and didn't let go. And I've got to applaud you for it. You're fearless. You know what you want. That's why of all the people in this room you're the only one I feel certain will make a success of himself as a writer. And yet . . . of course there's an "and yet," isn't there?' (Still more laughter. Flint's smile disappeared.) 'I fear for you, Bauman. You are eminently corruptible. You can tell a story, but you haven't become serious, and worse, you don't seem to care about becoming serious. And once you're out there, in the market-place . . . I'm sorry to say it, but it's easy for me to imagine you turning into a hack, settling for cheap success, and not because you're greedy, but because you desire too desperately to please.' All at once, to my shock, he took my hand. 'If you prove me wrong, I'll jump for joy. If you don't, I ask you only to remember this voice. Remember that I've never said a word to you out of self-interest, or told you only what you wanted to hear.'

The room went silent. Quietly Flint removed his glove-leather hand from mine. 'And now,' he said, turning away from me, 'I bid you all farewell. Stay in touch. As you know I don't give out my home address. Nonetheless you can always reach me care of the English department here. The magnificent Mrs Hall, the department secretary, has promised to forward everything along.'

Standing, he put on his coat.

'Aren't you staying for the party?' Mittman asked.

'No, no,' Flint answered sadly. 'I—' And shaking his head, he left. We were alone suddenly, with all that food, and in my case, a consciousness that I was being stared at – not with envy, no longer with envy – but with pity.

Pleading a final to study for, I fled. I went back to my room, where I started packing: in just a few days I would be leaving for New York, where I'd begin that summer internship at the publishing house for which I (and not Lopez) had been selected. And yet I couldn't concentrate on my suitcases tonight. Instead, sitting at my desk, I pulled from the drawer the letter I'd just received from the news reporter, congratu-lating me on my prize. 'Your story is both delightful and professional,' he'd written, just as Flint had said that of all the students in the class, I was the one most likely to find success as a writer: words at the utterance of which a current of pride had surged through me, a sensation of heady potency that I now tried to revive, to re-*feel* in its original purity, before his subsequent admonishments had snuffed it out.

Anyway, *were* Flint's warnings fair? Leaning back, I tried to analyze my behavior over the course of the semester. All I had done, it seemed to me, was write a story he had liked, and win a prize; yet now he reproached me . . . and why? *People forgive talent everything except success*: Flint himself had told us that. Wasn't it possible, then, that in castigating me, he was merely illustrating his own maxim, giving voice – he whose work had come to so little – to an envy not only of me, but of all of us, of all that earnest potential, so far unsullied by spite, that I and my classmates, in our eager youth, personified?

That night, I committed the first of the many acts of betrayal that would punctuate the next twenty years of my life. Not that I denounced Flint, or called up Lopez to tell her she had been right all along: I did neither. And yet it is often the subtlest forms of defamation that prove, in the end, the most pernicious. For Lopez's campaign against Flint, at least, had had the advantage of being up front and bold. My own, on the other hand, was underhanded, and consisted chiefly in telling the many people I met that summer in New York that though, of course, Flint was a genius – this went without saying – he was also a demagogue, petty and self-interested, and always trying to make his students dependent upon him, so that when or if they became successful, *he* could claim credit for their fame, and thus steal a portion of the recognition his own work had never earned him. (Partly true – which in no way absolves me of the charge of defamation. Anyway, the truth was not my goal. My goal was revenge.)

The next afternoon I took the bus into New York, to have lunch with the young woman who had hired me for the summer internship at Hudson House Publishers. It was raining. As the bus entered the Holland Tunnel I thought casually of Flint, how tirelessly he'd trekked in and back from our school every Wednesday, no matter the weather. 'For you, my children, I'd brave the fiercest storm,' he'd said once, in that voice to the timbre of which I'd thrilled . . . No more. Already I was listening for other voices, ones which, because they belonged to a future that was for the moment fictive, a thing of my own imagining, I could make say whatever I wanted, like the stuffed animals that as a child I had imbued with personality. *A joy to read*, one said. And another said, *the next J. D. Salinger.* And the third said (I curse to remember it, I curse to repeat it), *The truth and what you want to hear are the same.*

2

The Glass-Bottomed Boat

HIGHER EDUCATION, my mother used to say, is wasted on the young. A zealous autodidact, shamed, in that overachieving meritocracy that was the town in which we lived, by her single year of nursing school, she feasted on literature, history, and politics, first to prove her worthiness, later for the sheer joy of it. And at the beginning, I suppose her enthusiasm must have been infectious, for in high school I professed to be idealistic about learning; I even caused a small uproar one year by writing an editorial for the student paper protesting the English department's decision to offer SAT Review as an alternative to Shakespeare on the electives roster. And yet, this idealism cannot have been long lasting, for in college I myself never took a Shakespeare course, though I did receive full credit for a seminar called Theory and Practice of Gossip. Moreover, thanks to some convenient Advanced Placement tests in Biology and Calculus that I'd passed in high school, I managed to 'A.P. out' of my math and science requirements. What I did study were English Literature and Art History, in part because literature and art were the things I loved most, in part because these were the only subjects in which I felt sure I could get A's. Even here, however, my education was full of holes. For example, as a student I never read Dante. I never read Joyce. In the end, thanks to a permissive system of requirements that I managed to manipulate to my advantage (not a single course in American or European History, Philosophy, Economics) I graduated from one of the finest universities in the land without knowing the causes of the First World War, or what Romanticism was, or the meaning of the term 'Reformation.' All this has to be admitted. I didn't go to college to learn; I went to college to achieve.

My troubles started very early in my childhood, when I was given my first I.Q. test. As it happened, I grew up both in the age and the land of the I.Q. test; my elementary school was even named after its inventor, which may explain the almost occult significance with which the adults I knew – teachers and guidance counselors and parents of my friends and friends of my parents – endowed its results. For in our community, flanked on one side by the university where my brother was a student and on the other by the incipient battlements of Microsoft, where my father would eventually go to work, everyone knew his I.Q. by heart, though few people spoke it, out of shame, or modesty, or because they feared lest by its very utterance such a mystical figure – calculated, as in numerology, according to ancient and secret formulae, in the halls of mysterious temples – might lose its potency. I honestly believe that if at that time an incipient Albert Einstein had appeared in our midst, bearing his theory of relativity in one hand and a low test score in the other, the test score would have carried the day.

When I was very small, of course, I understood none of this. Instead my life consisted mostly of play: endless games of crazy eights with my sister, of Candy Land and Chutes and

Ladders, Barrel of Monkeys and Pick-Up Stix, with my peers. Even school was mostly play, a perpetual round of drawing turkeys at Thanksgiving, and snowmen at Christmas, and hearts on Valentine's Day. Holidays shaped the pleasant year – as soon as one was over we'd start planning for another – until one afternoon (it was the very beginning of second grade) I was taken out of class and sat down in a small room across from a young woman with horn-rimmed glasses who spread out a series of blocks that I was supposed to fit one inside the other, and asked me to complete a story about a little boy whose glass of water was half-full, and wanted me to tell her which of four pictures did not belong with the other three. None of this seemed to me worth taking very seriously at the time; after all, back then I had no idea what a test was, much less that the results of one could ramify fatally into my future. Nor had I any reason to believe that in contrast to the thousands of rounds of crazy eights I'd played with my sister, the scores for which we simply tossed away when we grew tired, my score for *this* game would be carefully notated and preserved in some inner sanctum of the school, where in conjunction with other scores it would be used to determine the course of my education. Yet this was, as it turned out, exactly what happened, as I discovered one morning on the bus when a tiny girl named Jana Scott (she had recently taught me to tie my shoes) asked me whether I was planning to bring my lunch for the field trip or buy a sandwich at the dock. What field trip? I asked. What dock? The one next week, she answered, to ride the glass-bottomed boat into Puget Sound. I blinked. Of this field trip I knew nothing. Yet from Jana Scott, I now learned that all my friends were planning to go.

At recess that morning I asked my teacher about the field trip. Yes, she confirmed, it was to take place the following Wednesday. And was I to be included? She shook her head. No, I was not. Why not? I asked.

Then she rubbed her hands together and in a somber voice explained to me certain facts of which, up until that moment, I had never been apprised: first, that in our state there existed something called the Mentally Gifted Minors, or MGM, Program; second, that according to the terms of this program, for every student who scored above the ninety-eighth percentile on a certain test, the school received money from the state to be spent on special MGM activities, such as the glass-bottomed boat ride; finally, that as I myself was not an MGM, there was no money to pay for me to go on the trip. To put it crudely, unlike Jana Scott, I hadn't made the cut.

That afternoon I arrived home in a state bordering on hysteria. Because I was not to be allowed to go, the glass-bottomed boat ride had swollen in my mind to mythic proportions, as if what was to be viewed through the boat's crystalline floor was not merely the depth of the ocean, but that very realm of intellectual delectation after which even at that young age I felt myself, in some intuitive way, hankering. What outraged me was the perniciousness of a system that granted to a single test the authority not merely to judge intellectual capacity, but actually to dictate the dispensation of rewards. Exclusion was the consequence. How I dreaded the prospect of the upcoming week, during which my friends would no doubt taunt me with their anticipation, not to mention the day of the field trip itself, my solitude at the bus stop, the morning after when I would be regaled with accounts of those pleasures of which, by virtue of my inadequacy, I had been deemed unworthy!

So began a dark and tormented period of my life, one that would last until I graduated from high school, and even then leave its dense residue in my psyche, like the pulp that remains once olives are pressed for oil. Because of the test, for instance, when I entered junior high school I found myself 'laned' (such was the vocabulary of the day) in classes the numbers for which, instead of ending with A for 'Advanced,' had no letter whatsoever appended to them. No matter that my teachers agreed that these classes were too easy for me: the test overruled. I was not an MGM. And though pleas on the part of my mother eventually led to my being allowed to 'change lanes' in two subjects – English and Science – nonetheless there would remain in my record forever not only the ineradicable result of the original test, but those of its spawn: the PSAT (which I was due to take the following year), and the SAT, and beyond that other tests, more tests. All of them were designed to quantify the ineffable: in keeping with the American paradigm, not learning, but the 'capacity to learn.' A poor score on the PSAT or SAT, I knew, would bar me from the prestigious East Coast education on which I had my heart set, just as my score on the MGM test had barred me from the glass-bottomed boat ride.

Although I had been writing stories ever since I'd learned *how* to write – indeed, my desire to invent must have actually predated my acquisition of the skills required to give it issue, for I remember trying to copy letters out of books well before I knew what they meant – it was not until late in my child-hood that I first cognized the idea of 'being a writer.' In part I was responding to yet another test that my test-happy school had compelled me to take, this one purporting to adjudge 'vocational aptitude,' according to the results of which the two careers for which I was best suited were those of (a) hair-dresser and (b) forest ranger. Writer wasn't even an option. Yet from my mother I knew that writers existed. Often I would look at their pictures on the jackets of the novels she checked out from the library. And I had my own writer-heroes, chiefly the theologian C. S. Lewis, a boxed set of whose *Chronicles of Narnia* my brother had given me as a Christmas present. Writing, at first, was pure imitation for me, an effort to prolong the reliable joy of reading once the last volume of the beloved *Chronicles* had come to an end. And yet, curiously enough, the more I tried to write like C. S. Lewis, the further I ventured from his Christian vision: writing, it seemed, though it might begin as a way out of the self, finally led one back into it.

Still, the fact that when I wrote, no adjudicators stood between me and the blissfully blank page – not yet, at least – did not free me from their influence in other arenas. For instance, according to my mother, in order to be a writer you still had to have a degree (as she did not) from a prestigious university. More importantly, you had to know the sort of people you were only likely to meet, or at the very least who were only likely to pay attention to you, if you had a degree from a prestigious university. In order to lead a life unencumbered by the test givers, in other words, you had first to placate them. This was the bargain I was offered, and to the compromised terms of which – unnecessarily, as it turned out – I ended up agreeing.

Now, as once I had not taken tests seriously enough, I took them too seriously. Most of my nightmares were about tests. Likewise most days after school, at the local bookstore-cum-coffeehouse, where, under happier circumstances I might have been discovering stories by Raymond Carver or Grace Paley, I labored for hours on 'Test Your Own I.Q.' booklets. Only pride kept me away from those schools the dedicated purpose of which was to 'prepare' students for tests that by their professed nature cannot be prepared for. Instead, with my allowance money, I bought a volume of practice PSATs (the letters stood for Preliminary Scholastic Aptitude Test), which I administered to myself with the fervent dedication of a sacristan, in an atmosphere of almost sepulchral gravity: closed up in the kitchen, the oven timer set for twenty minutes, I would try to sharpen my mind to the same pinpoint of exactitude to which I had sharpened my number-two pencil. If I did well, I would reward myself with a moment of repose, a willed cessation of anxiety that by morning would have eroded, unable to withstand the onslaught of worry, which my mind produced as feverishly as a congested nose produces mucus. If I didn't do well, however – and this was more often the case – then a heated panic would seize me, during which I would go back through my answers, trying to figure out where I'd gone wrong. Sometimes, it was true, I'd been slap-dash, or hadn't known the meaning of a word. More often, though, fear itself waylaid me, provoking me to look for tricks or traps where none existed. Thus, when asked to choose which of four words – *liberty*, *exile*, *imprisonment*, and *theft* – was the correct antonym for *incarceration*, I selected *exile*, because *exile* meant a state of *external* imprisonment, whereas *incarceration* referred to a state of *internal* imprisonment, i.e. in a jail. The answer, it turned out, was *liberty;* yet when, in my indignity, I asked my mother whether she wouldn't have answered the same way, she replied with the clear-eyed fas-tidiousness of a crossword-puzzle aficionado, 'I see your point. Still, I would have put "liberty."' (Unlike me, she was the sort of student of whom standardized testmakers dream: measured, literal, with a mind as precise as an X-Acto knife.)

The day of the actual PSAT neared. A week before, my anxiety pitched over into a kind of apoplexy, after which, in a last-ditch effort to defend itself, my body shut down com-pletely. For two days I stayed at home in a sort of fevered coma, from which I emerged only on the Saturday morning of the test, dry-eyed and eerily calm; bicycling to the school (not my own) where the test was to be given, I even wondered what my mother would have waiting for lunch when I got back. The other side of terror is numbness. Now that I'm an adult, now that I've been through psychotherapy and taken serotonin reuptake inhibitors, I recognize the truth in Forster's pairing of panic with emptiness. I didn't then.

Instead – innocent of Prozac – I locked my bicycle and walked into the cafeteria, where the test was to be given. A guidance counselor checked my name off the list, making sure first that my parents had paid for this privilege, then assigned me to a desk and handed me a narrow card on which were printed a series of empty circles, each corresponding to one of the four multiple-choice answers to each question. These cards, I knew, would in turn be tabulated by a computer – at the time the very idea of this amazed me – which was why it was very important, the counselor told me, that I use only number-two pencils, never number one or number-three pencils, which were in the one case too light and in the other too dark for the computer to read.

The hour approached. In preparation, the guidance counselor handed out the test booklets, which we were told not to open until instructed to do so. He had seated us in alphabetical order, which meant that I was behind a girl named Susan Barrett, a very tall and cool girl who had been one of the participants (their names were forever etched on the surface of my memory) in the notorious glass-bottomed boat ride. Unlike the rest of us, Susan Barrett appeared fairly unruffled by the prospect of the PSAT; indeed, she arrived just as the test was about to begin, out of breath, pushing hair from her eyes. 'I overslept,' she whispered as she took her seat.

Then a bell rang. We opened our booklets.

Today, of that test itself, I recall few details – certainly no specific problems or solutions. What I do remember is finding myself, at a certain point, imperiled by a moment of wavering between two possible answers. One or the other, I knew, was correct; yet if I chose what was to me the more obvious of the two, might I not fall into a trap, as I had in the case of *incarceration*?

Stretching, I glanced at the clock, then allowed my gaze, for a microsecond, to move downward, to the little card on which

Susan Barrett – who was already finished with her test and staring dreamily at the blackboard – had written her answers. It all happened so swiftly, it seemed as if I'd done it before I'd even decided to do it; my gimlet eye, the sharpness of which I had never previously tested, zeroed in fleetly on the appropriate line, the circle Susan had filled in. All at once I saw that I had given the wrong answer, the needlessly complicated answer, and with a sudden, silent 'Of course!' I quickly corrected myself, my pink eraser alone bearing witness, by the black smudge on its tip, to this criminal act. And meanwhile a sensation of reassurance flooded me that was at once so profound and so pleasant that I could not help but cede to its flow.

So began my career as a cheat – a career to which, like my homosexuality, I would never have admitted even if confronted with the most damning evidence, and about which I felt little compunction for the simple reason that, so long as it remained secret, so long as I never got found out, it had no reality for me. Because cheating was never an activity I planned in advance, but rather fell into spontaneously, little anxiety preceded it; yet because it was also an activity at which I never got caught, no anxiety followed it, either, only the calming certainty that for once I had defied a corrupt system.

From then on, the assurance that if need be I could always cheat became for me an anodyne, an analgesic against the dread that the prospect of, say, a French exam provoked in me. As it happened French and Math were the classes in which I cheated the most, probably because I approached them from the same point of view. French, for example, I looked upon less as a mode of communication and expression than as an aggravatingly inconsistent construct the complexity of which I could never quite master. Years later, when I went to France, I learned the language easily, and by the most natural method possible: by shopping in the grocery store, and falling in love with a French boy, and chatting with the lady who ran the dry cleaning shop on Rue St.-Martin. When I was in high school, however, French was merely a mess of irregular verbs and illogical rules so daunting that every time I opened my textbook a terror would seize me; suddenly it would seem as if I were looking at the page through distorting glasses, or a sheet of tears. Nor could I take these exams any less seriously than the evil PSATs, for I knew that in a high school as competitive as mine, a B in French or Math would significantly lower my chances of getting into the East Coast university, famous for its English department, on which I had set my sights.

I don't think that my French teacher, Madame Hellier, who was from Nîmes and raised rabbits in her backyard, had any idea of the anguish that her tests provoked in me. She was an affable woman who took little interest in proctoring exams, preferring instead to lead us in dialogues in which one of us would take the role of M. Thibaut, the other of M. Dupont, or to stage scenes from Molière farces and absurdist comedies like Ionesco's *The Bald Soprano*, or to host potluck dinners to which we would bring frozen croissants, casseroles filled with some *Joy of Cooking* version of *boeuf bourguignonne*, and store-bought 'French bread,' and to which Madame Hellier's own contribution, no doubt intended to appall and amuse us, was invariably something repellent to our sensitive American palates – snails served in their shells with garlic butter, or frogs' legs, or a stew prepared with one of her adorable rabbits. Still, she had to give the tests; it was part of her job.

Cheating, I should add, was easy in Madame Hellier's case, as the room in which our class took place was furnished not with ordinary desks, but rather with round tables at which we sat in groups of four. Also, because she was neither savvy nor dictatorial enough to take precautions, but on the contrary often left the room altogether during tests to smoke a cigarette with Frau Blumenfeld, the German teacher, it was a fairly simple matter not only to make sure I was seated across from a boy named Erik, who was half Swiss and had a flair for languages, but also to glance across the table whenever I came to a question that stumped or worried me – not so much, I told myself at the time, in order to steal his answer as to assure myself that my own was not incorrect. And yet, more often than not, Erik would turn out to have eluded some snare into which I had fallen blindly, or to have remembered a subtle kink of grammar that I had failed to pick up on; and once alerted to my own error, how, after all, could I leave the wrong answer on the page?

No one noticed, either, or at least no one said anything, although once, handing back the corrected tests (I had gotten an A), Madame Hellier did remark casually, 'I can't help but notice that you and Erik gave all the same answers – even the wrong ones.'

Cheating, of course, leads to lying: opening my mouth, I affected an expression of indignation that must have been highly convincing, for Madame Hellier immediately retracted her innuendo, apologized, and continued passing out the corrected tests.

After that my cheating became both flagrant and chronic. Always I gave myself pardon, afterward, by reminding myself that my motive was not to pillage the labor of others so much as to obtain a degree of relief for myself. After all, for me the sense of escalating panic that marked the days leading up to a test was nothing compared to the apprehension I felt once the test (if I had not cheated on it) was finished, the sleepless nights during which I would try to recollect every question, to reassess my strategies, to determine, as best I could, how I had done; indeed, I remember waking, too many times, at four in the morning from a dream in which I'd suddenly recognized the wrong turn I'd made in some calculus equation, getting up and going to the kitchen table, where, on one of my mother's notepads, I'd try to reconstruct both the problem and my solution in the hope (ever waning) that I might turn out, in the end, to have solved it correctly. So lost would I become in this futile, obsessive procedure that often at daybreak, when my father came in for his toast and coffee, I would still be sitting there in my pajamas, surrounded by scraps of paper, under a light as oppressive as the ones used by the police during interrogations.

Now I wonder whether cheating is like taking drugs or gambling; that is to say, whether, as taking a puff from a joint is supposed to lead inexorably to shooting heroin, or putting a quarter in a slot machine to staking your life savings at a Roulette table, looking over your shoulder at a friend's French exam will necessarily lead to one's graduation into what might be called the major modes of cheating, such as buying answers, or breaking into a professor's office to steal copies of an exam, or writing crib notes on the inside of your wrist. Which is to say nothing of posteducational cheating: price gouging, insider trading, adultery. In my case, at least in a literal sense, the answer is no; I was neither bold nor clever enough to take such risks. Still, what I lacked in daring I made up for in persistence. Indeed, if I were to add them up, I'd have to say that in addition to the standardized tests that I took, I probably cheated on as many as a hundred exams. And as a result, I got what I wanted. I did well on my SATs. I earned straight A's and was admitted to the university from which I was so slavishly determined to graduate. Now, as I finished high school, the future that lay before me was one in the potentialities of which I could revel, for it was a blank page, as yet unsullied by the smudges and erasures, the torn edges and ink blotches, of its own experiencing. And in this future, I told myself, I would never cheat. What would be the need? Cheating had been merely the means by which to attain this much-deserved end, this guarantee of inclusion in a world where cheating would no longer be necessary.

Alas, it was not to be. Indeed, today I'm fairly certain that it was my career as a cheat itself which sowed in me, as its dark legacy, the drive to succeed, the 'readiness to pounce on a sure thing' that would despoil the writer's life of which it had been my hope, through cheating, to assure myself. Yes, if I had it to do over again, I'd do it differently. I'd take German and Physics and Philosophy. I'd study to learn, and I'd learn with joy.

I am often startled by the extent to which the public and the private, the life of our times and the life of our days, reflect each other. As an adolescent, I used to like to think of myself as being out of sync with the age in which I was growing up; I saw myself as an iconoclast, at once too urbane and too tender to thrive in the world into which I'd been born, when the truth was that my zeal for success, not to mention my neurotic obsession with tests, made me the perfect citizen (despite my protests to the contrary) of that epoch in which SAT Review was offered as an alternative to Shakespeare; in which the so-called 'Back to Basics' movement campaigned for the return both of prayer and corporal punishment to the classroom; in which the parents of a schoolmate of mine promised him a BMW upon graduation, but only if he got into Harvard. (He didn't.)

This is the public side, the 'sociological' side, if you will, of the story; there is a private side too. Today I cannot help but deplore my habit, from very early on, of endowing teachers and institutions with the capacity to validate not only my intelligence, but my right to exist. Why, I ask myself now, did I crave so urgently these tokens of approval? In part, I suspect, because I wanted, by means of them, to distract attention from what I perceived to be the single great blemish on my curriculum vitae – my homosexuality. This was especially true where my parents were concerned. By preceding the inevitable revelation with a catalogue of my successes, I hoped that I might elide their inevitable disapproval and grief. Thus even before I had admitted my homosexuality to myself, I was already gathering my trophies together, building a sort of arsenal against future encroachments.

When I was in college, I used to tell people that given the choice, I'd always take fame over money. (Now, of course, I've learned that money is the more valuable of the two commodities, because it can buy you the one thing that fame steals: privacy.) In making such a lofty and ludicrous pronouncement, I thought I was affirming my opposition to the politics of greed that characterized those years, the Reagan years. Yet the assertion reflected equally my faith in fame itself as a real-world equivalent of straight A's, less the natural consummation of God-given talent than an advantage obtained through connections and luck. And this was why, though I grew to admire, even to love Stanley Flint during the semester I spent under his tutelage, I also continued to view him not only as a literary genius, but as the holder of some golden key by means of which I might at last gain entry to that magical city from which he arrived by bus every Wednesday, and in the stratosphere of which I too longed to shine. Without admitting it to myself, I nurtured the hope that I might be the next student for whom, on the basis of a single sentence, he obtained a publishing contract, as no doubt did most of my classmates. For though I was now riding on the glass-bottomed boat, of course there are always other glass-bottomed boats, ones with more limpid floors, that drift on richer seas.

At that time my university was going through a brief and

peculiar period (one, no doubt, never to be mentioned in its official histories) during which it had a reputation as a 'gay school.' This reputation was not merely a matter of undergraduate gossip. On the contrary, it was so widespread as to prompt an article in the *New York Times*, the author of which titillated her readers with such details as the distinction, in campus lingo, between 'lipstick lesbians' and 'crunchies': the former glamour girls who smoked and painted their nails, the latter more likely to wear flannel than Ferragamo, and fond of granola (hence the epithet). And though, in the final analysis, the article was somewhat exaggerated – for instance, it gave the impression that the campus was literally overrun by queers, that boys went to class in drag, that girls sucked marijuana smoke out of each other's mouths in the library – it was also something of a milestone, in that it represented the first public acknowledgment of open homosexual life at a university where for decades gay men and lesbians had felt obliged to efface themselves. (Later, a simple advertisement in the alumni magazine announcing the formation of a new gay and lesbian alumni group would expose the latent strain of barbarity in the school's history by provoking an avalanche of outraged letters from graduates threatening to cancel their subscriptions, withdraw their financial contributions, even pull their children out of the school should the offending advertisement not be immediately revoked, denounced, obliterated.)

One result of this new 'gay visibility' was that, though I was still deeply closeted at the time I took Stanley Flint's seminar, nonetheless I'd already met several 'out' homosexuals, most notably a group of boys I'd sometimes encounter in the common room outside the dining hall, sitting at the piano and singing a parodic version of the theme from *The Patty Duke Show* that began: 'They're cousins, they're lesbian cousins . . .' Though they couldn't have been more than nineteen or twenty, these boys seemed to me incredibly sophisticated, and not entirely as a consequence of the skewed perspective of my own youth, which made a twenty-one-year-old appear to be an 'older man.' It was also because they broadcast – intentionally, I suspect – an affect of debauched weariness and ennui the likes of which I'd never previously encountered. For instance, all of them chain-smoked, and dressed in black or gray flannel. Most of the time they wore ties; one, I suspect, wore lipstick. His name was Philip Crenshaw, and he had the caved-in cheeks and kohl-ringed eyes of a vampire. He was very gaunt, with long, spidery fingers, and he talked a bit like Stanley Flint – that is to say, in a deliberately affectless, aristocratic accent that gave away little of his origins, in monologues punctuated with linguistic archaisms, the subject of which was usually the homosexual underworld of New York, to which he and his friends repaired on weekends. 'Girls, I was visiting the Mineshaft last Saturday,' he might say, 'when I had the most frightful misadventure. I'd just walked away from the glory holes – having discovered, to my horror, that the delectable member I'd only seconds before taken into my mouth had on its underside this alarming little wart – when, strolling by the piss tubs, who should I see receiving the sacrament of fifty streams but *my shrink*! There he lay, naked as the day he was born, and positively *glistening*. And the worst part was, our eyes met. Well! You can imagine my anxiety when I arrived the next day for my appointment. "And what did you think when you saw me in the piss tub?" he asked. "Did *you* want to piss on me?"'

Philip's best friend was a robust, sallow boy of Irish descent called Gerald Wexler. Short and hefty, he had the unlikely combination of blue eyes and black hair ('Black Irish,' he used to say by way of self-praise), and compensated for his lack of physical stature by projecting himself violently onto every scene in which he was a character. Though his physiognomy was less than appealing (at least to me), he managed, by boasting about the enormity of his penis, to persuade a lot of men (including, much later, myself) to go to bed with him. Even at that early age he was already cultivating the air of jaded, *bon vivant* languor that in subsequent years, when he lived in Amsterdam, would mature into a veneer of Proustian dissipation, as if at twenty-five he were a retiree from some long career of wantonness and carousal. I remember thinking him spiteful, and rather jealous; for instance, at a party once, long before I admitted my homosexuality, he sidled up to me, and said, 'So, Martin, have you come out yet?'

I was so shocked that I didn't even think to lie. 'No,' I replied miserably.

'I thought not,' he answered, and wandered off again to join his friends.

More sympathetic by far than Gerald, Philip, and their cohorts were the lesbians with whom I studied, most evenings, in the rear smoking section of the library. Most of these girls – Gretchen and Schuyler, for example – were, to borrow the blunt terminology of the *New York Times*, 'lipstick lesbians,' or a subvariety thereof; that is to say, they adhered to the chicly austere aesthetic of Manhattan's East Village, which in those years required of its disciples conformity to a code of strict minimalism. When they spoke – which was rarely – it was with an affectation of listlessness, as if to suggest the attrition of the spirit itself, a sort of psychic anemia. Thus Gretchen, puffing on a cigarette during a break from her interminable thesis, might observe to Schuyler in regard to one of their professors, 'He's *really* such a *lowbrow*, sweetheart' – stretching out the syllables to the very limits of their capacity for attenuation, as if on the lexical equivalent of a torture rack. All of this convinced me that they were worldly, these girls who had spent semesters in Paris, who smoked Gauloises and carried in their Prada bags little tins filled with lavender-flavored pastilles.

The member of this community with whom I felt the strongest rapport, however, was probably the one who took its tenets of fashion least seriously. This was a prelaw student, a few years older than myself, named Barb Mendenhall. With her spiky blond hair, the pectoral muscles into which her breasts (thanks to a stern program of weightlifting) were gradually disappearing, her unwavering wardrobe of plaid shirts and hiking boots, Barb would have seemed the epitome of the fifties diesel-dyke had it not been for the ironic current of delicacy that blunted her masculine affect, and of which the pair of pearl earrings she wore was only the most explicit emblem. For instance, late one night she arrived in our midst bearing as always her tidy stack of utilitarian economics and political science textbooks (in sharp contrast to the slim volumes of theory, the brutalized yellow Gallimard paperbacks with which Gretchen and Schuyler and their ilk littered the tables). Having first arranged her notebooks and highlighters across from my own mess of story, she sauntered over to the corner and, with a thunderous grunt, hawked a wad of phlegm into the garbage can. 'Oh, Jesus, Barb,' Gretchen muttered.

'Thanks for sharing that with us, Barb,' Schuyler added, stubbing out her cigarette in a plastic coffee cup, while Barb herself swaggered back to the table, her thighs as thick as a cowboy's, a bemused smile playing upon her lips.

Unlike Gretchen and Schuyler, Barb was not a regular fixture in the library. On the contrary, she graced us with her presence only on those occasions when she could find a few hours to spare from her strict regimen of studying, computer work, and the sports to which she was so assiduously devoted: fencing, basketball (she was on the varsity team), even, toward the end of her senior year, boxing. I remember encountering her there one sunny spring morning, at an hour when the rear smoking section was empty except for me, because most of the lesbians were still asleep. Taking the seat across from mine, she pulled from her backpack her stack of morning mail, including a large envelope out of which she proceeded to tear, with great impatience, the latest issue of a magazine called *Woman Athlete*. 'Oh, man,' she said, rolling her eyes and licking her lips in what might have been a parody of masculine slavering, and showed me a photograph in which a sleek German pole-vaulter stood poised to leap. 'Hubba-hubba.' She laughed. Yet I was sure I could detect alongside her evident lust a quality of wistfulness in her voice, an intimation of what I might have called, had I read Proust (which I hadn't), the '*tristesse d'Olimpio*' of sapphism.

Barb was very beautiful. I remember seeing her from behind one afternoon. Her lustrous blond hair, newly buzz-cut, might have been that of a Roman soldier's. When she turned around, her eyes – mournful, lucid, deliquescent, cold and gray (the gray of certain rare mushrooms) – suggested depths of yearning at which her outward air of pragmatism barely hinted. In those eyes one could read not only a child-hood marked by unintelligible longings, but the adolescence into which that childhood had segued, and during which those longings had coalesced, as it were, into the idealized image of the woman she desired both to possess and to be. (The conflation of the desire to have and the desire to be – which can lead you to feel simultaneous jealousy and envy toward a cheating lover whose paramour you also find attractive – is probably the aspect of homosexuality with which heterosexuals have the most trouble empathizing.) Their exotic melancholy not only undercut Barb's macho posturings, it lent to her stony countenance an unexpected shadowing of vulnerability.

The extent of that vulnerability, however, became evident only during the spring of my senior year, after I had finally come out and was helping to organize the university's annual

'Gay and Lesbian Awareness Days,' or GLAD. This was essentially a weeklong series of dances, lectures, panels, and 'gay-straight raps,' culminating in an enormous rally during which thousands of balloons emblazoned with pretty pink triangles would be released into the sky.

An aside, now, about that pink triangle: although I was fully aware, then, of its evil origin – that in German concentration camps homosexuals had been forced to wear these pink triangles in the same way that Jews were forced to wear yellow stars – nevertheless its omnipresence, during GLAD week, did not have the intended effect (at least I think it was the intended effect) of making me contemplate the horrors of Nazism. On the contrary, whenever I carried my pink triangle balloon or brandished my pink triangle button, it was my own boldness in making such a display that intoxicated me, so much so that I barely registered the triangle's implications, which were of course the implications of evil itself. In this way, for my generation, the pink triangle became gradually dislocated from history. The minute it was turned upside down by its designers to signal its new function as an emblem of power and pride, there began a process of degeneration that would eventually reduce it into what it is today, a sort of politically correct fashion accessory, streamlined and natty, like the ubiquitous red AIDS ribbon that in a decade or so would be sprouting on every Hollywood breast, in some cases picked out in rubies.

Today the red AIDS ribbon, like the pink triangle, provokes little reaction in me when I pass someone wearing one on the street; it is neither frightening nor chic because it is not new. And yet in the early eighties, when AIDS was still a vagueness, a rumor on the periphery of things, to carry a pink triangle balloon was to make a daring proclamation. Parading up and down the college walkways, giddy and at the same time frightened, my friends and I would attract stares from boys and girls who loathed us, as well as from those who wanted to but could not quite muster the courage to join us. Theirs was a position I understood well, as it had been mine until the year before; then I'd gone to the gay-straight raps as a *straight* participant. Now I organized and led them. A surprisingly large number of students always showed up, though curiously, Barb was never among them – not, I suspect, because she was closeted (far from it; she was the most intrepid among us), but because she saw her own ardors as things too fragile, too exalted, to be able to survive the harsh light of a public airing.

Alas, it was at one of these raps that I became the involuntary agent of her downfall. I remember that I was standing near the front of the common room, listening while my 'cofacilitator,' an earnest crunchy named Erica, introduced the proceedings, when I noticed among the faces in the crowd that of a sophomore already famous among my friends, as she was considered a likely contender for the Olympic swim team. This sophomore, Tammy Lake, had jet-black hair and a friendly, oblong face. Although I knew her slightly – we lived in the same dormitory – I had no idea at first if she was a lesbian, or had simply come to the rap for the same reasons that other straight girls came to the raps: to prove her open-mindedness, or to expiate some childhood guilt, or because a boy on whom she had a crush had just come out to her. Nor, I think, would I have given the matter any further thought, had some recruitment instinct not compelled me to reappraise certain aspects of her appearance – short hair, muscled body, androgynous preppy garb – in light of their more obvious connotations. Was Tammy Lake, the proto-Olympic swimmer, gay? I found myself wondering. I certainly hoped so, because if she was, then her presence at the big rally on Saturday – that of a bona fide campus celebrity, a future face on the front of a Wheaties box – could prove a great boon to us, almost as much of a boon as if the TV star who had enrolled the year before (and of whom I had so far caught only a glimpse) were to give a speech. And yet this TV star, though rumored to be a fixture at the off-campus parties that Gretchen, Schuyler, and their friends threw most weekends, had so far kept a low profile so far as GLAD week was concerned, whether out of discretion or disinterest I hadn't a clue.

As for Tammy, when the rap ended she made a point of coming up and saying hello to me, much to the annoyance of Erica, who was dying to meet her. Ignoring the importunate glances of my cofacilitator, I mentioned that I would be manning the GLAD information table outside the dining hall the next evening, a remark to which Tammy responded with a smile so open and frank that, emboldened, I went a step further. I asked her if she wanted to help out.

'Sure,' she said. 'What do I have to do?'

'Just sit with me there for an hour or so, answer questions, sell buttons and balloons and T-shirts. Oh, and take signatures on our petition to support gay marriage.'

Crossing her arms, Tammy seemed to consider the implications of my offer – but only for a moment. 'Okay, why not?' she said. 'I think I should be able to handle that.'

After we had agreed to meet in the common room the next day at five, Tammy left. Very swiftly Erica began buttoning her jacket. 'By the way,' she said, 'I'd appreciate it if in future, when referring to the information tables, you'd use some other verb besides *to man*. It's sexist.' And she strode out the door.

The next afternoon found me, as promised, in the common room outside the dining hall, arranging on a folding table all those balloons and buttons and T-shirts and petitions, in what amounted to the leftist equivalent of a bake sale. Indeed, I was just smoothing out the black and purple banner (festooned, of course, with pink triangles) that hung over the edge of the table, when to my mild surprise Barb walked in. This was unusual only insofar as she lived off-campus and almost never ate at the dining hall.

'Hi, Barb,' I said.

Unsmiling, fists curled in her pockets, she bore down on me, her gray eyes wide with an urgency.

'Is something wrong?'

'Tammy can't come,' she said. Then, in a softer voice: 'You shouldn't have asked her.'

'But she—'

'You shouldn't have asked her,' Barb repeated. 'When she said she'd come, it was only because she felt pressured. Afterwards she had second thoughts. You have to realize, she has her future to consider.'

'I'm sorry. I didn't mean to step on any toes.'

'Don't ever ask Tammy to do anything like this again,' Barb went on. 'She's not like other people. And please – don't tell anyone I came here tonight.'

'Of course not.'

'Thank you.'

Turning around, she left. I sat down in my folding chair. What I was experiencing was not so much surprise as a sense of corroboration: that famous *of course* that comes when the solution to a murder mystery is finally revealed, and you slap yourself for not having seen it coming. For suddenly I understood not only that Barb and Tammy were having a love affair, but that through her lover Barb was living out that fantasy the long gestation of which I had read, almost from the day I'd met her, in her face. Now, for the first time, much of her behavior made sense to me: her furtiveness, her isolation, the distance she kept from the festivities attending GLAD week. I recognized the masochistic nature of her longing, the sacrificial pleasure she took in this romance of which duty required her never to speak, but rather to cherish in secret, silent in the anonymous stands while by the pool, as the climax to that hallowed ceremony in which love itself forbade Barb from taking any role, a medal was draped around Tammy's golden neck.

After that, I assumed that Tammy would keep a low profile for the rest of GLAD week, that Barb would make sure she remained sequestered, in some sanctuary of her own devising, at least until the celebrations were over. Instead she was behind me in line the next evening in the dining hall. 'Hi,' she said casually. 'Sorry about last night.'

'No problem.'

'Barb just didn't think it was a good idea. Hope you understand.'

'Sure.'

To my slight bewilderment, Tammy suggested that we eat together. At a small banquette on the side of the dining hall she interrogated me for half an hour as to my own history, the lesbian community on campus, the presence (or absence) of gay and lesbian professors on the faculty. Not far away, in the center of the room, Gretchen and Schuyler were having dinner with a friend of theirs, a pretty, pale girl with a dissolute affect who was rumored to have just ended a love affair with the TV star. Stubbing out cigarettes into their largely untouched plates of soy bean casserole (all three were vegetarians), they did not speak, not even one another; instead they seemed intent on providing for the audience of other diners a *tableau vivant* of metropolitan boredom, enervation, and glamour.

'Who are those girls?' Tammy asked, indicating their table with her long neck. 'I've seen them around.'

'The two on the left are named Gretchen and Schuyler. I think Barb knows them.'

'Are they lovers?'

I nodded. 'Or at least they used to be.'

'And the other one?'

'I think her name is Lauren.'

'She's pretty.'

'Yes.'

'Introduce me to her.'

The authority with which Tammy issued this command – and it was a command, not a request – startled and bemused me, even as it made me fear for Barb, whose portrayal of her girlfriend as naive and requiring of protection I now recognized as saying more about Barb's needs than Tammy's. So I stood, and led her to the table where the three girls were sitting. Like wakened sleepers, they blinked at us, as if our approach alone had roused them from drowsy stupefaction.

'Hi,' I said. 'Mind if we join you?'

'It's a free country,' Schuyler said.

Pulling up chairs, we sat. 'This is Tammy,' I said.

Introductions were made. Between Lauren and Tammy there passed only the vaguest 'Hi,' the most fluttering glance across the table and the food; and yet above the hum of conversation I was sure that I heard, as in one of those frequencies beyond the range of the human ear yet audible to dogs, an assignation being agreed upon, to take place later, in the dark, in one of their rooms.

The next day was bright and sunny. Just after lunch I was standing outside the library with some friends of mine, with Erica and Donald Schindler and a few others, all of us holding our pink triangle balloons and enjoying the new sensation, after winter, of sunlight and warmth, when from the direction of the Economics department Barb came striding toward us. 'Hi, Barb,' we all said in chorus, smiling, eager to share that good humor the warm weather had brought out in us.

Without so much as a word she yanked the balloon out of my hand and with a powerful fist punched it into smithereens. I jumped. Her breath ragged, she moved toward the stairs that descended into the library.

'Oh for God's sake, Barb!' Erica shouted. 'What's eating you?'

'Jesus, Barb!' Donald echoed, and turned to me. 'Are you okay?'

'I'm fine,' I said, gazing at the shriveled remnants of my balloon. Unlike Donald and Erica, I wasn't angry, probably because – alone among the witnesses – I understood the reason for Barb's outburst. No doubt, without much in the way of ceremony, Tammy had just dumped her. And yet at the same time, I remained uncertain as to one detail: had she chosen my balloon at random, because it was the first one to hand? Or was she protesting the role I had played, albeit unwittingly, in the quick decimation of her idyll?

For surely it was the loss of this numinous ideal, more than of Tammy herself, that Barb was mourning that day. Like many young homosexual men and women, she had invested her vast and secret stores of erotic longing not simply in a dream lover but, as it were, in a dream *scenario*, one in which that longing, instead of terminating in barren solitude as we are taught that it must, finds issue in love. Certainly this was the happy ending for which I hoped; and indeed, if I felt such a strong identification with Barb's fantasy of lovemaking in the Olympic Village, it was probably because her scenario, though differing from my own in every particular, nonetheless shared with it a common foundation in the desire to be redeemed by an exalted, even sacred passion.

For instance: the other day, browsing in a record store, I happened to hear a fragment of music in response to which – though my mind could remember nothing of it – my body issued a tremolo of adolescent nostalgia the likes of which I hadn't felt in years. Immediately I asked what the music was, and learned that it was the slow movement from Vivaldi's Concerto for Guitar and Strings in D; the reason I recognized it, I soon realized, was that it had been part of the soundtrack of a movie I had gone to see over and over again during my senior year in high school, a movie in which a rich American girl, living in Paris with her parents, falls in love with a poor French boy. In the movie an old man (played by Laurence Olivier) tells the pair that according to legend, two lovers who kiss in a gondola beneath the Bridge of Sighs, at sunset, when the bells of the campanile toll, will love each other forever, at which point they decide to run away together to Venice. And though everything about this movie besotted me, what gave me the greatest pleasure were the images it offered of Paris and Venice in the spring, lush and green, and providing such a contrast to the drought-ridden landscape of my adolescence, a landscape in which the greedy soil, when my father aimed his garden hose at it, lapped up the water and was instantly dry again. At home my sister and I had to share bathwater, at school notices thumbtacked above the toilets read, IF IT'S YELLOW, LET IT MELLOW, IF IT'S BROWN, FLUSH IT DOWN, yet in the film water was everywhere: it plashed laxly in Paris fountains, in Venetian canals it flowed with a lassitude from which even the recklessness of the gondola, in the climactic scenes, could not seem to wake it. By contrast, the theater where I went to see the film – that theater with its brown upholstered walls, its acid smell of popcorn – contained only drinking fountains, and these had been shut off by order of the fire commissioner for the duration of the drought.

How that film obsessed me! Soon I had seen it so many times that the old lady who took the tickets started looking at me with suspicion, as if she smelled inside my fervent attendance some unwholesome motive, such as a psychotic crush on one of the teenage stars. She was only partly right. What I desired wasn't anything so clear-cut as that beautiful American girl, that handsome French boy; instead I wanted somehow to embody the very essence of their romance, to be . . . not her, not him, but rather the wood of the boat, the moss on the walls, the tug of the water through which the gondolier's pole propels them toward the sighing bridge, as bells toll. Thus my own dream scenario was born in a movie theater, as perhaps Barb's had been, years before, in a high school locker room, where a beautiful runner was toweling off her limbs.

My scenario ran as follows: I would be in Europe, in some rapturous and lovely place – a monastery, say, where monks sang Vespers, or a cathedral where the sunlight refracted through the many-hued stained-glass windows, or one of the museums where I hoped someday actually to see the master-pieces of Italian Renaissance art the titles and locations of which I had memorized, along with Baylor, in the year of Stanley Flint – when across the vastness another pair of eyes would fix upon my own. It almost didn't matter to whom the eyes belonged; what was important was the chanting, the light in the windows, in essence the noble and benevolent cir-cumstances under which my friend and I would meet, and which we could recount, fifty years later, without compunc-tion.

Needless to say, none of it ever came to pass. Oh, some-thing like it came to pass: that is to say, one summer I did go to Europe, and in a museum (the Brera in Milan, to be exact) I did meet a boy, a very handsome boy named Gianluca, American of Italian extraction, an architecture student at NYU. This Gianluca had thick hair, black eyes, a weak chin darkened by an incipient haze of beard, and I remember thinking: he is the one I have been waiting for. His name is Gianluca. He has a weak chin. It was as if the subject of a por-trait for which the background has already been painted, and from which only the sitter himself is missing, had suddenly appeared, and by taking his place before the snaking river and olive groves, proved the foresight of the artist in knowing exactly how to frame a face he had never seen. But in the end nothing happened. I was too shy to make a pass at him, while he must have had bigger fish to fry, for he merely took me on a walk through the courtyard of the Brera, where the statues of the great architects stand, and said, 'Someday I intend for my statue to be placed here next to theirs.' I clucked in awe, after which we shook hands and parted. I never saw him again.

When I was young, I used to believe that delving into the past was necessarily like returning to a house in which one has spent the early part of one's youth, only to be stunned at how much smaller everything seems than it did in childhood. In truth, I have since learned, the emotions rarely respect those laws of perspective that govern memory. Thus, though I've gone on to suffer worse humiliations than I did in Milan, just as I've had to wait for the results of tests far more consequential than the PSAT (and on which it was impossible to cheat), I won't begrudge my adolescent self the legitimacy of his suffering. For in the end, all the experiences about which I've written here were rehearsals for those later hijackings of the spirit, vaster in extent if not intensity, that awaited me then, and await me still. (How trivial the PSAT seems when one has waited for a PSA!) In other words, 'Practice,' as my mother used to tell me, 'brings perspective' – the perspective of wisdom, which, while acknowledging the triviality of youth's preoccupations, also refuses to underestimate its pain: something of which I try to remind myself whenever I recall those weekends when she was awaiting the Monday results of a Friday biopsy, and I the Monday results of a Friday math test, and in my arrogance I believed our anguish to be equal.

3

Because Very Few Mice Know How to Dance

I HAVE A FRIEND, an antiquarian bookseller, above whose desk hang two credos. (1.) 'Never judge a book by its contents.' (2.) 'The worst thing you can do to a book is read it.'

No doubt this friend would have loathed my mother, a great lover and destroyer of books. Because she liked to knit while she read, before she started a new book she would first break its spine, so that it lay flat on her lap. And the sharp, bone-cracking noise that the book issued when she did this – if truth be told, with real brutality and pleasure – was enough to make my brother grind his teeth and afterward regard the book with genuine pity, the way a compassionate nurse might regard a wounded soldier whose sufferings it is not within her power to allay. Our shelves were full of books my mother had thus maimed, their split spines listing inward, or finely ridged with lines not very different from those that creased her own forehead, or spilling whole signatures where the seams, either of glue or thread, had been violated. (Likewise my sister was a torturer where books were concerned, albeit of a different stripe: she had a fondness for reading in the bathtub and was forever dropping paperbacks into the soapy water, causing their pages to warp and yellow.)

As a child I loved books as things, as well as things to read, and was inclined to endow them with sentience, the capacity to experience pain, to love, or to be lonely. Thus when I accompanied my mother to the library, and waited while she studied the newly arrived novels in the '7-Day' section, what captured my imagination more viscerally than any promise the books themselves might hold was a drama of my own invention in which the new books – which still wore their dust jackets – snubbed and sneered at the old books, which for reasons I did not understand had been denuded, stripped of their one garment, forced to sit naked and chilly in the bleak stacks, as neglected as the elderly men and women who lived in the nursing home to which my grandmother had been consigned in the last days of her senescence. In the library maltreatment and delinquency were common. Malicious youths manhandled or defaced the old books, some of which hadn't been checked out for decades. No doubt they envied their more popular and youthful brethren, the 7-Day books, for which women like my mother waited impatiently, and sometimes had to sign up weeks in advance.

She was the great reader of the family. In addition to novels, she read histories, particularly those of a domestic nature, the sort that catalogue, in lieu of battles fought and governments toppled, what people ate and drank and how they washed themselves in distant centuries. My sister read only three books, over and over again: *The Diary of Anne Frank*, *The Bell Jar*, and *I Never Promised You a Rose Garden*, all bath-bloated. My father alternated technical treatises with what he called 'airplane novels,' paperbacks of a suspenseful nature, usually with partially naked women on the cover.

Of all the members of the family, only my brother showed the instincts of a connoisseur. In a little room off the living room that we called 'the Hole' (and that would later, to his lasting regret, be annexed to my parents' bathroom to make space for a hydromassage tub), he kept his collection of science fiction and fantasy novels, their covers agleam with stars and starships and gaseous orbs circling triple suns. Not surprisingly, the Hole owed its name to the fact that it was both dark and cramped, no more than a closet, really, with one tiny window against which my brother had pushed his desk. To add to the effect of Hole-ishness he had stained the plywood walls and bookshelves the color of coffee.

After he went off to college, I used to sit sometimes by myself in the Hole, working on model cars and pausing occasionally to stare at the cover or read a few pages of one of the sci-fi novels. My favorite was called *One-Eyed Runts of Gamma Epsilon Five*, and told the story of a spacecraft that has had the misfortune to crash on a planet overrun with bald, single-eyed dwarves, all of them female and sex-starved. These dwarves, with their puckered pink lips and three-fingered hands, featured prominently on the cover, where they were depicted groping for a protagonist just outside the frame. That they had no visible genitals only added to my burgeoning confusion as to the construction of the female anatomy, a confusion about which I was too shy to inquire of my father and too shrewd to ask my brother, who in any case would have used the occasion only to make something up.

I give the wrong impression, however, if I suggest that *One-Eyed Runts of Gamma Epsilon Five* was in any way typical of my brother's collection, the vast bulk of which consisted of high-minded novels by authors for whom the ether represented less an end in itself than a framework within which to pose existential questions. Nor did all of these books look up to the stars; some looked downward, to a region of caverns and castle keeps and cobwebbed passages, books like *The Lord of the Rings* and *The Gormenghast Trilogy*, the musty covers of which seemed themselves to emanate the odors of a medieval dungeon. Holed up in the Hole during those lonely afternoons after both he and my sister had moved out of the house, I'd often thumb through the volumes of *The Gormenghast Trilogy*, absorbing without ever reading them that aura of gothic mystery of which the Hole itself seemed portion, as if it were a service entrance to some realm of Merovingian darkness.

Much of my early education about sex took place – ironically – in the Hole. For instance, on a low shelf, my brother kept a small assortment of *Zap Comix*, in the pages of which leering cartoon foxes, their fangs dripping with lust, pried apart the legs of buxom pig-women, while mares in high heels paraded down Haight Street, their human breasts spilling over the bodices of their tiny dresses, cinched at the diaphragm like the ones my sister made for herself on her Singer sewing machine. The world of the *Zap Comix* was infused with a marijuana haze, and could not have been more different from that of the novels my mother brought home from the library, in which sex figured more as an occasion for anger than burlesque. One, for instance, ended with its heroine buying pornographic pictures in Mexico – for some reason I remember vividly the sentence, 'An immense brown penis pushes against a pink breast' – while another described in visceral detail (and more radically still, in the present tense) the changing of a tampon. With their clipped, even clinical tone, their matter-of-fact use of dirty words ('prick' and 'piss' in particular), and, most tellingly, their atmosphere of ennui and short-temperedness, these novels gave voice to the same half-articulated feminist rage that must have underscored my mother's habit of snapping the spines of books (even '7-Day' books), or in the evenings cleaning the copper bottoms of her

Revere Ware pots with such ferocity they seemed literally to glower.

My brother and sister are much older than I am. Both of them had graduated from college well before I entered high school. They attended, one year apart, the university off the grounds of which we lived, and near which my father worked. Yet whereas my sister stayed on campus all four years, my brother, during his senior year, moved out of his dorm and rented a studio in an old Victorian house that had been divided up into apartments. I liked to visit him sometimes in this room to which he was gradually removing all his books, now that the Hole was in the process of being transformed into a hydromassage tub. There were always amusing things to look at there, such as a postcard on which one mouse says to another, 'Why do mice have such small balls?' and the other answers, 'Because very few mice know how to dance.' (I didn't get the joke; nor did my brother – probably because my begging amused him – ever enlighten me as to its hidden meaning.)

It was also in the house where my brother lived that I met my first novelist. I can't remember his name. He was an old man (at least from my perspective), oleaginous in aspect, with a large mole on his cheek. One afternoon when I was visiting he knocked on the door and presented my brother with a copy of his latest book, a paperback called *The House*. I remember he called me 'son' and patted my head. I suppose my brother didn't read *The House* immediately, however, because it wasn't until Thanksgiving that I heard it referred to again, this time as the subject of some inside joke between him and my sister: indeed, the mere mention of its title drove them both into fits of laughter. For as I soon learned, the house in *The House* was the very one in which my brother and the old novelist rented apartments. Nor were their fellow tenants at all happy about the rather pornographic use to which the novelist had put them. 'You're too young to understand,' my brother said, but loaned me *The House* anyway, which I read in a single night. The plot, of which I recall only the basic outlines, was episodic and multiform, as is often the case in books that take place in apartment houses, or hotels, or on cruise ships. I remember that in the first chapter one of the occupants of the house murders her husband, then chops up his body and feeds it to the garbage disposal. Another is an Indian who teaches his neighbors' neglected wives the pleasures of the Kama Sutra. Another – perhaps the novelist himself, in a rather idealized self-portrait – is a handsome, virile homosexual given to cruising the parks and alleyways of an unnamed city.

This was not the first time I had encountered homosexuality in a novel: I had read *Myra Breckinridge*, which was one of my father's airplane books, as well as most of Gordon Merrick's *The Lord Won't Mind*, when no one was looking, at the local bookstore. *The House*, however, more than either of these books, I savored, in particular one scene in which the gay hero, cruising a park, encounters another man dressed in jeans and a black leather jacket who stands before him, gyrates his hips suggestively and rubs his erection through his pants. Slowly the outline of the 'hardened member' is revealed, slowly the man unzips his pants, exposing black pubic hair – at which point a dog scares him away. (As for the author, a few months after the book was published he started receiving anonymous threats, presumably from his neighbors, and was compelled to move.)

Aside from novels and domestic histories, my mother's chief source of literary enlightenment in those years was a weekly magazine of immense prestige, so famous that it was known in our house simply as 'the magazine.' No doubt, if you are American, you have already guessed the name of the magazine; nor do I neglect to give it here out of coyness, but rather in deference to the sense of awe that name inspired in me, back in the days when the magazine enjoyed an almost sacred literary status, one that provoked both veneration and fear, as in those religious sects that perceive God's name as too holy to bear utterance. For in our kitchen, where brightly colored piles of the magazine's back issues lay everywhere, it really was a sort of cult, one into which my mother, from when I was very young, inducted me. And as a consequence, I viewed the magazine not, like other magazines, being as the product of discrete human labor in some New York office, but rather as a sort of immaculate conception that occurred weekly in our mailbox – an impression that its unusual policy of not printing the names of its editors, nor those of the authors who composed the brief unsigned articles with which each issue commenced, and which were written, as it were, by vapor, only served to intensify. In this magazine there were no biographical notes, no photographs of writers; instead their names – some famous, some obscure – appeared modestly, in tiny type, at the end of every article.

Today I cannot underestimate the importance of this magazine, which in those years really defined American literature, and not only positively, by what it published, but negatively, by what it did not. So vast was its influence that just as writers whose fiction appeared regularly in its pages became identified as ——— authors (a Faustian bargain, because it required them to trade, in exchange for this huge advantage, some of their independence), those whose work never appeared in the magazine were forced to define themselves in opposition to it, because it went without saying that every story the magazine did *not* publish it had necessarily rejected.

After my mother died my father told me something that surprised me. He told me that in the years just after my birth she had entertained, for a time, literary aspirations of her own; had even written half a novel, the manuscript of which he had discovered, one afternoon, in a kitchen drawer, and started to read, at which point she had snatched it out of his hands and eventually burned it. To me, she never mentioned any desire to write, though I do remember a peculiar incident that occurred when I was thirteen, and that in retrospect suggests the possibility of a latent and unfulfilled ambition on her part. At that time the *New York Times Magazine* – the famous Sunday crossword puzzle of which she filled in so religiously – was sponsoring a competition to finish a short story, the first half of which had been written by a writer famously associated with that other magazine, the one to which we were so in thrall. After reading the half story, I decided to enter the contest. I don't remember what I wrote, only that I took great pride in my pages, and showed them to my mother on the assumption that she would give my venture her seal of approval. To my bewilderment, however, she did not smile as she put the pages down, only pursed her lips and crinkled her nose, as if the dog had just farted. 'I'm sorry, honey,' she said, 'but this really is very immature. If you sent it into the contest, you'd only embarrass yourself.'

I was stunned. Nonetheless I obeyed my mother, who was the only authority on literary matters I knew, and consigned my pages – as she had those of her unfinished novel – to the back of a drawer. A few months later, when the winners of the contest were announced, I was dismayed to discover among the names of the runners-up that of a twelve-year-old boy from Michigan.

A long while later, when I was in college, my mother telephoned me one afternoon. 'You'll never guess who I met in the waiting room at the radiation therapy center,' she said. 'The nicest woman, from Tacoma. Her name is Leonie Kaufman. And her daughter – you'll never believe it – works for the magazine.'

I was sitting at my desk in the cold Northeast, before the

IBM Selectric typewriter I had saved up for months to buy, and that seemed to me so 'state of the art.' 'Really?' I said, slightly amazed to learn that *anyone* actually worked for the magazine – and more particularly, anyone with a connection to my mother.

This was the year after I took Stanley Flint's seminar. At the time I was taking yet another writing course, less demanding than Flint's, and taught by a novelist rumored to be a female-to-male transsexual. Until I heard this rumor, nothing in the novelist's appearance had led me to suspect him of having once been a woman, though on scrutinizing his physiognomy more carefully I did notice that his hands were smallish, his face unusually soft and round, his voice a bit high for a man's: evidence, perhaps, of the rumor's truth, or else of the degree to which I was susceptible to the power of suggestion.

In any event, my teacher's original gender mattered less to me than the fact that unlike Flint, he was encouraging me mightily in my pursuit of a story on which I was at work, a story based on events that had taken place at our university during the first semester of my freshman year. Back then I lived across the hall from a boy called Matthew Spalding – a very clever boy, a talented actor, good at doing imitations of movie stars and opera singers. Though I liked Matthew, I didn't think much about him – that is, until the afternoon a few weeks into the term when he walked into the men's room on the seventh floor of the main library, closed himself into a stall, and with a carving knife he had hidden in his backpack stabbed himself in the stomach, slashed his wrists, and slit his throat.

It is a commonplace that many would-be suicides, when they try to kill themselves, are less interested in dying than in making a 'cry for help.' Thus they climb to the tops of buildings where they know the police will try to talk them down, they swallow a bottle of pills and immediately announce the fact to their loved ones, they slash their wrists, but only at an hour when they can be certain that someone will come home and find them. And at first, because he had been rescued, we all assumed that Matthew had attempted a suicide of this sort; and yet if this was the case, he'd calculated very badly, for almost no one used the seventh floor of the library. Indeed, Matthew would probably be dead today, were it not for a fact of which I doubt he could have been apprised: namely, that this particular men's room, not only by virtue of its remote location, but because its door could actually be locked, was known among campus homosexuals as a good place to meet for sex. And as a result, only a minute or so after he went into this bathroom, someone else went in after him, someone who, upon seeing the blood pouring out from under the stall's partition, immediately summoned the police; the upshot of which was, miraculously, that Matthew was saved, and within a few days receiving visitors in the psychiatric ward of the university hospital. Most of these visitors were girls who had had crushes on him even before his suicide attempt. Now, one after another, they made the pilgrimage (I did too, once) to the hospital psych ward, with its double-locked double doors, only to return a few hours later, eyes lucid as those of witnesses to saintly miracles, and tell their friends, 'He's not the one who's sick. *We* are.'

This is not, though, the end of the story. A few days after Matthew's hospitalization a pretty girl named Pasha, more in love with him even than the others, tried also to kill herself so that she too could be admitted to the psych ward and be near him. Astoundingly, she was placed in the same therapy group with Matthew, who with his intelligence and wit had already taken a sort of leadership position in the odd little community of the ward. Later, Pasha went back to Oregon, while Matthew was transferred to a private sanitarium on the edge of the city, a place to which the girls in our dormitory continued to make their pilgrimages for a while, though fewer and fewer every week.

This, then – the story of Matthew, and Pasha, and the seventh-floor men's room – was the story I was writing that semester. Indeed, it was usually the thing over which I was laboring during the evenings I spent in the rear smoking section of the library, a locale that, as the months went by, was to become as popular as certain bars, despite the carpets into which cigarette butts had been ground, and the laminated tables yellowed by tar, and the brightly hued, vinyl-covered armchairs, pocked with burn marks, that lined the back wall. Sometimes it was so crowded there you couldn't get a seat and had no choice but to migrate across the way to the luminously clean nonsmoking section, where no one interesting sat, yet where – as in those regions of chic New York restaurants to which the unknown are relegated, and which are deemed 'Siberia' – you could always be sure of finding a place.

One evening, while I was working on my story, the TV star strolled in and took the seat across from mine. I glanced up surreptitiously from my notebook. She was less pretty than I remembered from the situation comedies in which she had appeared. Her famous black hair, which had appeared so lustrous on screen, was tied in a limp braid. She had slung an L. L. Bean jacket over the back of the chair, was smoking a Camel, and writing (to judge from her books) a paper on Faulkner. Her gaze never met mine, though a few nights later, at one of those edgy off-campus parties the lesbians were always throwing, we bumped into each other, literally, on the dance floor, after which, having first dusted herself off, she gave me a smile of recognition. Although she was a fixture at these parties, I still wasn't certain whether she was a lesbian herself, given that she never attended the monthly gay and lesbian dances, or the meetings of the various gay and lesbian alliances, or any of the events attendant upon GLAD week.

And yet a few weeks earlier my friend Eve Schlossberg, a photographer who liked to roam around the parties in order to capture the pictures of ecstatic dancers that would later make her famous, claimed to have had an altercation with the TV star, who had stormed up to her in a fury and demanded her film: 'As if I were some common paparazzo!' Eve added imperiously. Needless to say she refused to surrender her negatives, though she did promise not to print any shots in which the TV star appeared.

That fall I had a new roommate, Donald Schindler. A complex saga of love and disillusionment underlay this seemingly trivial change of circumstances. As I mentioned earlier, the previous year I had roomed with Jim Sterling, with whom I often spent weekends on Central Park West. Although Jim was the product of a genteel New York upbringing – as a teenager he had attended an exclusive East Side prep school, accompanied the daughters of the rich to cotillions, ridden taxis back and forth from violin lessons with a member of the New York Philharmonic – his coarse, reddish hair and thick fingers betrayed the fact that like me, he was a child of immigrants, Hester Street peasants who had risen in one generation from peddlers to captains of industry. Not that any self-consciousness about his origins ever marred his happy relations with the debutantes and bluebloods with whom he'd gone to school; on the contrary, he got along with them all famously. He got along with everyone famously. It was the only thing about him that I distrusted.

Jim was a major force in my life during those years. Avidly social, he stood at the center of a little circle that gathered most evenings around eleven in our room to eat chocolate chip cookies, or traveled en masse for pizza and hot tuna grinders at a local Greek diner. The members of this group, the founding of which dated back to the earliest days of our freshman year, had little in common save contiguity, the fact that we had all been assigned, that distant first semester, to the same dorm. Under normal circumstances such indiscriminate alliances – of which only the very young are capable – dissolve over time; and yet in our case, against the odds and thanks in great part to the vigorous energy with which Jim strove to hold us together, the little group had managed to maintain not only its integrity but its habits.

Nostalgia had a good deal to do with it. A burnished glow of childhood – nourished by Jim – irradiated most of our evenings together, and seemed to protect us. It didn't matter that during most of the hours of the day we were all off pursuing knowledge and sex and praise, itching to grow up; those evenings in our room, we drank hot chocolate instead of the gin that was what Gretchen and Schuyler served at their parties. No one smoked cigarettes, much less pot, for Jim had a puritanical aversion to all drugs. Indeed, he had not only vowed but kept his vow never to speak again to a former member of the group, a sly New York girl who had once fed him a pot brownie without telling him what it was.

But to get back to the saga of our breakup: the year before, we had made a new friend, a transfer student from the University of North Carolina called Ashley, or Ash, Barker, whom Jim had subsequently initiated into the little group. On the surface at least, Ash's most striking characteristic was his almost seraphic beauty. With his olive skin, blue eyes, and blond hair, he might have been an angel in a Botticelli portrait. His charm was androgynous and, for me at least, curiously without erotic power. Yet even though (in my view) he didn't hold a candle, say, to certain handsome and virile stars of the lacrosse team, he stood out in a way that these athletes never would, thanks to the very quality of inviolability that he projected, as if he really were an angel: a possibility to which the fact that he shaved but once a week lent credence, and as a consequence of which he always had dozens of suitors, most of them unappealing – homely Jane Eyres in search of their own personal Rochesters, or big-breasted seductresses who wanted to mother him, or more disturbingly (at least to Jim and me) boys, most notably a jaded member of the Philip Crenshaw circle who lived upstairs from us, in one of the rooms designated as 'psycho singles' because they were reserved for students with whom no one else was willing to live. This boy was forever showing up uninvited in Ash's room, where he would lie on the couch and stare at Ash while he studied. His method was relentlessness; it was as if he hoped by sheer force of will to breach the battlements of Ash's resplendent virginity. For Ash, by virtue of his good nature as much as his good looks, was serious business, worthy of labor, and yet at the same time naive, unsuspecting, always willing to take at his word, say, the physics grad student who offered to give him clown lessons, then in the course of one of the lessons tried to kiss him. Also, his character was such that he could not bear to disappoint, and therefore accepted invitations on which he would otherwise have preferred to pass. One afternoon, for instance (and this sort of episode was typical), he received a letter from a girl he didn't know, in which she explained that her roommate, who was in his Shakespeare class, had become so besotted with him that the writer feared she might do herself in if Ash didn't ask her on a date. Upon receiving this bizarre communication his immediate and panicked response was to pick up the phone and prepare to do as bidden, for there was more than a trace of chivalry in his nature; but Jim, to whom he had read the letter aloud, wouldn't hear of it. Instead *he* picked up the phone, dialed the number of the student psychiatric service, and gave to the psychiatrist who answered the names both of the girl and her roommate. Relieved to have the matter thus taken out of his hands, Ash could not express fervently enough his gratitude to Jim – a gratitude from which Jim, in turn, walked away with pride, glib in the assurance that because he at least would never be mistaken for a predator, he now possessed what all the predators wanted: Ash's trust.

The crisis, if that is not too strong a word, came during the spring. Because I was taking Stanley Flint's seminar that term, I was spending less time with Ash and Jim. Instead I was hanging out in the rear smoking section of the library, in the company of lesbians and cocaine snorters and other depraved sorts of whom Jim obviously (though silently) disapproved. More and more that semester, Stanley Flint and the lesbians had begun to captivate my attention, diverting it from Jim's little group. For instance, instead of eating in the dining hall with Ash and Jim, I would go on occasion to little off-campus dinner parties. Instead of having pizza with them after the library closed, I would sit with the lesbians in their dark apartments, watching them smoke joints. I suppose I should have taken it as a sign when one weekend Jim invited Ash – and not me – to travel with him to New York. And yet it is perhaps in the nature of friendship, as opposed to love, that we think of it as a constancy that requires no nurturing, and from which we can withdraw when we choose, certain that, like the affection of our mothers, it will be there to welcome us back whenever we return.

Alas, this is not how it is with friendship, which in the end is more like love than most people admit: a truth I learned late that semester, when one night Jim came up to my table at dinner (I was eating alone) and asked if he could sit down with me. Of course, I said.

Visibly nervous, he pulled out a chair. In a few weeks, he reminded me, the room draw was coming up. We would have to choose our roommates for the following year.

'Yes?' I said.

'Well,' Jim went on, 'I've been talking it over with Ash, and we've decided that we'd like to room together.'

I blinked. 'Oh,' I said, 'you mean the two of you,' for the dormitory included a few triples.

Jim looked away. 'Yes,' he said. 'The two of us.'

I pretended not to care; in truth, however, I was both shocked and hurt. After all, I'd introduced Jim to Ash. That they should now have established, between themselves, an intimacy from which I was to be barred seemed both unjust and fated. Nor did I give much thought to my own negligence in the matter, the degree to which I had ignored, in recent weeks, Jim's friendship. For it seemed to me in those days that I was forever introducing people, boys and boys or boys and girls, only to see them form impregnable couples, to which I would become at best a sort of annex, a substitute child, wanted because the couple in question needed an audience before whom they might perform their little dramas. And though, in the case of Jim and Ash, the coupling was not erotic, nonetheless the result was the same: not only was I alone, I feared that solitude was to be my lot in life. More practically, I had only a few weeks in which to find someone else to room with, or face exile in a psycho single. Unfortunately, nearly all the boys in my dormitory had already made their arrangements, with the result that only 'the scrapings,' as my mother might have put it, were left to choose among.

That was how I ended up with Donald Schindler. Not that there was anything wrong with him – that is to say, he didn't smell bad or have terrible acne, he wasn't a member of the National Rifle Association, or the Dungeons and Dragons Club, or the Fundamentalist Christian Alliance. Instead he was simply a midsized Jewish boy from Long Island who at least on the surface conformed to every stereotype of the midsized Jewish boy from Long Island. Indeed, that was the trouble. With his freckled skin and chestnut-colored hair he was a walking cliché, robust and dull and responsible, the classic mensch of whom mothers dream when they plan their daughters' weddings. And for this reason no one liked him.

I have always thought it must be a terrible thing to be the living epitome of a type. This was particularly the case with Donald, who had been for too many years denied the opportunity to reveal the breadth and dimension of his character, shunned too often by peers who, presuming him to be *only* what he appeared, had never taken the trouble to get to know him, so that in the end he had had no choice but to close himself off, grow solitary and self-supportive, in an effort to protect himself from what he perceived to be the certainty of social failure. And this was, ironically, the other reason why no one wanted to live with him: he radiated a hostility of which he himself was unconscious, and would have accepted exile in a psycho single without protest had I not come up to him one morning to inquire whether he might want to consider rooming with me. His answer, to my mild surprise, was an instantaneous and smiling yes.

Having hesitantly decided to pair up – relieved, as well, no longer to be among those poor dregs of humanity still without roommates at this late date – we made a plan to have dinner together that night. An Economics major, he told me that he intended to go to law school when he graduated, not because he loved the law, but because he felt it incumbent upon himself to maintain that level of family affluence for the sake of which his grandparents – like mine, poor immigrants, children of pogroms and shtetls – had endured so many years of hardship. A while later, when I met Eli Aronson, I would witness an even more intense variation on this theme: the theme of the immigrant family which, having struggled to attain prosperity, guards that prosperity almost jealously. Such families (Donald's was exemplary) often lead a sort of split existence, in which the desire to assimilate does battle with a heritage they are determined, after so many years of diaspora, to entrench. Thus Donald's parents, who belonged to an exclusive synagogue, who had sent him every week for Hebrew lessons when he was a child, and who would have been scandalized had he dated a gentile girl, also lived in a white Georgian house, resplendently colonnaded, and situated on a verdant lane dotted with maple trees and yew hedges called Maidstone Court. His father was Seymour, just as mine was Herbert. Seymour, Sydney, Herbert, Bernard: growing up, I'd always assumed these to be ordinary Jewish first names, when in fact they were stolid British last names, selected by our grandparents – all those Shmuels and Yettas, Shlomos and Saras – to ease their sons' social acclimation. Nor would it have ever occurred to them to think how swiftly their new homeland would slot these names right back where they belonged in our assumptions, leaving in their wake Uncle Bernie, Uncle Sy, Uncle Herb, those consummate Yids.

The self-awareness that Donald displayed during that dinner surprised and impressed me. Somehow I had never expected him to be so consciously sardonic about his own status as an avatar, a status the very fact of which effaced, at least in other people's eyes, the possibility of his even having a personality. And yet his private self, which he revealed shyly but without reluctance over the course of the next semester, proved to be much more complex than this outward aspect had led me to believe. For instance, as the term progressed, and as I began to receive more and more phone messages from smoky-voiced lesbians, an unsuspected strain of bohemianism began to expose itself in him. He was full of curiosity about my disreputable friends, their habits and hangouts. Once, after Schuyler had called to invite me for drinks at a seedy bar that she and her clan had recently colonized, he even asked me whether I made it my habit to frequent such louche environs: not disapprovingly, but in a tone of genuine curiosity, behind which there resonated a shy desire – not hope, he had been excluded too long for that – to be invited along.

I asked him what he had planned for that evening. He shrugged. 'Nothing. Maybe the tailgate party,' he said, referring to one of those large, dull gatherings the dormitories threw on weekends, the sort of dreary fêtes to which boys like Donald paid admission, only to stand together loutishly on the periphery, talking about football.

A sudden surge of generosity claimed me, and I asked him if he wanted to join us. He looked astonished; clearly he was so used to being left out of things that actually being invited along had never occurred to him.

In a state of high excitement, he hurried into the bathroom, from which he emerged a few moments later emanating the bitter odor of Listerine, the cloying perfume of Arrid Extra Dry rolled on too lavishly. For a moment I regretted my impulsive kindness; what, after all, would the lesbians, with their Samsara and patchouli oil, make of this boring boy, this boy whose very smell, so antiseptic and oppressive, suggested suburban drugstores? I feared lest Donald, in his plainness, should stand out in their atmosphere of opium-den lassitude as rudely as Gretchen, with her pearls and nose ring, would have stood out at the Schindlers' synagogue. Yet as it turned out I had nothing to worry about – or rather, as is so often the case, I was worrying about the wrong thing.

In due course we arrived at the bar. Its low-voltage green glow revealed, at a front booth upholstered in red vinyl, the faces, both dissipated and exotic, of the lesbians drinking and smoking with a claque of gay boys. No one was talking; they wore on their faces expressions of boredom that seemed well suited to the dilapidated condition of the bar, so unlike that of certain spiffy establishments closer to campus, where well-heeled undergraduates gathered to guzzle Pimm's Cup and sing old college songs. This bar, on the other hand, had never been a student hangout; indeed, until the lesbians had taken it over, it had remained the exclusive and dreary domain of ill-tempered old men, professional drunks who lived in the single-room-occupancy hotels that punctuated the outskirts of the campus, some of whom now sat near the television, staring glumly over their beers at the peculiar and noisy party that had intruded upon what had been up until then their private sanctum.

Slumming, usually looked down upon, must be thanked at least for this, that it pumps economic nutrition into dead locales. It didn't matter that the wallpaper was smoke-stained and peeling, or that the television had bad reception, or that the vinyl booths were splitting in places, exposing their yellowed foam rubber innards: what was important was that suddenly, because of the lesbians, the bar was happening. Thus Dolly, the waitress, had a fresh dye job, and knew each of her new clients not only by name, but by drink. 'Stoly and tonic, right, Laur?' she asked in her husky voice, while Mel, her stoic partner and possible husband, mixed daiquiris. Meanwhile Donald, approaching the crowded booth, smiled like someone who has finally, after years of searching, found his element.

Amazingly enough, he hit it off with everyone. Nor did the fact that some of the girls were making out with each other faze him in the least; instead he seemed not only to accept this homosexual ambiance, but to delight in it – which did not, I think, mean that he himself was gay; on the contrary, I suspect that it was more the bohemian character of the situation that appealed to him, at least to judge from the exuberant way he was looking at everyone, especially Lauren, the girl to whom the TV star was purportedly linked at the time, and Eve Schlossberg, who was not herself a lesbian (yet) and seemed perfectly willing to return his attentions. She had brought a friend with her, a boy named Lars whom I thought very handsome and arrogant, with his sleek nose, his lean legs and pouty eyes. This Lars made me nervous for the precise reason that unlike Philip and Gerald and their crowd, nothing in his appearance, his voice or clothes or countenance, gave away the fact that he was gay. Homosexuality as a self-declaring state made more sense to me, for though I was spending most of my free time, that semester, with a gay crowd, among young men and women who, I supposed, took it for granted that I too was gay, nonetheless even at this late date I clung to the belief that so long as I neither spoke of nor acted on my sexual impulses, they would fail to implicate me. Which, as it turned out, was not the case at all, as I learned the evening I came back to my room from the library only to find that someone had written on the door 'Martin Bauman is gay' – words I wiped away furiously, in the middle of the night, fearful lest someone should happen upon me in the throes of erasure.

Given the situation I was in, you'd think I would have admired Lars, who in his 'normal guy' masculinity provided such a contrast to Gerald and Philip's self-mocking and repellent faggotry; and indeed, if Lars had cultivated me, if he had even so much as acknowledged my existence, I might have done just that; my entire life might have gone differently. Instead, from the moment we were introduced (by Eve, with a knowing wink), Lars refused to give me the time of day. Not only did he seem not to like me, he seemed actively to dislike me, so much so that soon I began to perceive his virile athleticism less as an ideal to be emulated than a challenge to which I – not a queen like Philip Crenshaw, but at the same time incapable of serving a volleyball – could never possibly live up. Worse, his rebuff implied that the campus was full of boys who were neither scrawny and intellectual like me, nor lisping and faggotty like Philip, into whose fraternity of masculine pleasure I could never hope to gain admission. Yet if they existed, these boys, who were they? Why had I never met them? Where were they hidden?

Lars's refusal that night even to acknowledge my presence did not surprise me. What did surprise me was that even as he ignored me, he paid enormous attention to Donald; flirted with him outrageously; even, as the night drew to a close, put his arms around him and whispered something in his ear that made Donald wriggle with laughter.

Afterward, on the way back to our room, slightly envious that my charitable gesture had led to such a huge success, I asked Donald what it was that Lars had said to him. 'That he has a crush on me,' Donald answered, his lips turning upward in a smile. Once again an act of kindness, an act of introduction, had ended, perversely enough, in my own exclusion.

From that night on, Donald became an integral member of Gretchen and Schuyler's circle. The degree to which they embraced him stunned and slightly offended me. Now it was Donald who Lauren called to invite to parties; Donald who offered to take *me* along; Donald who sat alone with Lars at a banquette at dinner, engaged in a laughing tête-à-tête. Dressed in his usual uniform of white T-shirt, jeans, and outmoded tennis shoes, smelling always of Listerine, he went to every party, accepted every invitation, laughed at the irony that after so many years as a wallflower, he had finally found social success – but in a circle where every girl was gay! Well, not *every* girl, I said, and reminded him of Eve Schlossberg, always skulking through those parties with her opportunistic camera. He yawned. Yes, he said, it was true, there was Eve Schlossberg; and yet that hair of hers! . . . His blasé attitude puzzled me, even made me wonder if Donald might be gay after all, until it occurred to me that Eve was quite possibly the first girl who had ever expressed a genuine interest in him, in which case it might be more exciting to rebuff her advances than to respond to them.

Meanwhile his friendship with Lars deepened. At parties they made a habit of dancing together, for Donald had no qualms about dancing with other boys. Once Lars even asked him to slow dance, an invitation to which Donald responded first by balking, then, after a pause, by boldly stepping into Lars's arms – a gesture of bravura on his part that made me slightly queasy with envy. The late arrival of this chance to reveal the hidden wildness in his personality appeared to delight Donald, especially at party's end, when the breaking dawn found him ensconced in Lars's lap, smiling broadly, as if he were simultaneously answering a challenge and issuing one, proving his openness and flouting the narrow mores of his mother, who, if she'd seen him in such a posture, would have burst into tears.

And yet I doubt Donald ever accepted Lars's more intimate invitations, the ones I myself had hoped to receive. If he did, he certainly never told me. Not that this dissuaded Lars from continuing to make them; on the contrary, Donald's rebuffs appeared only to fuel Lars's determination to win him over. And this I found confusing. For by courting Donald so unabashedly, Lars had called into question what I took to be some of the fundamental rules of sex: namely, that very good-looking people naturally gravitate only toward other very good-looking people; that if Lars showed no interest in me, it wasn't because of who I was, but because I simply wasn't of his echelon; finally, that to fall in love with very beautiful people (as, for instance, so many disgraced girls and boys had fallen in love with Ash) was necessarily to invite humiliation and embarrassment. Better, much better, to focus one's attention on those whose attractiveness was more or less on a par with one's own – or so I told myself, until the day that Lars, whom I grouped with Ash in the very highest echelon, fell in love with Donald, plain Donald, who washed his hair with Tegrin and had a greasy forehead. In so doing, he shot my theories to hell.

A question remains: if what made Donald so attractive to Lars and the lesbians was the disparity between the image he projected and the interior self to which it provided such a contrast, then what made the lesbians attractive to him? The answer, I think, was their very inaccessibility, the fact that unlike the women with whom he'd grown up, they were so utterly self-sufficient: rich, capable, smart, and, more significantly, oblivious to, unneeding of, men. Not that they disliked men; they simply didn't require them. My presence, or Donald's, or Lars's, either in the rear smoking section of the library or at Dolly's bar, was fine, was amusing and delightful. It just wasn't necessary. I suspect Donald appreciated that, and respected them for it. I suspect he also found it sexy.

As for Lars, months passed and he still didn't give up on his efforts to seduce Donald, even though, quite naturally, the unglamorous reality of their friendship had by now eclipsed, even defused, the erotic frisson of their flirtation, in the process infusing their banter with a joking quality, as if it were all simply a game (albeit a game to which the unlikely but never relinquished possibility of sexual consummation lent an edge of tension). For Donald, it was becoming clear, no matter how flattering he might find Lars's invitations, was in the end no more likely to accept them than Eve Schlossberg's. Nor was Lars single-minded in his pursuits, as I learned when, during a break in our Milton seminar one afternoon, Eve announced to me (with the smug pride and fake offhandedness of the confidante), 'By the way, have you met Lars's new boyfriend?'

'I didn't know he had one,' I answered.

Eve nodded. 'A graduate student in History. They haven't had sex yet,' she added intimately, 'they've only cuddled.'

My response to this news (a response of which I felt ashamed) was again envy. In contrast to Lars, for whom it was no doubt ordinary, the prospect of cuddling as a prelude to sex (not to mention sex) made my mouth water. For whereas he, at nineteen, was already a sexual sophisticate, who had had, or so Eve told me, countless lovers, including his high school music teacher, I was at nineteen a virgin in every sense: a truth I had so far admitted only to Donald, who had confessed in kind that he had done it just once, with a 'slow' girl in his high school. In such worldly, even world-weary circles we wandered like neophytes, admiring and awestruck, yet finally lost in the wilderness.

I realize now that I have not yet said anything about music, which played such an important role in our lives back then. These were the years – those immediately following the advent of punk rock – when the antisocial shrieking of Johnny Rotten and Sid Vicious and the Sex Pistols was in the process of giving way to that more palatable, less threatening version of itself that was known as 'new wave.' Essentially, new wave assimilated the violent ravings of punk into the fold of a more melodic affability, neutralizing both its originality and its power to disturb. And it was to this rather ambiguous music – songs by bands like the Human League, the Thompson Twins, Culture Club – that Donald and I danced so gleefully, both at the parties we went to and on certain wild evenings at Dolly's bar. Remote were the high school gyms where girls had stood anxiously in clusters waiting for boys to ask them to dance, and in which only discrete pairs, captivated by the push and pull of their private orbits, circled that glowing orb, the rented disco ball, as it tossed over the floor, the walls, even our hands and faces, bits of confetti made from light and color that we would chase as aimlessly as a dog chasing a sunbeam. Here, on the other hand, pairdom was not a requirement of danc-ing. You could dance alone, or in a group, and when you danced in a pair, such was the promiscuous fluidity of the crowd that it might hurl a stranger into your arms, or pull your partner from you. Thus in those warrenish apartments where Donald and I danced together, those apartments where all around us girl couples smoked joints and made out on Salvation Army couches, it meant nothing that suddenly he might part from me and yank an annoyed Eve Schlossberg, who was in the middle of snapping a picture, into a jitterbug; or that Lars, appearing out of nowhere, should suddenly run up to him and lift him into the air; or that even the TV star herself, perhaps as a consequence of too violent a shove, should come flying toward me at such speed that the two of us would end up literally on the floor, laughing and only slightly wounded.

Sometimes when we were alone in our room, or in the common room late in the evening, making tapes for a party, Donald and I would 'slam-dance': hurl our bodies against each other with such insolent energy, such youthful and ecstatic recklessness, that in the morning, when I got up to shower, my arms and hips would be covered with bruises.

Then, only a few months into the term, and despite all our fondness for each other, we had a terrible falling out. The source of this breach, surprisingly, was politics, a subject of which I have heretofore made little mention not because it was irrelevant to our lives, but because the degree of its relevance was something of which most of us had remained unconscious, until that fateful November evening in 1980 when Ronald Reagan was elected president. His victory was an outcome that neither my mother nor I, in our wildest dreams, would have ever predicted, having as West Coasters witnessed too many years of gubernatorial ineptitude, too many failures on his part to win the Republican nomination, even to be able to imagine the idea of 'President Reagan.'

Of course we were wrong; and not only wrong, but hugely wrong. For Reagan not only whipped Carter that fall, he whipped him so thoroughly as to leave us numb, horrified to discover the extent to which, in our little liberal enclave, we had been living in a dream, remote from a national disgruntlement that in the form of votes now threatened to undo, as one of my mother's friends put it, 'everything we achieved in the sixties.' Now I laugh at the hysteria to which Reagan's election drove some of my mother's friends, one of whom went so far as to buy an open ticket to France, in the event that a sudden wave of fascism should sweep the nation. In 1980, however, my ideas were more simplistic. I took it as a given that if on a personal or social level two people found sufficient common ground to enjoy each other's company and become friends, then by necessity they must also share the same political perspective. Yet this was not the case at all, as I learned a few weeks before the election, when in reply to some remark I'd made about 'those assholes who'd actually vote for Reagan,' Donald looked me square in the eye and said that if I thought everyone who planned to vote for Reagan was an asshole, then I'd better revise my opinion of him, because he had every intention of voting for Reagan himself.

I was shocked. 'But you're a Democrat,' I said.

'Why should that matter?'

'Because – well, look at the people you hang out with! Do you think any of our friends are voting for Reagan?'

'Lars is voting for Reagan.'

This was too much. 'But Lars is gay!' I protested.

'So?'

'But if Reagan had his way he'd put every homosexual on the planet in a concentration camp!'

'You're exaggerating,' Donald said blithely. 'Anyway, there are plenty of gay Republicans. There's even an organization of gay Republicans in Washington.'

This I refused to believe. To my view, if homosexuality had a genetic origin, the gay gene had by necessity to be linked to the leftist gene. 'I don't see how you can sit there and say all this so casually,' I said. 'You *and* Lars. I mean, look at Reagan's social policies—'

'Look at his economic policies. America can't afford four more years of President Peanut. We'll be bankrupt. We'll be at Russia's mercy.'

Yanking my chair away from the table where we were eating, I fled. Tears filled my eyes. I wondered how I could even endure another night in the same room with Donald, and wanted to call my mother for comfort; to call the dean and ask that Donald be assigned immediately to a psycho single; to call Eve and ask if it was true – if it was even possible – that Lars was a Republican.

In the end, however, I did none of these things. Instead I cold-shouldered Donald, even as we remained roommates. Short of agreeing to change his vote, he did everything he could to remedy the wound. I was the one who refused to budge. For suddenly I found myself disillusioned not only with Donald himself, but with that entire crowd that studied in the rear smoking section of the library, the political viewpoint of which, I was quickly discovering, was essentially one of apathy. Gretchen, for instance, said she had no intention even of registering to vote. 'I'm apolitical,' she told me drowsily. Eve insisted she was a libertarian, while Lauren refused to discuss the subject at all. Their lack of engagement in the electoral process, though not out of keeping with the generally lethargic affect they cultivated, saddened me, and cast in a new light those very aspects of the circle that had attracted me in the first place. No longer did blasé smoking call up, for me, Paris cafés on rainy afternoons: instead it made me cough. Likewise at the parties – so crowded and fume-riddled – where once I had danced in a rapture, I found myself growing claustrophobic and bored. Even Dolly's I didn't enjoy anymore, so edged with contempt did the rapport between owner and clients suddenly appear to me: evidence not of freedom or imagination, but of that Weltschmerz in which only those who have both time and money can afford to indulge.

If I owed my rather rigid ideas about politics to anyone, it was my mother, an entrenched enemy of the status quo, who had voted several presidential elections in a row for an obscure independent candidate, a black lady with a lisp called Shirley Chisholm. I'm still not entirely certain what prompted, in the early seventies, my mother's transformation (at least in my eyes) from docile housewife to troublemaker; I suspect it was some confluence of feminist dogma and dissatisfaction with her lot in life. All that is sure is that at a certain moment she started infuriating my father with her habit, at dinner parties, of refusing to stay silent when some of his more right-wing colleagues made remarks along the lines of, 'If you ask me, the simplest solution is just to drop a bomb on Moscow.'

'I understand that you had to think it,' my father would remark afterward, crabbily undoing his tie, still reeling from my mother's outraged and withering reply, 'but did you have to *say* it?'

The fact was, unlike my father, who counseled in almost every circumstance the avoidance of conflict, my mother believed with equal avidity in speaking her mind. Sometimes I thought this tendency innate to her character; on other occasions I suspected that she was fomenting discord for the express purpose of vexing her husband. In any case his anxiety lest she say something explosive to someone, coupled with her resentment of his desire, in her words, to 'shut her up about politics,' lent to all social occasions they attended together (and especially to the parties they threw at home) an aroma of panic and hostility that infiltrated the house for days before and afterward. For instance, I remember a costume party they gave one year at Mardi Gras, to which my father had invited, among others, a particularly reactionary colleague, and my mother a friend of hers from the hair-dresser's, a woman with peroxide blond hair like Dolly's, whose husband showed up wearing a Nixon mask. My father's colleague, offended, left in a huff. 'It's disgraceful,' he said, 'mocking the president of the United States like that' – a remark to which my father responded by paling, my mother by smiling, ever so slightly.

Though my mother had hated Nixon vehemently, cursed him through the Watergate years, vowed that as soon as her cancer was diagnosed as terminal she would 'take him out,' she looked upon Reagan less as a villain than as a buffoon. Indeed, when he won the Republican nomination that year, her initial response was to breathe a sigh of relief, since in her view the choice of such a cretin as the Republican candidate simply ensured Jimmy Carter's reelection. Not that she liked Carter, either, having taken his decision to reinstate draft registration as a personal betrayal. For the Vietnam War was not, then, so far off that she didn't still have nightmares in which she went to visit me in boot camp and found me with my head shaved, being subjected to humiliations that were to me (I must admit) exciting to contemplate, because I could not do even a single push-up. Also, my poor brother, toward the end of the war, had had the misfortune of drawing the number 4 in the draft lottery, which meant almost certain conscription. In a panic he had bought a ticket to Canada, though in the end the combination of a heart murmur and a college deferment (one of the last given out before the war ended) saved him from being shipped off.

As my eighteenth birthday approached, the decision as to whether I myself should register for the draft became a source of contention between my parents. Curiously enough my father, who took the matter far less seriously than my mother, advised me simply to ignore the call to register. My mother, on the other hand – imagining, I suppose, a scene in which the police dragged me handcuffed from my dorm room, and furthermore having discussed the matter at great length with the other women in her local chapter of Mothers Against the Draft – believed that I *should* register, but only after sending a letter to our senator asserting my moral opposition to all war. In addition, I was supposed to cover the draft registration card, which I had to fill out at the post office, with stickers expressing my intense resentment at being legally compelled to sign up for a military with which I was not in sympathy: stickers graciously printed up, and paid for, by Mothers Against the Draft.

In the end, more timid than my father (or perhaps he simply feared the ramifications of my mother's strategy) I took the latter course. Meanwhile my mother, since Reagan had won the Republican nomination, found herself in the uncomfortable position not only of having to vote, but to campaign for a candidate by whom she felt personally betrayed.

If she derived comfort from anything at this time, it was the assurance that Carter's reelection was a *fait accompli*. Yet as the summer progressed – exposing, in its merciless heat, the irritable mood of the country – even that assurance became more and more tenuous. I think we were both holding out for some last minute resurgence of sanity that would prove all the pollsters wrong, as had occurred when Truman beat Dewey. Instead the wave crashed over us. Reagan won by a landslide. That night at my university huge, impromptu parties sprouted up everywhere, at which friends of mine whom I would never have dreamed capable of such perfidy opened bottles of champagne and smugly toasted not only the election of 'President Reagan' (how hard it was for me to get my mouth around those words!), but the age of illusory prosperity, of cocaine and wild parties and rampant greed, of which – graced with that peculiar sagacity of which only the young are capable – they were taking with each glass of champagne a first, bloody gulp.

Now, of course, I see that my mother's great misjudgment (and mine) was to assume that, contrary to what Donald had argued, it would be on the basis of social issues – such trivialities as their positions on human rights, war, poverty – that Americans would make up their minds as to which candidate they should elect. Instead, at my university, numerous young people voted for Reagan simply because they intuited that under his leadership they would stand a greater chance of getting very rich. And this, as it turned out, was exactly what happened.

As for me, threading my way through a crowd of revelers on the way to my room that night, I felt not the slightest surprise, only a sense of digestive unease, to observe among the celebrants Donald and Lars, clinking glasses and laughing. When our eyes met they smiled at me pityingly, as if I were one of those aging hippies, throwbacks to a dead era, who can be found even today on Telegraph Avenue in Berkeley, shouting through bullhorns about the demise of People's Park. *Come join us*, those smiles urged me. *Give up your piety, which is out of fashion anyway, and accept that this is good for you.* And they were right; it would prove to be good for me.

Still, I wouldn't join them. Instead I knocked on the door of my old and diehard allies, Jim and Ash, from whom, for a period of months now, I had been estranged. Jim grinned as he let me in. He didn't seem surprised to see me; indeed, from the look on his face, I got the impression that he had been expecting my return all along.

Without a word he shut the door behind me, shut the door on the outside revelry. Here music was playing too – the Supremes singing 'You Can't Hurry Love.' Most of the members of the little group were there, eating chocolate and graham crackers with a vengeance, drinking tea and Coke and in a few cases beer. For as it turned out, we did all have something in common, all of us in that little group, something that it had taken the mayhem outside, from which we had sought collective shelter, to illuminate: a horror at the outcome of the election. And though Jim welcomed me unhesitantly into this cozy atmosphere, though he made not a single allusion to that dissipated mob for the sake of which I had forsaken his reliable friendship, nonetheless I could hear beneath his hospitality the stern drumbeat of disapproval, the echo of unspoken words: 'Why didn't you listen to me? I could have told you they were no good.'

Certain things had changed during my months of exile. Most notably, Ash now had a girlfriend, a very pretty sophomore named Julia Loomis who was unquestionably, according to my old way of looking at things, in his echelon, and who now sat to his left on the sofa, shaking her head sorrowfully even as Jim clucked with a curious admixture of regret and maternal satisfaction.

After that, for a while, I stopped studying in the rear smoking section of the library; instead I sat in Jim and Ash's room and finished my story about Matthew Spalding, of which I was very proud. The story, like the one my mother had dissuaded me from sending to the *New York Times Magazine,* seemed 'adult,' for I had a great imitative faculty, and therefore had written it not in the intimate, conversational tone that came naturally to me (and of which, I hope, this narrative is an example), but rather in a style displaying the hallmarks of what would be labeled, a few years later, literary 'minimalism': the stark, pared-down present tense, bereft of description, the third person voice that adopts no point of view but instead lets events 'speak for themselves.' (If I put this last phrase in quotation marks it is only because

I have learned that events rarely speak for themselves; instead, in most cases, they speak for people, for ideologies, for profit.)

Because my transsexual professor responded to this new story with the sort of exuberant and substanceless praise from which one can extract little benefit or learning, I decided I would send it to Stanley Flint. Though we had not been in touch since the seminar had ended, I knew from Baylor that he was now teaching at a small, posh college in Vermont. Unlike me, over the intervening months Baylor had maintained a steady correspondence with Flint; even sent him a few stories, to which he had responded with his usual mix of passion and attack. She said that in his letters Flint often asked after me, which surprised me, and made me wonder whether he might still be unapprised of my decision to break with him, to remove myself from the cult, to trust him no longer. I suppose I imagined that because, during my summer in New York, I had sometimes spoken ill of him, word of my badmouthing must have necessarily gotten back to him; or even if it hadn't (and in this supposition I revealed an unspoken truth, that I had not broken with the cult at all) that he must have intuited from a distance (for such was Flint's capacity to pillage his students' minds) my secret treachery.

Yet if Baylor was correct, and in his letters to her Flint had asked after me, and even wrote of me with fondness, then perhaps I was wrong: a possibility, surprisingly, which filled me with hope, for in the intervening months I had started to miss the passionate engagement Flint brought to the teaching of writing: an enthusiasm that my current professor, for all his intelligence and charm, simply could not muster.

Armed, then, with Flint's temporary address, I typed up a fresh copy of my new story and sent it off to him. His reply arrived by post four days later.

'Dear Bauman,' he wrote:

Thank you for sending me your story. I'm sorry to say I'm not impressed by it. The problems are multiple, nor do I have time right now to go into every last one of them – that is a task for which I would require a class-room, a table and you in the hot seat across from me (but more about this later). Instead I shall say only that in attempting to emulate the so-called 'minimalist' style you have mauled your natural tendencies (which are warmer than this), in effect, stifled your voice for the sake of mimicking the 'fashionable' – in your case especially, a most dangerous habit.

What I would suggest is that you start lobbying immediately to get me a new post at your great university, bearing in mind that should you succeed your place in whatever room I am assigned will be guaranteed. Really, Bauman, I'd like to conk you on the head, or conk myself on the head, for failing to drum enough of the truth into you when I still had you as my *élève*.

I enclose a copy of the lit mag from this godforsaken little college where I have been exiled, and featuring a story by Baylor which I managed to get into it. But most of the other pieces therein are unrelenting shit.

I beg you to accept my apologies for the abruptness and, I fear, hardness of this letter. Please know that I have written so only because I care about you.

Yours,
Stanley Flint

Reading this letter over again today, I'm struck by its wisdom and sincerity. Reading it then, in the arrogance of my youth, I took offense at it – and not merely because Flint had not liked my story; also because I interpreted his rejection, fundamentally, as a rather sneaky attempt to persuade me that my chances for success as a writer depended utterly on him, and that therefore for my sake (as opposed to his) I should immediately, and almost single-handedly, arrange for him to be rehired. What frustrated me was the sense that he was more interested in getting back his old job than in helping me – which might well have been the case, at least in part. And yet by grabbing onto his desire to return to the university as a justification for ignoring every valid thing he said, I gave in again to the shoddy, cheating strain in my character. I also made a mistake – one that, as the years passed, I would come to regret more and more.

All of which is a long way of saying (nervous, Mr Flint, I am now committing the sin of 'throat-clearing') that I never answered the letter.

Ahem.

Then history, as it occasionally does, knocked me over and trod upon my back, intruded upon my naive belief that by necessity large events occur at a distance from ordinary life, in remote regions from which foreign correspondents report them in newspapers.

One cold day, a few weeks after I failed to answer Stanley Flint's letter, a madman shot the president of the university. Apprehended, the madman said he had done it to prove his love for the very TV star across from whom I had sometimes sat in the rear smoking section of the library, or bumped into at parties. Suddenly journalists and plain-clothes detectives mobbed our quiet campus. Coming out of class, I'd see a fixture of my mother's little kitchen television screen, the man who delivered the news to her faithfully every weeknight before dinner, asking Jim Sterling's opinion of the affair.

In the library someone told me that the FBI had called Gretchen in for questioning – not because they suspected her of having any involvement in the assassination attempt, but because, as one of the TV star's friends, it was thought she might be able to shed some light on the lunatic's motives.

I worried (and perhaps rather hoped) that the police would call me in for questioning. Instead they called in Donald.

By a freakish coincidence, the weekend after the shooting, the TV star was scheduled to appear in a play, her first on-campus theatrical outing. The director the play happened to be Stanley Flint's son, who was a member of the university's thespian club. At first everyone assumed, in the wake of what had happened, that the performance would be canceled, or short of that, that the TV star would be replaced by an under-study – until it became clear that the president would recover, at which point the TV star, displaying that 'show must go on' fortitude so characteristic of good actors, announced through her press agent that she had no intention of reneging on her obligation. This decision only brought more attention to the play, tickets to the opening night of which suddenly became as sought after as those to one of Vladimir Horowitz's rare concerts. Fortunately Jim Sterling, with uncanny foresight, had bought four in advance, three of which, after great pondering and analysis, he decided to give to Julia, to Ash, and to me.

I remember that night vividly – and not for the reasons you might think. Yes, of course, pushing through the clutch of reporters that had gathered outside the auditorium, I enjoyed the heady sensation of importance with which the occasion was invested, as if we were key witnesses going into a court-room. I also enjoyed (why not admit it?) the knowledge that in having a ticket I had become, very briefly, part of an elite, someone who, for this night at least, held power in his hand, in the form of a tiny stub of paper I could have sold for hun-dreds of dollars if I'd chosen to. Not only that, but Jim had managed to get us the best seats in the house. To our right sat the same reporter who had endowed the fiction prize I had won, while a few rows behind us (in the worst seats in the house) I could glimpse Lars and Eve and Donald, to whose friendly waves I responded brusquely. And then there was the empty seat in the row in front of ours, the one we kept eyeing with curiosity until at the last minute, quite literally as the lights dimmed, Stanley Flint himself hurried in and claimed it.

At the sight of him my heart began to race. Suddenly I worried that he would rebuke me, scream at me, as he had in class, for never answering his letter. The matter of where I might hide during intermission preoccupied me until the end of the play's first act. Then the lights came up: I watched carefully to see in which direction Flint was going, so that I might go in the opposite one.

And of course, because I was staring at him, our eyes met; I smiled and waved. Flint's gaze was out of focus. He waved back, though uncertainly, and put on his trench coat. Was it possible that he hadn't recognized me?

Suddenly I did an about-face and approached him. 'Hello,' I said.

He turned. As always he smelled of steam and cities.

'Bauman,' he said in his slight southern lilt.

'Very nice to see you,' I continued, not sure what to call him now – Stanley? Flint? Mr Flint? – as well as astonished by the surge of affection rising in my throat, by that need for his attention which I had made such an effort to suppress in myself, and which, by never answering his letter, I had more or less ruined any chance of seeing fulfilled.

He was not looking at me. He was looking over my shoulder.

'Terrible, what's happened,' I said.

'Mmm,' he answered, distracted, though not necessarily by me.

'Your son's a wonderful director,' I went on. 'I think he's done a fantastic job.'

'Really? I can't tell, myself.'

'Take my word for it.'

He coughed. 'Listen, Bauman, I must be going, I see over there some other former darlings of mine, to whom I need to offer salutations. Good to see you, young man.'

Patting me on the shoulder, he left. I watched him disappear into the crowd. And why was it that a feeling of bereavement suddenly stole over me, one that made no logical sense, since Flint's words had been kind – too kind, even? For they were not the words one used when speaking to a friend, they were the words one used when bidding farewell to someone going off on a voyage from which he will very likely never return, final words, from which I was able to extract either what Flint, in his clever cruelty, intended me to extract – that he had given up on me; that he had no hope for me; that I was no longer one of his 'darlings' – or else (and this was to me an even less palatable possibility) that I simply didn't matter to him anymore; that I was nothing to him; one face among hundreds.

I wandered away. In a corner near our seats Jim and Ash and Julia were dissecting the play. What I wanted more than anything, right then, was to run up to them, to tell them what had happened, to see reflected in Jim's eyes the pity he would no doubt feel for Flint, or at least the Flint I would paint for him: self-serving, jealous, giftless. 'It's all rather sad,' I could hear Jim saying – and indeed, he might have said those very words, except that this time I did not hurry over to him; I did not camouflage my regret with anger, as I had so many times in the past. Instead I stayed where I was, watching the back of Stanely Flint's head grow ever more remote, as once again, and not for the last time, he was lost to me.

4

Titles Not to Be
Read Beyond

ONE WINTER MORNING during my junior year I found a letter
from the magazine in my mailbox. At first I assumed it would
turn out to be one of those cut-rate subscription offers that as
a student I was always receiving, until I noticed that my name
and address had been typed using an old-fashioned typewriter
on which both the 'a' and the 'm' jumped up. Inside, typed in
the same manner, and corrected in one spot with Liquid Paper,
was the following note:

Dear Mr Bauman,
This is a fan letter. I have just read your story 'Weight'
in *Watermark* [a student magazine], and it is terrific.
You have a great ear for dialogue and an eye for detail.
Also, you've pulled off something difficult: putting
yourself not only in a woman's shoes, but in an older
woman's shoes, with utter conviction. Others around
here have read the story too and are equally impressed,

and if you write any more, we hope you'll let us see them.

    Sincerely,
    Edith Atkinson

Rereading this letter nearly twenty years later (in the interval the magazine has undergone upheavals and reincarnations that in those days would have been unthinkable; Edith is long retired; of those 'others' to whom she refers so coyly, none remains) I see in it all the hallmarks of the magazine's old sense of itself as an institution too firmly rooted in the soil of American culture, too canonical, if you will, ever to fall prey to commercial realities. This confidence is evident, for example, in the seemingly effortless transition from 'I' to 'we' that Edith makes in the last sentence, a transition intended, I now know, to underscore the fact – made manifest also in her decision not to indicate her title nor to say how she came to read a story published in an undergraduate magazine in the first place – that the letter, though signed by one 'Edith Atkinson,' has in fact been drafted by the hovering spirit of that self-incarnating entity, the magazine itself.

Another aspect of this letter that today takes me by surprise: even in 1981, when such usages were already out of fashion, the telephone number is given according to the old formula OXFORD 3-1414: a testament (along with Edith's stubborn refusal to exchange her old Remington for one of the new IBM Selectrics then coming onto the market, and that would soon themselves be rendered obsolete by the earliest versions of the personal computer) to the magazine's view of itself as exempt from, perhaps even beyond the reach of, technology, time, history.

The first thing I did after I received the letter was to run over to Jim and Ash's room and read it to them. Then I telephoned my mother. Then I typed out a polite note to Edith Atkinson, indicating that I would like to send her more stories.

Her reply arrived the following week. Yes, she said, she would be delighted to read more of my work. Hastily I pulled together my oeuvre, which at that point consisted of four stories, the latest of these, 'String,' being the saga of Matthew Spalding's suicide attempt. (I had a fondness for one-word titles in those days.) It was a story of which, despite Stanley Flint's blandishments, I felt especially proud.

Ten days later they all came back. 'Dear Mr Bauman,' Edith wrote:

> We've read these with interest. They're good, but there are several problems. First, the stories are too memory-oriented, and we are off recollection these days. Second, in all four your tone is sometimes condescending. Also, there aren't any likable characters, by which I mean characters with whom we can sympathize, whose points of view we want to share.
>
> In the end it seems to me that you're writing in a voice that's too cold for you, and while objectivity is fine, that first story of yours suggests to me that your natural tendency is toward a more intimate tone.
>
> I'm sorry not to have better news. Do keep sending me your work!
> Yours,
> Edith Atkinson

The letter did not distress me particularly, for the simple reason that over the last several weeks I had been coming around myself to much the same opinion that Edith expressed here, and that Stanley Flint had expressed about the last of the stories in *his* letter. Not that I felt inclined to write a belated note of thanks or apology to Flint, with whom I was still a little angry. Probably I should have, and yet the truth was, I no longer felt that I needed anything from him, since now it was upon Edith Atkinson alone – a woman who existed for me purely as a prose style, who had no face, voice, or age – upon whom I was pinning my hopes; she, and not Flint, would become my mentor, my sage, my guide to that mysterious and enviable universe, New York.

Accordingly, I decided to write a new story, keeping Edith in mind as an ideal reader: someone remote, intelligent, and finicky, whose enthusiasm would matter.

As had become my habit, I didn't go home for spring break that year. Instead I stayed at school, where I spent every afternoon in the rear smoking section of the library, quiet and empty during this period when everyone else was off on vacation. The new story was oracular in nature, in that it described a scene I had not yet enacted, much less come to recognize as the essential prerequisite to my adulthood it was destined to be: namely the scene, now almost iconic, in which the young homosexual comes out to his parents.

Some further information is necessary here. Although, by this point, I was spending much of my time with Lars and Gretchen and their crowd, I still did not conceive of myself, at least consciously, as homosexual. This is a difficult state to explain to anyone who has not lived in it. Suffice it to say that instinct makes itself felt less strongly when it is indulged than when it is betrayed. For years I had tried to convince myself that the starstruck reverence I cultivated for certain girls and women really amounted to erotic love – a sleight of hand I could sustain only so long as the girls and women in question refused to take my passions seriously, as had been the case until the spring semester of my freshman year, when one evening I found myself sitting alone in the residential common room with flame-haired Nina Reilly, whose affections I had been cultivating, the lights switched off and her locks pressed into my nostrils. Even though we said nothing, even though we did not so much as look at each other, still, I could feel forming over our heads, like a cartoon speech bubble, the prelude to a kiss.

Pleading a paper to finish, I fled – the reality of what was expected of me overwhelmed me – after which I stopped pretending to have fallen in love with girls. Instead I adopted a pose of sexual nullity: so long as I didn't declare myself, I reasoned, I would remain at least in principle heterosexual, this condition being the default program in the same way that 'female' is the default program for the human embryo when the hormonal influence of the Y chromosome is suppressed. And yet on some level I must have wanted to be found out, for in a course I took on the sociology of Japan, I wrote my term paper on Yukio Mishima – but purely, I told myself, out of intellectual curiosity. Visiting my parents one Christmas, I checked out John Rechy's *The Sexual Outlaw* and H. Montgomery Hyde's *The Other Love* on my mother's library card – but only because I was open-minded and wanted to learn.

With the story it was the same ruse: what I told myself was that I was writing about a young man who flies home to tell his parents that he is gay not because *I* was gay, not because I knew that soon I would have to fly home and make the same declaration to my own parents, but because I found the situation 'interesting.' It was interesting to contemplate the dramatic consequences of such a revelation. It was interesting to piece together, with that same detached empathy that had guided me in writing about Aunt Lily, or Matthew Spalding, or my mother, those ordered emotions it takes but a single truthful utterance to scatter.

What I did not admit was that in telling such a story I was also engaging in one of those acts of literary palmistry by means of which writers so often predict or rehearse their own futures. Thus, even though half a year would pass before I would bring about the scene of revelation that lay at the story's heart (and for which – irony of ironies – the story itself would serve as the springboard), even though half a decade would pass before I would bring Eli Aronson home for one of our ersatz Jewish Christmases and we would scandalize my father by kissing under the mistletoe, nonetheless I was able to write these very scenes, in large part thanks, I see now, to the solitude of that spring break, that ugly, empty library, which, in its tranquil amplitude, provided for my imagination a model of spaciousness it had not known since childhood: a blank page. There I felt myself freed, for the first time, from the fear lest some suspicious figure – my mother, Donald, myself – should peer over my shoulder and deduce, from a few scrawled sentences, what it was that the story and I shared. Or is this disingenuous of me to say, when I was writing the story for Edith Atkinson, for the one magazine on which every literate American (and in particular my mother) depended as a source for fiction? I'm still not sure. What is certain is that I could never have written the story had that library not swathed me in its cool, protective, and effacing cloak.

Not that I wrote with ease; on the contrary, the construction of the story (if it could even be called that) was slow and ornery, consisting chiefly in a nervous sequence of steps backwards and forward, false starts, interruptive bouts of panic and despair. 'Flow,' when it happened, never happened for long. By the end, my notebook was a mass of illegible marginalia, fierce erasures that made holes in the paper, all in sharp contrast to the tidy legal pads that Barb Mendenhall, my only companion, arranged each morning across the table from me, the textbooks over which, with methodical industry, she dragged her yellow, pink, and blue highlighters.

I finished the story just as the break ended. By then I felt as bruised as the pages themselves for even though I had typed out a fresh copy, I still winced whenever I looked at the lumpy sentences, the infelicitous turns of phrase. Indeed, even in those instances where I had attempted literary first aid and covered over the offending passage with a bandage of rhetoric, I grimaced, for now I recognized the 'repairs' to be about as seamless as the grafts that Dr Frankenstein affixed to his monster's face. To each repair I would then make further repairs, which would necessitate, in those years before the personal computer, typing out yet another fresh copy. Bandages piled on top of bandages until I could no longer distinguish the wound from the cure, until I was as bleary-eyed as a surgeon emerging only half-satisfied from the operating theater, his gloves stained with the patient's blood.

The season of midterms took me out of myself for a time. After a week I reread the story and, to my surprise, found it not nearly so bad as I had feared. Accordingly, and with a bravado I could never have mustered had I not shut down the part of my brain that worried over consequences, I sent it off to Edith Atkinson. Several weeks passed without a reply. Each morning, when I went to check my mail, I fully expected to find in my box the requisite thick envelope of rejection. Instead I found nothing, or even worse, one evil morning, a *thin* envelope printed with the name and address of the magazine, which I tore open in a riot of hope, only to discover inside the cut-rate subscription offer with which I had confused Edith's original letter in the first place.

It was now the end of March. Nearly a month had passed since I'd sent the story. Was no news good news? Did the fact that Edith was taking so much longer to respond than she had on previous occasions mean that the story's merits were being debated? That it had gotten lost in the mail? That she was on vacation? Or was the delay simply an indication (this seemed the most likely scenario) that it was being circulated among those 'others' for whose collective opinion Edith served as mouthpiece? Indeed, perhaps Edith didn't even exist; perhaps hers was simply the name the 'others' used when they wanted to make cautious inquiries without jeopardizing their precious anonymity. (As I later learned, such a scenario wasn't far off the mark.)

Then one Monday afternoon, while I was studying in my room, the phone rang, and Donald (with whom, despite our political differences, I was still living) picked it up. 'It's for you,' he said, handing me the receiver.

'Martin Bauman? Edith Atkinson.'

'Oh, hello!' I said.

'Your story's terrific. We'd like to publish it.'

I looked at Donald. He was cleaning his ears with a Bic pen.

'Wow. Really?'

'There is some work I'd like to do on the story, though – if you're amenable. Tell me, do you ever come to New York?'

'Sure. I mean, I could.'

'Why don't you come next week and I'll take you to lunch? We can talk.'

'Great.'

'Is Thursday okay? I wouldn't want to take you away from your classes.'

'No, Thursday's fine. I don't have class on Thursday.'

'Come by the office. Ask for me at fifteenth-floor reception. Oh – is one o'clock all right?'

'Fine.'

'By the way, you should be very proud. It's a wonderful story, a very important story. We're thrilled to be doing it.'

She hung up. The entire conversation – which changed my life irrevocably (and not only for the better) – had taken all of a minute. And now it was over, and I was still sitting on our familiar sofa with its shot springs; across the room Donald was sniffing the clot of ear wax impaled on the end of his pen.

'What's up?' he asked.

I told him that the magazine had bought my story. He snorted. 'I don't believe it,' he said.

'Neither do I,' I answered. And why should I have? Probably when I arrived next Thursday at the offices of the magazine, I decided, it would be to be told by the fifteenth-floor receptionist (no doubt a pitiless harridan, deaf, after decades, to the pleas of a thousand, a million, young aspirants) that some mistake had been made, that Edith Atkinson had made no appointment with me, that Edith Atkinson was on extended leave, that there was no Edith Atkinson.

'So what's the story about?' Donald asked next.

I opened my mouth. I thought.

'It's about family,' I said after a moment.

'Good subject, good subject.'

I worried that Donald might press for specifics, but he didn't. Instead my vague answer seemed to satisfy him, just as it satisfied all the other people with whom, over the next few days, I shared my news, including my writing teacher of the previous year. 'Do you want to read it?' I hazarded, not really certain what I'd do if he said yes.

'No, no,' he answered. 'I'd rather wait and see it in the pages of the magazine.'

If there had been any chance my mother might have said the same thing, very likely I would have told her too. And yet I knew my mother: such an imprecise answer as 'it's about family' would never satisfy her. She would nag at me until I gave her details. So I decided not to tell her, or at least to wait until I went home at the end of the term to tell her, ostensibly because such news was far too monumental to deliver over the phone, in fact because I was trying to postpone as long as possible the moment when I would have to reveal to her and my

father what the story was about – which would be tanta-
mount, I knew, to coming out to them. For my mother was at
once too clever and too suspicious to be taken in by those
feints of purely 'intellectual' interest by means of which, while
writing the story, I had managed to delude myself.

Still, I started preparing. In my mind I rehearsed over and
over the scene of inquisition, imagining any number of possible responses on the part of my parents, and for each one
readying a strategy of self-defense.

If, for instance, my father said to me, 'I'm so disappointed
in you,' I decided that I would respond by listing all my successes: a catalogue of prizes and encomia so impressive that in
its wake he could not possibly remain disappointed, especially when reminded of that catalogue's crowning glory, the
acceptance of my story by the magazine.

If he said to me, 'Are you sure this isn't just a phase you're
going through?' I would first tell him about Nina Reilly, then
by way of chastising him for his narrow-mindedness read
aloud some heart-stopping words on the subject (from the
story, of course) that would put an end to this line of questioning altogether.

If my mother burst into tears, and said, 'It's all our fault' –
but here I faltered. What *could* I say if my mother burst into
tears? The very idea made me angry. 'How dare you not
admire me, how dare you cry?' I decided I would shout,
thereby shaming her into a more dignified posture.

And finally, if my parents persisted in wailing and shaking
their heads, if they refused obstinately to accept the news of
their son's homosexuality except in terms of tragedy, then, and
only then, I would use my secret weapon: the boyfriend I was
determined to have found by then, a boyfriend so handsome,
well-spoken, and respectable that they would have no choice
but to smile, wipe the tears from their eyes, and acknowledge
that even my sister could not have done better. Yet this

boyfriend – so far – had failed to materialize, no matter how diligently I crisscrossed the campus in search of him, my heart held out as if it were a Geiger counter that would beat more loudly, and with greater frequency, the closer I came.

The Thursday on which I was to have lunch with Edith Atkinson arrived. The evening before, not sure what to wear, I summoned Donald, who advised a flannel jacket and a pair of green corduroy pants that my mother had given me on my last visit home. He had worn a similar outfit, he told me, to a summer job interview, and it had done the trick perfectly.

That night he headed off, as usual, to Dolly's bar, leaving me to try to get some sleep. But I couldn't, and at six the next morning, already showered, shaved, and dressed, I took an early bus into New York. For several hours I wandered through midtown, stopping occasionally to stare up at the many-eyed red brick edifice in which the magazine maintained its offices, not really very distinguishable, I saw now, from all the other many-eyed red brick edifices crowded together on that street, nor even the exclusive domain of the magazine at all, which I had always assumed would own its own building. Instead, if the directory posted on the lobby wall was to be believed, the magazine occupied only three of the twenty-five floors. On the others, real estate agents, advertising copywriters, accountants and dentists and the consulates of African nations went about their business, presumably unconscious of, or perhaps in some way spurred to great thoughts by, their proximity to a myth, an icon, to what was in short the quivering spirit of American literature itself.

In any case, that morning I ate too many doughnuts, drank too much Coca-Cola, browsed at Coliseum Books until I had a headache. Finally at ten to one I returned to the building, entered the great rectangular lobby, got into the elevator, and rode to the fifteenth floor. Here the doors opened onto a cramped waiting room with no windows. The walls were putty-colored. Next to a reinforced door – electrified, like the ones at the psychiatric ward to which Matthew Spalding had been banished after his suicide attempt – a young girl wearing wire-rimmed glasses, vaguely pretty and bearing not the slightest resemblance to the heartless crone I had envisioned, sat behind a bulletproof glass partition, busily depositing pills into a seven-sectioned box labeled with the days of the week.

It seemed to take her a moment to register my presence.

'Can I help you?' she asked, after I had cleared my throat.

'Hello,' I answered, eager to assure her that I was not merely some hopeful with a manuscript to deposit. 'I have an appointment with Edith Atkinson.'

'Your name?'

'Martin Bauman.'

She picked up the phone. I waited. 'Edith? A Martin Bauman to see you . . . Okay. Edith will be out in a second,' she told me as she hung up.

I sat down on one of the hard little chairs that were lined up against the wall, as at a police station, or outside a school principal's office. Across from me posters in brass frames depicted covers of the magazine dating back to its inception in the last century. And how long would Edith keep me waiting? What would she look like? Because one naturally creates a face to match every voice, whenever I'd talked to her I'd imagined a woman with disorderly hair, her glasses hanging from a cord around her neck. A smoker, I assumed. And indeed, as I thought about it, I realized that this image was not invented at all, but excavated from memory, the image of my mother's piano teacher, Helen Risko, of whose no-nonsense voice – '*one*-two-three, *one*-two-three,' while my mother clunked out a Chopin waltz – Edith's own voice, over the telephone, had reminded me.

Then the door buzzed open and someone walked in. 'Martin?' the familiar voice asked.

I looked up. The woman who was apparently Edith Atkinson had white hair, silky and fine, pinned behind her head with a barrette. She wore pearl earrings, a beige tailored suit, sleek pumps. She was tall and svelte.

I stood. 'I'm Edith,' Edith said, holding out a hand without rings, without nail polish, soft from moisturizer. From between thin, coral-colored lips smallish teeth gleamed. Her age I had trouble deducing: somewhere between fifty and seventy, I guessed. I thought her beautiful.

'Let's go to my office,' she continued, and led me through the forbidding electrified door. Here a yellow corridor divided into further yellow corridors. The paint on the walls was thickly slavered, full gloss, as in hospitals. On a bulletin board next to a coffee machine someone had posted an advertisement for free kittens.

We walked by countless cubicles, in which a number of people – men and women, middle-aged and old – were sitting before antiquated typewriters, writing or talking on the phone. Some of them smoked. Next to one woman's desk stood a plastic garbage can piled high with crushed Diet Coke cans. It suddenly occurred to me that these people were probably writers, and that these cubicles were the offices that the magazine gave to those among its contributors whom its legendary editor prized the most. (Such lore I had learned from my mother.) Unfortunately Edith – my Edith, the Mrs Risko Edith having been all but destroyed – led me along at too fast a clip to gawk. 'Did you have a good trip?' she was asking. 'I assume you took the train – or was it the bus? Do you have a car?'

'I took the bus. I don't have a car.'

'My son wants a car in college. He's very insistent about it, but his father and I don't think it's a good idea. Here, come in.' We stepped into her office, which was narrow and wedge-shaped, with only a sliver of a window. 'I mean, what's the point of a car, when you're living on campus? Sit down.'

I did. On her desk, next to a pile of manuscripts, sat yet another elderly typewriter – the one with the jumping 'a' and 'm,' no doubt. Above it, several pieces of magazine stationery thumbtacked to a cork bulletin board announced TITLES NOT TO BE READ BEYOND ('The First Time'), SENTENCES NOT TO BE READ BEYOND ('Morning call came early at Auschwitz, but Baruch didn't care; he was a morning person'), WORDS NOT TO BE READ BEYOND ('myriad').

We talked for a while. She inquired after the president of my university, whom it turned out she had once dated – 'Eons ago.' She had three sons, she said, the youngest of whom (the one who wanted the car?) was currently applying to college. And where had I gotten those handsome corduroy pants? I told her I didn't know, that my mother had bought them for me, at which point she had me stand up so that she could pull out the waistband in order to read the inside label.

After that we went to lunch at a hotel long associated with the magazine's staff, one that in the thirties had been a famous gathering place for literary intellectuals but that in the intervening years had fallen on hard times, eventually escaping the wrecking ball only thanks to a bailout on the part of a Japanese conglomerate. Now, where once writers had exchanged witticisms, tourists photographed their food.

Although in subsequent years I would meet many people who came from Edith's milieu – the milieu of the original bluebloods, old Protestant money, a direct chain of descent leading back to the *Mayflower* – at the time she represented something relatively new to me. Not that I hadn't previously met adults who were rich – I had – and yet these adults had tended to be Jews, avatars of upward mobility like Jim Sterling's father, whose own father had been an immigrant from Lithuania. (Shulevitz, his original name, he had changed at Ellis Island in homage to British currency.) Inherited wealth, of course, is something entirely different. For instance, as I learned over lunch, Edith's family had had an association with the magazine from its birth: indeed, her grandfather had been one of its first backers. She divided her time between an apartment on East End Avenue ('we bought it thirty years ago, when real estate was cheap') and a 'drafty old summer house' in Maine, part of a compound of houses that had been in her husband's family since the First World War. Her husband, whose name was Beavis, was a lawyer. The oldest of her sons was also a lawyer. The middle one was an artist. The youngest, the one who was applying to college, and for whom she had coveted my green corduroy pants, hadn't decided yet. All of them went by nicknames: Whiff, Lanny, J.A.

Our main courses arrived. Over the years, I'd come to associate the term WASP with poached salmon, dessert forks, prudish portions; indeed, so concerned was I lest I should make a gluttonous impression on my new editor that I'd ordered more modestly than I might have in other company – an entirely unnecessary measure, as it turned out, for Edith tucked into her own ample lunch with gusto. She picked up her lamb chops by their bony handles and chewed on them. She ordered an ice-cream sundae for dessert. Such casual hedonism made me think wistfully of my mother and her friends with their bowls of sugarless Jell-O, their draconian diets and rigorous exercise routines. None of them was as thin as Edith, however, who clearly had no peasant blood in her, who radiated the hale health, the natural grace, of the aristocrat. She had garden dirt under her nails. In lieu of a purse she carried a canvas bag, battered and patched, from L. L. Bean.

After she had paid the bill – 'We'll let the fellow with the top hat pick up this one,' she said – we went back to her office to talk about the story. 'Homosexuality is such a hard subject to handle!' she told me, taking the manuscript from the pile on her desk. 'And yet you manage it so effortlessly. That's what I like. I've read plenty of homosexual stories, and the trouble is, they all seem sociological. They all say, "Look, I'm about homosexuality as a category," instead of just being about people, which is what yours is. And the mother's a great character. Incidentally, Mr ———' (she named the magazine's famous editor) 'is particularly keen to be publishing it. He wants to run it as soon as possible, which is high praise given that a lot of stories sit around here for a year or more before they make it into print. Are you all right?'

'Fine,' I said. How could I explain that if I looked stunned, it was less because Edith's remarks had included an element of praise, than because up until that moment I hadn't realized I'd written a 'homosexual story'? This was a troubling matter. Before I had a chance to brood on it, however, Edith had pulled some galleys out of a manila folder and handed them to me: my story, already typeset in the magazine's unmistakable face, with suggestions penciled in the margins. 'The ones in red are mine,' she said. 'The ones in green are Mr ———'s. You'll notice he's constantly putting in commas. He has a thing about commas. He thinks people don't use them enough anymore. The third set – the ones in blue – are Anka's. I'll be taking you in a minute to meet Anka.'

I stared open-mouthed at my story's title, at the distinctive typography, at my name at the end.

'Oh, one thing before I forget,' Edith went on. 'In the story we've got three "fuck"s and a "piss." Now Mr ———'s willing to forgo the "piss" – he says there's no way around it – but he draws the line at "fuck," so we'll have to find an alternative to that. I'm afraid we're a bit fuddy-duddy around here,' she added, winking. 'As for the contract, it should be ready in a few days. Do you have an agent yet?'

'No,' I answered, my eyes still fixed on the galleys.

'You'll probably start getting inquiries once the story's

published. Or I could make a few recommendations. Not that
you'll need an agent with us – more for book contracts. Oh,
and you'll be receiving a check within a couple of weeks.
You're probably wondering how we pay. Most authors do.
The system's not really all that complicated. Basically, everyone around here reads the story and gives it a grade, like in
school, A to D. Then the grades are averaged together – naturally Mr ———'s counts more than the rest – and based on
that we work out a price per word. Fairly straightforward, in
the end.'

'Fine.'

'And I love the bit about the woman whose hair is like a
brioche. That's a great bit. Plus the scene under the mistletoe!
Oops, we'd better go see Anka before she leaves for her shrink
appointment.'

Standing briskly, she walked out of the office. I followed
her down yet another long corridor – clearly the domain of
the lower orders, for the offices were both darker and smaller
than the ones I'd passed earlier, some with frosted windows,
some with no windows at all.

At one of the doors, which was open just a crack, she
knocked.

'Who is it?'

'Edith!'

We entered. A plump woman in her early thirties, with a
hooked nose, flushed cheeks, and long blond, gray-streaked
hair rose from her cluttered desk.

'Anka, this is Martin,' Edith said.

'A pleasure to meet you,' said Anka, holding out her hand.
'Sit, if you can find a chair.'

Her office was a chaos. I had to take a coat, a purse, and a
string bag of onions off the extra chair before I could sit
down. Edith, having pooh-poohed my insistence that she sit
and I stand, disappeared briefly, returning a few seconds later

with a folding chair of the sort my parents kept in their basement next to the card table.

'I really love your stories,' Anka was telling me. 'I don't
know if Edith told you, but I was the first one around here to
discover you. That story about your mother and the radiation
therapy center. At least I presume it's your mother.'

'Yes,' I said, rather amazed, yet at the same time refreshed,
by the boldness of her inferences.

'It may be personal,' Anka continued. 'You see, we have a
lot in common. I'm from Washington, too. And my mother
also goes every week to a radiation therapy center.'

A dim idea seized me. 'Which hospital?' I asked.

She named our town.

'But that's where my mother goes!'

'You're kidding. What's her name?'

'Carolyn.'

'Your mother's Carolyn? But that's amazing! My mother
adores Carolyn! She talks all the time about Carolyn!'

'What's *your* mother's name?'

'Leonie. Leonie Kaufman.'

'From Tacoma?'

'Yes.'

'Isn't it a small world?' Edith threw in, perhaps not
realizing that what was amazing wasn't so much the small-
ness of one world as the fact that two I had always thought
irretrievably distant – my mother's and the magazine's,
the one in which I lived and the one for which I longed –
had just collided.

Before I left to catch my bus, Anka gave me a sheaf of her
own stories, seven of them, all photocopied from small literary quarterlies. 'Every one of these was rejected by the
magazine,' she said, 'in case you were wondering if I get pref-
erential treatment because I work here.'

'Thanks. I can't wait to read them.'

'Call me the next time you're in New York,' she added. 'I'll have you over for dinner.'

I explained that I intended to be in New York two weekends hence, as the guest of my friend Jim Sterling. 'Great,' Anka said. 'Maybe we can arrange something for Saturday. Only remember – when you call, let the phone ring once, then hang up. Then call back and let it ring twice. Otherwise I don't pick up.'

I promised to follow these instructions, after which I bid Anka and Edith good bye and headed to the Port Authority. On the bus I studied the tricolored suggestions in the margins of the galleys. Generally speaking Mr ———, as Edith had alerted me, confined himself to inserting commas, while Edith offered what she called 'judicious cuts,' most of which, when I made them, led instantly to the elimination of those very awkwardnesses over which I had sweated while writing on the story. Indeed, so self-evident did I find her solutions that I wanted to hit myself on the head for not having seen them myself – much the same sensation as when, in high school, our math teacher would map out on the blackboard the elegant answer to some thorny algebra problem on which, after hours of struggle, I had finally given up.

Anka's suggestions, the ones in blue, were murkier. For instance: 'I feel the need for some *meanness* here,' she wrote at one point in the margin. And: 'Are you sure this is the right metaphor?' And: 'Why editorialize? The facts speak for themselves.' Such criticisms, I found, were harder to respond to than Edith's, for the simple reason that they came in the form of questions rather than answers. As for Anka's own stories – which I devoured – they described the ups and downs of a young woman's complicated relationship with her equally young husband, whom she has married straight out of high school. In the last of the stories, the young woman has an affair and leaves the husband. In order to avoid his perpetual, pleading calls, however, she must instruct her friends and colleagues in an elaborate telephone code . . .

As I soon learned, Anka's relationship with the telephone, in life as well as in fiction, bordered on the paranoid. For instance, even though she had given me along with her stories a sheet of magazine stationery on which she had scribbled her home address and phone number, whenever I tried to reach her at her apartment I got an answering machine – something of an innovation in those days. Later, she explained to me that she never answered the phone when she was at home, preferring instead to 'screen' calls and pick up only for those friends with whom she felt up to speaking. For Anka had a lot of people she wanted to steer clear of: not only, presumably, her ex-husband, but the agents of a credit card company with which she was having a dispute, several lawyers, her landlord, even, depending on the state of their relationship, her mother. Needless to say, the last thing I wanted was to be added to her 'don't answer' list, which I imagined as being akin to the list of titles not to be read beyond that I had seen posted above Edith's desk. And yet I had a favor to ask. Ever since I had discovered that her mother was the famous Leonie with whom my own mother cracked jokes at the radiation therapy center, I'd been worrying lest Leonie – having learned from Anka of my story's acceptance – should congratulate my mother, with whom I hadn't yet shared the news. Accordingly, a few days after our meeting I called Anka at her office, following the elaborate instructions she had dictated. The second time she picked up. 'Hello, Anka,' I said.

'Martin, how are you?'

'Fine. Good.' I paused. 'And you?'

She made a noise that does not translate easily into print: a sort of digestive whinny, signifying disgust or frustration or both. 'So what's up?'

'I'm afraid I need to ask you a favor.'

On the other end of the line I heard palpable, even eager silence: Anka was listening. Yet once I had explained the situation, she neither interrogated my motives, nor sputtered that it was too late, that she had already told Leonie, that Leonie was at that very instant on the way to the radiation therapy center to chat with Carolyn. Instead she said simply, 'Don't worry, I haven't breathed a word to Mom.'

I was relieved. 'Thank you,' I said.

'At the same time, I wouldn't advise your putting it off for long,' Anka continued. 'I mean, eventually your mother's going to read the story. It can't be avoided. I know. I've been through the same thing.'

I figured that she was referring to the affair she had had – or rather, to the affair I presumed her to have had, judging from her stories, which I had taken to be autobiographical. Yet what surprised me even more than Anka's frankness in alluding to her own 'personal life' was the ease with which she drew conclusions about mine. For if I interpreted her correctly, then she not only took it for granted that I had read her stories as autobiographical, she also took it for granted that she could read mine the same way; in other words, she had deduced, from the story, that I was gay, and to this deduction, because it was accented neither with hostility nor self-righteousness, I hardly knew how to respond. After all, since my childhood bus stop, only two people had ever confronted me publicly about my homosexuality: Gerald Wexler, and the author of the anonymous graffito on my door. In both cases the motivation had been malice. Anka, on the other hand, seemed to be acting only from friendly concern. I cannot overstate how much I liked her. Today I have no idea where she is; a dozen years ago she quit the magazine, gave up her apartment, and disappeared off the face of the earth. The last time I spoke to Edith even she hadn't a clue what had become of her. When I was young, however, she changed my life. More important by far than the first person to whom one comes out is the first person to whom one does not need to come out. Her support precluded confessions. For that, Anka, wherever you are, I thank you.

The following week I met with Edith a second time, to go over the galleys. At lunch she asked me which writers I admired. I mentioned Grace Paley and Raymond Carver, whose work at that point had not yet been published in the magazine. As it happened I'd met Carver a few years earlier, at the same community college writing workshop where I'd encountered the poet of the yellow river. I explained that I had told him my idea (still vestigial then) for a story about Bo and Peep, then confided that at seventeen I doubted whether I knew enough to communicate the sort of despair that would lead someone to abandon her life and go off to meet a space-ship. To which he replied, 'Once you've known one despair you've known every despair': an observation with which Edith, by nodding, indicated her quiet accord.

'And what are you reading at school?' she asked next.

'*Howards End*,' I said. 'For my class on the Edwardian novel.'

'Lionel Trilling thought it was his best book – though personally I'd plump for *A Room with a View*. As for Morgan, he told me he preferred *The Longest Journey*. Isn't that odd? It just goes to show you that writers can be the worst judges of their own work.'

'You mean you knew him?'

'Not well, but yes. He was friends with Mr ——— back when I worked as his secretary.'

'Wow,' I said. It was hard for me to conceive of someone actually having known Forster. 'What was he like?'

'Extremely kind. And honest. In fact sometimes he could be so honest that people would get offended. Not the sort who suffers fools gladly.'

'How did you meet him? Excuse me, I hope I don't sound like I'm interrogating you.'

'You don't. It was at a luncheon party that Mr ——— and his wife gave one weekend at their place on Long Island. I remember I was incredibly nervous – meeting the great man and all. But then Morgan put me at my ease almost at once. He was good at that. You see, there were all these writers there, all hell-bent on making a positive impression, and they were talking so much he couldn't get a word in edgewise. So he just sat there, and I just sat there, because I was too shy to say anything, and then he winked at me, I suppose because we were the only two people at the table who weren't flapping our gums.' I laughed. 'Anyway, at some point the conversation turned to why people write, and someone there suggested that maybe fiction writing was only a matter of wish fulfillment, like dreams – we were all armchair Freudians in those days – and suddenly Morgan sort of raised an eyebrow at me. Back then I assumed the look meant that he thought Freud was a lot of hooey and didn't I agree, only I've been thinking about it recently, and now I wonder whether it was because when he did all his best writing, he was so young. After all, he was only in his twenties when he wrote *A Room with a View*, he hadn't experienced anything, really. He'd always been trapped with that mother of his, in addition to which there was his homosexuality – homosexuality you just couldn't do much about in those days. And so in a certain way his early novels *were* pure wish fulfillment. Anka thinks that George is the most cardboard character in the book, but I think that's because George was Morgan's beau ideal, the love he was always looking for but gave Lucy instead. What he couldn't live, he wrote.'

These remarks filled me with vague alarm. In speaking this way of Forster's youth, I wondered, was Edith offering me a warning? After all, I too was young; I too wrote of experiences I had never had, while having experiences of which I never wrote – in particular, the experience of living always on the margins of other people's dramas, as chronic sidekick, go-between, or counselor.

That evening I arrived back at school determined (a) to lose my virginity and (b) to come out, both before the term ended. In essence, I had simply reached the point where I could no longer bear the weighty life of pretense to which I had previously consigned myself. For such a costume, paradoxically, is not only cumbersome but flimsy. It seems always to be coming unpinned. I wanted to be off with it, and therefore vowed that by the time my story appeared in print, I would have, as it were, caught up with myself, become the sort of person who could have written such a story from experience.

It was now April; this meant that only a week remained before the GLAD festivities began. Accordingly I decided to make the closing ceremony my deadline, and with the same industry that had marked my preparations for the PSAT, began to devote my energy to the task of convincing someone to seduce me, which is in and of itself a form of seduction.

But who? Lars, obviously, was out of the question. So were Gerald, Philip, and their crowd, though in retrospect, I realize that I probably could have gotten any of them to do me the favor just by asking. Nor would I consider even for a minute visiting the gay bar that operated a few blocks from campus, a squalid and cheerful little hole in which the owner's mother was rumored to wash the glasses, for I was puritanical, and therefore determined to find another 'nice boy,' someone who, like me, would never set foot in a gay bar – a fact of which, in future years, when we were a couple, we could boast.

I had now narrowed my criteria. The next step was to investigate the most likely source for the sort of boy I was seeking: namely, the membership (thirty in all) of an elite all-male choir at my university, one that was famous all over the world, and which year to year, though its members changed, remained ineluctably itself, bringing to the ears of nostalgic alumni its familiar repertoire of madrigals and fight songs, always in the same delicate a cappella arrangements, always performed by lovely, clean-cut, eager-eyed boys in white tie and tails. Of the group's members that year, six, so far as I knew, were gay. I decided that before GLAD week ended, I was going to have slept with one of them.

It is a testament to the awe Edith Atkinson inspired in me that even now, nearly twenty years after our first meeting, I still cannot bring myself to use the word 'myriad.' Likewise the presence of 'The First Time' on Edith's list of 'Titles Not to be Read Beyond' forbids me from going into detail about the process by which I ended up sleeping, the Tuesday of GLAD week, with Theodoric Vere Swanson III – the member of the chorus on whom I had decided to set my sights not because I found him the most attractive (on the contrary, of the six candidates he was the least my 'type'), but because I judged him, on the basis of his looks, to be 'on my level,' and therefore less likely than the others to humiliate me with rejection. Here, of course, is the beginning of a significant drama: the scissoring of the erotic from the romantic, and my consequent evolution into a much worse kind of cheat than I had been in high school. This story, however, remains to be told in future chapters. For the moment my goal was simpler, and I achieved it: over the course of a single night's sexual gamboling in which pleasure, at least on my side, played little if any role; a night marked by embarrassing stabs, on both our parts, at the sort of 'sophisticated' erotic dialogue we had read in books (for instance: 'tastes good, huh?' Theodoric Vere Swanson III said as he guided his penis into my mouth, his lovely tenor voice as unsuited to these words as mine had been when, at the age of thirteen, my own voice not yet cracked, I had played the psychiatrist in a junior high school production of *Equus*); over the course of this night I managed at last to cross a border I immediately recognized to have existed only in my own mind. Now, at last, I could come out, which I did the following day, investing my solemn confessions with a lilt of pride that mimicked the official tone of GLAD week. One after the other, over pious cups of tea, I exposed myself to Donald, to Jim Sterling, to Ash and Julia, none of whom seemed the least bit ruffled by my news, because in fact I was merely confirming a truth of which they themselves had been conscious for years.

The next weekend Jim and I went into New York. As requested, a few days before our departure I called Anka, who invited me to dinner that Saturday at her apartment. It turned out that she lived not far from Jim's parents, in a rambling old flat just off Columbus Avenue, a neighborhood that is now glamorous, but that was in those days in the throes of transformation: no longer the exclusive domain of poor yet industrious Jews, butcher shops with GLATT KOSHER stickers in their windows, piano and violin teachers; no longer, even, the realm of immigrant squalor that had in the sixties begun to encroach upon all this middle-class Jewish orderliness, replete with smelly bodegas that sold sugarcane juice, tropical fruits over the hairy rinds of which flies crawled, questionable-looking meats; and yet not the crowded corridor of sushi bars and shoe stores it would become a decade later, Columbus Avenue in those years was simply a street trying to maintain a breakfront of brave resistance against incoming tides of change; and that breakfront, by 1982, was beginning to buckle.

In a sense, as Anka told me later, it was all her fault – or rather, the fault of all those artistic young men and women who in the mid-seventies, wanting a lot of space but having little money, had begun quietly emigrating uptown, moving into huge, vacant apartments for which the rent was still astonishingly low. Soon the neighborhood had a reputation as cutting edge, which meant that with the economic boom of the Reagan years people with a lot of money, attracted by the heady smell of the creative, began to follow the pioneers across the park, upping the rents and effectively putting an end to the old orders, to the delis and butcher shops and bodegas. Buildings went co-op, and Anka, who had lived in her six-room apartment for nine years and paid a rent of three hundred and seventeen dollars a month, found herself sharing the morning elevator ride with investment bankers, Broadway directors, and rock stars, all of whom had purchased their apartments for prices in the six figures. Like many rent-controlled tenants, she was, not surprisingly, the bane of her landlord's existence, especially since, in sharp contrast to those of her neighbors who were already in their eighties and nineties, she was neither likely to die nor move any time soon. And as a result, she said, the landlord was out to get her. 'He wants to get rid of me because he knows that once I'm gone, the others will go,' she told me that evening as she led me through the big, drafty apartment, along hallways with creaking parquet floors, past bathrooms in which huge tubs with feet squatted next to cracked ceramic basins. Because the immense rooms had hardly any furniture in them (or perhaps because I was used to the highly specific room distinctions that characterized the middle class milieu of my childhood), I found it hard to tell one from another; we ended up in what might have been the living room, but could also have been the study, or the dining room. Here what I would later learn to recognize as four original Arne Jacobsen kitchen chairs surrounded a Formica table with a typewriter on it. Against the wall was an old sofa over which Anka had thrown a beige sheet.

She walked me to the window, the pane of which was broken, sealed with cardboard and tape. 'See this?' she said. 'My landlord did this. Or one of his goons. Threw a rock.'

'Are you sure?'

A cat came into the room, sinuous and fat, with an immense, raccoonish tail. 'There's no evidence,' Anka went on, picking up the cat and holding it protectively. 'Still, it doesn't take a rocket scientist to put two and two together. I mean, think about it. I'm a complainer. I've taken him to court twice already. He knows he can't throw me out, so he's always looking for creative ways to get back at me. For instance, there's been a leak in the bathroom ceiling for months. I call and call, but he won't have it fixed. Also, there's a law that says he has to turn on the heat by November first. Well, remember how cold it got last October? He wouldn't switch it on, at least not in my apartment. And now he's trying to evict me over the cat. He says the cat attacked a neighbor, when the poor old thing can't even use his claws anymore. Would you like anything to drink?'

I asked for water. While Anka fetched it from the kitchen the cat, with a forthrightness I had never before witnessed in a feline, climbed onto my stomach, put his forepaws on my shoulders, and with a loud purr began rubbing his whiskered cheeks against my own.

The doorbell rang. 'I've invited some friends to join us,' Anka said, handing me my glass of water, then pushed the admission buzzer. Brushing off the cat (its claws pulled my sweater), I stood politely to greet the new arrivals, who turned out to be a pair of young women, one tall and slightly paunchy, with blond hair, the other dressed in jeans and an oversized lumberjack shirt. She had an oddly asymmetrical face that reminded me of Liza Perlman. In fact, she was Liza Perlman.

'This is Janet Klass,' Anka said, and kissed the cheek of the blond girl. 'Janet's doing her dissertation in Cognitive Psychology at Columbia. It's a statistical study of the work habits of writers, which means that every month those of us poor slobs who were dumb enough to agree to take part have to fill out these tedious questionnaires that delve into the most intimate aspects of our lives.'

'Oh, please, Anka,' said Janet. 'A pleasure to meet you, Martin.'

'And this is Liza Perlman. She's in the study too.'

'It's a thrill to meet you,' Liza said, offering me her hand, which was both moist and limp. 'Anka gave me a copy of your story – I hope you don't mind. It's really great.'

'I loved it too,' Janet added.

'She's probably going to try to rope you into the study now,' said Liza.

'Hey! Don't spoil my game plan!'

It took me mildly aback that Anka had been sharing my story with so many people; and yet, when I thought about it, I could see no reason to be offended, given that within a matter of months the story would be in print. 'Oh, I wouldn't mind at all,' I said to Janet. 'Only I'm hardly a writer. I mean, I've only written a few stories—'

'Oh, you're a writer all right,' Anka said, patting me on the back.

'You're what I'd call a natural writer,' Liza concurred.

'And what is that supposed to mean?' asked Anka.

'You know – someone to whom it just *comes*, like breathing.'

We sat down at the table with the Arne Jacobsen chairs. A warm flush of satisfaction was running through me, its center point the spot on the small of my back where Anka had touched me.

'Liza, I'd be disingenuous—' I said. 'Or would I be ingenuous?'

'Ingenuous,' Anka interrupted, 'if you're going to say what I think you're going to say.'

'Okay. I'd be ingenuous if I didn't tell you that I read your novel last year. I really loved it.'

'Sorry. In that case you'd be *dis*ingenuous. I thought you were going to say something else.'

Anka was right. I *was* disingenuous – and more than she realized, since in truth I'd read only the dust jacket of Liza's novel, from which I'd learned that it concerned the relationship between a bulimic girl and her fat mother; even then I was becoming an adept at the New York art of flattery.

Liza pulled at her earlobe – a tic to which, over the years, I would grow accustomed. Praise, as I soon learned, delighted her, yet she was never quite sure how to muster the blend of gratitude, pride, and humility that is the proper response to it. Instead her cheeks flushed when people said nice things to her. 'Oh, thanks,' she said – a little pompously, I thought, as I gave her the once-over. In fact she was much prettier (and smaller) than her jacket picture would have led one to assume. Also, since the picture had been taken she'd cut her red hair short, which suited her. Even under her shapeless clothes, I could see that she had a slender, girlish, graceful body, one that seemed curiously disconnected from her freckled, oblong face with its frame of red hair ('Jewish red,' Eli later specified) as in a book I'd had as a child in which the heads, bodies, and nether regions of various animals could be combined in any number of hilarious ways.

Anka removed her typewriter from the table and disappeared into the kitchen. 'Even though we never met, we went to school together,' Janet was saying to me.

'Really? When did you graduate?'

'Last year. Do you know Gerald Wexler, by the way?'

I said that I knew him vaguely.

'Is he a friend of yours?' Liza asked. 'I've met him a few times through my friend Eli. Eli used to go out with his twin brother. Do you like him? Is he smart?'

'I don't know him well enough to judge,' I admitted, then added boldly, 'though I do have to confess, I find him kind of obnoxious.'

'I'm so relieved to hear you say that! We do too!' Laughing, Liza clapped her hands together. And who were *we*? I wondered. Liza and Janet? Liza and Eli, who had gone out with Gerald's twin brother – which meant, presumably, that Gerald's twin brother was also gay? (Gay brothers was a possibility I had not previously contemplated.)

Anka returned. In her arms she carried two large bottles, one containing Diet Coke and the other white wine, which she deposited onto the table. Then she spread out a fan of take-out menus: pizza, Chinese food, falafel, hamburgers. 'I'm afraid I don't cook,' she said, 'so order what you want.'

An uncertain smile claimed Janet's lips. 'Oh, what a cool idea,' Liza said. No doubt she found Anka's rather novel way of throwing a dinner party, to say the least, amusing, the stuff of later tales to be shared over other dinners, more proper dinners, cooked by their hosts or by caterers. And yet to me the stack of take-out menus was pure delight; the only dilemma was what to choose amid such bounty.

In the end I settled on Chinese food: cold sesame noodles and 'pot sticker' dumplings. (How daring, I thought, to order *only* appetizers!) Anka and Janet elected to split a large mushroom pizza, while Liza, who suffered from various food allergies, said she would just have a Greek salad.

Once Anka had phoned in our orders, she returned to join us at the table. Liza wanted to know what I thought of Edith. 'I've heard she's really lovely,' she said, pulling once again at her earlobe.

'I've only met her twice. She's been wonderfully encouraging.'

'Edith is a saint,' Anka said. 'She's a substitute mother for me.'

'You know, everyone's saying yours is going to be the first gay story the magazine's ever published,' Liza continued. 'How do you feel about that?'

I barely had time to register the implications of this question – not to mention of the phrase (which I would hear a thousand times in the coming years) 'gay story' – when the doorbell rang. The first of several delivery boys, this one bearing Liza's Greek salad, stood sheepishly on the threshold. Two others followed in close succession. By now, to my relief, the topic of conversation had shifted from Liza's difficult question (attention spans are short in New York) to Janet's study, the methodology of which Anka was playfully challenging. 'I mean, how can statistics harness something so ineffable as the creative mind?' she asked, slicing up their pizza.

'Oh, I'm sorry,' Liza interrupted, 'but before I forget, I've just heard some amazing gossip!' Eager silence. 'Yesterday my mother was having lunch with an editor at Holt, and he told her that ——— just bought Sam Stallings's first novel for two hundred thousand dollars.'

'Two hundred thousand!'

'She couldn't believe it. We both hate his work!'

'I must have rejected fifty of his stories at the magazine,' Anka said. 'The worst sort of I'm-a-macho-guy-and-I'm-gonna-prove-it-by-going-out-to-shoot-rabbits crap.'

'Do you think he might want to take part in my study?' Janet asked.

Both of them stared at her. She blushed.

'Did I tell you I met him last year at Club Bread?' Liza resumed. 'At first I tried to be friendly, but he came off as such a phony! For instance, he does this whole "I'm just a regular, working-class guy" shtick – you know, acting as if he finds literary life disgusting and snobbish and all that – and yet at the same time he's the ultimate operator! I mean, he was always repairing his truck. Every time you saw him his legs were

sticking out from under his truck. He never came to any of
our readings, but then when Galway Kinnell visited, he
showed up in a tie and blazer.'

'How pompous.'

'And that's not all! I've got a friend, Ellen Garber – have
you read her novel, Anka? You should, it's really wonderful – anyway, she was at school with him. One day they had
a lunch date. Well, as it happened, that same week Stanley
Flint was visiting. Flint was sitting alone, eating a sandwich,
at the table behind Ellen's. So up walks Sam with his lunch
tray, smiling at Ellen, who stands up to greet him, when suddenly he notices Flint, by himself. And you know what he
does? He pretends not to even know her. He walks right past
her, straight up to Flint, and says, "Excuse me, sir, mind if I
join you?"'

Anka laughed.

'What's Club Bread?' Janet asked.

'You know, Bread Loaf. The writers' conference.'

'Stanley Flint was my teacher, too,' I said.

'Really? Did you like him? I know him a little through my
mother. As a teacher I've heard he's brilliant but mad.'

I've heard. How many thousands of times, over the course
of that evening – and a hundred evenings to come – would
this seemingly innocuous, ultimately pernicious little phrase be
used: 'I've heard she's a really bad writer.' 'I've heard she got
a huge advance for her last book, but the publisher was disappointed by the sales.' 'I've heard he's always trying to
seduce his women students.' Later, I too would become skilled
at such subspeech. At the time, however, I still believed that in
New York writers got their nourishment from intellectual
exchange, when in fact all anyone did was gnaw at the bones
of hearsay and hindsight.

When the evening ended (early) Anka saw us to the elevator. Once downstairs, Janet, who was going uptown, got into

a taxi. As Liza was planning to take the subway downtown, I offered to escort her to the station. This did not surprise her. She seemed to take it for granted that I would want to stay in her company.

Briskly we headed toward Broadway. Even now the phrase 'gay story' was echoing in my head – this despite the fact that Liza's flip observation was hours old, cold under the weight of all those other manic subjects that had been heaped atop it during the dinner, like coats piled on a bed at a party. Curious: earlier I'd wanted to leave the subject alone. Now, however, in the silence of our walk together I found myself straining for a way to return to this topic, about which I longed to converse with Liza, with whom even then I felt a mysterious kinship. And why? I hardly knew her. Worse, she had already revealed herself to be a terrible gossip, the sort of person one should never trust with secrets. And yet I see now that I wasn't looking for someone to keep my secrets. I was looking for someone to free me from my secrets.

We had arrived at the 72nd Street station. 'I hope you'll stay in touch,' Liza said, once again offering me her limp hand. 'Are you planning to move to New York when you graduate?'

I said that I was.

'I could probably get you a job teaching at the New School – if you're interested. Oh, have you got a book yet?'

'A book!' I shook my head.

'Don't worry, I'm sure you will soon.' And she handed me her visiting card. 'Call me the next time you're in town. I have a friend I'd like you to meet. My best friend, Eli Aronson. Did I mention him already? He's got this thick, luxurious blond beard, very soft – the sort of beard a woman would have if women had beards.' And with this quite extraordinary offering she smiled.

Now I wonder: was there something knowing, perhaps

even questioning, in that smile? And if so, what was the question? When Liza talked of Eli Aronson, was she speaking in a code of omissions as complex as Anka's code of telephone rings, offering me a clue – as in the crossword puzzles to which both she and my mother were addicted – by means of which I might fill in the answer that would in turn provide the key to the other answer with which it intersected, the one that addressed the mystery not of Eli's homosexuality, not even of my homosexuality, but of her own?

Not that this was really such a mystery. Indeed, I think I probably knew from the beginning that Liza was a lesbian, if from nothing else than from the surface details: her loose jeans, her short hair, the fact that she wore only one earring. And yet, as I subsequently discovered, it would have horrified her to find out that anything in her appearance 'gave her away.' Even more than for me, the process of coming out was for Liza fraught with torment, mostly because her natural eagerness to share every detail of her life so perpetually militated against her terror, as she put it, of being 'pigeonholed,' or mistaken for 'some horrible, hideous, fat old dyke.' Now I can't help but suspect that she was using Eli – the promise of Eli, the threat of Eli – to nudge the nervous revelation into voice.

We had been standing for five minutes on the sidewalk in front of the subway station. Even though it was the time for good-bye, however, we didn't say good-bye. Instead, as during that moment after a date when one partner waits for the other to ask if he or she 'would like to come up for a drink,' we hung fire. Hesitation gaped between us, for we were both shy; yet in the end it was Liza who took the plunge and suggested we go and have a cappuccino at a little café she knew.

Then I puffed out clouds of relief (it was a chilly night) and with gratitude followed her up Amsterdam Avenue to the dark, smoky little café where over cake and steamed milk (I still didn't drink coffee) I poured out my heart to her, confided to her my worries about my parents, admitted my longing to find, someday, a great love, and by doing so mortared an intimacy the implications of which I am still today excavating, and will probably be excavating until I am old.

In such small, unexpected ways our lives change irrevocably, and I am a fool (but a natural fool) to try to tease out of the past the directions my own might have taken had I had the foreknowledge to let Liza simply disappear down the damp steps of the subway station that night, into the train and out of my life forever.

When the semester ended, as planned, I flew home to visit my parents. My mother was in a good mood because the brutal course of radiation therapy treatments that she was then undergoing appeared to be paying off: that is to say, the small tumors that pocked her body were shrinking, and in one or two cases had disappeared altogether. My father considered this, along with my return from college, cause for celebration, so the night after I got home we went out to dinner at a French restaurant – this despite my mother's anxiety over her hair, some of which had fallen out, and which she had recently had 'recrafted' by a hairdresser who specialized in clients undergoing radiation therapy. 'It was that nice Leonie Kaufman who recommended him,' she added. 'You know, the one whose daughter works for the magazine.'

I said nothing. I even managed, for the duration of the dinner, to steer the conversation away from such literary subjects. Then we got home, and as was their habit, my parents changed into their robes and lay down on the bed to watch television. I remember I was extremely jittery, almost bursting with the need to get the ordeal over with, to tell them once and for all about my story, at which point, I imagined, I would be free, the last hurdle would have been cleared, my life, from then on, would be a clean, straight path down which I had merely to stroll, enjoying all the sequential pleasures that lined it. And this need to unburden myself must indeed eventually have beaten back fear, for around ten I went into their bedroom, and said, 'Mom, Dad, I have something I need to talk to you about,' at which point my father turned to me quizzically and my mother, adjusting her eyeglasses, said, 'Can't it wait until a commercial?' which was just like my mother. So I sat down at the foot of the bed and waited until the commercials came on. My father had a remote control – at that time still something of a novelty – which he aimed at the screen to mute the volume. Inside the television cats pranced silently toward bowls of Little Friskies. I stood.

'You said you wanted to talk to us about something?' my father asked, his face open and relaxed, as was my mother's. And why shouldn't they have been relaxed? Neither of them had reason to expect, at that moment, that their youngest child, his chest puffed out like a pigeon's and his hands plucking at the lint on his sweater, was about to spring on them two intertwined revelations either one of which would have been enough to leave them reeling with astonishment. Yet there it was: into the quiet of their nighttime bedroom, during a commercial break, this child had strode, screwed up his eyes, and uttered a sentence it would take both of them several seconds to unpuzzle. 'Mom, Dad' – pausing, he issues a deep and alarming breath that is meant to start the adrenaline pulsing in their veins, to alert them to the fact that this is a serious matter, that at last, before silent cats, their boy is going to unmute himself – 'Mom, Dad, guess what? I'm coming out in the magazine.'

5

Dear Mr Terrier

A COUPLE OF months ago, while cleaning out a basement, I happened upon something I had no memory of saving: one of the surveys Janet Klass sent me every month as part of her doctoral research, and that every month I filled out as dutifully as the good student I had recently been. The survey consisted of twenty-four multiple choice questions, the first of which ran as follows:

> What is your chief motivation for writing?
> (a) Personal satisfaction
> (b) Financial reward
> (c) Public recognition
> (d) Desire to communicate
> (e) Other (please amplify below)

How did I answer? I can't recall. Probably (a), personal satisfaction, the rituals of a child trying to write the Narnia Chronicles. Or perhaps (d) or (c). Not (b). I would never have admitted to (b). Now I can see that within me there coexist two radically different beings, the artist and the fame seeker. Without the artist, the fame seeker would have nothing to peddle. Without the fame seeker, the artist would have no audience, no career, most crucially no money; the fame seeker – from whose embrace of the public the shy artist shrinks – is also his enabler. For just because art is the opposite of commerce doesn't mean that it lives outside its influence. Indeed, Janet, if I were to fill out your survey today, the only answer I could give to this question would be (e) other. Please amplify below, you say; all right, I will. But I must warn you, it will take more than a paragraph. Indeed, you might say this very novel is my amplification.

Ahem. But where was I? Oh yes.

After I graduated from college I moved to New York, where I went to work for the publishing firm of Hudson House, in whose editorial department I had once been a summer intern. In the interval a paperback company called Terrier Books had acquired Hudson, fusing the two entities into the rather ungainly 'Hudson-Terrier.' Hudson had then sold its old offices on Fifth Avenue, with their battered mahogany writing desks and leather armchairs, shipped its staff and files downtown to Terrier's vast and loftlike 'space,' and removed the word 'House' from its spines, so that they bore only the name 'Hudson.' New joint stationery was printed up, on which the famed wirehaired dog that was the symbol of Terrier appeared to be barking at the oil lamp that had been Hudson's logo since its inception in 1883.

In my childhood, Terrier books had always been my favorites, for no other reason than because my family always kept fox terriers, creatures of great tenacity and loyalty, whose obsessive habits in many ways mirrored my own. Thus whenever my brother and sister initiated a round of that game wherein people are likened to foods, machines, flowers, etc., when the category of 'animals' came up I was always a terrier. The little black-and-white dog on the spine of the books, so similar in affect and posture to the ones with which I lived, was a mascot: all my earliest literary dreams ended with publication by Terrier, which was probably why I so delighted in the prospect of working there.

My job required me to be at the office three days a week, which I thought ideal, because it left me plenty of time to write. As it happened, the publication of my story the previous spring had caused a small stir in literary circles: that is to say, it had piqued the curiosity of readers, become the subject of speculation among writers (particularly homosexual writers), provoked a barrage of letters to the magazine, most of them negative, etc. And yet, curiously enough, this little storm that the story had generated barely touched me, its author, mostly because the magazine's policy of not printing the biographies of its contributors meant that none of the speculators knew who I was. Also, at the time of the publication I was out of the country, traveling in Europe and enjoying (if that is the right word) the heady regret of being absent from my own great moment. I remember that the week of July 11, when the issue of the magazine featuring my story hit the stands, I was in Rome, staying in a little hotel near the Spanish Steps – a more expensive place than I could afford, really, except that there happened to be a single single room, without a bath, and about the size of one. And there, on the floor next to the narrow bed, my head on my suitcase (there was no space for a desk, much less a chest of drawers), I would half sit, half lie in the afternoons, writing until the sun went down, at which point it would be cool enough that I could go and wander the old city, bored and friendless yet too shy to strike up a conversation with strangers.

What I didn't know was that across the ocean, my story was taking on its own life. In gay circles, writers who had struggled for years to get their work into the magazine were making aghast and disbelieving telephone calls to one another, asking if anyone knew who 'he' was, this Martin Bauman who had stepped out of nowhere to one-up them. No one knew anything, though, except that there *was* a Martin Bauman listed in the Manhattan telephone directory, a gay Martin Bauman, in fact, who worked as an interior decorator. Many years later, at a party, I met him. Thrown into sudden intimacy by the mysterious bond that is a common name, we retreated together to a corner, where he told me, 'You can't imagine the calls I got. And the invitations I turned down!' No one guessed that the Martin Bauman who had actually written the story had already stepped back into that nowhere from which he had emerged briefly – or more correctly, a new nowhere, that of a tiny, telephoneless room in Rome, the one window of which looked out onto a cramped *cortile*, and in which, on hot nights, it was impossible to sleep.

And yet, so brief is the American attention span that by the time I got back to school in September the issue of the magazine containing my story had already been buried, in dentists' waiting rooms and in Upper East Side living rooms (as well as on my mother's kitchen desk), under stacks of more recent numbers. Even my mother's friends, from whom she had been having to endure a barrage of undesired commiseration all summer ('Poor Carolyn! Did you know before you read it?') started leaving her alone, their interest caught by fresher scandals – a child on heroin, a husband surprised in panties and high heels – all of which came as a relief to me. As it stood I had too much to do – my senior thesis, a photography course I was taking, the perpetual possibility of love – to be able to contend with such an ambivalent variety of fame. Instead I became political; I met, and briefly ruined, Barb Mendenhall; I went to bed with a handsome art student, and enjoyed myself a little bit. For a while even New York faded into the background; even Liza Perlman, with whom I was in the incipient phases of becoming intimate, disappeared, subletting her apartment and taking a two-year teaching gig at a tiny college in Minnesota.

From Stanley Flint, on the other hand, I heard nothing, and this surprised me. That he hadn't read, or at least heard about the story, seemed improbable, for I knew that he subscribed to the magazine, and kept abreast of the fiction it published, seventy-five percent of which he dismissed as 'unmitigated shit.' Did his silence mean, then, that my story had not qualified as part of that minority he considered worthy? Or was the letter he never wrote (and I checked my mailbox every day) merely a snub – further evidence that he had not forgiven me for my failure to get him his old job back?

One afternoon during my last semester I ran into Baylor in the rare book room of the library. Though she had graduated a year earlier, she was still living near campus, having taken a job as an editorial assistant at the university press. 'Hello, Bauman,' she said when she saw me. 'Congratulations on your story.'

'Thanks,' I answered.

'I can't pretend I'm not jealous as hell. I am. In fact, I wish I hadn't liked it as much as I did.'

'And you – are you writing much these days?'

'All the time. Every spare minute.' She checked her watch. 'Oops, I'd better get back to work. Nice seeing you.' And she hurried out the library doors.

It was mid-April when this meeting took place. The forsythias were in bloom; my senior thesis was finished, typed, turned in. With graduation only weeks away, I suddenly realized that I could no longer put off dealing with certain realities I'd been trying to avoid for months, chief among them the knowledge that at summer's end I would no longer have a secure little dorm room to return to, no longer a cozy schedule of lectures and seminars to keep me busy and vary my days. Instead I would have to make a life for myself and by myself – a task upon which, with that concentrated and pleasureless determination that had characterized my preparations for the SAT, I now focused my energies: I started looking for an apartment, a job, an adulthood. At school most of my friends were in a better situation than I was. Donald Schindler, having deferred Harvard Law School, was going to work on the stock exchange; Jim Sterling had landed a job as an editorial assistant at *Time*; Ash, who always made odd choices, was planning to enroll in clown school. As for me, my sole ambition was to move to New York and write. And yet despite Baylor's jealousy, even where writing was concerned, things were not going nearly as well as I had hoped. For though the publication of my story had netted me a few thousand dollars and half a dozen letters of vague inquiry from publishers and agents, it had not, as I had dreamed it might, led to the publication of a second story in the magazine, and then a first refusal contract, and finally one of those coveted writers' offices past which Edith had led me before our first lunch. Instead everything I'd sent her since the previous summer – seven stories in all – she had, for a variety of sensible reasons, rejected – which meant that I could no longer count on the magazine to make my career. Nor could I count on it to pay my rent. So I decided to look for a job. Because I knew people at Hudson, Hudson was the first place I called, and Hudson was where I ended up working.

Through Janet Klass I found an apartment not far from Riverside Park. In fact, it was Janet's apartment: she was giving it up in order to move across town, where her mother had bought a co-op 'as an investment.' The place she passed on to me cost nine hundred dollars a month, and was located on the fifth floor of a tenement walk-up that belonged more to the Lower East Side than to the amplitudinous blocks of West End Avenue on which it perched, sordid and forlorn. On either side red-brick apartment houses rose up, grand and stolid, the epitome of West Side gentility with their gynecologists and piano teachers, their service entrances, their conscientious lack of thirteenth floors. Our grimy little edifice, by contrast, had neither elevator nor elevator man. Its stairwells smelled of unwashed hair. Bugs lounged in the ceiling fixtures.

Because much of this and the next chapter will take place in that apartment, I shall now describe it. It was L-shaped. When you entered, you found yourself in a corridor too narrow for most pieces of furniture to pass through. Three doors opened off this corridor, the first onto a tiny bedroom with a loft bed, the second onto an even tinier bathroom with a miniature sink and tub, the third onto a second bedroom that could only have been called spacious when compared with its neighbor. All three of these rooms looked out onto the vestibule in which the super kept his pile of used car parts and pit bulls.

After that the corridor turned a corner. Here there were two larger rooms (by larger I mean nine feet by nine feet), both of which faced west, smack onto other apartments. The 'view' was of a young woman who came home every afternoon in tennis shoes, her pumps in her shoulder bag, and spent her evenings smoking joints in front of the television. One of these rooms I used as a bedroom, the other as a living room. At the far end of the corridor was the kitchen, with its bottom-of-the-line appliances and wood-grain laminate breakfast table.

I had two roommates, Dennis Latham and Will Gibson. Dennis, who came from Atlanta, was the plump, intelligent, soft-spoken boyfriend of a girl with whom I had become friends toward the end of my senior year, Wendy Stone. Evenings he sold tickets at the old Thalia movie theater, which showed revivals; mornings he spent reading avant-garde philosophers such as Benjamin, Derrida and Adorno.

Will was tiny, at least when compared with Dennis and me: five foot two in his tennis shoes. Although he was twenty-one and in his first year at NYU Law School, he looked every inch the adolescent, with a hairless chest and spotty chin. From what we could tell he didn't own a razor. Privately we wondered whether some drug his mother had taken during her pregnancy had stunted his growth. Yet he was far from sickly. Indeed, his nervous, animate athleticism put both of us to shame. While we slept late on weekend mornings, he would be up at dawn, riding his bicycle to the Columbia gym. In the afternoons he ran in Central Park. Not surprisingly he was much in demand in certain circles, and maintained a coterie of older admirers who took him to dinner at Le Cirque, or to Paris on the Concorde. To these gentlemen Will must have seemed a precious rarity – an articulate, *legal* alternative to the risky dalliances that had undignified the greater part of their lives – yet the only thing he really shared with his suitors was the very taste for 'unripe fruit' that drew them to him. (Such is often – and ironically – the case.)

Despite our differences in temperament, the three of us made up a cozy, not uncomfortable little household, and though our divergent schedules meant that we rarely ate or socialized together, nonetheless we managed to pay our rent on time and keep the bathroom clean. Nor did we lack for company, especially on weekends, when we seemed always to have houseguests: Wendy Stone, down from the university, where she was finishing up her incompletes (she was a troubled girl, a brilliant rebel, whose parents – affluent pseudo-WASPs – had changed their name from Stein); or Dennis's friend Teddy, up from Washington, where he was working as a congressional page; or someone Will had picked up at the monthly Columbia gay dance, an undergraduate usually, smallish and stylish, and a study in contrasts with the older, richer men into whose elegant East Side and East Hampton lives he sometimes disappeared on weekends.

He is dead now. Two years later a bus ran him down on his bicycle near Lincoln Center. And Dennis is teaching English in Texas, and Wendy is married to a man who dared question, once, the purpose of books in the video age, thus ruining our friendship forever. And Janet – I haven't a clue what's become of Janet, or her study. Years and miles separate us all from one another, as well as from those nights when we roamed the city in a pack, eating in coffee shops in groups of twelve, or going to double bills at the Thalia in gangs of fifteen, or flowing in and out of parties: it seemed that every weekend, somewhere, there was a party, given by a friend or a friend of a friend. And how many friends I had! Maureen and Ron and Tom S. and Tom R. and Josef and Elise and Melora . . . the names roll off my tongue easily today, even though I don't remember much about any of them. Some of them I spoke to for only minutes at a time, some of them I never spoke to, yet they were my dearest friends, with whom I rolled like a puppy in the intimate, indiscriminate heap that was New York, to me, in those years.

It's hard for me to imagine that there was ever a time when I didn't drink coffee, but there was. No doubt a certain resistance to adult habits – of which another symptom was my aversion to wine – underlay this curious abstention; for though I was old enough to vote, pay taxes, and go to prison, in those years it comforted me to think of myself less as a grown-up than a child on the outer edge of childhood, whose father could always be counted on to rescue him from difficulties, and whose missteps would always be excused as the foibles of youth. Coffee would have spoiled the effect, which was why, on the Monday, Wednesday, and Thursday mornings when I rode the subway downtown to Hudson-Terrier's offices – they were located in the east teens, in a region of warehouses and lofts to which the publishing industry, driven from midtown by exorbitant rents, was gradually migrating – I always brought a can of Diet Coke with me, the contents of which, once I had settled into my tiny cubicle, I would empty into a mug emblazoned with the old pre-Hudson-Terrier logo (that ubiquitous oil lamp), where, once the bubbles had settled, it did a passable imitation of joe. In this way I could indulge my own morning habit without upsetting those of my colleagues who could not stomach the idea of a Coke at eight A.M.

My chief responsibility at Hudson was to deal with what is known in publishing circles as the 'slush pile': specifically, that stack of unsolicited manuscripts, most of them addressed to 'Dear Sir' or 'Dear Editor' or even 'Dear Mr Terrier,' that is the bane of every editorial department, and that never seems to get any smaller, no matter how diligently the eager-eyed slush reader (invariably a kid like me) struggles to keep it in check. And if at Hudson the slush pile was particularly huge, this was in large part because a dozen years earlier another slush reader had plucked out of the heap a novel you are certain to have heard of, one that went on to become the biggest bestseller in the company's history, and because of which Hudson now enjoyed a reputation for sympathy among the naive and unconnected – one to which Harry Hudson III, its owner, had only added when in an interview he'd once vowed that no manuscript would pass through the portals of *his* house without getting a fair reading. (This was the sort of thing Harry Hudson III had a habit of saying, and that annoyed his employees, who knew he had never read a slush manuscript in his life. Nor did his edict last long; a few years later, in his late eighties, nearly blind and hugely rich from the buyout, he gave up his nominal title of 'president' at the company he no longer owned, as well as the grand and ceremonial office that was always kept on the ready for him, even though he never once, in my tenure, visited there. After that, Hudson ceased to employ a slush reader, choosing instead to enforce the policy – already in place at other publishing houses – of returning every unsolicited manuscript unopened. The job I once held, as a result, has disappeared.)

At first I laughed a lot over the slush pile, the manuscripts and letters I was always skimming, of which a typical (though invented) example might be the following:

Dear Mr Terrier:
Several years ago I was abducted by aliens and taken
aboard their spacecraft, where I was subjected to surgi-
cal procedures in the private regions of my body. Since
then I have tried to interest the police, FBI, CIA,
Surgeon General, even the President himself in my
experience, to no avail. Now my phone is being
tapped. Rocks have been thrown through my window,
the brakes on my car fixed. In sum, there is a conspiracy afoot to squash the valuable information I have to
share. *Taken: The True Story of an Alien Abduction*
recounts not only my experiences aboard the craft but
the subsequent attempts on my life by government
agents determined to keep me silent . . .

No, I am not being fair: this is not a typical example. I include it only to alarm and amuse. Much more typical (and sadder) were the badly written memoirs of adolescence through which at first I slogged dutifully, then later, as I grew more jaded, threw into the reject pile after reading only a sentence (shades of Edith); the children's books with titles like *Deirdre the Dodo*, *Fred the Fox Goes to the Doctor*, *Pete Puppy's Day Out*; the trashy novels about rich people written by poor people; the volumes of confessional poetry (one of them was called – quite memorably, I thought – *Probing the Abscess*); the trashy novels about poor people by rich people; the exposés of corruption in obscure industries that promised to be 'timely.' (This latter adjective, which I encountered in nearly every letter I read, infuriated my friend Carey Finch, the youngest of the editorial assistants, and an idealist of the most irascible variety. 'Don't they understand?' he'd say, quite literally tearing at his hair. 'The point is to write something time*less*!')

Most of these manuscripts were not timeless. Instead, in their coarse sincerity, they foretold the confessional talk shows that would become so popular in the nineties, the ones on which (for example) women whose sons had died from auto-erotic asphyxiation would describe the horrifying scenes they'd happened upon, in bedrooms decorated with posters of baseball stars. Even so, I gave each one of them my faithful consideration, in the naive hope that if I dug long enough I might discover somewhere a piece of real literature by some winsome unknown: a fresh Flannery O'Connor, a proto-Paley, a child Salinger; instead of which I found junk – boring junk – most of which I sent back swiftly, with only a form rejection letter paper-clipped to the manuscript, in the self-addressed stamped envelopes that its authors, careful to follow the guidelines listed in the *Writer's Market*, almost always took the trouble to enclose.

And yet when, on rare occasions, I did happen upon a letter that merited, at least in my view, a more considered response (if for no other reason than because its sincerity broke my heart), I would take the trouble to send a personal reply. Thus, to the girl from Cincinnati who had written *The Michael Jackson Diet Book: How The Inspirational Music of Michael Jackson Can Help You Lose 50–100 Lbs.*; to the English professor from El Paso who had gone to the heavy expense of photocopying and mailing his twelve-hundred-page, heavily annotated biography of James Elroy Flecker; to the ex-hippie in the East Village who wrote freshly and urgently about her boyfriend's periodic habit of emptying everything they owned onto the sidewalk and trying to sell it, yet whose work was marred by her bizarre refusal to use punctuation; to these people I wrote letters – sometimes long letters – that I signed in a purposefully illegible scrawl, a vague streak of nothing that would be impossible to decipher, and behind which I could remain safely anonymous. For as Carey had pointed out, even though I had the least power of anyone at Hudson, to those authors who sent their books in over the transom (some of whom might be psychotic) I had the most.

As I was rapidly discovering, I had come to work at Hudson during a transitional moment in its history – indeed, a transitional moment in the history of American book publishing. To understand the nature of this transition one needed only consider the layout of the Hudson-Terrier offices. The northeast corner, into which no natural light ever crept, was the domain of 'Hudson Editorial,' where the assistants wore tartans, worked under brass lamps with green glass shades, and thumbtacked postcards of Virginia Woolf and James Joyce over their typewriters. The southeast corner, on the other hand, belonged to 'the terrible Terriers.' Here the sunlight poured in so liberally you had to squint against it. The terrible Terriers wore contact lenses instead of glasses, went to the gym, and talked on the phone. It seemed that they were always talking on the phone. Horrifying neologisms peppered their conversations: 'privish' (as opposed to 'publish'), 'midlist,' and perhaps most upsetting of all, 'impact,' which they used as a verb, in sentences along the lines of: 'How do you think the sale of Scribner's is going to impact the industry as a whole?' (My mother's son, I grimaced every time I heard it.)

Working there was a little bit like trying to drive in one of those medieval European cities where powerful BMWs jostle tiny Fiat 500s, or worse still, ass-drawn carts on the narrow streets. Thus, though there *was* a computer in the office, only one person knew how to use it. At Terrier the editorial assistants at least had self-correcting IBM Selectric typewriters. At Hudson we made do with Liquid Paper. Also, because Harry Hudson III was essentially a kind man, the Hudson staff included a number of rather useless old people he had never had the heart to fire. There was a short, white-haired lady named Mrs Brillo who had been with the company for thirty years, and who performed, from what I could tell, only two functions: first, she talked to the photocopier, which like all the machines at Hudson was both old and ornery; second, at her little desk she maintained a large stock of off-brand supermarket cookies and pastries, of which everyone was invited to partake. I liked her. During my breaks I would often stroll over to her desk for a Danish or a few creme wafers from a fifty-for-a-dollar-ninety-nine pack, or a generic Mallomar. Then one afternoon she was fired; given two hours to clean out her desk. Nothing more. After that, no one talked to the photocopy machine, while the brisk young woman who appropriated Mrs Brillo's desk not only kept no treats there, she ate only carrots and breadsticks, and later had to be hospitalized for bulimia.

Of course, if we had been wiser, or less blind, we might have seen in the firing of Mrs Brillo a grim omen for the future, just as we might have foretold the grosser hijackings to come, for example, from the memo that went around the office the week of my arrival, announcing (as if it were news) that the staff was always welcome to buy Hudson-Terrier books at a forty percent discount, but really warning us to put a stop once and for all to a practice by means of which editorial assistants had been supplementing their paltry salaries since time immemorial: namely, taking books from the office and selling them at the Strand. Upon reading this memo my young colleagues groaned and shook their heads, just as they groaned and shook their heads when they learned that our new boss, Marjorie (or Marge) Preston, had been given a mandate by Terrier – which had itself been given a mandate by its 'parent' corporation, a murky multinational based in Germany – to 'increase revenues and decrease spending.' And though no one was quite sure just what, on a practical level, this frightening edict might mean, nonetheless we made all sorts of doomsday predictions – less out of fear than in the spirit of the paranoid flyer who imagines that by constantly envisioning a crash he can keep the plane aloft. For when one is standing on the cusp of a new age, what is difficult to grasp is not the fact of change, but its extent. Thus, decry though we might the demise of the all-cloth binding in favor of the cardboard binding with only a strip of cloth on the spine, I doubt that any of us could have foreseen the day when books would have no cloth on them at all. Nor would we have believed him had someone told us that in a dozen years the old Scribner's Bookshop on Fifth Avenue would have become a Benetton, or that closer to home, the terrier would have consumed the oil lamp at which he currently only barked, leaving 'Hudson' a tiny imprint of Terrier, with a staff of two. For Hudson was Hudson; to suggest that one day it might simply be put to sleep was as ludicrous as to imagine that someday CDs might eclipse records, or that Mr ——— would be fired as editor of the magazine. Our cynicism, in other words, had limits; the world did not.

Still, we were stoic. In the face of the gravest indignities – for instance, the purchase for a million dollars of a trashy novel ('a *commercial* novel,' the terrible Terriers corrected) no better and no worse than any of the hundreds that had come in via the slush pile – we put on a brave face. Nor did I flinch when asked to type, on behalf of a long-standing editor (who was in turn acting on orders from Marge), a wad of letters to authors long published by Hudson, of which a typical example was the following:

Dear Nancy,
What a delight it was running into you the other night at Billie Eberhart's dinner! I must say you're looking terrific, in addition to which we're all thrilled here at how well the Terrier reprint of *Soldiers and Sisters* is doing – 3,300 copies sold at last count!
By the way, you owe us $142.33 for copies of your books above and beyond those specified in your contract, and if we don't receive payment soon, a collection agency will be notified.
Well, that's all for now. Hope your work's continuing apace, and that George and the kids are well. Oh, and has Lucy finished Brearley yet? She's scrumptious!
Yours with affection,
Lorna

Later, when things got worse, a lot of my colleagues left publishing. Carey Finch, about whom I shall have more to say presently, got a Ph.D. in Comparative Literature, and became an avatar of Queer Studies. Others went to business school or law school, and ended up a lot richer than the editors for whom they had once worked – those editors whose habit of going out for expense account lunches at pricey restaurants they had found, in the days when they could barely afford to buy a carton of yogurt, so galling. Only one has stuck it out in publishing: Sara Rosenzweig, the assistant to our editor in chief, and hence, back then, the editorial assistant in chief. In her late twenties and very smart, Sara was not only a Jew, but an Orthodox Jew, who lived with her mother on the Lower

East Side, had to leave work early on Fridays in order to be home before dusk, and dressed, even on the hottest of summer days, in blouses the sleeves of which dropped below her elbows, pantyhose, knee-length skirts. Sara's hair was so stiff and blond that at first I wondered whether she was compelled to wear one of those wigs that married Orthodox women must put on so that men cannot see their tempting locks. In fact, the hair was hers, and she was single. This was a problem, for though she insisted that she could never marry a man who wasn't Orthodox, she also couldn't bear most Orthodox men, whom she considered boorish. 'Well, why not marry a Conservative Jew, then?' I'd ask her during the lunches we sometimes ate together. Why not eat shrimp, or wear pants, or cook meat with milk? To which she would respond that the arbitrariness of Orthodox practice was exactly its point: precisely *because* the rules were outdated, their acceptance was the ultimate proof of faith.

It was through Sara that I was introduced into a substratum of Manhattan society of which I might otherwise never have learned anything. This was the culture of middle-class Orthodox Jews, the tendrils of which, though firmly rooted in the Lower East Side, also reached into the most remote neighborhoods of Upper Manhattan. These Jews had their own restaurants, at which Sara and I often ate: in addition to the French-kosher La Difference, there was the Chinese-kosher Moishe Peking, and the Japanese-kosher Shalom Japan, the owner of which sang karaoke on Thursday nights.

It was here that I told her, one Thursday evening, that I was gay. She remained nonplused.

'And yet I'll bet there aren't any gay Orthodox Jews, are there?' I challenged.

'Sure there are.'

'So how do they reconcile their sex lives with their religion?'

'Well,' Sara said, 'the ones I know – because biblical law says you can't lie with another man, they do it standing up.'

The ingenuity she described – an ingenuity that was at once Jewish *and* gay – made me laugh. In this way our friendship was secured.

After that we had lunch together most days, either at the office, or at one of the kosher restaurants, or on Tuesdays at a cheap Chinese place nearby, with all the other editorial assistants. Because Sara could not eat the food served here, she always brought along a bottle of fruit juice and an apple that she would peel primly, while the rest of us spun the lazy Susan in the center of the table, piled our bowls with greasy noodles and kung pao chicken, guzzled Tsingtao beers. Conversation at these lunches tended to devolve quickly into complaint: the dissipation of literary values was lamented, as were our pitiful incomes. (Average starting pay in those days was just under twelve thousand dollars a year.) Or we would tell rude stories about our bosses, one of whom – a new recruit from Random House – did not know the difference between Tom Wolfe and Thomas Wolfe. This horrified his assistant, Jane, an earnest Vassar graduate of twenty-two. 'I mean, can you imagine?' she'd say. 'An editor at one of the most illustrious publishing houses in New York, and he doesn't know who Thomas Wolfe is.'

'My boss can't spell "separate,"' a colleague chimed in.

It is worth pointing out here that like the new arrival from Random House, the editor who couldn't spell 'separate' was one of the ones Marge had hired upon her arrival, and as such to be distinguished from the few remaining old editors, the ones who had been with Hudson twenty years or more, and not only knew the difference between Thomas Wolfe and Tom Wolfe, but had edited both of them. *These* editors had lunch at their desks, in contrast to the new kids, who ate out every day with agents at fancy restaurants – meals from which they returned moaning that the food had been too rich. 'These days when I go to the Four Seasons I just order a green salad with lemon juice,' Marge herself was wont to say, to the horror of Sara, whom she had never once invited out for a meal, kosher or otherwise.

All struggles, I'm convinced, come down in the end to food. My colleagues, I saw, were in the process of becoming Marxists; they were experiencing alienated labor; they were smarting at the unequal distribution of wealth. And yet a vestige of their old literary idealism must still have survived in them, for toward the ends of our Thursday lunches, a little drunk from too much Tsingtao beer, we would always end up vowing that someday, together, we would quit Hudson and form a new publishing company, one that cared about literature, and that would be called (after the Chinese restaurant) Round Table Books. And at this new company the old values would be resurrected. Young authors would be taken on with an eye toward the future – tiny Hemingways, miniature Whartons, junior Faulkners! A backlist would be built to rival that of Scribner's or Knopf – exactly the sort of backlist that these days Hudson seemed to care less and less about replenishing; yes, for a moment, hope would brighten our young faces, until it was time to pay the bill (so poor were we that we divvied it up to the penny), after which, slightly urpy, we would return to our cubicles and wait for the editors, who had big offices with windows, to come back from their equally big lunches.

As for Marge Preston, her insistence that she ordered only a green salad when she went to the Four Seasons must have been spurious. Either that, or she simply did not possess the aristocratic genes of lamb-chop-loving Edith Atkinson, in comparison to whom she appeared bookish, lumbering, and coarse, all at once: a peculiar mélange of Marianne Moore and Estée Lauder. Though she was not yet forty, it was to her

that the powers that be not only at Terrier, but at the conglomerate that owned Terrier (of whom the most daunting
was no doubt her own immediate superior, the elegant Mrs
Fairfax, whose soft-spoken manner and impeccably tailored
suits belied a certain professional implacability) had entrusted
the perilous job of dragging fuddy-duddy old Hudson House
into the twentieth century; nor, I think, could they have found
a better person to take on this onerous task, for though Marge
was an instinctive and somewhat ruthless businesswoman,
she was also the author of a biography of I. Compton-Burnett,
which meant that the more literary members of the Hudson
staff could not help but respect her erudition. I remember her
as a mass of flying yellow hair, cigarette smoke, and L'Air du
Temps, always in a rush, always late for something, yet never
too busy, even in the midst of giving orders to two or three
people at once, to offer some nugget of witty and allusive
commentary. 'This manuscript,' she might say, 'makes me
remember what Dr Johnson said about the dancing dog: the
thing is not that it is done well, but that it is done at all.'

The same might have been said of Marge herself. Though a
shrewd editor, capable of inspiring awe in Nobel laureates,
several of whom had dedicated books to her, she was also
hopelessly disorganized, forever losing crucial documents and
missing deadlines and failing to return phone calls. In this
regard she posed a startling contrast to the sleek and efficient
Mrs Fairfax, whose presence of mind always seemed to put
Marge to shame. Worst of all, she often broke down at critical moments, at which point the responsibility for running the
editorial department would fall – unbeknownst to anyone –
onto Sara's capable shoulders. Without Sara, Marge might
have been fired by Mrs Fairfax months earlier. Yet rather than
acknowledge this debt to her assistant, or express to her any
form of gratitude, time and again she passed Sara over for
promotions. Her excuse was that Sara did not possess the

'intellectual qualifications' necessary to become an editor, which meant in essence that she had graduated not from Radcliffe or Smith, but from the City University of New York. Instead, she disparaged and abused her assistant, much as in old novels the 'distressed gentlewoman' will often heap opprobrium upon the paid companion without whose assistance she cannot so much as get out of bed in the morning.

As I mentioned earlier, Marge's mandate from Terrier had been to transform Hudson from a sleepy and genteel backwater into a 'major player,' and toward this end she had not only gotten rid of all the 'dead wood' (people like Mrs Brillo), but made it clear to her underlings that their future at the company depended on their capacity to generate profit. It was a decree at the very mention of which the old timers cringed, for by and large they were mild, unambitious men and women who lived in rent-controlled apartments, and were content to publish every year a familiar assortment of first novels, French cookbooks, and detailed guides to bird-watching. None of these books sold very well (or cost very much), yet in the old days this hadn't mattered much, since as everyone knew Harry Hudson III had such deep pockets that he never looked at the balance sheets; the whole company was for him merely a tax write-off; in short, he *preferred* that Hudson lose money. To the old-timers, the bestseller was a distasteful, even lurid animal, one to which, when on rare occasions they did produce a specimen (always by accident) they referred with wistful regret, as if success were an unfortunate and rare mutation in the literary gene.

Of course they were wrong – and not merely in their estimation of Harry Hudson III's attitude. For as it turned out his pockets weren't nearly so deep as everyone had thought, which was why he'd had to sell the company. And now the powers that be had given Marge deadlines and numbers to match. Rumor even had it (though this Sara refused to corroborate) that at the end of the coming year she was supposed to fire all the editors whose books had failed to make a profit – in which case, as Carey Finch noted ruefully, she'd have to fire every editor in the house. This she didn't do. And yet it was true that recently a few editors – including Carey's boss – had rather abruptly decided to take early retirement. In their place terrifying 'hot shots,' such as Jane's recruit from Random House, were hired. This was particularly troublesome to Carey, who had liked his boss, a fiery leftist whose list consisted mostly of statistic-driven studies by political scientists who wrote earnest analyses of urban decline, environmental decline, social decline – in short, books that proved, beyond a shadow of a doubt, that our culture was in decline. But now this affable and somewhat tipsy gentleman had suddenly (and under duress) 'left,' and though Marge assured Carey that he himself would be kept on, she gave no indication as to who it was he would be working for: someone flashy and vulgar, no doubt, who would laugh at his idealistic advocacy of the timeless.

Carey was an angular young man of twenty-one, graceful less in the manner of a bird than of a squirrel; and indeed, it was of a squirrel that I usually thought when I ran into him in the corridor where he went to smoke, lifting the cigarette to his lips with that same blend of appetite and precision that marks the aforementioned rodent's demeanor when eating acorns. Everything about him, now that I think of it, was squirrely: his fine-boned hands, his silky fawn hair, even his eyes, which were the size and color of hazelnuts. I thought him very handsome. Whenever he strode down the hall past my desk, his gaze intently focused, his body spry in its never-changing uniform of jeans, tweed jacket and Oxford shirt, my response was invariably one of attraction mixed with envy. For I recognized that despite whatever comparisons one might draw between him and backyard animals, Carey possessed, and would always possess, the very thing I lacked: namely, that cohesive admixture of self-knowledge and taste to which we refer when we say that someone has a 'look.' I knew. I didn't have a look. Instead, with my wrinkled shirts, ill-fitting glasses, and shaggy hair that when uncut (which was most of the time) lifted off my head in rolling waves, I must have given an impression as ill-defined as that of Marge Preston, when she hurtled by in one of her weirdly conceived and oddly touching outfits: a pink Chanel suit, say, with Birkenstock sandals.

What made Carey's look work, on the other hand – what made his perfect manners and faultless fingernails signify so much more than merely a dull adherence to convention – was the current of short-temperedness, even violence, that under-scored his idealism, and that revealed itself whenever, at Round Table lunches, the topic of literature came up. Then he would become both testy and argumentative, especially if a writer he considered to be overrated (for example Forster, my own favorite, whom he thought a sentimentalist) received what was, in his opinion, undue praise. For unlike the terrible Terriers, he really loved literature, and not as a writer manqué, but as a reader. He read with epicurean gusto. He read the way a gastronome eats.

Carey lived not far from me, in a studio apartment on West 110th Street, which meant that sometimes we rode the subway home together after work. Because we never talked about anything except books, I had no idea that he was gay until one Saturday evening when, quite by accident, I ran into him with some of his friends at the monthly Columbia gay dance. The occasion, which might have been awkward, turned out to be utterly cordial; indeed, not only was Carey not flummoxed by my presence, he appeared genuinely pleased to see me, and immediately invited me to join the little group of boys, with whom he was sitting at one of the tables on the periphery of the dance floor. These turned out to be mostly old pals from college: one was a graduate student in Biology, another worked as a legal clerk, a third managed a gourmet food shop. None of them seemed to be remotely on the make, which rather surprised me. Instead they spent the duration of the festivity happily planted at their little table, never dancing (it was hard to imagine Carey dancing), just chatting, mostly about some mutual friends, a couple named Richard and Susan, whose doings they seemed to find endlessly fascinating. And how safe, even cozy, I felt in the little nest that Carey's friends formed, especially when, from a distance, a man I had noticed at another Columbia dance started staring at me. The trouble was, there was something slightly mad about the way this man stared; it gave me an instant erection. He was probably thirty – years younger than I am now. He had thick hair, broad shoulders, just the tiniest bit of a beer belly. From where he stood leaning against the wall, his hips slightly bucked, drinking a Corona into the neck of which a lemon wedge had been shoved, he cast me a look so frankly lewd and assessing I almost giggled. No one had ever looked at me that way before. And yet such brazenness only left me shy and at a loss for words. So I stayed where I was, safe behind that social border across which, I knew, decorum would forbid this man from dragging me by the hair, no matter how much I might want him to. Even when he went to the toilet, casting a glance over his shoulder as he walked, I didn't follow.

When the dance ended, we all went out for hamburgers at Tom's Diner (later to be made famous by Suzanne Vega), where I saw a lot of people I knew: Philip Crenshaw, as gaunt as ever with his kohl-ringed eyes, and Lars with Eve Schlossberg, who was studying photography at the New School, and my roommate Will with one of his boyish amours. The man who had been staring at me I did not see: he had gone home, apparently, or moved on to some other venue. I remember feeling relieved, and at the same time disappointed. Secretly I hoped that when I left the diner to go back to my apartment, I'd find him waiting around the corner, at which point I would have no choice but to submit to his bold gaze. But I didn't. Instead I walked home alone, looking back now and then to see if by any chance he might be lingering on a stoop.

That night it was too hot to sleep. Naked and unsheeted in my bed, I tried to imagine what the stranger with the questioning eyes might have done with me, or to me, had I gone with him. Part of me lamented not having approached him – the part of me that was tired of crossing only when the crossing guard told him to. And yet that spare, brutal room to which, in my imagination, the stranger led me was a place I feared as much as I desired. There, I knew, I would be stripped not only of my clothes, but of my very self; the crossing guard would fall to the pavement, and in his place would rise up a creature of pure, pleading appetite.

We were having a terrible heat wave in New York. Though the sky was always gray and heavy, no rain fell on the dirty sidewalks for weeks at a time. Each workday, on my way to and from the subway, I'd find myself pushing through a death-of-the-rain forests heat that might have been a rain forest. And yet even on Sundays, when the streets were empty, and everyone sensible had gone to the beach, I stayed behind, too grateful at last to be a leaseholding resident of Manhattan even to want to contemplate stepping off the island of my dreams. Anyway, I reasoned, why fight the crowds at the beach, why endure sunburn and sand flies and pebbles in my shoes, when I could just as easily spend the day at Jim Sterling's parents' cool apartment, reading, or watching television, or playing Monopoly? This was my preferred method of repose. Quintessential city people, the Sterlings owned no 'little place on the shore,' no country house. Instead Mrs Sterling joked that they had invested their money in first-class air-conditioning. 'Our unit's a Cadillac,' she told me. Nor had she any truck with the claim that too much conditioned air was bad for the lungs. On the contrary! She kept their apartment so cold we had to wear sweaters.

Hot Sunday mornings, then, while all our friends were lugging beach umbrellas, ice chests, and suntan lotion to Penn Station, Jim and I would meet at the corner of 86th and Broadway (he too was renting a cramped apartment), then walk together to his parents' building on Central Park West. Up we'd ride in the elevator, noting carefully, whenever it made stops to pick other people up or let them off, the styles in which the various foyers were decorated. One, I remember, brought to mind old ocean liners; another, all chintz and bullion fringe, resembled a Victorian powder room; a third had gleaming white walls and a chrome-edged table I recognized from the Museum of Modern Art's furniture collection.

Soon we'd arrive at the twentieth floor, which belonged in its entirety to the Sterlings, and where the walls of the foyer were painted a crisp butterscotch yellow. The floor was marble, as was that of the dining room, which was unquestionably the most impressive room in the apartment, with walls covered in Zuber paper, hand-blocked and painted, and in this case depicting a vaguely Eastern river landscape, replete with rose-colored peacocks and ginkgo trees. At the mahogany table an individual saltcellar with its own tiny spoon sat behind each place setting. Until I'd met the Sterlings I hadn't known what a saltcellar was. Now I dismissed the salt-and-pepper sets of my childhood as yet further evidence of its cultural poverty, and vowed never to 'shake' salt again so long as I lived.

Of course, if the Sterlings themselves had been as stuffily formal as their dining room – if, for instance, Mrs Sterling had set her table with four forks and three spoons, or kept a little bell by her plate to ring for the maid (indeed, if she'd *had* a maid, as opposed to Gussie, who came in three times a week to fry chicken and wore an old pair of Jim's underpants on her head) – then probably I wouldn't have liked them nearly as much as I did. And yet this Jewish couple who had grown up in Yonkers were amazingly (considering the elegance of their apartment) blasé. Except on those nights when Gussie fried them chickens, they ate only take-out, most of it from Zabar's, that West Side emporium to which, in the spring and fall, Mrs Sterling liked to go herself to do the shopping. (In summer and winter she had everything delivered.) Sundays in particular were days of ritualistic excess, the table littered with little plastic Zabar's tubs containing lox and flavored cream cheeses, platters of rye bread, bagels, and bialys, sheets of wax paper layered with lacy slivers of pastrami, half cakes in half-cake-shaped plastic receptacles. Jim and I would eat – brunch, not lunch – then afterward retreat to his room, where we might amuse ourselves by playing old board games, or watching reruns of 1950s science fiction movies. When you are twenty, childhood has yet to season into memory; beneath the bark the wood is still green. Hence we could happily waste the whole day in an inertia of television. Or he might read, while I reverted to my adolescent habit of drawing maps for nonexistent subway systems. Or we'd take on projects in Mrs Sterling's kitchen, preparing from a cookbook called *Cocktail Food* (it was the only one she owned) such dainties as 'cucumber-filled flowers filled with caviar,' 'lemon swans,' 'pink-salmon-soufflé-stuffed zucchini boats.' Now I see that if we threw ourselves into these activities with such fervor, it was only because we knew they were the last little gasps of a dying thing, as in the final weeks of August children will often seem to play with greater intensity, as if to protest the leaves that are already starting to change, the 'Back to School' ads in the newspapers. For soon we would reach a point where we could no longer muster the enthusiasm needed for such play, we would jump full-force into adult habits and tastes: strip poker instead of Monopoly, coffee instead of Diet Coke. Ours was the zeal that precedes nostalgia, which was why, when we shook hands at the corner of Broadway and 86th Street at day's end, a blush of shame would sometimes creep over our faces – evidence that the pleasures in which we had been indulging were at once too ludicrous and too intimate to bear articulation.

Probably the sense that has eroded most steadily in me, as I've grown older, is that of certainty. When I was young, I felt *certain* that I would live the entirety of my life in New York City; I felt *certain* that I would never own a house, only an apartment; I felt *certain* that the city was – no, not my choice – my fate. Instead of which, almost two decades later, I live as far from New York as you can get, amid patient cultivations, on an unpaved road where the only traffic is caused by passing flocks of sheep. These days it's hard for me to believe that I could have endured summers in New York – yet I not only endured them, I thrived on them. After all, there was so much to do! Shakespeare in the park (hours waiting in line), Ethiopian restaurants where one ate mysterious pulses with one's fingers (risk of salmonella). Everything was always open. You could get cold sesame noodles at two in the morning if you wanted to. (Cold sesame noodles – a dish I had never tasted outside Manhattan – were my chief gastronomic passion; for two weeks straight that summer I ate nothing else, only slurped, every night, those delicious chilly threads and their peanut butter dressing from the aluminum tins in which the local Chinese restaurant packed them.) Or you could go to any number of clubs, or travel from party to party, or stay home and watch reruns of *I Love Lucy* until dawn.

City life became, for me, the source of mad daydreams. For example, it thrilled me to contemplate the fact that just a few inches away from where I sat, say, reading in the Sterlings' living room, someone else, a stranger, was very likely also sitting. And who might this stranger be? A movie star? A man who forced his wife to dress in a rabbit suit? A girl who drew pentangles on her bedroom floor? That I didn't know enraptured me, and made me regret those expanses of lawn and tree that in my parents' neighborhood separated one family from the next. Here, on the other hand, variety was layered, as in a club sandwich. People lived atop one another, and beside one another, and all around one another, in a series of boxes inside other boxes. It made me feel ensconced, protected, saved.

That summer, with the exception of Jim, I was spending less and less time with my old friends and more with Carey's – a coterie of intelligent, well-educated young men who wore tweed jackets, had their hair cut at old-fashioned barbershops, and spoke incessantly, whenever they were together, of this couple, this Richard and Susan, with whom they were collectively obsessed, and about whom they were always saying vague and tantalizing things along the lines of: 'The thing about Susan is that she's just so . . . but what can you say about Susan?'

Apparently you could say that she loved sex; that once she had told Carey she pitied men, because they could never experience the bliss of being fucked simultaneously from front and back; that a *parfumeur* in Paris had been so taken with her, he had mixed a special perfume in her honor.

As for Richard, he was a great fellow. Everyone loved Richard. At NYU Law School normal straight guys scrambled to be his friend. (Later I asked my roommate Will if he knew Richard. 'That guy?' Will said. 'He never talks. I hardly notice

him.') Richard was sometimes the subject of salacious speculation among the group, chiefly regarding the size of his penis.
(Whenever this matter came up, I noticed, Carey would grow
gloomy, silent, and the subject would change.)

He had other reasons to be gloomy. At Hudson, Marge
was taking her time replacing the editor he had worked for,
which meant that he found himself in what was for him the
unenviable position of not having enough to do. Carey was
one of those people who is only happy when he has tasks to
which he must attend (a convenient excuse, I have found, for
the avoidance of self-examination). Accordingly, in the days
following his editor's 'retirement,' he would often wander
over to my desk and linger there idly, in much the same way
that I had often lingered at Mrs Brillo's desk, hoping she
might offer me a second doughnut. One day he even asked if
he could help out with the slush pile. Sara was so shocked
that Carey would actually volunteer to take on such an onerous task that she asked Marge to give him a project to keep
him busy until she hired the new editor, at which point
Marge saddled him with a 750-page fishing encyclopedia to
edit.

Secretly I was disappointed. While they'd lasted, I'd enjoyed
Carey's visits, the frustrated energy he radiated when idle.
The truth was, I had become a bit smitten with him – or to
put it more accurately, I had *decided* to become a bit smitten
with him, not because he attracted me physically (in his agile
wiriness, he could not have differed more from the dark
stranger at the dance), but because he seemed to me the sort
of person with whom I ought to fall in love: one whose evident respectability, when the time came to enact that visit
home with a boyfriend that was my story in the magazine,
would distract my mother's attention from the fact that he
was male. Obviously this was neither the first nor the last time
I would fall in love in such a calculated way, for in those

days, as I have said, I could divorce the erotic from the romantic as neatly as my sister separated the yolk from the white of an egg. Lust, I believed, could also be an offshoot of love, one that evolved slowly, over years. It was the same trick I'd played in high school, when I'd convinced myself that I had 'crushes' on certain girls, only this time the object of my artificial affection was not a girl, but a boy whose very decorousness obviated the necessity of thinking about desire.

On the subway, meanwhile, brutish men, versions of that leering beau ideal at the dance, would sometimes look my way. Because they recalled the stare of the stranger at the dance, their glances, even when casual, excited me. Around them I built erotic scenarios as elaborate as the imaginary subway systems I still invented at Jim Sterling's on Sunday afternoons. In the fantasies I spun around Carey, on the other hand, the two of us never took off our clothes. Instead, wearing cashmere sweaters and ascots, we would sit side by side in leather armchairs, in the living room of the village brownstone owned together. A fox terrier (homage to Terrier Books, of which Carey was now editor in chief) lounged between our feet. What I was enjoying, in these fantasies, was what Mrs Patrick Campbell called 'the deep, deep peace of the double bed after the hurly-burly of the chaise longue' – yet I had never known the hurly-burly of the chaise longue. I had skipped a crucial step. And meanwhile Carey and I remained only friends. I was far too timid to make advances. Also, we were never alone together. Instead, whenever we went out it was in the company of other people – Carey's college buddies, or the Round Table crew, or Eve Schlossberg, with whom he'd turned out to have gone to high school.

Was it because of shyness that he was trying to avoid being alone with me? I wondered sometimes, but could not say for sure. The nervousness he radiated blocked out all signals, collected around him like a woolly darkness. In his company motives were obscure, distances distorted, perspectives blurred.

At work, meanwhile, the period of limbo continued. Candidate after candidate for the open slot Marge interviewed and rejected. Nor was she quick in the process. Lackadaisical in the least pressured of situations, she grew panicked under the gun, and ground to a halt. Without Sara's aid I don't know what she (or Carey) would have done; she simply could not make up her mind. And then one Friday, in response, perhaps, to some unspoken signal of helplessness, Sara stepped in and took over. She was really extraordinarily efficient. By the end of the morning she had every one of Marge's meals booked for the following week: breakfasts, lunches, and dinners with prospective editors, some of whom Marge herself had approached, some of whom Sara had chased down on her own.

Monday the rush began. Not that we had any idea who the candidates in question were. Sara was nothing if not discreet. Only she knew to what restaurant Marge went hurrying off at the end of every morning, invariably twenty minutes late, and invariably not in possession of some crucial item or document: her wallet, or a catalogue, or an umbrella, with which Sara would have to run after her, calling 'Wait!' as the elevator doors shut on Marge's face.

The strategy worked, however. By the end of the week Marge had gained five pounds from all the meals, but was also down to three finalists. Or so Sara confided in us without divulging a single name. After all, it is by only sharing just enough information to keep others hungry that you can secure for yourself a small power base.

That Friday, meetings were scheduled with all three candidates. Because at least two of them already had other jobs, these meetings had to be conducted in secret, not at the office, but in Marge's living room. Even though Friday was usually one of my days off, I came in after lunch, if for no other reason than to give Carey moral support. Especially for him, a palpable halo of worry surrounded Marge's empty office as the afternoon waned, and no call came. By the end of the day, we realized, a decision would most likely have been made. But what decision? Who? Only Sara might know, and Sara wasn't talking.

Dusk fell. 'Has she called?' we asked Sara, who was putting on her raincoat, readying herself for the hurried trip home before the sun set. But she only shook her head. 'Sorry, kids,' she said, and went. Carey packed up his fishing encyclopedia. I asked if he wanted to have dinner with me, and though the invitation seemed genuinely to please him, nonetheless he asked if he could take a rain check: his mother was in town, and he was going with her to her favorite sushi bar.

Monday I arrived at the office before nine. Sara and Carey were already there, which didn't surprise me. What did was that Marge was in her office with the door closed.

'According to the janitor they've been locked up together since six-thirty,' Carey said.

'Who are they?'

'Marge, Mrs Fairfax, and Mr X,' said Sara

'Or Ms X,' Carey added. 'We won't know until they come out whether it's Mr or Ms.'

For a moment the three of us simply stared at the closed door. Then Sara said, 'Well, no point in standing around, let's get to work.' And she sat down at her desk. Reluctantly, Carey slunk off to his fishing encyclopedia. Getting ice for my Diet Coke, I passed Marge's office a second time. The door was still shut.

Eventually I too sat down, and was just reading the first page of a 'young adult' novel called *Don't Hate Me Because I'm Retarded* when a spasm of adolescent hunger seized me, and I decided to go and get something from the candy machine – checking on the way, of course, to see if Marge's door was open; it wasn't. I ate the Hershey's bar I'd bought, then retraced the path to my cubicle, which took me yet again past Marge's door, still closed. Then I went to the men's room, where I was just unzipping my fly when someone walked in and stood at the urinal next to mine. I turned to see who it was, and found myself eyeball to eyeball with Stanley Flint.

'Bauman,' he said casually. 'What are you doing here? They're not publishing you, are they?'

'No, I work here,' I answered.

'Really? What a coincidence,' Flint said. 'Because as of today, so do I.'

6

Law of the Jungle

ALTHOUGH I SAW very little of Liza Perlman that fall – for the duration of her stint at Babcock College in Minnesota she had sublet her New York apartment, and flew back only on holidays – nonetheless we talked all the time by phone. This was not merely due to distance; as I quickly discovered, Liza's preferred mode of communication was the telephone. When she woke up in the mornings, even before she got out of bed, she always called one of her friends – usually the famous Eli, or else a boy called Ethan with whom (strange as it may sound) she watched *Jeopardy!* over the phone. Sometimes she even slept with the phone cradled in her arms, the way that a puppy will sleep nestled against an alarm clock wrapped in a blanket.

Our conversations were usually about books. 'Any news?' Liza would ask me, meaning news about publishing. (She took it for granted that my job at Hudson gave me access to all manner of inside information.) Yet usually in Babcock, Minnesota, she knew more than I did in New York. She knew, for instance, at what salary Stanley Flint had been hired, having learned this 'extraordinary' scoop from her mother: eighty thousand a year 'plus stock options,' which seemed a staggering figure. For Flint, as it turned out, was one of Sada Perlman's clients, as were Leonard Trask, Nancy Coleridge, and most of the other writers he admired. 'You could say he made my mother's career,' Liza explained. 'I mean, before that she was just a housewife in New Jersey. Then she left my father, and with one client – this black woman from Cincinnati no one had ever heard of, but whom Stanley admired – she decided to become an agent. One client! If nothing else, you can say this about my mother: she has a good nose.'

If there was no news, we talked about Liza's teaching. She was miserable in Babcock, she said, where no one had ever heard of a bagel. To a one, her students were 'imbeciles.' She longed for home – for Chinese food, and movies, and all-night grocery stores. In Babcock, everything closed at five. People actually went to church on Sundays; even her colleagues in the English department went to church. To make matters worse, because she did not drive, she had to depend on her few on-campus friends to get anywhere – chiefly Lucy Ellington, a poet, and head of the Babcock Creative Writing department. 'Do you know her work?' Liza asked, and sighed before I could answer. 'It's wonderful. I don't know what I'd do without Lucy. We play Scrabble together every weeknight.'

Toward the end of our conversations Liza sometimes made a perfunctory inquiry as to how my 'personal' life was going. Was I finding my way? Had I 'met' anyone?

Reluctantly I told her about Carey, with whom I seemed incapable of getting anywhere beyond infatuation. 'I really ought to introduce you to my friend Eli,' she responded absently. 'I've told you about him, haven't I?'

'Yes.'

'Next time I'm in New York . . .' But not surprisingly, the next time she was in New York, she was so busy we had time only for coffee, and the promised meeting with Eli never materialized. In truth, I hardly noticed. A few days earlier, a huge distraction had walked into my life: my roommate Dennis's mother, Faye, who had showed up at the end of August for a two-week visit and never left. A tiny woman – shorter even than Will – she dressed in espadrilles and washed-out sundresses that gave her a curiously tragic aspect, as if she were the doomed heroine of a Tennessee Williams play. She had shoulder-length streaked hair, gravel-colored eyes that seemed always to be on the verge of filling with tears, a weak chin that quavered when she laughed.

From the evening of her arrival she insisted that we call her Faye and not Mrs Latham. 'I can't stand Mrs Latham,' she said. 'It makes me feel so *old*.' She also insisted that we 'pretend she wasn't even there,' a rather disingenuous command, it seemed to me, since despite her diminutiveness she took up enormous amounts of space: both in the cramped bathroom, every surface of which she had soon covered with her eye creams, face creams, leg creams, lipsticks, pills, soaps, and scrubs, and in the living room, where she slept on the foldout sofa and hung her dresses from a piece of tricolor laundry cord purchased at Duane Reade. Also, she smoked, which none of us did, leaning her head out the window into the vestibule, from the depths of which the super's pit bulls growled up at her.

Sometimes I wondered why she wasn't staying at a hotel, as my own mother most certainly would have done under the circumstances. Lack of money seemed an unlikely reason, as Faye had a walletful of gold credit cards. Loneliness for her son, then? Yet Dennis's work schedule meant that he was away most evenings, and he spent his afternoons locked in his room, sleeping or reading. Nor did his remoteness appear to strike his mother as anything out of the ordinary. Indeed, from her behavior you would have thought she was in New York only to see New York. Most mornings she rose early and went to museums, or on 'looking' expeditions at Saks and Bergdorf's from which she returned laden with perfume samples the odors of which mingled humidly in our unventilated corridor.

At first I couldn't quite tell what she made of our squalid little nest – such a far cry from her ranch house in suburban Atlanta, with its swimming pool, its central air-conditioning, its wall outlets (of which she spoke rapturously) into which a vacuum cleaner tube could be plugged directly. ('It makes cleanup so easy!') Yet if our yellowing linoleum and dirty walls disturbed her, she never let on. Instead, while Dennis sold tickets at the Thalia, she cleaned. In the bathroom she scrubbed the mildewed grouting with Tilex. In the kitchen she put on heavy gloves and removed forty years of encrustation from the old stove. 'If there's one thing you boys need it's good old-fashioned mothering,' she told Will once, before presenting him with one of the elaborate meals she was wont to prepare, meals consisting mostly of homely American dishes, for which she thought we might be nostalgic: cracker salad (iceberg lettuce, saltines, tuna, and mayonnaise); chicken and dumplings; casseroles into which she mixed ground beef, Kraft Macaroni and Cheese mix, and canned cream of mushroom soup. Such dinners, from which Dennis was generally absent, at first delighted Will and me; after all, we were still boys, with huge appetites. But then on the second Friday of her visit, when we had both come home early with the intention of taking showers before going off to dinners with friends, she announced that she had been laboring all day to make us spaghetti with her 'special' sauce. The combination of her wet eyes, quivering chin, and tomato-stained sundress proved too much to resist: dutifully we sat down and ate her spaghetti, neither of us mentioning the other dinners with which we would have to follow this one. Faye herself did not eat, only watched. 'Is it good?' she asked. 'Is the pasta over-cooked? I try to make it *al dente*, which is how Dennis likes it. His father likes *his* mushy. That man has no culture.'

No, we reassured her, the spaghetti was perfect; the sauce was not too dry; she had not added too much oregano. With our own mothers, of course, we would never have been so polite, just as Dennis, arriving home in the middle of the meal, was not polite, snarling 'I'm not hungry!' before slamming into his room, leaving his mother with welling eyes and garlic on her fingers.

All told, such a vital female presence in our midst both awed and fatigued us, so much so that as the date of her planned departure neared, we found ourselves looking eagerly forward to the resumption of our ordinary rhythms. But then the Saturday morning when she was supposed to leave came, and passed, and Faye was still there. Nor did she offer any explanation for her continued residency; instead, as usual, she was cooking. ('Oyster stew,' she announced when I walked in the door.)

Dennis, taciturn at the best of moments, was reading in his room. His silence hinted at grim possibilities, and when the discovery that we had no onions sent Faye running out to the corner grocery, we confronted him where he sat behind a volume of Derrida. Point blank, Will asked him how long his mother intended to stay.

Putting his book down, Dennis ran his fingers through his hair. 'I don't know,' he admitted. 'All she says is for a while.'

'But doesn't she miss her vacuum cleaner outlets? Doesn't she miss your father?'

'The one thing I'm sure of is that she doesn't miss my father.'

'But it's already been such a long visit . . .' Will could not

have hinted more loudly that he wanted Dennis to *ask* his
mother to leave. . . . Then keys sounded in the lock. 'I'm
back!' we heard Faye calling in her singsong voice.

'We're in here!' Dennis yelled.

Her little face appeared through the crack in the door.
'Having a powwow?' she asked cheerfully. 'Mind if I join in –
or is this one for boys only?'

It was now September. Although the first day of fall was
fast approaching, the heat wave that had shrouded
Manhattan for most of the summer hung on. Even so, Faye
cooked furiously, which did nothing to cool our already stuffy
apartment. Sundays I fled to the Sterlings' icy perch with more
than usual enthusiasm, only to return at twilight to a corridor
in which the smells of frying meat and perfume commingled
stiflingly. I went early to work and left late, while Will stayed
most evenings at the NYU library until it closed. As for Faye,
whereas previously she had spent much of her time window-
shopping and going to museums, now she almost never left
the apartment, only sat in the kitchen, smoking and reading
suspense novels of great length and gruesomeness, most of
which centered around the kidnapping, torture, and murder
of small children. It was now becoming rapidly clear to us that
she had left her husband, a fact to which only her husband –
a man whose phone manner was so mild it bordered on the
sinister – appeared not to have caught on. Because we both
knew that we could not have thrown out our own mothers
under such circumstances, however, Will and I gave Dennis no
ultimatums. Instead we simply tried to make the best of the
situation. We were kind to Faye. We pretended not to hear the
screams that emanated from the television set, on which she
was always watching made-for-television movies about the
kidnapping, torture, and murder of small children.

At last autumn came, with a sudden gust of brown leaves
and chilly weather. Because, in previous years, this would

have been the season for returning to school I found myself dreaming most nights that I still had tests to take, papers to finish. During the day an acute nostalgia claimed me. I missed the old ritual of choosing courses, missed my dorm room, in which some stranger was now sleeping, missed Gretchen and Schuyler, Barb Mendenhall, Eve Schlossberg. They should have been sitting, once again, at that yellowed Formica table in the rear smoking section of the library. Instead Gretchen and Schuyler were in Paris and Berlin, respectively; Barb was in law school at Stanford; Eve, who was trying to make a go of it as a photographer, was sharing a tenement flat with Lars on the Lower East Side. People whose faces I wouldn't have recognized now occupied those chairs that for me would forever carry the imprint of my friends' behinds, and this knowledge made the one visit I paid to my old stomping grounds that September almost as difficult to endure as the longing it was meant to assuage.

To compensate – and to keep myself away from Faye's burdensome presence – I threw myself with more alacrity than ever into the slush pile; yet even the offices of Hudson-Terrier, thanks to the unexpected arrival of Stanley Flint, were no longer the haven they had once been. Not that Flint was unpleasant; on the contrary, he could not have been more cordial. Whenever he passed my desk he patted me on the back. He called me 'young man' or, as in the old days, 'Bauman.' No, the problem was that he refused categorically to acknowledge my existence as a writer. Not once did he ask me how my real work was going. Not once did he congratulate me on the story I had published, or make reference to our past student-mentor relationship. In his spare time, I knew, he continued to teach two nights a week. Sometimes his students would come by to visit him in his office, which he kept dark even on the brightest of afternoons, the shades drawn, his desk awash in lamp glow.

His arrival at Hudson had not been without its attendant fanfare. Indeed, so newsworthy had the *New York Times* considered his hiring that it had run his picture on the front page of the arts section, alongside an article in which Marge had expressed her delight that 'this genius of American letters' was 'joining the Hudson team.' Such press gushing had been enough to ensure Flint's popularity with the terrible Terriers, for whom what was impressive was not that he was great but that he was 'hot.' At the same time, his long-standing affiliation with good writers made him popular with my Hudson colleagues, who were at the very least relieved to be working with someone connected to literature. Even Carey got along with Flint, of whose tastes he approved, and when Flint made his first acquisition – just a week after our meeting in the men's room – he made a point of smuggling me a photocopy of the manuscript. The book in question, a collection of stories by a Park Avenue divorcée who had once been one of Flint's students, intimidated me not only because of its wit, but its concision: here was the vaunted 'minimalist' style that he championed, and that in the coming years would be first revered, then vilified. My writing, on the other hand, was neither clever nor succinct; indeed, as Flint had indicated in his offending letter, its main virtue was warmth, which did best when given room to breathe. I wished I could have been wittier, a Fran Lebowitz whose mailbox would always be crammed with party invitations. (Everything comes down to food: according to Liza, you could eat so well as publishing parties that once you got on the A-list you'd never have to buy groceries again.)

Flint worked like a demon. In his interview with the *Times* he'd vowed never to take more than a week to respond to a manuscript, and he kept that vow. Not once did I arrive at the office when he wasn't already there, nor did he once leave before me, which made his cold-shouldering (either intentional or – even worse – the result of his simply having forgotten who I was) all the more difficult to bear. For the truth was, as in college, I craved his attention, only now I was competing for it not with Acosta or Mittman, but with writers who taught at my university, or were members of the American Academy of Arts and Letters. So far as reading manuscripts went, Flint's policy was to cast a wide net, then throw back almost everything he caught – which meant that almost from the moment of his arrival, publication by him was looked upon as a prize of great worth. More manuscripts now landed on his desk than on that of any other editor, some of them by novelists whose agents would have laughed, just a few months earlier, had a colleague suggested they submit to a backwater like Hudson. Even more shockingly, Flint was turning down books by authors who were much more famous than he was. At editorial meetings battles erupted over his rejections: not only was he saying no to Pulitzer Prize winners, he was dismissing their work as 'baby talk' or 'unmitigated shit.'

His decisions occasionally raised the hackles of management, whom Marge was always having to placate. 'I trust his instincts,' she declared, when on the same afternoon he turned down a new book of stories by a writer with an office at the magazine, and paid fifty thousand dollars for a first novel by a woman no one had ever heard of. 'Bauman, it's great,' he told me. 'I'm flabbergasted. This girl – she's from Mississippi, and she works, believe it or not, carving headstones. Her husband's family runs a headstone business. I don't know where she learned to do it, but she writes like an avenging angel. Extraordinary stuff: long, long sentences, but so gorgeously crafted it's as if they're made from gossamer. She tells the most gruesome stories and makes them beautiful, as opposed to all those tedious people who tell beautiful stories and make them gruesome.'

The news of this acquisition was followed by another announcement: he had bought the rights to a first novel that Marge hoped would become 'a major bestseller.' The author was one Julia Baylor.

She came in the next day, looking both thinner and more elegant than at school, and very pleased with herself. As it happened I was sitting at the front desk at the time, filling in for the receptionist, Dorell, who was out to lunch. 'Martin,' she said, 'what on earth are *you* doing here?'

'I work here,' I answered meekly.

'How wonderful,' she said. 'Then it'll be just like the old days.'

It was not. In the old days, I was the favorite. Now I was a menial, manning the reception desk, while Baylor and Flint chatted in his office.

A few minutes later they reemerged, laughing to show their teeth. 'Take my calls, will you, Bauman?' Flint said. 'I shouldn't be more than a couple of hours.' And they sauntered off toward the elevator.

That afternoon I went home in a state of despondency. Old feelings of inferiority were creeping over me: why Baylor and not me? I found myself asking. Was it because of the letter I had failed to answer? Because Flint hated homosexuals? Because he and Baylor had had an affair? Or was the truth quite simply that Flint had lost interest in my writing, concluded that whatever potential he'd once seen in me had, as it were, evaporated? Such, I had to admit, was the most likely, if least palatable, explanation for his behavior – or more accurately his lack of behavior, given that his comportment with me was never, for all its neglectfulness, anything less than courteous.

As it happened, my own work was not going very well right then. The trouble was that I kept getting stuck, sometimes for weeks, on a single sentence, like one of those wind-up toy robots that walks into a wall and keeps walking. Faye provided the ideal excuse for this inertia, since in the past, on the days when I hadn't gone to Hudson, I'd almost always had the apartment to myself. Now, however, Faye not only never went out, she made such a show of not disturbing me that in the end her attempts at silence served only to wreck my concentration, until finally I decided that I would do better if I took my typewriter down to Hudson and set it up in the empty office of one of the fired editors. At least there I could write undisturbed, and even better, glance up, whenever I wanted to, and see Carey at his desk, a pencil in his mouth, his pressed shirt folding in on itself in such a way that the contours of his chest were obscured. For my crush on Carey – which in recent months I had allowed to lapse – had of late resurfaced, not as a result of any change in his attitude toward me, but because my roommate Will had just fallen in love and was forever describing to me the dreamy evening walks that he and his paramour, an NYU freshman named Vincent, took through Riverside Park, where under the stars they kissed for the first time. Vincent and Will shared chocolate bars in our kitchen and, most romantically of all, had for almost a month been putting off the actual act of sex, in order to make the event, when it happened, that much more exalted. The only problem was that Vincent lived in a dormitory, while we had Faye. How would she react, Will wondered, were she to bump into a half-naked stranger in the bathroom? Did she even realize that we were gay? (Knowing Dennis, it seemed unlikely that he would have told her.)

Eager to be of service (as well as to gain a vicarious experience of Will's love affair by functioning as its facilitator), I offered to talk to Dennis on his behalf – an offer Will accepted at once, perhaps in the hope that threat of embarrassment to his mother might motivate Dennis, at last, to ask her to leave. As it happened Dennis was working that evening at the

Thalia, which meant that there was no chance of Faye interrupting our conversation.

Accordingly, after having dinner (cooked by Faye, of course) I strode down to the theater, which was on 95th Street, and rapped on the box office window. Behind bulletproof glass Dennis was reading *Beyond Good and Evil*, which seemed oddly apposite. 'Hey,' he said, smiling vaguely as he got up to let me in.

'Hi, Dennis,' I said, stepping inside the ticket booth.

'What's up? Want some popcorn?'

'No thanks. I need to talk to you about something.'

'Oh?' He sat down on his stool.

'You know that guy Vincent that Will's been seeing?'

An elderly woman now stepped up to the booth and asked for a ticket.

'Sorry, go on.'

'Well, Will's invited him to sleep over tomorrow night.'

No response. Dennis was making change.

'Is that okay with you?'

'Why wouldn't it be okay with me?'

'Because – with your mother here . . . we thought that maybe—'

'I told her from the beginning, as long as she insists on staying with us, she's going to have to accept our living our lives the way we always do.'

'But does she even know that Will's gay? That I'm gay?'

'Is it any of her business?' Dennis handed the old woman her ticket. 'Tell Will to have anyone over that he wants,' he added, when it became clear that I wasn't leaving. Yet Wendy Stone, I noticed, hadn't been down for several weeks now. Was this because of Faye? (No, as it turned out: she had met someone else, the man she was going to marry, which further explained Dennis's bad mood.)

The next night I had dinner with Anka Kaufman, after

which I arrived home to find the apartment quiet. From the living room the light of the television flickered: Faye, I saw, had fallen asleep while watching a video of *Brief Encounter*.

I went to bed, only to be roused an hour later by the sound of the deadbolt turning; then, around dawn, by the familiar gurgle of a flushing toilet, a shower switching on. When I woke, around nine, it was to the smell of maple syrup. In the kitchen, a rather stunned-looking youth wearing only a pair of white Calvin Klein underpants sat at the Formica table; Faye, flipping pancakes, was chatting with him amiably about Princess Diana; Dennis, in his ratty bathrobe, was staring grimly into Nietszche. We had been foiled again.

In October, amid wind and unexpected frigidities (yet our landlord, like Anka's, refused to switch on the heat), Carey finally introduced me to Richard Powell and Susan Bloom, the couple of whom he and his friends made such a cult. Though both were scions of wealthy Upper East Side households – habituated, from early in their childhoods, to shopping at Barney's and Christmas vacations in Gstaad – they now lived in a squalid railroad flat on West 87th Street with several deaf white cats. Their furniture, most of which they had dragged in off the street and draped with Indian bedspreads, brought to mind opium dens, as did the smell of incense, cigarettes, and curry that infused the crumbling foam rubber of the sofa. Later I would come to recognize this particular variety of dereliction as merely another version of that 'slumming' instinct that had driven my college friends to Dolly's bar; at the time, however, I thought it wonderfully bohemian, this atmosphere that was to me as cozy and smelly as that of the box in which a litter of kittens has just been born.

From our first meeting what struck me most viscerally about Richard and Susan was their languor. Whenever Carey and I went to visit them, for instance, they seemed always just to be getting out of bed. Sometimes a diaphragm lay quivering on their kitchen table – further proof, I thought, of the degree to which they had thrown off outmoded niceties. (Today such a gesture strikes me as pure exhibitionism.) Also, though both of them were ostensibly graduate students (Richard in law, Susan in French) they showed no evidence, at least in my presence, of studying. Like their cats, they were sinuous and wayward.

At first Susan herself disappointed me a little. This was because Carey's descriptions, before I met her, had led me to expect a modern-day Circe, one whose beauty and charisma could reduce men to swine; instead of which here was this stoop-shouldered girl with rubicund, slightly spotty cheeks, big hips and unshaven armpits the odor of which mingled curiously with the oils she was always dabbing on her neck – utterly unremarkable, I thought, especially when compared to Richard, who was classically good-looking in a *Mayflower* sort of way. And yet perhaps it is a mistake to assume that Circe must be beautiful. After all, she was a witch. She had charm, in the most old-fashioned sense of the word. So did Susan. Most of it came down to smoke and mirrors, I am convinced now, a brilliant mix of motherliness and glamour that beguiled men, and to which women remained utterly indifferent; not that this mattered, for like Marge, Susan was the sort of woman for whom the opinions of other women are largely irrelevant.

Richard was mild, even shy, in comparison. Smaller than Susan, he had fine, chestnut-colored hair, a snub nose, skin that burned easily in the summer: in short, just the sort of complexion that you would expect from a boy with an unblemished Anglo-Saxon pedigree, whose mother could trace her ancestry to a fourteenth-century Scottish laird. As children, people like Richard, when they are asked to draw their family trees, find themselves faced with a snarled root structure that goes back centuries, even intertwining, at times, with crucial historical events, such as the beheading of queens. Susan, on the other hand, came from a cutting. Beyond her immigrant grandparents she knew nothing of her ancestors, which did not mean that the offspring of those grandparents had not managed to ramify, over fifty years, into every branch of American commerce. In other words, her family tree, though young, was top-heavy, whereas Richard's was elderly and dying. If he was the classically uptight WASP, she was the exemplary undisciplined Jewess, all erotic pungency and chthonian ravines, forever counteracting his good breeding with outrageous public outbursts along the lines of: 'Last night Richard came seven times. I had to stop – I was getting sore – but he could have gone on all night.' Such remarks hardly seemed to faze Richard, however, who responded to them merely by blowing smoke rings. Like so many sons of Park Avenue, he knew how to keep his cool. Indeed, only once in my presence did he ever show his hand, and that was when Susan, rather indiscreetly, referred to 'the days when Carey was always trying to get Ricky into bed,' at which point his eyes widened, his mouth froze, a blush ascended his cheeks like a climbing rose.

In those years I used to make it my habit to ride the subway uptown well after midnight. When I mentioned this to my father on the phone one afternoon, he became so alarmed that he decided to start sending me a monthly 'taxi allowance' – which, instead of using for cabs, I stowed away in the bank: why waste money, after all, when reports of subway dangers were so obviously exaggerated? I reasoned. Instead I took bolder risks. Finding myself stuck on the East Side at two o'clock in the morning, I would walk alone across Central Park instead of waiting for a bus, and could not fathom what all the fuss was about: after all, the park was bursting with people, only some of whom were junkies. In retrospect, the nonchalance with which I risked my life regularly, both in the subways and on the streets, rather stuns me, especially given my extreme wariness where sex and drugs were concerned. Drugs especially. Even in the cocaine heatstroke that was Manhattan in those years, I never so much as puffed on a joint, ostensibly because I was too much of a 'good boy' to break the law, really because I feared the loss of control, the ecstatic rein-loosening, to which drugs were supposed to lead.

As for sex, the distaste I claimed to feel for the sort of quick encounters with which homosexuality has always been associated was really a cover for my deep attraction to those very leather bars and porn emporia of which in public I voiced such old-maidish disapproval. For the truth was, I worried that if I stepped even once down those corridors of pleasure, I might never again find my way out.

This did not mean, however, that I avoided gay bars. On the contrary, most Friday and Saturday nights I invariably went (by subway, of course) to Boy Bar on St Mark's Place, sometimes with Will and, on rarer occasions, alone. For here, as at the Columbia dances, I was almost always certain to run into friends from school, with whom I could fall into easy conversational groupings that would protect me from that fidgety ritual of staring and dancing that is every gay bar's *raison d'être*; and yet sometimes, when no one I knew happened to be hanging out at Boy Bar, and I found myself standing alone with my mineral water on the fringes of the dance floor, then my carefully arranged fig leaf of sociability would suddenly fall away, exposing that basest and most unbecoming of motives: libido. Now I was no different from anyone else at the bar. I looked and longed. Sometimes people looked back. Once I even worked up the courage to approach a man with maple-colored hair who had winked at me, only to find that when he moved his manly jaw the voice that emerged from his throat was that of Gale Gordon, Mr Mooney on *The Lucy Show.*

'You're a *writer*! How *fascinating*!'

'And you?'

'I'm a *window dresser*!'

What is it about those two words – 'window dresser' – that causes them to connote the very opposite of sex? 'Well, it's been nice talking to you,' I told the window dresser, whose coppery chest had made my mouth water. 'I'd better be getting home.'

'But *I* was hoping you'd come home with *me*!'

Go home with Mr Mooney! How was it possible? All night visions of red-haired Lucy, Lucy past her prime and up to no good, would dance wildly in my head. No, I could never go home with Mr Mooney; I was holding out for love; for Carey. And yet whenever Carey and I were together somehow I could never seem to find the words to clue him in that I was 'interested.' Nor did he, in his furious prosecution of the day, give me anything in the way of opportunity. I assumed that he was shy and that to compensate I would simply have to work that much harder. But how? So sexless and sociable was our friendship that if I asked him out to dinner he would assume I meant at Tom's Diner, or with ten other people. On the other hand, if I made it obvious that I had a crush on him (difficult in the best of circumstances) the result might be rejection – a prospect I did not much relish.

The trouble was, in those years I still had no natural feeling for courtship; no instincts guided me; in the language of the human heart I remained, and would remain for some time, illiterate. As an adolescent it had been easier. Back then, whenever I'd had a 'crush' on a girl, I'd simply slipped a letter asking her to 'go steady' through the grille of her locker, or deputized a friend (usually another girl) to deliver the message in my stead. Nor had I matured, at twenty-two, beyond such methods, which was why, that Sunday, I called up Susan and invited her for a corned beef sandwich at Barney Greengrass. As she was a passionate eater, and Richard was off with his family in Aspen, she accepted at once. We met, and devoured our sandwiches in a frenzy. Mustard dripped from our chins. Afterward, because there were no men present, we split a slab of chocolate cake.

It was only once the cake had been finished, the crumbs picked from the plate, our lips licked clean, that we started talking. Lighting a cigarette, Susan gazed at me. I had on my sad face. 'What's wrong?' she asked, as I'd hoped she would.

'Oh, it's nothing.'

'Are you sure?' She leaned intimately across the table. 'Because if something is wrong, I hope you know that you can trust me.'

I looked at her assessingly. Her dark eyes were veritable pools of solicitude, her voice unctuous with the longing to advise.

Then I cleared my throat, and said that I had fallen in love with Carey. Her lips convulsed, baring her big front teeth, on one of which a speckle of parsley glinted. 'You're kidding,' she said. 'You've got the hots for *Carey*?'

'Have the hots' seemed the wrong phrase to express my idealized (and largely manufactured) passion. Nonetheless I nodded.

Susan clapped her hands together. 'But that's fantastic!' she said. 'I can't believe I never thought of it myself. You and Carey! Perfect!'

'Do you think so?'

'Of course. I can see it now – editor and writer. You'll take literary Manhattan by storm! Not to mention *gay* Manhattan.' She stubbed out her cigarette. 'Confidentially, Richard and I have been hoping something like this would happen, only . . . well, it hasn't been easy for Ricky with . . . you know . . .'

I remained silent. I didn't know. She told me. It seemed that Carey's history with Richard had not been an entirely happy one. Oh, things had begun cordially enough, when the boys were roommates and best friends in college. But then, rather out of the blue one evening, Carey had announced that he was in love with Richard – a declaration to which the bewildered Richard had responded first by apologizing, then by reaffirming his essential heterosexuality, then by assuring Carey that this would in no way affect their friendship; all of which had only fueled Carey's determination to seduce his roommate, whose denials he took as further evidence of suppressed desire.

After that, Carey's passion had grown unmanageable. At night Richard dared not fall sleep for fear lest he should crawl into his bed and try to kiss him. Susan's appearance on the scene only made things tenser, and might have led to a full-fledged rupture had she not adopted, quite cleverly, the strategy of taking Carey on as a confidant, and thus deflecting any feelings of antipathy. They became a trio, and for a while even lived together in the apartment on 87th Street, Carey sleeping on the living room couch, until the loud noises of Richard and Susan's lovemaking drove him to despair and he moved, alone, to the spartan studio he now rented on 110th Street.

'But even with that, he's always at our house,' Susan said. 'You've seen how it is. He comes over for supper, or to play a game of Risk. And of course we can't throw him out, even when we *would* like a little privacy. I keep saying to Richard, the only solution is for Carey to get a boyfriend, yet he never seems to, he's always pining after these ridiculous men who won't give him the time of day.'

'Really?' This was the first I had heard about the ridiculous men who wouldn't give him the time of day. Still, I was determined to take Susan's encouragement to heart. 'So what should I do?' I asked. 'I mean, if he doesn't know, how do I make him know?'

She pursed her lips. 'Well, one possibility,' she said, 'is that I could talk to him . . .'

I didn't smile – though of course this was exactly what I was hoping for. 'Do you think that would be a good idea?' I asked.

'Sure – if I'm subtle, which I will be. I'll feel him out first so that you can feel him up later.' She giggled.

'Would you do that for me, Susan?'

'For both of you, dearie.'

The bill had arrived. 'I'll pay it,' I said.

She did not object.

The next morning I had just returned from the Korean grocery on the corner when Faye, who was smoking in the kitchen, told me that Richard had phoned. This surprised me: it was Susan, or Carey himself, from whom I was expecting to hear. Nonetheless I called back eagerly. What Richard told me was that earlier in the morning, examining his Week-at-a-Glance, he had discovered that today was his and Susan's 'half anniversary.' By way of celebration, he and Carey were organizing a spontaneous party, inviting some friends to have dinner with them that evening at Susan's favorite Chinese restaurant. Yet this was not all: to mark the event, each of us was to surprise her with a half present – he, for example, was going to give her a set of half-moon pearl earrings, while Carey was giving her the first half of a two-volume biography of Lytton Strachey. Might I bring something equally 'half-baked'? he asked, his voice nasally genteel, to which I responded that even if it meant treading the avenues of Manhattan to its very edges, I would find the perfect thing.

After I hung up Faye wandered by my door. 'And what are you up to this morning?' she asked wistfully. 'Off to work?'

'No, it's my day off.'

'Oh, of course. Stupid of me to forget.' She sneezed delicately. 'Imagine that, a young man, a day off, all of Manhattan to enjoy. So what's it going to be? A movie? The Met? A stroll in the park?'

'Actually, I have to go shopping for an anniversary present – a *half*-anniversary present,' I said, and explained the situation.

'But isn't that charming,' Faye said, 'doing that for the girl he loves.'

In a burst of sudden generosity I invited her to come with me on my shopping trip. The invitation appeared both to stun and delight her; after all, not once since her arrival had Will or I (her son need not even be mentioned) deigned to include her in any of our extra-apartmental activities. Cheeks flushed, for the first time in weeks, with pleasure, Faye hurried to get dressed. We rode the subway together to Macy's. 'Now, let's see,' she said as we headed through the revolving door, her voice tremulous at the prospect of actually being able to help, 'a half present . . . let's concentrate . . . let's give it all our attention . . . or half our attention!'

In fact my own attention kept wandering to other items, such as a pair of cufflinks in the form of plume pens, or a putty-colored Ralph Lauren shirt that I thought might beautifully complement Carey's eyes. 'How about a half-slip?' Faye suggested. 'Or a half-tester? What is a half-tester? Or half a gallon of half-and-half?'

In the end we settled on half a pound of Godiva chocolates and a tape of the soundtrack to *Half a Sixpence*: nothing so good as Carey's gift, but true to the theme. Then we went back home; I showered and shaved. 'What are you going to wear?' asked Faye, who was now sitting in the kitchen, reading a novel the cover of which depicted a child's ball bouncing into a wading pool filled with blood.

'I'm not sure yet.'

She put her book down. 'Let me help you! I love helping people pick out clothes. You know I've always regretted that I never had a daughter.'

We stepped into my room. 'Uh-uh, nope, nope,' Faye muttered, pushing aside the hangers in my closet. 'Too conservative.'

'What about this one?'

'Ugh! Anyway, there's a stain on the lapel. What you need is something with oomph, something . . . Wait a minute, what's this?' And she pulled out a rather outrageous shirt I had bought the month before and still not worn, on which climbing roses made their way up a trellis of pale blue stripes.

'Do you like it?'

'Oh, yes. It's so – new. Now try it on. Black pants, if you've got them.'

Crossing her arms, she stared at me. For a few seconds I stood helplessly before her, until she got the hint, and burst into a fit of laughter. 'Oh, I see,' she said, clapping her hands over her mouth. 'Dennis doesn't like to undress in front of me either. Well, don't worry, I'll skedaddle.' And she shut the bedroom door behind her. Taking off my bathrobe, I put on clean underwear and socks, the flowered shirt, a pair of black jeans, black socks, and Doc Martens, then strode into the living room, where Faye was watching the news. Muting the volume, she stood. 'Now let me see,' she said. 'Almost perfect . . . the only thing you need . . . ah, I know.' And she rummaged in her purse.

'Here,' she said, pulling out a little vial of perfume. 'It's the new Calvin Klein.'

'But I never wear—'

'Ssh. Bend your neck.'

I did. Standing on tiptoe, she spritzed me. The cologne both burned and chilled.

'Now you're ready,' Faye said, patting me on the arm. 'Go and have fun.'

Picking up my bag of half presents, I headed out the door. Appropriately, I was running half an hour ahead of schedule. Because no one else had arrived at the Chinese restaurant, I had to wait alone at the big table with its pots of soy sauce and hot pepper sauce, studying the menu, until Carey walked in. (He too was prone to be early.) 'Hi,' he said, taking the seat across from mine.

'Hi, Carey.' I put the menu down.

'Wow, that's quite a shirt you're wearing.'

'Thanks.' I wasn't certain I'd been complimented. As for him, to judge from his Oxford shirt, he'd come straight from work.

Somewhat irritably he lit a cigarette. 'Have a good day?' I asked.

He shrugged.

'Marge on the rampage?'

'Stanley on the rampage. He's threatening to quit because she won't let him buy a six-hundred-page poem by a taxidermist.'

Richard and Susan now entered the restaurant, both out of breath. Standing, Carey kissed each of them on the cheek, and was about to reclaim his place across the table from me when Susan said, 'No, don't sit there, sit here, next to Martin.'

Uneasily, he picked up his jacket and moved. She winked at me.

'That shirt's so – vivid,' Richard said.

'Do you like it?'

'It reminds me of my parents' bedroom curtains,' said Susan. 'Gosh, I'm hungry. Who else is coming?'

'Amos and Ingo.'

'They're late.'

Soon enough, however, Amos and Ingo arrived, and Susan was presented with her gifts. 'All you have to guess,' Richard said, 'is what they have in common.'

'What they have in common,' Susan repeated. And paused. 'Richard, darling,' she said after a moment, 'I find every one of them enchanting, but I can't for the life of me guess what they have in common.'

'Here's a clue,' Carey said. 'It's today.'

'Today – but what is today?'

We all laughed. Finally Richard gave in and told her. Bursting into a smile, she kissed him, kissed all of us. For such attentions as these – perhaps even more luxurious than the gifts – Susan, I saw, could afford to take for granted. I wondered what it would feel like to be so affluent – and not merely in terms of money, but of love.

When dinner ended, having bid farewell to Ingo and Amos, the four of us climbed into an old-fashioned Checker Cab and headed to the West Side. This yellow behemoth, the manatee of the automotive world, was one of the last of its breed, with jump seats, on which Carey and I sat. First we stopped on 87th Street, where Richard and Susan got out. 'No, no, you two ride on,' Susan scolded, when Carey tried to get out too.

'But I thought you might want to play a game of Risk,' he pleaded.

'Not tonight. I have to give Richard a thank-you blowjob.' Again, she winked. 'Now, you two behave yourselves. Don't do anything *we* wouldn't do.'

'Good night, Susan,' Carey said, and withdrew into the taxi. '103rd Street,' he told the driver as Richard slammed the door.

'Let's get off at 110th, and I'll walk back,' I suggested.

'No, I'll walk up. No need for you to walk.'

'Okay, if you want.'

I got up from the jump seat. The slapping noise it made as it hit the partition startled me, bringing to mind as it did a trip I'd taken to London with my parents when I was a boy, when I had loved sitting on the jump seats of black cabs. Now, however, it made no sense to remain on that childish little platform and, taking Susan's place on the more comfortable bench, I looked at Carey expectantly. He stayed where he was.

I opened the window a crack. It was one of the only times I could remember that the two of us had actually been alone together. Yet we did not talk. Back rigid, Carey stared at the Broadway traffic, the slurred reflection of car lights and street-lamps sweeping across the plane of his glasses.

'The dinner was fun, wasn't it?' I said.

He nodded, mumbled words I didn't catch. Recalling Susan's wink, I asked myself whether his silence might not be a sign that he was hoping I might make some first move that he himself was too timid to attempt . . . and yet, if this was the case, he gave no clue as to his wishes. Indeed, he gave no clue as to anything. So I stayed where I was, my face palsied in a clown smile, breathing in the cigarette and cinnamon smell of his jacket, until the taxi arrived at 103rd Street. He paid and got out. On the street we stood together, hands in our pockets, like duelists waiting for a signal.

Then I was brave. 'Listen,' I said, 'if you're not—'

'I suppose Susan's been bugging you about it too,' Carey interrupted.

'About what?'

'This crazy idea she has, that you and I . . .'

I was silent.

'Fixing us up,' he went on. 'And it's so ridiculous! Not that she doesn't mean well – it's just that, have you noticed the way straight people will sometimes assume that just because two people are gay, automatically they're meant to be a couple?'

'Oh, I have,' I lied.

'And then this making sure we sat together, and leaving us alone in the taxi. She can really be so *coarse.*'

'Coarse, yes,' I repeated. Yet my voice, despite the immense effort I was making to be jaunty, remained hollow, and my eyes were as wet as Faye's. I could not hide the disappointment I was suffering, not even from Carey, who stepped a little closer.

'There's something I need to show you,' he said.

Taking off his jacket, he rolled up the cuff of his shirt; held out his forearm. 'Look.' From where his fingers spread out, each with a dusting of hair above the knuckle, veins fanned the length of the hand up to the narrow wrist, around which rope burns coiled like ribbons. I blinked.

'This is what I like,' Carey said, flexing the muscles of his arm. 'Do you understand?'

'I think so. I think.'

He unrolled his cuff and covered up, once again, his wrists; once again put on his jacket. 'There's only one thing I need to ask you,' he said, 'and that's not to say anything to Susan and Richard.'

'Of course I won't.'

'It's not that I make a secret of what I do. It's just – with some people it's easier not to talk about it. You know what I mean?'

'Of course I know what you mean.'

'Good. I'm glad. Well, good night, Martin.' He held out his hand. 'See you at the office tomorrow. I hope you – understand.'

'Good night. I do,' I said. And shaking hands, we parted. Oblivious to traffic, I lunged out onto Broadway, not noticing that the light was red; a car swerved to avoid hitting me; from the screeching of horns, the ranting of the driver who had stepped out of the car and was shaking his fist, I fled into an all-night grocery store, where a Korean girl stood moistening lettuce heads with a spray bottle. In the cool silence, waxy red and yellow peppers glistened amid coriander beds. There were packages of Chinese noodles of the sort my mother had made me for lunch when I was a child, stirring a raw egg into the soup; bars of the expensive Swiss chocolate that Will and Vincent liked to share; boxes of Entenmann's chocolate chip cookies, before a display of which I now paused, caught my breath, waited for my heartbeat to steady. Well, I thought, at least it's not that he doesn't like *me*, and picking up a box of cookies, went to pay. Wraithlike, the girl with the spray bottle floated across the store, took her place behind the cash register, studied, as if they were some sort of riddle, the cookies I had selected.

By now someone else had come in – a stocky man dressed in loose jeans and an open shirt. His hair was cut short, as short as his day's growth of beard. When I looked at him, he looked back. It took me a moment to recognize him; after all, at the Columbia dances, the light had never been this bright, nor his hair this closely cropped.

I gave the girl money. From where he stood by the beer cooler, the stranger stroked his chin, grabbed, as if unconsciously, the crotch of his jeans, smiled at me. His smile burned. Astonished, aroused almost to the point of hurt, I took my change and hurried out of the store. Yet I did not go home. Instead I loitered on the corner, pretending to examine my receipt. Inside my head a voice of prudence – that crossing guard whose commands I had always heeded – was urging me to hurry back to my apartment, to flee this temptation as fast as possible. Resistant, I stalled, until the stranger emerged. He was carrying a pack of cigarettes. Striding to the corner, he stood next to me, close enough so that I could feel the heat of his bicep.

'Hi,' he said.

'Hi,' I answered.

He stretched his arms over his head. 'So who are you?'

'Martin Bauman.'

'Pleased to meet you, Martin Bauman,' he said. 'I'm Joey.' He held out his hand. His teeth, I noticed, were crooked and smoke-stained, yet this flaw – which under other circumstances would have troubled me – I found easy to edit out, so captivating was the scratching sound his fingers made as he stroked his chin.

Then the light changed. We crossed. 'I've seen you before, haven't I?' he said.

'Yes. At the Columbia dances.'

'Oh sure, that's where it was. I missed last month.'

'It was good, it was a good one.'

'I try to get to them whenever I can, which isn't that often.' He rubbed his hands together. 'So what are you up to tonight, Martin Bauman? Got anything up?'

'On my way back from a party. An anniversary party.'

'Yeah? Whose?'

'Some friends of mine. Richard and Susan. Actually, it was their half anniversary. Richard threw it, and we all got Susan half presents.'

'Cool.'

Silence, for a moment. 'And what are you up to?'

'Oh, nothing much.' He stopped walking. 'To tell the truth, I was feeling kind of horny.'

'Oh?'

'Feeling in the mood to fuck.' And he looked at me hard, in the eye. 'Are you into that? I mean – getting fucked.'

I shrugged. 'I guess so.'

'Where do you live? Could we go to your place?'

'I've got roommates.'

'That's okay. We can go to my place. That is, if you don't mind the dirty underwear on the floor.' He winked.

'Where do *you* live?'

'Just a few blocks from here. Come on.' And turning around, he walked back the way we'd come, toward the grocery store. I followed. 'Smoke?' he asked, offering me a cigarette.

'No thanks. But I don't mind if you do.'

'Doesn't matter.' He put the cigarettes away.

After that we stopped talking. At the end of a dark block, he led me to a building the door to which had apparently been broken open by vandals. Graffiti covered both the stoop and the walls. *Hurry*, I wanted to say as we stepped into the vestibule, for just as in a long car trip the last few minutes are the most difficult to endure, so now, after years of patience, I was finding even the prospect of waiting for an elevator almost unbearable; what I wanted was to watch him put his key into the door, hear the deadbolt unlatching, feel, finally, the pressure of his big fingers unbuttoning, without restraint or ceremony, the flowered shirt that Faye had helped me pick out – when was it? – hours, days ago?

At last the doors creaked open. We stepped inside. In the brief privacy of the elevator, Joey leaned toward me and kissed me on the cheek. The sweetness of the kiss made me smile. Very delicately, he lifted my glasses off my face, held them over his head, and waved them. 'Give me the fucking money,' a voice shouted suddenly, to which another voice – my own – shouted back, 'All right, only please don't hurt my glasses.'

'Give me the fucking money!'

I handed him my wallet. The doors slid open. On the landing, he pulled out the cash, tossed the wallet into the elevator, threw my glasses to the floor, and crushed them with his foot.

Then he was gone, leaping down the stairs in a riot of footfalls that bred echoes of footfalls, until in my ears I could hear the cicadas screaming in my parents' garden.

A door slammed. I picked up my wallet and stepped into the hallway, where I retrieved what was left of my glasses. The lenses were in pieces, which was inconvenient, because without them I could hardly see at all. Even so, I didn't want to get back into that elevator. Instead, gripping the handrail, I began to make my way down the stairs.

Curious: for some reason, in that percussive moment, what I was remembering was an afternoon in seventh grade when during science class (we were doing dissections) a tough boy named Dwight Rohmer had dropped my three-ring binder into a vat of cow eyeballs. 'Fuck off!' I'd shouted as I fished the slimy notebook from the formaldehyde, at which point Dwight's friends had let out a collective groan, a sort of '*Oooh, oooh!*' under their breaths, as if I were a girl they had happened upon peeing under a tree. Only Dwight did not say, '*Oooh, oooh.*' Instead, when class ended, he grabbed me by the arm, dragged me into the boy's room and, pushing my face into the piss-smelling cement, kicked me hard, over and over. His kicks were bracing. They knocked the fear out of me. 'No one tells me to fuck off!' he cried, while behind him that Greek chorus, his friends, smoked and observed the proceedings pitilessly. 'Law of the jungle, man,' one of them murmured, as Dwight lifted me to my feet and hurled me, hard, against the wall; after which I ran bawling from the bathroom, through the cafeteria, and into the office of my guidance counselor, whom I told, in tears, what had happened. This guidance counselor, a young man who cultivated a goatee in the days when such things were not fashionable, gave me a glass of water, which I drank, and summoned Dwight. To my surprise, he sat us down next to each other. Dwight wore an expression of implacability, as if brutal experience had hardened him beyond fear. 'Did you hit Martin?' asked the counselor.

He shrugged.

'Why?'

'He told me to fuck off.'

'And he threw my notebook into a vat of eyeballs,' I added in fury.

The counselor now announced that he had some photo-copying to do, and left. We were alone. Through tears I looked at Dwight, who indicated, with a subtle gesture of his forehead, the door, through a crack in which the counselor's eye could be plainly made out, as huge and stupid as that of any cow.

By now I had reached the bottom of the staircase. Stepping outside, onto the stoop, I saw people whose faces were only brushstrokes. Suddenly it occurred to me that I no longer had my cookies. What had happened to the cookies? Their loss, for some reason, aggrieved me much more than that of the glasses, the money. And meanwhile those strangers were look-ing at me. I could feel them looking at me. Did they guess, from my appearance, that in an instant I had been robbed and blinded?

Still, it could have been worse, I reminded myself. I could have been dead.

Slowly I made my way down the street. Without my glasses the city was lovelier than ever. Streams of yellow light arced and spluttered against the backdrop of the sky. Above my head streetlamps were puddles of lime blurring into cherry, around which swift little banners swam, schools of them, like illuminated fish. Even the darkness itself seemed palpable, an element through which I had to dig my way, hands thrust in front of me, scooping up fistfuls of the cool, charcoal-colored air.

And then I was crossing Broadway again, stumbling down

103rd Street, where the lights of a hundred apartments winked at me. Fitting my key into the door to my own building, I noticed that my hands were shaking. Why were they shaking? My mind felt calm, and in any case I was home now, safe, stepping into my apartment with its familiar smells of old grease and perfume. I hadn't had, and therefore hadn't lost, much money. I hadn't lost . . . The hall light was off. 'Who's there?' A frail voice called.

'It's me. Martin.'

'Oh, Martin, honey!' Faye stepped out of the living room. She was in her dressing gown, her pink backless slippers. 'But you're ashen. What happened?'

'I was mugged.'

'Oh my Lord, are you all right? Do you need a doctor?'

'No, I'm fine. Is Will here?'

'He's out. Dennis is working. Come on, come with me.'

Putting an arm around my shoulders, she led me into the kitchen, where she poured me a glass of water. I drank it greedily, in a single gulp. 'Sit down. You *look* all right,' she said.

'I'm fine. I just lost my glasses.'

'Oh my poor darling, do you have an extra pair?'

I shook my head.

'Well, don't you worry, yesterday I passed a shop that does them in an hour. We'll go over there first thing in the morning and get you shipshape. Now what would you like? A shot of whiskey, maybe?'

'Just some more water, thanks.'

She poured out another glass, sat down across the table. 'Tell me what happened,' she said.

I told her that walking home from the Korean grocery store, I'd been knocked to the ground by two figures whose faces I could not make out. 'Give me the fucking money,' one of them had shouted, after which I had handed him my wallet, from which, to my relief, he had taken only the cash; in the course of the fracas, however, my glasses had been knocked onto the street, where a car had run them over.

'Well, bless your heart,' Faye said. 'How much did you lose?'

'Fifty dollars.'

'Shouldn't we call the police?'

'There's no point. There's nothing I can tell them. I didn't see their faces.'

Pleading fatigue, I got up and went into my room, where I undressed. My flowered shirt, I noticed, had a tear in one elbow. I threw it into the trash. Pulling off my pants, I observed dispassionately the drying streaks on the front of my underwear, which I took off as well, before lying down on the bed and closing my eyes. Somehow I did not want to switch off the light.

Soon I heard a knock on the door. 'Who is it?' I asked softly.

'Faye. I noticed your light was still on. Are you sure you're all right?'

'I'm fine. You can go to bed.'

'Okay, just wanted to check.' A pause. 'Well, good night, honey.'

'Good night.'

'Listen, if you need anything, even if it's the middle of the night, just holler. Don't worry about waking me.'

'I won't,' I said, and, switching off my own light, listened to the quiet swish of Faye's slippers as she padded down the hall.

The next morning Faye took me, as promised, to the optician's shop she had passed, the one that produced new glasses in an hour. It was unseasonably warm out. Holding my arm firmly, she led me through mazes of daytime traffic, down into the subway and back up again. Then in the shop, because I couldn't see well enough to make a selection on my own, she picked out a pair of frames for me. 'And you know what?' she said, sitting down next to me. 'These ones are nicer than the ones you lost – so maybe this cloud has a silver lining after all.'

'Maybe.'

'Silver lining! How funny, since they're silver glasses! By the way, there's a coffee shop next door. Can I get you anything? A Coke?'

'No, nothing.'

'To tell the truth, I'm not really thirsty either.'

From a little table next to my chair she picked up a copy of the magazine. Without my glasses, everything looked cottony, even Faye's arm, the slender trunk of which obtruded into my peripheral vision every time she turned a page. And yet, like the truly blind, I could hear more clearly than ever: the voices of a woman and her daughter trying on sunglasses, someone doing scales on a piano, the quiet hum of traffic. Also Faye's voice: 'It's time for me to go, I think . . .'

I turned. 'What?' I said.

'You're sweet to pretend,' she went on, 'but I know you can't wait to get rid of me. I'm not dumb. I realize when I've overstayed my welcome.'

'But you haven't—'

'So I guess it's back to Atlanta.' She laughed. 'You're lucky, Martin. You haven't screwed your life up – yet. You only look forward, not back at every bad decision you ever made.'

The 'yet' upset me. 'Are you saying I'm destined to make bad decisions?'

'Sometimes I think everyone is. And what can you do in the end but live with it? That's my conclusion, at least. Anyway, God knows I can't keep on burdening you boys with my tiresome—'

'Mr Bauman!'

I glanced up, startled. 'Yes?'

'Your glasses are ready.'

'Oh, great.' And I strode toward the desk where the optometrist, her arms open as if for an embrace, held them out to me, slipped them onto my face. With a kind of grave finality, not untouched by regret, the world came back into focus – teeth, lipstick, rows of frames, and when I turned, Faye's eyes, which looked as usual as if they were about to fill with tears.

After I paid, we stepped out onto the street. 'Well, good-bye,' she said sadly, peering into my newly corrected eyes. 'Tonight may be the last time you see me.'

'I hope not.'

'That's kind of you. Even so—' Her lips twisted, as if she were trying to smile. 'What I mean is, I hope your day goes well. I hope all your days go well.'

'Thank you. Yours too.'

'Be sweet.' And lifting herself onto her tiptoes, she gave me a kiss on the cheek that surprised me almost as much as Joey's had, not twenty-four hours earlier. Then she left. For a moment I watched her moving into the distance, her hair undone, her tragic sundress swaying, until a brilliant swag of light cut across the sky, and I had to cover my eyes. When I opened them again Faye was gone. I looked at my watch. 'Late for work,' I said aloud, and, turning, headed back into that city, that jungle, the laws of which I was finally beginning to learn.

7

At the Children's Table

AROUND THIS TIME I started writing a novel. This was not entirely an artistic choice: of the half dozen agents from whom I had received letters of inquiry after the publication of my story, all but one had told me that it would be impossible to launch my career with a story collection. Stories, the agents explained, simply didn't sell, the only editors who were interested in them being those at the magazine, which of course did not need to concern itself with such trivial matters as profit – and yet from the magazine I was finding myself, with every rejection letter I received (there had now been twelve), feeling increasingly estranged. Even Anka sounded different to me on the phone, as if my calls wearied her, as if it would be only a matter of time before she changed her hang-up code and added my name to the list of people with whom she preferred not to speak. For like any great aristocrat, the magazine was both ill-tempered and eccentric, with many curious little likes and dislikes (no dream sequences, no phonetic renderings of demotic speech, exclamation points only when absolutely necessary), and now, despite my zealous adherence to her unwritten codes, the old dame had apparently decided not to be 'at home' to me anymore. A novel, I saw, would at least bring me into a literary arena in which the magazine, by virtue of its very devotion to the story form, held less sway; and this realization, combined with the discovery that Stanley Flint was going to publish Julia Baylor, had the effect of jump-starting my literary ambitions. After months of lassitude I itched, once again, to write. I would call my novel *The Terrorist*, I decided; essentially, it would conflate the history of my own family with that of the Kellers, some neighbors of ours, a well-intentioned if weakly idealistic couple whose daughter had tried one afternoon to blow up the state capitol.

My hope was that the story of this family would provide the novel not only with dramatic backbone, but with a vehicle into which I could deposit all the lore of my sixties childhood; yet as I wrote on (and I wrote with remarkable fluidity) every day found me divagating further from my original conception. The great difficulty of constructing a novel is that one has to maintain, at the same moment, two radically different perspectives: the first that of the entirety, the book as it will be remembered by a reader who has long since finished it (and what a difficult point of view this is to adjudge, requiring an act of projection not only across space, but time), and the second, that of the thousand minutiae – details of place, expression, smell, nuance – which proliferate in this ocean of story, yet seem always to be swimming off in the wrong direction, leading you toward dead regions, or even worse, regions that prove to be far more lively than those to the exploration of which you have committed yourself. Process, in other words, begets unexpected (and not always pleasant) discoveries, and the 'theme' turns out to be not the thing with which you began, but the thing with which you end.

One afternoon Baylor called me at work and invited me to have lunch with her. At her suggestion we met at one of the expensive restaurants where I often made reservations for editors. No longer the owlish girl I'd met the first night of Stanley Flint's seminar, she had her long blond hair pulled back into a chignon, wore a natty navy blue jacket and a Hermès scarf, and, most dramatically, appeared to have lost, somewhere along the way, the big glasses through which she had once scowled at her German worksheets. Now her blue eyes, which I had never really seen, accented the sculptural beauty of her cheekbones, so much so that I wondered which was the mask, this Manhattan chic or the schoolgirlishness of university days.

Almost immediately we fell into a conversation about Flint. 'The thing is, when we were in school everyone used to make such a cult of him,' she said. 'His origins, his family, everything. Remember the stories in class?' She laughed. 'And of course the truth is always so much more banal – which, when you think about it, is one of the basic tenets of Flintism, isn't it?'

'So what *is* his history?' I asked, trying not to sound too curious.

She shrugged. 'Southern. He comes from the Carolinas, I think. The limp's from some accident he had as a child. For a long time he worked on newspapers.'

'And has he been much married, like what's-her-name – you know, "silvery" – said?'

'Well, twice, which isn't *that* much, comparatively speaking. With his first wife he only had sons. With Ursula – she's a psychiatrist – he has a little girl. Naomi. She's ten.'

'Have you met them?'

Baylor shook her head. 'Flint still maintains a very strict separation between church and state. But he talks about them. From what I gather, the healthiness of the whole arrangement

embarrasses him, because he's afraid it'll take away from his
reputation as an outlaw.'

'Where do they live?'

'Upper West Side. West End and . . . 104th, I think.'

I gawped. 'But I live at West End and 103rd!'

'Do you now.'

'But that can't be! I've never seen him once on the street.'

'Why should that be so surprising?' Baylor asked. 'New
York's an enormous city' – which was true. Yet if Flint lived
not, as I had always assumed, in some remote and glittering
corner of the East Side from which all but the wealthy and
famous were barred; if, rather, he lived within spitting distance of my own daily life, in that same neighborhood where
every afternoon, unconscious of his proximity, I ordered take-
out Chinese food, and did my laundry, and bought groceries,
then the cosmopolitan world with which I'd always associated
him was both more navigable and less distant than I'd
thought. And this discovery, while dulling the luster of his
aura, also gave it a patina of identity to which the connoisseur
in me responded with zeal.

That evening I did not go home after work. Instead, climbing out from the subway, I walked a block north of my own
apartment, then stood for a few minutes on the corner of
West End and 104th, gazing at the buildings that defined the
intersection: four staunch brick edifices, impenetrable and
murky, cozy only to their occupants, for whom they were
the trees in which nests awaited. Out of one of the doors a
little girl carrying a tennis racket now hurried: Naomi Flint?
If so, she looked nothing like her father. And yet why should
she have been Naomi Flint? Each of these buildings had a
population the size of a small town's. It was as unlikely that
tonight I should see Naomi Flint, I realized, as that I should
ever, in all my months on West End Avenue, have run into
Stanley Flint.

Even so, in the foyer of one of the buildings (the only one without a doorman) a brass plaque proclaimed the presence within of

URSULA FLINT, MD
PSYCHIATRY
Please Ring 6-A

which meant that Baylor was right; Flint did live here. Standing in the foyer, fearful lest someone walking in might accuse me of loitering, I studied rows of tiny buttons on the intercom. 6-A: FLINT, I read. And across the way, beneath one of the mailboxes: FLINT, S. & U.

So this is it, then, I remember thinking: the glass door with its security bolts through which he walks each morning and each evening; the lobby, with its Naugahyde benches and sand-filled ashtray, where he gathers his mail; the old-fashioned elevator in which every day he rides up to that apartment wherein, presumably, he had read my first story, and Baylor's novel, and the stories by the girl who designed headstones. That I could get no closer appalled and excited me, and fearful lest he should stumble upon me gaping at his name, I fled, retreating to my own humble digs. Later, though, stepping outside for some air, I couldn't help but linger on Flint's sidewalk for a while, staring at the illuminated sixth floor of his building; and likewise the next morning, at five, ostensibly because I wasn't sleepy, I went out and stood on the corner of 104th Street until, just as dawn broke, he emerged, as shocking in his reality as one of those monuments, the leaning tower of Pisa or the Eiffel Tower, the impact of which a history of postcard views and miniature statues blunts so much less than we think it will; indeed, in the nakedness of selfhood, these spires startle all the more for their many cheap approximations. Unaware that his every move was being witnessed, relieved (albeit briefly) of the burden of a public image, Flint was at that moment both more himself – and less. He scratched his head, bent to tie a shoelace. Then he turned the corner. I followed him. Because he did not see me he was not, at the moment, Stanley Flint at all: instead he was simply the 'I' to which all of us are reduced at those instances when we have no need to exist for other people.

Leaning on his cane, he headed for Broadway, where at a kiosk he bought a *New York Times*. He went into a coffee shop (I watched through the window) and sat at the counter. I thought briefly of following him in, taking the seat next to his as casually as if it really were by accident – and yet to do so, I knew, would be to spoil that brief caesura, that nameless solitude in which he was tarrying. So I waited patiently on the corner, and when he stepped out of the coffee shop and hailed a passing taxi, from behind the display of porn magazines festooning the news kiosk I watched until his cab was gone from view.

Not long after this something occurred that was destined to have far-reaching effects on my relationship with Flint. One morning I was filling in, as usual, for the receptionist at the Hudson-Terrier front desk, feeling rather bored and wondering when she would get back from her break, when the elevator doors opened and a florid woman in her mid-forties walked out. A mass of pale curls framed this woman's face, which was overly made-up and somewhat damp. Although she was fat, her weight sat well on her, in contrast, say, to that of Marge Preston, which tended to settle in her behind and thighs. This woman, on the other hand, had the sort of firmly overstuffed body to which we allude when we describe someone as 'zaftig' or 'Rubenesque.' Under her green parka she wore a pink satin cocktail dress. Her lips, which were painted coral, she pursed confidently as she stepped up to me, head erect, bosom thrust forward in the manner of a Miss America striding down the runway. 'Good morning,' she said.

'Good morning,' I answered. 'May I help you?'

'Yes you may. I'd like to speak to the editor.'

I drew my back up. So here it was at last, I thought thinking – human slush, slush in the flesh – and was preparing to show the woman the door when another door – the one to Hudson Editorial – clicked open, and Flint walked out. 'Bauman,' he said, 'I was wondering . . .' And he stopped in his tracks. 'Hello,' he said to the woman. 'May *I* help you?'

'Good morning,' she repeated. 'As I was just telling this young gentleman, I'm here to speak to the editor. About a book I've written.'

'I'm the editor,' Flint answered. 'Won't you step this way, madame?'

Then, casting a conspiratorial glance in my direction, Flint led her toward his office, from which they reemerged about twenty minutes later. 'Thank you very much,' the woman said breathily, shaking his hand.

'You're very welcome, my dear,' he answered, and pushed the elevator button for her. She stepped inside. Patting me on the shoulder, he winked at me, then returned to his office.

The door clicked closed. I flinched. *Well, what was that about?* I remember asking myself. Had I just witnessed Flint the womanizer in action? Or was it, on the contrary, Flint the editor who had come to the fore that afternoon, somehow recognizing in the very carriage of this overdressed woman the faint resplendence of unrefined genius?

That morning I gave in, once again, to love. Nothing would do, I decided, but Flint's praise, and with my heart in my throat, I resolved to ask him to read the eighty pages I had so far written of *The Terrorist*. And yet how to approach such a daunting figure? Here lay the trouble. At first, from shyness, I tried writing him a letter, then tore it up; after all, wouldn't a letter seem oddly impersonal given that three days a week we worked thirty feet from each other? A phone call, then – but that would be cowardly. Or perhaps I might ask Carey to talk to him on my behalf, as previously I had asked Susan to talk to Carey . . . only in that case the results had been disastrous. No, I decided, the only thing to do was to confront him directly, and accordingly, at the end of a long day about a week after the episode of the woman in the parka, I knocked at his door, which was as usual half-open. (Or should I say half-shut? Dimly I recollect intelligence tests from my childhood.)

'Come in!' he called.

I peered inside. 'Hello,' I said sheepishly. (I still didn't know what to call him. Stanley? Flint? Mr Flint?) 'I wondered if I might—'

'Oh, Bauman.' Pushing aside a manuscript he was in the throes of red-penciling, he motioned me in. 'And what can I do for you this fine day? Don't just stand there, come in.'

I did as bidden. 'Thank you,' I said, clearing my throat. 'Actually, I wanted to ask you a favor. You see, for the last couple of months I've been working on a novel, my first novel. I've got about eighty pages now. And given the fact that at school you were pretty enthusiastic about that story I wrote, I was wondering whether you'd mind—'

'You mean you want me to read it?' He grinned. 'But I'd be delighted to. And what are you doing in the doorway like that? Sit down, sit down.' He pointed to a chair in the corner. 'Is that what you're holding in your hands? Your manuscript? Bring it here.'

Approaching him, I did as commanded. He scanned the first pages. 'Nice title,' he said. Then he skipped to the last page; looked at the final line; said nothing.

'I must confess, Bauman,' he continued, vaguely flipping through my pages, 'that I did read that story of yours in the magazine. And I hope you won't be offended' – he glanced up at me suddenly, guardedly – 'if I tell you I wasn't much impressed.'

'I'm not offended.'

'The trouble was, it read like a public service announcement. Also, you write as if homosexuality itself was interesting. It's not interesting. All that's interesting is individual experience.' He scooped my pages back into a pile. 'I didn't say anything earlier because in our capacity as coworkers, I felt it wasn't my place. You understand, don't you? As for this novel, *The Terrorist* – really a nice title – of course I'll be more than happy to give it a look-through tonight—'

'Tonight!'

'Why waste time? Then we can talk tomorrow, how does that sound?'

'Fine.' I hesitated. 'Oh, and by the way, please don't feel you have to be gentle just because—'

'Have I ever been gentle? You sound like a girl about to be fucked for the first time.'

'Oh, well . . .' I laughed, embarrassed. He waved. I backed out of the office. Gathering up my coat, I left. What was surging through me was the same sensation of dread that in high school had always preceded the mornings when I would get the results of a test; I hardly slept that night, and when dawn broke, hurried to work, where I hoped that Flint, encountering me as he arrived, might take me into the office and get the business over and done with. Yet as luck would have it, though I got in at half past seven, he had beaten me to the punch and was already holed up in his office. As usual his door was ajar. Dare I knock on it? I asked myself, then decided not to: after all, if he had come in so early, it was probably to get some reading done without being disturbed. So I drank my Diet Coke, settled down at my desk, tried to concentrate on *The Horror of Hilton High* . . . only my eye kept wandering to the clock. Eight approached. Once again, as if casually, I swung by Flint's office, the door to which remained ajar. Still I didn't knock. For he had merely said that he would talk to me 'tomorrow,' and there was still the whole of the day left. No doubt the best course of action would be simply to wait until he summoned me. Only he didn't summon me. The morning waned. Passing by his desk around eleven, I asked Carey if he was in a meeting. 'No, he's alone,' Carey said. 'Do you need to see him?'

I shook my head, checked my watch. Panicked now, I waited ten more minutes, then puffed up my chest and knocked on the fatal door.

'Yes?' Flint called.

'Hello,' I said, peeping my head through the crack.

'Oh, Bauman. Come in.' I did. Atop his desk my manuscript sat, pristine, looking as if it had never been touched. Perhaps he hasn't read it yet, I thought with relief, which would at least mean that he didn't hate it (hate me).

'What can I do for you today?'

What can I do for you today! The question hardly seemed apposite, given the circumstances. 'I wondered if you'd had a chance to look at the pages I gave you,' I said.

'Pages?'

'The novel.'

Flint appeared confused. 'What novel? You didn't give me a novel.'

'But I—'

'Oh, you mean this?' He pointed to my manuscript. 'But this isn't a novel,' he said, laughing gently, as if at a display of idiocy. 'This is just paper with little black marks on it! A novel,' he went on, lips closing over teeth, 'is an act of chemical bonding. A novel sparks. Atoms in orbit, sending off electrical charges that yank them into structure. Whereas this' – again, he indicated the manuscript – 'this is just letters combined into words, words into sentences, one sentence after another, blah-blah-blah. Too much plot, too much subject matter, too much jerking off, in both senses of the phrase.' He pushed the manuscript toward me. 'I know you can do better than this, Bauman. You did better than this once. As you may recall I wrote you a letter several years back indicating that you needed my guidance, and that it would be in your best interest to persuade that august institution from which you recently graduated to invite me back for a semester – and to this letter, I don't need to remind you, you elected never to reply. Well, some time has passed since then, and now, it seems, you're able to admit that you need me. Which is fine. I'm not a vindictive man.' He stood. 'As you may know, I'm teaching a private seminar these days, twice a week. Not under the aegis of a university – that's far too restrictive. What I'd suggest is that you apply for the winter term – not that I can guarantee you admission, that will depend on the quality of the other submissions, since of course, the seminar is strictly limited to eighteen participants. Baylor will be attending – she won't pay, she'll be a sort of auditor. Well, think about it. As I said, you have little choice.' He handed me my eighty pages of little black marks. 'I know you're disappointed. I know you were hoping for an offer of publication. Unfortunately, you're nowhere near that stage yet, as far as I'm concerned, nor is there any guarantee that you ever will be. Well, good-bye, Bauman.'

'Good-bye. Thank you,' I said. And snatching the manuscript back, I hurried to the men's room, to one of the stalls, where I sat down. The fact was, it had taken me a few moments to grasp the full import of Flint's monologue. And how amazing, I thought (with that detached tranquillity of mind that so often immediately follows a shock) that I had actually reached a point with him where I would have been glad to hear one of those familiar epithets, 'baby talk' or 'unmitigated shit': anything but this relegation to successively lower echelons of attention (and yet how the purity of his standards still thrilled me, awed me!), this demotion from favorite to merely another undistinguished voice in the roaring mob!

I left the men's room; I hobbled back to my perch. Before my eyes the slush grew blurry, turned literally to slush. It occurred to me, rather dimly, that I would now very likely have to quit my job. For how could I continue to work at Hudson, when Flint occupied an office only a few feet away from where I sat, and through the door to which I could always catch, if I craned my neck, a glimpse of his cruel, unforgiving, beloved face? Nor did it help much that pride was already rushing in to ameliorate the damage, that around the wound the helper cells of pride were erecting a scab of pep talk and testimonials, reminders that despite whatever Flint had said there still sat in my desk drawer half a dozen letters from agents all eager to represent me, all admiring of my story in the magazine. (And had Baylor ever published anything in the magazine?) For the injury, despite all pride's efforts to subdue it, still gaped. Flint refused to budge from the throne upon which I had placed him. His praise remained the only reward that mattered to me, which meant that so long as he reigned, every blessing he bestowed upon other people would be a knife between my ribs.

And then, almost before I had made the decision to stand, I was on my feet again. I wasn't sure where they were taking me, only that when I found myself outside Marge Preston's office, my being there seemed somehow inevitable. Sara was away from her desk. 'Excuse me, Marge?' I called through the open door.

Raising her eyes from her own desk, the surface of which was a chaos of letters and spreadsheets, she glanced up at me; took off her half glasses. 'Hello, Martin,' she said, pleasantly if a bit impatiently. 'What's up?'

'There's something I need to talk to you about.' I had my hands twisted one around the other. 'May I?' I indicated the door with my head.

Marge straightened her back. 'Of course,' she said, stood, and shut the door behind me. 'Is something wrong? You don't look well.'

I had never before noticed how short she was; she came up only to my shoulder. 'It's just . . .'

Putting her arm around me, she led me to a conference table, where she sat me down.

'I don't know where to begin,' I said. 'Something happened recently that I've been worrying about, that I feel I need to tell you about – and yet . . .'

Her lips were grim. 'Go ahead,' she instructed. 'And don't worry, this will stay between us.'

'But that's just it, I'm not sure if . . . You see, it's about Stanley Flint.'

She rubbed her temples. 'Oh dear. Go on.'

Then I told her about the woman who had appeared at the front desk and asked to see 'the editor.' I told her about Flint's unexpected entrance, and their subsequent disappearance together into his office. I assured her that of course I had no reason, no reason at all, to assume that by inviting the woman in Flint was doing anything other than offering encouragement to a fledgling writer . . . yet there were rumors. Even back when I'd studied with him, there had been rumors.

To all this she listened quietly, without expression, chewing on the left temple of her glasses.

'I thought you should know,' I concluded.

Marge got up. She strolled over to a bookcase, from which she extracted a volume of poetry by Wallace Stevens. 'Martin, as I'm sure you're aware,' she said, flipping through the poems, 'I've worked in book publishing for a number of years. Fifteen years.'

'Yes.'

'More importantly, I've worked as a woman in book publishing for fifteen years. I know the kinds of things that go on. I have to. If I didn't I'd never have gotten as far as I have.' She shut the book. 'Part of my job is keeping my ears open. You'll have to trust me on this, but there's very little that happens at this company of which I'm not aware. All of which is a way of saying that what you've told me today – it's nothing that comes as a surprise. Nothing. No, all that's a surprise to me is that Martin Bauman should turn out to be the kind of person who'd use information like this to try to get back at someone.'

'But I'm not trying to get back at anyone!' I countered, stunned not by the falsehood of her accusation, but its truthfulness. 'Anyway, why should I want to get back at Flint?' (This in a quieter voice.)

'You tell me.'

'I don't.'

'Still, it must have hurt when he bought Julia Baylor's novel. And yet you've got to realize, Martin, that just because Julia's reached, shall we say, a certain level of maturity, that doesn't give you the right to try to spoil her chances, or ruin Stanley's career.'

'But I'm not jealous! Baylor and I are friends. We had lunch together.'

'Then why are you here?'

'From a sense of duty.'

Marge smiled benevolently. 'I think, Martin,' she said, sitting across the table from me, 'that maybe now is the time for you to consider whether it's in your best interest to keep working at Hudson. After all, you're a writer. Publishing's no career for you. As I've often said, when writers get too involved in publishing, they're ruined by it. You ought to be off on an island, where there's nothing to distract you but the sound of the surf against the rocks – not here, in this dreary office, with all these tiresome people. And publishing's not what it used to be. Nor, I fear' – she sighed dramatically – 'will it ever be again.'

'But plenty of writers have worked as editors. Doctorow was an editor. Toni Morrison—'

'If you need a job, go work on an oil rig, or at a zoo. Something that feeds your creativity. Anything but some miserable old publishing house full of backstabbing and gossip and details you'd probably be better off not knowing.'

'But I like working here . . .' My voice trailed off, for I was close to tears. 'Excuse me if I'm dense,' I said, 'but am I being fired?'

Smiling sweetly, Marge nodded.

I said nothing, only breathed deeply, to contain the sob I felt rising in my throat like a hiccup. Then I stood.

'Are you all right?' Marge asked.

'Yes,' I said. 'In fact – it may sound strange, but I want to thank you. I can tell you're doing this for my own good. I feel humbled. I hope you won't continue to think badly of me . . . And of course I won't say anything to anyone else about what happened.'

'I'd appreciate that. Please don't think I've ignored these problems. Believe me, I'm dealing with them in my own way. But sometimes effectiveness requires, shall we say, a certain amount of discretion.'

I nodded. She stood and opened the door for me. We shook hands.

In the interval Sara had returned. 'What's wrong?' she asked under her breath. 'Why were you and Marge locked up in there?'

I told her I had just been fired. 'Oh dear,' she said, in a

voice that betrayed neither surprise nor any great displeasure.
'I'm sorry, Martin.'

'I am too,' I said meekly. Then I returned to my desk, where
I gathered together the few possessions I kept there – a box of
Kleenex, a comb, the mug from which I drank my Diet Coke –
and left Hudson-Terrier forever. I went home. The apartment
seemed oddly empty without Faye, who was just about the
only person to whom I could have confessed, at that moment,
what I'd been through. I even considered, briefly, phoning
her in Atlanta, but checked myself in case she should interpret
my distress call as a plea for help and catch the next flight up
to New York.

I spent the rest of the day watching television: a flurry of
soap operas and game shows, talk shows and grainy cartoons
whose characters I remembered from my childhood, the Road
Runner and Bugs Bunny and Pepe Le Pew, out of whose
amorous arms a black cat painted with a white stripe had con-
tinually to wrest herself. No one came home. For dinner I ate
delivered Chinese food, as at Anka's so many months ago,
then went to bed, eyes red and limbs heavy, successfully anes-
thetized by so much TV. I hoped I would sleep without
dreaming, for hours, for days, only some time during the
middle of the night the sound of keys in the lock startled me;
I woke, and to my surprise found myself privy to one of those
moments of self-understanding that come upon us so rarely
when we are young (and only with slightly greater frequency
when we grow older). For just as, in the aftermath of that
seduction that had turned into a robbery, the absence of
glasses had brought the familiar Manhattan landscape, as it
were, into a fresh and unexpected focus, so now – bereft of
those dependable correctives, optimism, and self-confidence –
I saw my own motives . . . not more clearly, just differently.
And what I saw upset me more than anything Stanley Flint or
Marge Preston had said. I saw a boy so desperate for approval

that, having failed to win it from one source, he had rico-
cheted immediately to another, which had also denied him.
Worse, in the second go-round, he had been perfectly willing
to try to ruin someone with the suggestion of indiscretions no
worse, in the end, than any of his own, in order to attain,
almost as a by-product of his reassurance, a dose of vengeance.
Yet the worst part was that when, in return for this effort, he
had suffered humiliation, he had actually offered thanks for
that humiliation, strained to recalibrate it so that in his own
mind, at least, it would signify approval. Indeed, so base (and
so self-abasing) did the behavior of this boy seem to me that
I wanted to kick him hard, as once Dwight Rohmer had
kicked me.

I got out of bed. Just as I no longer felt sorry for myself, I
no longer felt grateful to Marge, whose disparagement of the
publishing industry I now recognized for that insider's cynicism, both fatuous and arrogant, by means of which the more
entrenched try to convince the less entrenched that their
exclusion from the corridors of power is a blessing. After all,
if things were so bad, why wasn't Marge trying to change
them? This was, I knew, a grim diagnosis, yet curiously it did
not move me to despair. Instead, as dawn broke, a mysterious
energy coursed through me. To my surprise, I discovered that
my ambitions, though somewhat bloodied, had survived the
night intact; indeed, they were crying out for me to do some
things I'd been putting off for months, and that morning, in
keeping with their demands, I made an appointment to meet
with the one agent who had not told me I had to write a
novel; I arranged a lunch with Edith; I even sat down in a
coffee shop and read over those pages of mine that had
received, at Flint's hand, such a drubbing, and found that I
was as eager to return to work on them as I was pleased by
what I'd already done.

The following week I got a new job, not on an oil rig, but

at a snooty bookshop on the Upper East Side, the ill-tempered owner of which prided himself in the influence he wielded over his clients, most of them New York society ladies, who depended upon him to sell them exactly those books the presence of which on their ebonized Sheraton consoles would be sure to convince any party guest that he or she had walked into a truly intellectual home. Because the taste of the owner was both eclectic and obscure, he was also much beloved by certain authors whose novels, had it not been for the energy with which he promoted them (though he could be equally capricious in withdrawing his favor), would have sold only a few hundred copies: writers like Geòrges Perec (crafter of the famous e-less novel), W. M. Spackman, George Steiner, Kennedy Fraser, Gilbert Adair. For taste trickles down, and the party guests who took note of which books were sitting on those Chippendale étagères and in those Biedermeier cabinets always made a point not only of buying them and pretending to read them, but of recommending them vehemently to their sisters-in-law, interior designers, and psychiatrists, all of whom then felt themselves duty-bound to follow suit. In this way a few people who might not have otherwise done so discovered literature, so the owner of the bookstore can be credited with actually having done some good.

In any case, of my tenure at this bookstore (which was even briefer than my tenure at Hudson-Terrier) everything I need to say can be summed up in a single anecdote: as a sop to those of his employees who were, like me, far too educated to take any pleasure in the operation of a cash register, the bookstore owner had set aside a shelf for the display of those volumes that we designated 'staff recommendations.' This shelf was near the table on which he exhibited, in gleaming stacks, his own favorites. Best-selling pieces of trash (excuse me, commercial novels) were relegated to a remote corner, as at small-town newsstands the pornography is always hidden far in the back, next to the gun magazines.

One afternoon during my first week at the bookstore a woman in her early sixties, expensively though inelegantly dressed, came up to the front desk and asked for the owner, who was at lunch. 'Can *I* help you?' I offered, at which point, rather hesitantly, she inquired whether I might be able to recommend a novel to her.

As it happened, that very morning I had made my first contribution to the employee recommendation shelf: Sybille Bedford's *A Favourite of the Gods*, which Obelisk (now defunct) had just brought back into print. 'It's really wonderful,' I said, handing her the book, which she regarded dubiously. 'It's about a young girl growing up between the wars, with this awful mother. Most of it takes place on the French Riviera.'

'Oh, the Riviera,' the woman said, lifting her eyebrows. 'All right, I'll give it a try.' And she took the novel away with her.

The next morning she was back. Again she asked for the owner. 'He's in the back,' I said. 'Would you like—'

'No, no, that's all right,' she answered hurriedly, and removed *A Favourite of the Gods* from her purse. 'I'm afraid this just isn't working for me. Could I exchange it?'

'Of course.'

Very cautiously, then – looking first over her shoulder toward the door of the office, from which the owner had not emerged – she moved to the back of the shop, where she picked a book off the trash shelf. 'I'll take this,' she said, scurrying up to the desk and handing me Judith Krantz's *Mistral's Daughter*.

At that instant the owner stepped out of his office. 'Hi, Fritzi,' he said.

'Good morning, George,' Fritzi answered, and looked at me

helplessly. But to her relief, I had already slipped the book into its plain brown wrapper.

I am now going to break one of Stanley Flint's cardinal rules. I am going to write a scene set at a cocktail party.

If it is any justification, Flint himself was a guest at that party; indeed, he was one of the principal guests, having once taught the author in whose honor it was being thrown. But to tell the story correctly requires some backtracking. Near the middle of December – I had been working at the bookstore about a month then – I received a call from Liza Perlman, who had just gotten back to New York for her Christmas break. 'What are you doing tonight?' she asked. 'Because my mother's gotten me an invitation to this huge publishing party. It's for this really hot young writer, Sam Stallings. Do you know him?'

'Isn't he the one you were talking about at Anka's?' I asked. 'The one you thought was so arrogant?'

Liza hedged. 'Oh, I'm not saying I like him *personally*. Personally I think he's a jerk. Still, the party should be great. Have you read his book, by the way?'

'Not yet,' I admitted, carefully eliding the fact that though, indeed, I had not read *Rodeo Nights*, I had thumbed through it a dozen times at the store, in that way of literary New Yorkers who, before even turning to a novel's opening page, will first examine the author's photograph, check the back cover to see which other writers have given him blurbs, look at the dedication, scan the acknowledgments (to see who the author's friends are, as well as by which institutions he has been awarded grants, residencies, and 'financial assistance'), and finally skim the small print on the copyright page, whereon are listed the names of those magazines in which a portion of the book in question (usually 'in somewhat different form') has previously been published.

'I have to confess, I haven't either,' Liza said. 'I mean, it all sounds so macho, you know, one of those books in which guys are always calling each other by their last names. Not my cup of meat, as my friend Eli says of Arnold Schwarzenegger ... Still, it's going to be *the* party, my mother says. It's at ——'s.' (She named the editor of a well-known literary magazine, a rich man who lived in a townhouse overlooking the East River.) 'Everyone's going to be there. My mother, by the way, was the one who suggested I invite another writer along, so I thought I'd ask you – that is, if you're not busy.'

As it happened I wasn't busy; nor could I deny the curiosity – far more intense than my irritation at Liza's pretentiousness – that those dangerous words *everyone's going to be there* had aroused in me.

We agreed to meet at seven on a specified corner of Sutton Place, after which I got dressed and hailed a taxi: a rare indulgence, but then again, this was a rare occasion. Liza was already waiting when I arrived. Dressed in a jean jacket, black silk pants, and a pale cashmere sweater – an outfit that, I would later learn, like so much else in her life, represented a concession to her mother, who could not abide what she called 'dyke clothes' – she was leaning against a lamppost, a shapeless purse slung over one shoulder. Her red hair, I noticed, she had grown a bit longer since we'd last seen each other; tufts of it dipped shaggily into her eyes.

Having said hello and kissed each other on the cheek, we walked toward the little cul-de-sac at the end of which the editor lived. I asked Liza how her semester at Babcock had gone. 'Yuck,' she said. 'I think I'd go crazy if it weren't for Lucy. Only next term she's on leave, so I don't know what I'll do.'

We had reached the editor's house. By the open door a crowd was gathering; just inside, an efficient-looking young woman was checking the names of the guests off a list attached to a clipboard, while behind her a liveried servant took their coats.

Liza stopped speaking. She seemed distracted, as if she were looking for someone who might recognize her. No one seemed to, however, and when we reached the head of the line and the efficient young woman said, 'May I have your name, please?' her answer sounded more like a question – 'Liza Perlman?' – as if she wasn't entirely sure who she was.

The young woman scanned her clipboard. 'How do you spell that?'

'P-E-R-L, no A.'

'Ah, yes.' With a yellow highlighter she sliced Liza off the list. 'And you?'

I stammered.

'He's my guest,' said Liza.

The young woman nodded. We passed. The servant took my coat (Liza kept her jacket), after which we walked up a flight of stairs the treads of which were painted pale pink, to match the pink-striped paper on the walls. 'Wow,' I said. 'Imagine owning a whole house in New York City.'

'Haven't you ever been in a townhouse before?'

I shook my head. She smiled, as if my innocence (which was in fact largely manufactured) had touched her. By now we were at the top of the stairs; in front of us an immense living room spread out, its parquet floor covered with an equally immense (and genuine) Aubusson carpet.

'Do you know most of these people?' I asked Liza, gazing out at the little islets of furniture that punctuated this seascape, and upon which the party guests, like exotic marine specimens, were writhing and feeding, as in those rock pools that the ebbing of the tide brings into view.

'Some,' Liza said. 'That's Nadine Gordimer. She's doing a reading at the 92nd Street Y tomorrow. And over there's John Irving.'

I peered. 'He's shorter than I thought he'd be.'

A waiter approached us, bearing a tray on which filled roundels of puff pastry had been arranged. 'Brie and ham tartlet?'

'Thank you.'

'No thank you.'

'Champagne? Sparkling water? Ginger ale?'

We each took a glass of ginger ale. 'Say, isn't that Stanley Flint?' Liza asked, pointing across the room.

I followed her finger. To my horror, I saw that she was right: near the back of the room, where a pair of damask curtains, heavily fringed and pelmeted, framed a view of the East River, Flint was drinking and laughing with Marge Preston and two women I didn't recognize.

My first impulse was to flee, or short of that disguise myself – as I might have done as a child – within the copious folds of the curtains. Because I knew that to behave in this way would be to lay bare certain emotions of which I preferred that Liza remain ignorant, however, I held my ground.

'By the way, how's your friend Eli?' I asked.

'Don't you want to say hello to him? He was your teacher, wasn't he?'

'Later, if you don't mind.'

'I wonder where my mother is,' said Liza, whose concentrated perusal of the crowd appeared to have eclipsed her focus on Flint.

'Why didn't he come tonight?'

'Who?'

'Eli.'

'Oh, he doesn't like parties. Do you want to walk over to the bar?'

'Stuffed mushroom caps? Buffalo wings?' a waiter called – this latter item, I suspected, a nod to the setting of Sam Stallings's novel. I took a sample of each, then followed Liza to the bar, next to which more hors d'oeuvres were displayed on a long table, all elegantly overwrought, and a far cry from the 'cocktail food' Jim Sterling and I had prepared in his mother's kitchen. It was here that we stationed ourselves, for the table, we soon discovered, provided the ideal post from which to observe the party's many tropical atolls, not to mention those inviting currents into which others, braver than we, were now diving headlong, while we stayed rooted to the shore.

Or at least this was how I felt. Liza – less innocent than I, though more timid – appeared merely to be searching for a face in the crowd at once familiar and friendly, the face of someone who might offer a hand to ease her in. And soon enough this face appeared. 'Oh look, there's Janet!' she cried, and began waving frantically. 'Janet! Over here!'

From the throng Janet Klass extricated herself. 'Hi, Liza,' she said. 'Hi, Martin.' She picked up a leaf of endive stuffed with crab. 'Boy, am I glad to see you guys! I don't know anybody at this party.'

'Neither do we!' Liza cried gleefully.

'Sam only invited me because he's in my study. What are you drinking, by the way?'

'Ginger ale. You know what this reminds me of, the three of us here? It reminds me of the neighborhood parties my parents used to take me to, when all the kids would have to sit at the children's table.' And indeed, to the insiders working the crowd, those seasoned veterans of a thousand New York parties, what children we must have seemed, with our soft drinks and giggling intimacies! A year or so later all this would change, there would be born that cult of youth (a by-product of the Reagan years) of which the high priests were those Wall Street whiz kids who seemed always to be earning their first million before turning twenty-two (their number included both Barb Mendenhall and my old roommate

Donald), and to whom Liza and I, as well as Sam Stallings, would come to serve as a sort of low-rent analogue, a 'literary brat pack,' to borrow the language of the press, the members of which, it was said, shared a fondness for nightclubs, a link to Stanley Flint, and a penchant for the so-called 'minimalist' style. Straight out of graduate writing programs, already armed with lucrative contracts, the members of the brat pack would soon be taking over parties like this one, as well as magazines, publishing houses, PEN committees . . . and yet for the moment all this was still far away, and it was just Liza, Janet, and I standing at the fringe of the hors d'oeuvres table, gazing out at a scene that seemed to have been going on for a hundred years, like one of those soirées that Proust takes so many pages (and so much pleasure) in describing.

But I have digressed. It so happened that while we were waiting there, staring meekly (if this is possible) at the roaming crowd, a pair of eyes had picked us out for special scrutiny. These eyes belonged to a tall woman of middle age, cleanly suburban in her tartan skirt and ruffled white blouse, and now bearing down on us, speaking even as she walked, though I couldn't make out her exact words. As she approached – back straight and bosom high – the expression of questioning anxiety that had marked Liza's face since our arrival suddenly gave way to a grimace in which relief and worry were admixed. 'Liza,' the woman said, shaking her head disapprovingly.

'Hi, Mom,' Liza said.

Then Sada Perlman, having first kissed her daughter on the cheek, stepped back, put her hand on her heart, and sighed.

'Mom, please—'

'At least you could have done the buttons right. And that jacket! What's the point of wearing nice clothes if you're going to cover them up—'

'It doesn't matter! You remember Janet, don't you?'

'Of course. Hello, Janet. My, that's a lovely skirt. A pity my daughter doesn't take tips on how to dress from you. And how's your study going?'

'Very well, thank you, Mrs Perlman. I'm hoping to finish collecting my data by spring, at which point I can start the computer analysis—'

'And this is Martin Bauman, the young writer I was telling you about. Martin, I'd like you to meet my mother, Sada Perlman.'

'Hello, Martin.'

'How do you do,' I said.

'How do *you* do,' she answered. 'I'll tell you straight off, I read that story of yours in the magazine, and I thought it was terrific.'

'You did? I'm glad.'

'It must have been upsetting for your mother, though. I know it would have been for me.' She stared rebukingly at Liza, who turned away. 'So tell me, are you kids having fun? I noticed that Stanley's here. Liza, have you said hello to him yet?'

'Not yet.'

'And what about Sam? He certainly is the toast of the town. Ellie Dickman just told me his book's entering the best-seller list next week at number nine, isn't that fabulous?'

'Really? Number nine?'

'Listen, honey,' Sada continued, taking her daughter by the hand, 'Nora's over there – you know she can't walk very well these days – and I promised I'd take you by to say hello—'

'Oh, Mom . . .'

'Come on, darling, she's an old lady. You know she's always asking after you. It would break her heart if you didn't at least talk to her.'

'But she always gets me trapped in conversations that last for hours!'

'I promise to rescue you. Now be a good girl and go.' With which words Sada pushed Liza out into the crowd. Timorously Janet and I followed. From one of a pair of armchairs dressed in chintz slipcovers an old woman with bright white hair and a faint mustache smiled up at us. 'Liza,' she said warmly, trying to stand, an effort in which her legs, though braced by support hose and tennis shoes, refused to comply.

'Don't get up. Hello, Nora.'

'Sweetheart, let me look at you. You look wonderful.' Nora reached her arms toward Liza, who bent down obediently to be kissed. 'And how long has it been? So much time. People live too long.'

'Nora, may I introduce my friends? Martin Bauman and Janet Klass. Martin and Janet, Nora Foy.'

I gasped a little. From Sada's conversation I had assumed that this Nora would turn out to be some tiresome relative she had dragged along to the party, to whom filial duty required Liza to make nice. Instead of which here was Nora Foy, the poet and memoirist every one of whose books my mother had read faithfully, though never without the complaint that they were too 'whiny.'

The fact that the Nora of whom Sada spoke so familiarly was not merely any Nora, but a famous Nora, only fortified the perception – already burgeoning in me – that Liza had an impeccable literary pedigree; and yet it also had the effect, curiously enough, of highlighting the degree to which this party, for all its metropolitan glamour, was in the end not very different from the neighborhood Christmas parties to which I'd gone every year since I could remember, and at which my mother always accompanied the carolers on the piano. 'Sit down and tell me what you've been writing,' Nora said, patting the armchair opposite hers, while Liza, a ferocious smile planted on her face, stared after her mother, who had drifted away and fallen into conversation with a short young man in a purple jacket. Despite her promise, it seemed, Sada was not going to rescue her after all, and with a resigned sigh Liza acceded to her fate.

As for Janet and me, we found ourselves abandoned to the mercy of the crowd, the members of which seemed to be dancing all around us. And indeed, as previously I had looked upon the party as an exotic marine habitat, it was now as a dance that I conceived it, one in which strangers were constantly 'breaking in' and separating partners from each other, as Nora Foy had separated Liza from me. Faces were everywhere – faces, and smells, a skirmish of perfumes the likes of which I hadn't encountered since the days when Faye had filled our corridor with her samples from Bloomingdale's. There was John Irving, and Jay McInerney, and a woman I thought might have been Renata Adler . . . and Stanley Flint, again, at the sight of whom my heart started racing. As at the premiere of the play in which the TV star had acted, destiny had placed him directly in my line of vision. Our eyes met; confidently he strode up to where I was standing with Janet. 'Bauman,' he said warmly, and shook my hand.

Janet – the very idea of Stanley Flint, she later told me, intimidated her too much to bear even the prospect of being introduced to him – had fled. Flint and I were alone. He looked good – certainly better than in the Hudson offices, the fluorescent ceiling lights of which tended to lend to his harrowed complexion (well, to everyone's harrowed complexion) a pale, blotchy cast. Now, in the warm luminescence of the cocktail party, his beard hearty and weathered, he squeezed my hand, looked me intently in the eye.

'Hello,' I said, still not sure what to call him.

'A delight to see you, young man,' he said, 'a real delight' – which was a relief to me, because it meant at least that Marge hadn't told him about my attempt to get him fired. 'I must tell you, the offices of old Mr Hudson are a sadder place without your eager young face peering around every corner. We all talk about it. Rosenzweig and Finch and I. How else to put it? You brightened things up with your clumsy eagerness, your exuberant awkwardness.'

'Thank you. Work's going well, I trust?'

He shrugged. 'As a job, it's an ordeal to me. I see my function as essentially thankless – to be a midwife to literature. And every day the fight gets tougher, the fight to convince the money machines that greatness matters. You see, they have no vision beyond their balance sheets. To them the only books that matter are the account books . . . but that's neither here nor there. You're well rid of us. A publishing house is no place for a writer.'

I smiled; so at least he still considered me a writer.

'As for the new slush reader,' he continued, 'a tiresome girl, very literal-minded. No equal to you.'

'And Carey?'

'Wonderful. A godsend. I don't know how I'd live without him. But the truth' – here he stepped closer to me – 'and this, I trust, will remain between us, is that I'm not sure how long I'll be staying on at Hudson. Certainly long enough to see the books I cherish through to publication – my beloved Baylor, for instance. Only I've been writing myself quite a bit lately . . . a novel . . . Your friend Liza's mother's just sold it to Knopf, on the basis of half the manuscript.'

'Really,' I said, recalling with amazement the constipated stories I'd read in the university library. 'That's wonderful. Congratulations.'

'Well, I suppose. But you see, I'm not sure how I'm to manage it, the triple duty I now face, teaching my beloved ones, and my work at Hudson, and writing. Of course there are more hours in the day than one thinks at first. Still, at a certain point a man must choose his weapons. Two out of the three, perhaps . . . and speaking of teaching, I trust I'll be receiving a submission sometime soon from you for my seminar?'

'Yes,' I said, though privately I wondered whether taking Flint's seminar – that is, should I even be admitted to it – would really do me much good. For what I craved at that moment, more than anything, was freedom from all those judges in whom I had invested the power to bestow upon me a title I could really only bestow upon myself. Just as a few months earlier I'd grown weary of the magazine with its sometimes old-maidish likes and dislikes, now the idea of once again having to submit to Flint's tirades and blandishments, no matter how justified, wearied me, as it were, in advance.

'When's the deadline for submission?'

'January fifteenth – which gives you a little time. But please' – he lifted his hands into the air – 'nothing from that unspeakable manuscript you showed me on your last day at Hudson, which I trust you've disposed of! Something fresh, something worthy of your talent, my boy!' And he patted me on the back, hard. 'Well, I must go. Work – writing – awaits. I should never have let Marge convince me to come to this horrible party, such activities are a waste of time. You shouldn't be here either. Be well. Stay in touch.'

Waving grandly, he turned away from me. The crowd swallowed him up.

Suddenly Janet was at my side again. 'Stanley Flint,' she said. 'Wow. The very name makes my hands shake.'

'I didn't realize that old lady was Nora Foy.'

'Of course. She's been a client of Sada's forever. Oh, look, Liza's free again.' Janet pointed across the room to where Liza, pulling at her earlobe, was walking toward us.

'Sorry about that,' Liza said. 'I can't bear the way my mother's always forcing Nora down my throat. I had to pretend I was sick in order to get away.'

'What's wrong with her?'

'Long story. By the way, Janet, Nora says she's very interested to hear about your study. Why don't you go and talk to her?' And she pushed Janet in Nora's direction. 'Janet's sweet,' she added to me, having first verified that the missile had hit the desired target, 'but she can be so *boring*. Oh look, there's Sam Stallings. Wouldn't you like to meet him?'

Without waiting for a reply she pulled me away, toward the edge of the room, where a short young man in a sleek khaki suit and black T-shirt was standing at the center of a crowd. He wore on his face an expression of glib self-satisfaction that on reflection I realized I might too have worn, had a novel for which I had been paid two hundred thousand dollars just entered the bestseller list at number nine. I couldn't pretend I didn't recognize him, for I had studied his picture carefully at the bookstore, and though the reddish pockmarks that blemished his face – residue, no doubt, of teenage acne – had not been visible in it, at the same time it had not, as pictures so often do, falsified his good looks. (A few years later I would learn this lesson myself, when during my own brief moment of fame a young movie producer who had summoned me to his office to 'take a meeting' looked at me quizzically upon my arrival. 'But in your picture you look like the young Rupert Brooke,' he complained. 'You don't look anything like Rupert Brooke.')

To be fair, Sam Stallings, whose photo had made me think of Emilio Estevez, didn't look anything like that beau ideal either, though I wasn't about to write him off as a consequence. He had his own distinct appeal. By his side a thin girl in a satin sheath – a model, I would later learn – smoked a Virginia Slim and stared with ennui at the crowd, which, not being her own, offered her nothing. Later that evening I would learn from a profile of Sam in *New York* magazine that though he was only thirty, he already had two ex-wives. When asked what he wanted to do next, he'd answered, 'I'd like to direct.'

Liza introduced us. 'Oh, Bauman,' Sam said, shaking my hand so firmly I almost yelped. 'Yeah, I read that story of yours in the magazine. It was good. Really interesting.'

The subtle implications of the adjective 'interesting' – chosen on this occasion, I suspected, in order to make it clear that to Sam the very *idea* of homosexuality was as alien, say, as the Hindu practice of drinking cow urine – did not fail to have the desired effect on me. I grinned at him dumbly. 'Thanks,' I said. 'I'm afraid I haven't read your book yet, though I'm eager to.'

'Sam,' the model whispered, interposing herself.

'Oh, Liza, this is Amber. Amber, Liza. And Martin.'

Amber blew out smoke. 'Hi,' she said. 'Sorry, my boyfriend's really rude. He never introduces me to anybody.'

'I like your suit, Sam.'

'Oh, thanks. There's an interesting story behind this suit. It was a gift, if you can believe it or not, from Gianni Versace.'

'Versace loved his book, isn't that cool?' said Amber. 'You know it was published in Italy even before it came out here. We went over, and Sam was really the toast of Milan. They even lent him a Ferrari.'

'Really.'

'And then one day, I'm sitting in my suite, exhausted after, like, thirty interviews, opening a bottle of Brunello with Amber, when there's a knock on the door, and the bellhop brings in this box containing five Versace suits!'

'Who's your Italian publisher?' Liza asked enviously.

'Oh shit, there's my agent,' said Sam, who, though a Mississippian by birth (I had learned this from his book jacket), had long since mastered the New York art of getting swiftly out of a conversation. For there were hundreds of people at the party, and he wanted to preen before every last one of them. 'I'd better run,' he told Liza. 'Good seeing you. And Martin' – to my surprise, he winked – 'a true pleasure, buddy. Let's do lunch sometime. Come on, sweetheart.'

'Bye,' Amber said, grinding her cigarette butt into the Aubusson.

They strode away. 'You know who Amber reminds me of?' I said, turning to Liza, only to discover that she was gone. In her place an immensely fat and overrouged woman, eating a piece of cake, was grinning at me.

'No, who?' asked this woman, who must have thought herself very witty.

'Oops, sorry, I thought you were someone else,' I said – and hurried off in search of Liza. It turned out that one of those mysterious undertows that flow through parties had simply carried her off while I was gazing after Sam Stallings, so that now she stood near the periphery, in huddled conversation with a woman whose bleached-blond hair reminded me of Rocky's in *The Rocky Horror Picture Show*. I looked for Janet, but she was still embroiled with Nora Foy. ('People live too long,' Nora was saying in her loud voice.) Which meant that I was not only alone, but, I feared, conspicuous in my solitude, and on the theory that at least if I held a drink in my hand I'd *look* as if I had a reason to be at the party, I walked to the bar and got in line.

I had been waiting only a few seconds when someone tapped me on the shoulder. I turned. The young man in the purple jacket, the one for whom Sada had forsaken her daughter, now glared at me. 'Excuse me,' he said, 'but I couldn't help overhearing someone call you Martin Bauman. Are you *the* Martin Bauman?'

This locution rather stunned me. 'I don't know,' I said. 'Which one is *the* Martin Bauman?'

'Well, naturally, the one who wrote that great story in the magazine.'

'Oh, that one. Yes, I guess so.'

The young man clapped his hands together with childish delight. 'Oh, I can't believe it!' he cried. 'You don't know how incredible this is. That story – it was the story of my life. Roy!' – at the sound of which name, a handsome young black man disengaged himself from one of the atolls and approached. 'You're not going to believe it. This is Martin Bauman.'

'Really!' Roy held out his hand demurely. 'Congratulations! That was some story.'

'Thanks.'

'Forgive me if I sound like a raving fan,' his purple-clad friend continued. 'It's just – you don't know the lengths I went to, when the story was published, trying to find out who you were. And now you're *here*. So let me ask: who *are* you?'

I stammered. 'I'm not sure—'

'That's a very rude question, Kendall,' said Roy, clearly the more even-keeled of the two. 'Didn't your mother teach you manners? You're supposed to introduce yourself and offer the girl a drink *before* you pounce on her.'

'Oops, sorry. I'm Kendall Philips. I work at *House and Garden*. And this is my friend Roy Beckett, from the *Times* – publishing division.'

'Pleased to meet you,' Roy Beckett said. 'The fact is, if we both sound surprised, it's because we figured you'd be older. How young are you?'

'Twenty-two.'

'Twenty-two,' Kendall repeated, shaking his head as if in disbelief. 'Oh, baby. Look, there's Henry. Henry!' He waved his arms as if signaling a car to stop.

A stalklike man in his late forties now approached. 'Henry, you're going to die,' Kendall said. 'This is – ta-da – Martin Bauman.'

'Oh, what a delight!' said Henry. 'You know we've all been crazy with curiosity to meet you. All us gay writers, I mean. I'm Henry Deane.'

I shook his hand. Here was another name I'd heard, another writer whose books I should have read but hadn't.

The woman with the bleached-blond hair, to whom Liza had been talking, was the next to near. 'Hello, Henry,' she said. 'Isn't it marvelous about Sam's book making the best-seller list?'

I have never warmed to being told what to think is marvelous; neither, apparently, did Henry, who, ignoring this nonquestion, said, 'Oh hi, darling. Billie, you'll never believe it, I didn't believe he really existed, to tell the truth, but this is Martin Bauman.'

'Oh, the famous Martin Bauman,' Billie said, fixing her gaze not on my face but the staircase, up which, for all we knew, someone really important might at that very moment come reeling.

'I didn't know I was famous,' I said, when what I should have said – more honestly if less modestly – was 'I didn't know I was famous until tonight.'

I date from that party the beginning of an intimacy the sediment of which, despite its comparatively short duration – it lasted only a few years, until Liza's marriage to Ben Pollack estranged her from Eli, from whom I was soon after to be estranged myself – I can taste on my lips even today, years later, it is the flavor of the sugary batter left over in the bowl after a cake has been mixed – and that is exactly the sort of metaphor at which Liza excelled. For in memory taste, like sound, lasts longer than sight, which is why Liza's voice – charming, querulous, a chalky blue color (if voices have colors) – can be dictating these words to me today, even though I haven't heard it for more than a decade. As for her face, it is more or less lost to me: not surprising, given that since her wedding I've only seen her only once, from a distance. She was standing on the corner of East 64th Street and Second Avenue, the same shapeless purse slung over her shoulder that she'd been carrying the night of Sam Stallings's party, and dressed, despite the upheavals that had marked the intervening years – her marriage, my breakup with Eli, the birth of her child and deaths of our mothers – in exactly the same sort of vaguely masculine outfit about which Sada had always remonstrated. Then I wondered at the passage of time, which wears away the outer layers of experience while leaving the essential self intact. I didn't say hello, though. There was too much to explain, and as it stood, I was already late for an appointment.

It had been over the course of the week immediately following Sam Stallings's party – a week during which we talked or saw each other almost every day, until I had to fly back to Washington for the Christmas holidays – that my friendship with Liza, as well as my knowledge of her, really cemented. Most of our conversations took place over the telephone. Liza, who had a terror of solitude, more or less lived on the phone. Whether in New York or Minnesota, alone or with a lover, she never began her mornings without first making a call from bed – as I mentioned earlier, either to Eli, or a boy called Ethan, or in the absence of these two reliable confreres, as was the case that Christmas break, when Eli was bicycling in the south of France with his parents and sisters, and Ethan had gone off to visit a white Russian princess in Venice, someone else, some new discovery, in this instance myself.

The first call came the morning after the party, when in the stillness of my apartment – Will having already gone to the gym, and Dennis being asleep – Liza's voice provided a welcome interruption. 'Did I wake you?' she asked – which she had. Nonetheless I pretended to have been up for hours.

'Me, I'm still in bed,' Liza said. 'You can probably hear it in my voice, I'm still rubbing the sleep out of my eyes. Incidentally, isn't that a funny euphemism, calling the stuff that forms in the corners of your eyes "sleep"? I wonder where it comes from?'

I agreed that it was funny – such seemingly random asides, I would soon learn, were typical of Liza – then asked her if she'd enjoyed the party.

'Enough,' she said, 'but you know how it is with parties, there are so many people, and you run around so frantically trying to say hello to all of them, and in the end you come away hyperventilating and feeling as if you haven't talked to anyone at all.'

'That's true.'

'You were certainly a hit, though. Especially with Henry Deane. I'll bet you weren't expecting to get so much attention,' she added – a little jealously, I thought.

'Not really.'

'Well, if you want my opinion, you ought to strike while the iron's hot, put out a collection – oh, and of course follow it immediately with a novel. You are working on a novel, aren't you?'

I said that I was.

'Great. What's it called?'

'*The Terrorist.*'

'Nice title. What's it about?'

I explained to her. She listened carefully, though also with a slight edge of impatience – a lot of uh-huhs, and mmms – as if trying to hurry me along to the point at which politeness would require me to turn the question around and ask it of her.

'And what are *you* working on? Also a novel?'

'Mmm. I've never been much interested in short stories. For the moment – this is tentative, a working title – I'm calling it *The Island of Misfit Toys.*'

'You mean as in *Rudolph the Red-Nosed Reindeer*?'

'Yes, yes!' Liza cried gleefully. 'I'm so happy you recognize the allusion! Of course,' she added, her voice taking on an unexpected gravity, 'a lot of people think it's outrageous to call a novel *The Island of Misfit Toys*. Radical. But I think it's brave when serious literature takes on popular culture, don't you? Also, I love the Island of Misfit Toys. Remember the choochoo train with the square wheels?'

'And that doll. I never could figure out what the doll was doing there. She didn't have anything wrong with her.'

'Yes, yes! That's the point – the idea of *feeling* there's something wrong with you, when at least outwardly there isn't.'

'Is that what your novel's about?'

'Sort of. It's about a girl who suddenly develops a lesbian crush on her friend.'

Her voice grew a little pinched as she said this, as if she'd been worrying how I might react.

'That's a great idea. Very dramatic.'

'I only wish my mother felt the same way. But what she says that if I publish this book, it'll ruin my career.'

'Why?'

'Because when people read the novel, they'll assume I'm a lesbian and pigeonhole me as a *lesbian writer.* And I just don't see why that should be the case, do you? I mean, if you were to read a book about a woman who falls in love with another woman, would *you* assume the writer was a lesbian?'

'Yes, as a matter of fact.'

Liza squealed, sort of. 'But why?' she cried. 'I mean, couldn't the writer just be writing the book because she thought the subject was interesting?'

'Possibly, but that's not what you were asking me,' I said. 'You were asking me if people would *assume*, from reading the book, that the writer was a lesbian, and what I'm saying is that given the way the world is, people probably will.'

'But that's so stupid! And anyway, the book's in the third person. Originally it was in the first person. Then I changed it to third person. Now a lot of it's from the point of view of the heroine's boyfriend. Don't you think that should make a difference?'

'I don't see why it matters,' I said boldly, 'if people think you're a lesbian.'

'I know, I know. Eli says the same thing.'

'I mean, everyone at that party – Sam Stallings, for instance – took it as a given that *I* was gay. And my feeling is, so what? I am.'

'But that's the problem!' Liza said, her voice tinny with exasperation. 'I'm not – or rather, I'm not only. Oh, this kind of thing must really be so much easier for men! I mean, if you're a man, from what I gather, it's just a matter of, you either like to whack off looking at pictures of naked girls, which means you're straight, or you like to whack off looking at pictures of naked boys, which means you're gay. But with women it's never so simple. In my case, for instance, I've dated both men *and* women. As a matter of fact I'm dating a woman right now. But that doesn't mean I'm making a lifetime commitment to being a *lesbian*.' I heard her frown. 'What I don't understand is why people have to give everything a label. Because once you're labeled a lesbian, it's like, that's the end of it, you can never get married and have children, which I fully intend to do.'

'But lesbians do have children. Lesbians do get married.'

'Oh, please! Have you ever been to a lesbian wedding? Eli and I went to one last year, it was horrible. Both the "brides" wore tuxedos. Also, even though they registered, none of their relatives bothered to buy them any decent presents. Excuse me, I'm walking to the kitchen right now . . . I have a cordless phone . . . I'm getting a Diet Coke.' Suddenly her voice lowered. 'Hold on a sec. Hi, Mom.' There was a noise of muffling. 'Sorry about that,' she went on a moment later. 'I'm back in my room now.'

'You're staying with your mother?'

'My apartment's sublet until the spring, so I don't have any choice. It's horrible. There.' She pulled – I could hear it – the pop top off the Diet Coke. 'Anyway, as I suppose you've figured out, I'm pretty unresolved about this lesbian thing. All my friends tease me about it, this whole drama of, is Liza a lesbian this week, or isn't she? "The great debate," Eli calls it.'

I was already beginning to suspect that if Liza spent as much time discussing her sexual indecision with her friends as she had with me, whom she hardly knew, it was at least in part to ensure the centrality of 'the great debate' in their (our) conversations. Not that her suffering wasn't real: on the contrary, as I learned over the course of the next several days, ever since she had made the mistake, in high school, of confessing to Sada her love for her best friend, Kelly, her mother had been waging a vigorous campaign to stop her from making what she insisted would be the biggest mistake of her life. For Sada, despite the dismal state into which her own marriage had declined (she and her husband had not lived together for almost twenty years), remained for murky reasons the staunchest advocate of heterosexual monogamy on the planet; indeed, her enthusiasm for the ideal of coupledom seemed to have increased exponentially as the condition of her own union had degenerated, which meant that despite her professed feminism, she often found herself at odds with certain literary friends from whom her 'conservative' positions alienated her. In this way she prefigured some other feminists who in subsequent years would enter into a marriage of convenience with the Christian right, with which they shared nothing save the common goal of wanting to criminalize pornography.

'By the way,' I said to Liza during one of our telephone conversations, 'you never explained to me why it was that talking to Nora Foy upset you so much at the party.'

'Oh, it's not Nora herself,' Liza said. 'Nora's all right. It's just that my mother's always pushing her at me because she wants to rub in my face what it's like growing up to be an old lesbian.'

'I didn't know Nora Foy was a lesbian.'

'Of course. And my mother says that if I don't mend my ways, I'll end up just like her – miserable and alone and living in squalor with forty-seven cats.'

'But, Liza,' the gay-straight rap leader in me said, 'there are also thousands of lesbians who've made happy and successful lives for themselves, with other women.'

'I know. Eli tells me the same thing.'

'As well as thousands of women who fought their natural impulses and ended up in loveless marriages.'

'Eli says that too. You're a lot alike, you and Eli. I should introduce you. But for the moment it's a moot point, because as it stands starting in January I'm trapped again in Babcock, where there isn't a lesbian for miles around, and Jessica' – this was the woman, a ceramist, whom Liza was currently dating – 'she's here in New York. Confidentially, though, I've started seeing a man at school. On the side. Nothing serious, it's just to amuse myself. His name's Arthur – Art – and he teaches history. He has a really big penis. Do you like that? I find it hurts.'

'Well—'

'I do like men, you know. I'm not some man-hating bull dyke. I enjoy sex with them. And anyway, even if my going out with Art does please my mother, that's hardly relevant, because as it stands she couldn't be more unhappy with me on account of Jessica. I don't know why I'm telling you all this,' she concluded. 'I hardly know you. Yet somehow I feel as if we've been friends our whole lives. Isn't it funny the way that happens?'

I had to agree that it was funny, especially because I felt the same way – this despite those bursts of hysteria and hypocrisy that so infuriated me in Liza. For it was true that even after just a few days, our bond already seemed better established, more vesseled with intimacy, than many others I had shared for a much longer duration, so much so that sometimes it was hard to believe we hadn't actually sat together at that children's table of our childhood. There is no quicker shortcut to intimacy than the discovery of common ground, of which Liza and I had acres; what we didn't realize – what we wouldn't realize until we were older – was that it is upon the method by which that ground is cultivated, not the soil itself, that intimacy in the long run depends.

In any case, it became quickly evident that among the many things Liza and I shared was a whole vocabulary of nostalgia, the common grammar of the suburbs – in particular the television programs we'd watched – having made it possible for this New Jersey girl and this Washington boy, without ever meeting, to have what was in essence the same childhood. Eli was different. Though he'd also grown up in the suburbs, he'd disdained them in a way we hadn't, devoting his attentions not to TV, but to the reading of Shakespeare and violin lessons. Every Sunday he'd ridden the train into the city, where he'd wandered the corridors of the Metropolitan Museum of Art, searching for his soul mate. The *fin de siècle* was his ideal, the world into which he bemoaned not having been born, with the result that even as Liza and I, at the age of twelve, were both preparing 'cut-glass dessert,' following the recipe from the *Joys of Jell-O* cookbook, Eli, in his own mother's kitchen, was making *boeuf en gelée*, having read somewhere that it was a favorite dish of Oscar Wilde's. Eli, in other words, was an intellectual snob, whereas Liza and I were snobs of a different and perhaps more insidious order, the sort who grow defensive in the company of those for whom the love of serious art has rendered the unrefined flavors of popular culture unpalatable. Yet this is a natural process, in much the same way that it is natural to discover that the SpaghettiOs with sliced franks you loved as a child no longer seem quite so delicious after you have grown up and gone to eat *trenette al pesto* in a harborfront Ligurian trattoria.

In the end, I suppose you could say that Liza and I were voluptuaries of the SpaghettiO, epicures of *Room 222*, connoisseurs of *Airport 1975*, the entire cast of which – Karen Black, Helen Reddy, Linda Blair, Sid Caesar, Gloria Swanson (playing herself), and so on – both of us could recite from memory. Thus at dinner with Liza and Janet Klass, I could mention àpropos of nothing a band I remembered having seen once on *The Gong Show,* four geeky youths dressed in white gowns and pulling around IV poles while they sang, 'Hospital, hospital, like it, like it.'

'But wait, wait! I remember that too!' Liza had shouted, thrusting her hand into the air like a child overeager to answer a teacher's question. 'They were a sort of precursor of Devo. And Jaye P. Morgan gonged them!'

Television – a dubious heritage, to say the least – was the lodestar of our friendship. Our knowledge of its arcana amazed Janet, who had grown up in a more rarefied atmosphere, where TV was strictly banned. 'You guys are incredible,' she'd tell us. 'I never saw any of those programs, I was too busy reading *Little House on the Prairie.*' And yet the surprise, in my case as well as Liza's, was that we had read too: we had read *while* watching television.

The other topic of which Liza spoke obsessively was AIDS, over which, in those years, we both suffered even though we knew very little about it. AIDS had first come into my life several summers earlier, when, driving with my mother in her green MGB sports car (my mother disdained station wagons) to the inauguration of some enormous new super-market, I'd heard a voice on the radio speaking about 'gay cancer.' 'Purple lesions, previously seen only in elderly men of Mediterranean extraction,' the voice had said. 'Hopefully the disease has not spread outside the homosexual community.' My mother had chewed gum, kept driving. 'What's the world coming to,' she'd asked, 'when even on the radio people misuse "hopefully"' – my mother, ever the crossing guard of grammar, the layer-down of the 'lay' and 'lie' law, the wager of the one-woman war on the split infinitive.

This was in 1980, when no one knew anything about AIDS. By the end of 1982, when I met and befriended Liza, little had changed, except that the disease – no longer called GRID – was spreading fast. Our worry was blanketed in ignorance, fringed with denial. Nor, I suspect, would I have believed it if some prophet had told us that twenty years hence AIDS would still be with us, and that only the naive and demented would talk of a cure.

As for Liza, her distress was both exaggerated and to a certain degree touristic. It did not matter how many times I reminded her that so far at least, there existed only one proven case of female-to-female AIDS transmission. 'I know, I know,' she'd say, 'and yet what if – this is purely hypothetical – you have, say, a tiny cut on your finger, microscopic, and then you insert it, you know, into somebody? Couldn't you get it that way?'

'Theoretically, though the probability is almost nil.'

'A few weeks ago Eli told me that soon there's going to be a test available. He says that when it comes on the market we should all band together and refuse to take it, because if the government gets ahold of information like that, they'll start quarantining people, and from then on it'll only be a matter of time before we end up in concentration camps.' She frowned. 'I'm not sure, though. I mean, if there was a test, I think *I'd* take it, just to be on the safe side. Wouldn't you?'

'I don't see why you're so worked up,' I answered (carefully dodging the tricky question of my own attitude toward tests), 'since from what you've told me you don't have anything to worry about. And even if you did, would it really help to know you were positive for the virus, when clearly there's nothing anyone can do and you'll die anyway?'

'Oh, I'm so tired of this! Do we always have to talk about AIDS? Let's talk about something else,' Liza said, for she had the bad habit of forgetting, whenever a subject made her uncomfortable, that it was she who had brought it up.

'Okay. How's the famous Eli? Have you heard from him lately?'

'I got a postcard from Aix.' She sounded bored.

'He's a writer too, isn't he?'

'Well, yes. That is to say, he *writes*. He's never published a book.'

'And is he good?'

'Oh, not bad – but at the same time not what I'd call a *natural* writer, the way you and I are natural writers. For Eli it's more like he chose it instead of it choosing him, you know what I mean?'

I did. At the same time, I couldn't help but wonder whether Liza *wanted* to *keep* Eli from becoming a 'natural writer,' in which capacity he might have threatened her supremacy.

'Eli's an amazing person,' she continued, seemingly oblivious to the fact that she had just insulted him. 'The thing about him is that he's got this almost magical ability to make you feel cozy and safe in his company. He's a wonderful masseur. There's something very feminine about him. He's a sort of man-woman, really. You know when we lived together in college, we always slept in the same bed.'

'Really?'

'Yes. And it wasn't anything like sleeping with Arthur, who snores and flails. Instead Eli just sort of – shapes his body around yours. Also he's got this beautiful beard, but it's the sort of beard a woman would have, if women had beards. You could comb it with a Barbie comb.'

'You told me that the first time I met you.'

'Oh, did I?' Liza asked disingenuously, for as I soon learned, this was one of her favorite *mots* concerning Eli, whom it was in her interest to emasculate. Her mother, need-less to say, hated him; to Sada he was a demonic figure, forever beckoning her daughter with luscious apples to which she – merely the mother – could offer no alternative save the homey flavors, more wholesome if less delectable, of the domestic kitchen. For Liza was impressionable, and Eli, when he spoke of his own homosexuality, did so with the fervor of a rabbi and the charm of a mountebank.

Meanwhile, even as Liza disparaged Eli, she also depended on him. Thus she told me that though both of them had had lovers over the years, their friendship had always taken pri-ority over these mere affairs of the heart. I wondered whether I was supposed to interpret this as a warning, since in my typ-ical way, I was already looking upon my own love affair with Eli – whom I had not even met – as a *fait accompli*. And yet if this was the case, was Liza's intention to dissuade me, or simply to make sure I understood the parameters within which I could safely operate? So long as I respected her dom-inance, I suspected, so long as I gave wide berth to the primacy of *her* friendship with Eli, then she would be delighted to introduce me to him when she got back to New York in the spring. Yet if, on the other hand, what I sought was a relationship with Eli that might eclipse their own, I should look elsewhere, for it would never happen; not in a million years.

8

The Deviled-Egg Plate

THAT SPRING I finally met Barclay Eberhart, my new agent, with whom, until that time, I had communicated only by post. At first, based on his old-fashioned letterhead and signature, I'd assumed that Eberhart – whose clients were mostly obscure contributors to the magazine – would turn out to be a soft-spoken, elderly gentleman with fine white hair, in appearance rather resembling the learned professor whose advice Babar the Elephant seeks whenever he finds himself faced with a scientific or technological dilemma. Instead, however – as I discovered when I called him the first time to make a lunch appointment – Barclay, to judge from his (her) voice, was a woman – and not only that, but the same 'Billie' with the bleached-blond hair to whom Henry Deane had introduced me, and who had irked me by refusing to meet my eye. 'Fooled you,' she said when I went to meet her at her apartment. 'Barclay's a family name. I've been called Billie since I was a child. Come in.'

After giving me a brief tour of the flat – she did not yet have

an office, having then been in the business only a few years –
Billie took me out to lunch at Café des Artistes, which she
called her 'watering hole.' Here the waiter brought her an
ashtray and lighter almost as soon as we sat down. She
seemed anxious, which was not surprising, given the slightly
hostile caution I was broadcasting, having never forgotten
that initial bad impression she had made on me at Sam
Stallings's party; and yet context often influences actions more
than we would like to admit, with the result that the person
whom we find, in one setting, boorish or ill-tempered, can
reveal herself to be both charming and likable in another.
Certainly this was the case with Billie, who in her own words
'did horribly' at parties, yet was utterly winning one on one.
Nor could I deny the degree (of which I became conscious
only as the lunch progressed) to which I had made certain
assumptions about her character and intelligence based only
on her hair color, having inherited from my mother a set of
narrow prejudices, one of which held that a woman with
'loud hair' was necessarily 'L.C.' (low-class), whereas Billie
was not only decidedly 'H.C.' but the author herself of several
novels published in the late sixties and early seventies, all of
which, it turned out, my mother had checked out from the
library and read. 'They weren't very good, though,' Billie told
me, at lunch, 'which is why I became an agent. Because I
loved good writing, and if I couldn't produce it myself, I
decided, the next best thing I could do would be to sell it,
make writers I liked some decent money for a change.'

I was glad to hear it, just as I was glad to hear her dismiss
as 'idiotic bullshit' certain 'instant bestsellers' and 'review-
proof books' for which Hudson-Terrier and other publishers
had been recently paying vast sums of money. 'I mean, think
about it,' she said. 'You go to a bank, and say, "I represent the
estate of Grace Metalious—"'

'Who?' I interrupted.

'That's my point. She wrote *Peyton Place*. You go to the bank and say, "I represent the estate of Grace Metalious, and I want to borrow fifty thousand dollars," and the bank will laugh in your face. But if you say, "I represent the estate of Samuel Beckett, and I want to borrow fifty thousand dollars," the bank will say, "Write your own check."' She smiled aggressively. 'The problem with the direction publishing's going in is that publishers are always looking for the Grace Metaliouses, not the Samuel Becketts. And I'm changing that.'

Billie's integrity impressed me mostly because it was not merely anecdotal. For example, she told me she had recently sold to Simon and Schuster a work about the philosophical implications of animal training, written by a lady in her early eighties who had been on the staff of the magazine since the beginning of the Second World War, for the princely sum of seventy-five thousand dollars. On the other hand, just this morning she had refused to represent the author of what she called 'junky' historical novels that earned millions of dollars annually, because she could not abide his politics.

She was a peculiar admixture of enterprise, shyness, and principled gestures that sometimes worked against her own best interests. Sleek and muscular, with a supple complexion that seemed to belie her fifty-three years on this planet, and that was the envy of those among her colleagues who had endured all manner of plastic surgery in order to achieve a less convincing version of what for Billie was both natural and free, she came from a long line of New England bluebloods, a family the complex ramifications of which enwebbed several presidents and the author of *Gone With the Wind*, as well as Edith Atkinson, who was either Billie's third cousin or her cousin thrice-removed (she wasn't sure which). A protected girlhood distinguished only by an affair with a male teacher at boarding school had concluded, unsurprisingly, at Smith College, which she attended for two years before absconding to New York, where she joined Andy Warhol's circle and shared an apartment with Ultra Violet. It was during these years that she became, as she dispassionately put it, the 'junkie and drunk' she still was, though she had neither touched a glass of wine nor smoked a joint for almost ten years now. Finally, near the end of the sixties, she'd landed in a mental hospital, only to emerge from its protective barbarity a few years later, personality intact, at which point she married, had a girl child, now twelve, divorced, married again, and divorced again. All of which, she said, had worn her out so thoroughly that these days she preferred to lead a quieter life, devoting her energies exclusively to work and to the raising of the daughter – rarely to men, and never to drinking.

After lunch we went back to her apartment, where we sipped chamomile tea and got down to business. Having read my eight stories and the 150-odd pages I had written so far of *The Terrorist*, Billie told me, she felt fairly convinced that my work was ready to be sent out. Her game plan (if I approved it) was to seek for me a two-book contract, from a publisher on whom I could rely 'to keep your books in print for the rest of your life, and after.' She then handed me a list she had drawn up of houses and editors to whom she wanted to submit: Putnam, I read, Farrar, Straus and Giroux, Random House, Hudson-Terrier; at this last house, Billie added, she was thinking of showing the manuscript to Stanley Flint, whom she was sure was going to love it.

'Actually, I'd rather if you didn't give it to Stanley Flint,' I said, putting down the sheet.

Billie looked puzzled. 'Fine, if that's what you want,' she said. 'Only may I ask why?'

Because I didn't feel like telling her everything right then, I explained merely that Stanley Flint had once been my teacher, and that until recently I had worked at Hudson-Terrier as the slush reader. 'Enough said,' she replied, and crossed Flint's name off her list. 'Anyway, there's every possibility that Stanley won't be at Hudson for very much longer. You know Sada Perlman's just sold his first novel to Knopf for four hundred thousand dollars.'

'Four hundred thousand dollars!'

She nodded. 'I haven't read it yet. I'm told it's pretty dense. I think what they're banking on is his celebrity, his name. But who knows? Stanley's a genius, so the novel might be a masterpiece.'

By now it was May. Though a variety of activities had kept me busy since Christmas – most notably, my search for a new apartment, Dennis and Will having informed me on the same afternoon that they each intended to move out at the end of the summer – I still hadn't fallen in love. Moreover, with every week that passed in which I didn't fall in love, I found myself looking forward that much more eagerly to the day when Liza would come back and finally introduce me to Eli Aronson, on whom I had for rash and illogical reasons pinned my hopes.

Alas, this did not come to pass. For near the end of the month Liza, who had been offered last-minute residencies at both Yaddo and the MacDowell Colony, called to tell me that she had decided not to return to New York at all that summer, and instead to extend the sublet of her apartment until the beginning of September. (The fact that Jessica, the ceramist, was also going to be at Yaddo had no doubt influenced her decision.) This meant that if I wanted to meet Eli, I would either have to call him up myself – a frightening prospect – or wait until Liza reentrenched herself in the autumn.

I chose to take the latter course – a decision made easier by the fact that as summer began, and with it that annual exodus to the beach, I suddenly found myself the object of not one, but two amorous campaigns. First Kendall Philips, the editor at *House and Garden* who had introduced himself to me at Sam Stallings's party, started calling me on a regular basis and inviting me out on what appeared to be, from the way he conducted himself, 'dates.' This was bewildering only in that I wasn't really attracted to Kendall: I preferred his friend Roy, who, alas, showed not the slightest interest in me, being at the moment, at least according to Kendall, too furiously in love with a futures analyst on Wall Street even to notice anyone else. ('Roy's what we call a yarmulke queen,' Kendall explained. 'One of those black guys who only like arrogant Jewish boys.') Our three dates were uncomfortable occasions, mostly as a consequence of Kendall's refusal to take the hints I was always dropping that I didn't want to go to bed with him. His obduracy was all the more difficult to tolerate, in that it recalled my own behavior back when I was infatuated with Carey, and had ignored his signals of disinterest so will-fully. Now that the shoe was on the other foot, so to speak, I suddenly understood what a difficult position I'd put Carey in, and vowed to find some means of apologizing to him for what I now saw to have been a substantial error of taste as well as judgment.

In any case, this episode blew over – or perhaps I should say (more truthfully if less prettily) I stopped returning Kendall's phone calls – when one chilly evening at a Columbia dance a boy named Enrique Antonio Miguel Fernando Jiménez came up to me out of the blue and asked me to dance. This boy, as I learned, was twenty-four years old, lived with his parents in the Bronx, and was working at a branch of the Athlete's Foot in order to pay his way through City College, where he was studying drama. Ricky (or Tony, or Mike, or Nando; he moved among his many names as casually as certain people change their hair color) took such an instant liking to me that at first I found myself mistrusting his affection, which I assumed to have an ulterior motive; after all, in my experience so far, whenever people had claimed to want to kiss me or go to bed with me it had either been because they intended to steal my money (as had been the case with Joey) or because some demented fondness for my writing made them want to be able to say they'd slept with (even more than they wanted actually to sleep with) 'Martin Bauman, the author of such and such a story.' Yet it was, in fact, simply Martin Bauman whom Ricky really had asked to dance that night. Because he never read the magazine, he had no idea that I'd published a story there. Nor did he care much when I told him. Drama, he said, was his thing: Ibsen, Sondheim, Woody Allen (an odd trio, I thought). He looked at the magazine only for the cartoons.

I found him very attractive. Like Joey (whom I never again saw at one of those Columbia dances) he was both broad-shouldered and dark; like Roy he was bulky, even a little fat, with the sort of musculature that one acquires only through a lifetime of physical exertion, as opposed to that synthetic brawn – somehow too glossy and plasticized – that one piles on by means of weightlifting regimens and steroids (and that in so many cases seemed intended to provide an armature against AIDS); finally, like Stanley Flint, he had heavy hair and penetrating black eyes. I cannot tell you what a contrast he presented to the fixtures at that Columbia dance – for example, to Kendall himself, who had exercised the muscles in his upper body so much, and those in his lower body so little, that in the end, to borrow a memorable Henry Deane-ism, he was 'all man from the waist up, all woman from the waist down.' Genetics, on the other hand, had given Ricky a long torso, fleshy lips, and limbs strong enough to crush as well as to embrace. Like his manners, which were gentlemanly in the extreme, his face seemed to belong to a distant era, at once harsher and more courtly than ours, so that when he kissed me that night at the end of the slow dance – bright eyes shining, mint-smelling voice unctuous as he whispered, 'I could really go for you, Martin' – what I recalled were those brooding portraits of young noblemen, always in mail and codpiece, that Bronzino painted for the Medici court.

Afterward, at my apartment, we slept together. Unlike Will, who had made such a drama out of postponing the consummation of his love affair with Vincent, Ricky had no qualms about going to bed with someone on first meeting. Indeed, when (lying together on that couch that Faye had made into her bed) I stopped his hand on my fly, and asked, 'Don't you think it's too soon?' his answer was a simple and persuasive no. 'Why wait?' he reasoned. 'After all, if we don't do it tonight, we'll do it tomorrow night.'

He was right: we did it both nights. The second time he brought me flowers, and a little ring, made of colored glass, which I still have, and treasure more than either of the rings – one of jade, which providentially broke in half a year after we met, the other of silver – that Eli and I would exchange later on.

I have long believed that one can deduce more about a man's character from the attitude he brings to sex than any other mode of interaction. In my case, sex has always been a cerebral business, in which fetishistic props – those elements that lend to the act a quality, so to speak, of atmosphere – play at least as important a role as the person (or persons) I am with. Ricky, on the contrary, perceived sex as a purely physical – and purely *communicative* – pleasure. This meant, among other things, that he had no interest in pornography, which I hoarded. 'To me, making love just isn't a spectator sport,' he liked to say whenever I brought the subject up, thus employing one of those stock phrases with which – ashamed of his upbringing in a poor Hispanic neighborhood, by immigrant parents who barely spoke English – he was always peppering his conversation. Likewise he never wore underwear. 'What's the point?' he said. 'They only get in the way.' For he had no idea – and why should he have? – that probably as a consequence of some episode lost in the fog of memory (or the steam of a shower room) I attached great erotic importance to the pulling off of a man's underwear: a case, perhaps, of the wrapping paper mattering more than the gift. Now I suspect that if only I'd been brave enough to voice this desire, Ricky would have gladly acceded to it, for he was not prudish, and would have gone far to make me happy; and yet in those days fear of rebuke inhibited me far too often from speaking up. Instead, when I was with him as when I was alone, I resorted, in my mind, to highly specific fantasies by means of which I could be certain of arousing myself. Thus I would pretend that I was an athlete getting a massage from his coach, or that I was a grunt being punished by his sergeant at boot camp, assuming all the time that in doing so I was fooling Ricky, when in fact my closed eyes betrayed my absence, with the result that he got sad, for he knew that the pleasure I was experiencing was a private one.

But I have digressed, I see now, from the subject of love to that of sex, which is only a department of love. Ricky's conception of love was both simpler and more admirable than mine. That little ring – spontaneously offered, and none too costly – was its emblem. I think he never questioned love, which he perceived as an element both copious and free, upon which human circumstance sometimes acts as a pollutant or irritant. To me, on the other hand, love was the precious wand of sunlight that on rare days pierces the cloud cover of discord and strife under which all human dramas plays out, and to which as a child I had learned early to acclimate myself. In other words, I was (perhaps because of my upbringing) a congenital pessimist, whereas Ricky, for no good reason (and this made it all the more charming), had managed to retain not only his childish idealism, but the old-fashioned belief – no doubt Latin in nature – that loyalty is a virtue. Once he decided that he loved someone, he never strayed. Nor would he ever have tolerated my cheating on him, for jealousy is the one volatility a heart like his will allow itself. All that he asked in return for his malleability – his readiness, at any moment, to retune his needs in order to accommodate mine – was fidelity, which he saw as an easy enough thing to give. After all, sexual variety can have little allure (much less meaning) to one for whom pleasure comes as easily as breathing.

In retrospect, I wonder if I should have clung to him; and yet, if I am to be truthful, I must confess that his adoration – not to mention his tendency toward chivalrous self-sacrifice – annoyed me as much as it flattered me. This was in part because the very straightforwardness of Ricky's nature – which in the abstract I esteemed – also caused him to scorn the sort of tortured and analytical 'dissections' in which Liza and I took such satisfaction, and which were to him merely a waste of time. Because he felt no need for talk, he teased me about the hours I spent on the phone: the point of life was pleasure, he said, which he defined purely in terms of its own experiencing. Indeed, his only neurotic trait, no doubt derived from that perpetual wish to convince me that he was worldly, was his habit of filling his conversation with the stock phrases of which I have already given one example. Thus, if I were to mention my despair at knowing so few people with whom I could really talk about writing, he would reply, 'What am I, chopped liver?': an expression I found particularly galling not merely because it was so hackneyed, but because it called attention to my Jewishness, with which Ricky claimed to feel a great affinity on account of his fondness for Woody Allen, whom I loathed, yet at whose altar he presumed that I, being a Jew, must also worship. Here, as in so many volleys, he missed the target, and instead of persuading me that we were of the same milieu, only made me feel more acutely the distance that separated that apartment in the Bronx, full of incense smells and plaster saints from my book-littered room wherein, amid copies of the magazine and posters of the London Underground and the Paris Metro, his discarded pants, always carrying a faint whiff of Obsession for Men, appeared so out of place.

Yet there was a darker reason for my feeling that I could never make a life with Ricky, one that in those days I would scarcely have had the courage to articulate. It was this: he was the first man I had ever met who managed to embody both the dominant father figure by whom I longed to be ravaged, and the sweater-clad coeval by whose side I dreamed of reading *Middlemarch* on long winter nights. Such a fusion of traits, you might think, would have been the ideal after which I chased. Instead it frightened me. I'm not sure why this was. Perhaps I imagined that if I gave myself up to pleasure, as Ricky did, then my selfhood would slip away, as once a diamond of my mother's had slipped down the bathroom drain. Thus whenever he visited my apartment I always opened the windows after he left, in order to dissipate that odor of cologne and sweat – to me the very redolence of submission – in the wake of which I could not write.

That summer we 'saw' each other two or three times a week – I put quotation marks around the word 'saw' because my affair with Ricky constituted the only relationship I have ever had that I can fit under the traditional rubric of 'seeing someone' or 'dating.' Subsequently – and not only with Eli – my impatient need for instantaneous and total union led me to skip all intermediate stages and jump directly from first meeting to 'the deep, deep peace of the marriage bed'; only with Ricky did I experience that style of courtship – 'going steady' – toward which young people are supposed to lean. This was mostly his doing. Though he had no qualms about sleeping with me on the first date, in the long run, he said, he believed in 'taking things slowly,' not so much from a sense of caution as to maximize the pleasure he derived from process. It was the same with eating; while a desire for satiation compelled me to wolf down my dinners, Ricky savored each bite.

Also, because some scruple obliged him to wake every morning in his bed in the Bronx, even if it meant crossing Manhattan in the rain at four in the morning to catch a bus, he never spent the night with me. Probably some vestige of his Catholic education, with its emphasis on filial duty, underlay the obstinacy with which he enforced this rule, no matter how often I reminded him (nor could he deny it) that after all he was a grown man, whose parents had long since stopped believing he was in bed every night by eleven. For unreason can have its own peculiar logic. Thus each night, in spite of my vague pleas that he stay, Ricky would climb noiselessly out of my bed, dress in the dark, fumble for his watch and wallet. 'Don't go,' I'd call halfheartedly, at which point he would kiss me, whisper, 'Good night, baby,' tiptoe down the corridor (yet his tennis shoes, of which, thanks to his job, he had a dozen pairs, made the floor squeak), open and shut the door with great delicacy, so that it should not slam. There would be a sound of creaking that would resolve itself into the familiar click of the deadbolt, which meant that I was alone. I could get up, wash, brush my teeth. For despite protests to the contrary, I was always relieved when Ricky left, since in fact I had never once in my life spent a whole night in the same bed with someone else. Snobbery made me dread lest he should embarrass me in front of my roommates, while habit made me worry that if he did stay I would never get to sleep.

The truth was, despite my proclaimed longing for a great love, I had over the years grown rather inured to solitude, from which I even derived a certain consolation. Now I can trace the beginning of this process back to the Friday night during my sophomore year in high school when a girl named Kim Finnegan, a friend of all of my friends, gave a party and in a fit of teenage caprice made a drama of not sending me an invitation (because, of course, she had to have someone not to invite). My father was away; my mother, I seem to recall, was waiting for the result of some dire test. Lying in my sister's bed (for I liked to sleep, on weekends, in rooms other than my own), I listened to the thrum of the rain, and found in its very constancy a rhythm by which to construct my own solace; the knowledge that not far away my friends were enjoying themselves, perhaps at my expense, became itself a warmth against which I could nestle. Meanwhile I watched the little bar of light under the doorframe that meant my mother had not yet gone to bed. For hours it remained steady, as clear-edged as a gold ingot; then around two I heard her slippered feet in the corridor, the definitive flip of the switch, after which this bar of light – my touchstone, through that rainy night – disappeared and left me swimming in darkness.

I have mentioned that during that summer I was looking for an apartment: in late August, just before Dennis was scheduled to begin graduate school, and Will to move into the Lower East Side railroad flat he was to share with Vincent, I finally found one. This was, at last, the cabin in the sky of which I had so long dreamed, a studio nineteen stories up, with a view of both the Empire State Building and the Chrysler Building, and boasting a panoply of complicated gadgets installed by its former tenant, a gay electrician. Most prominent among these were an electrified Murphy bed that operated by remote control, and a venetian blind one could lower and raise using a garage door opener motor hidden beneath the window. Needless to say the presence of such low-tech gewgaws only added to the delight I took in my new home – the first in which I had ever lived alone – and to which, with Ricky's help, I moved, one humid afternoon, my few items of furniture (most of them made of unpainted plywood, purchased at a store in my neighborhood the sign for which – NUDE FURNITURE – made me think of strip joints) and many books. This turned out to be a fairly time-consuming procedure, since the new apartment was located far downtown from the tenement flat that Janet had passed on to me, in a building with a checkerboard and oak-paneled lobby, and that was named, as are so many in Greenwich Village, after one of the old Dutch masters.

At this point I became so involved in decorating the new apartment that in my frenzy to paint walls and purchase sheets, hang pictures and alphabetize novels, I almost forgot the fact that certain strange editors were at present reading my book of stories, which Billie had started, in her words, to 'shop around.' Or perhaps I should not say 'forgot,' since even in my delirium I called her twice a week. 'No news yet,' she always said. Even so I remained optimistic, for I liked my collection, at least one-eighth of which bore the magazine's seal of approval. In the end I had titled it *The Deviled-Egg Plate*, after a story about which I was shortly to have a fracas with my mother much greater in scope and longer-lasting than any my story in the magazine might have provoked. The problem was not that the story exposed a secret of mine, but one of hers: specifically, her early marriage, long before she had even met my father, to a handsome sailor who had subsequently abandoned her, and from which she had retained, for reasons never clearly articulated, all the original gifts, including the crystal plate for holding deviled eggs referred to in my title. What intrigued me was that my mother refused categorically ever to *use* this deviled-egg plate, which, at the same time, she would neither give away nor sell. Rather than ask her why this was, I decided to invent the reason for myself, and wrote the story – which probably made her at least as angry (the reason I invented bearing a startling similarity to the truth) as the fact that in doing so I was exposing to public scrutiny a matter that was 'none of my business.'

In any case, I did not have to wait long to get the news for which I was hoping. Indeed, only a few weeks after she'd sent the collection out, Billie, sounding surprised, called to tell me that an editor at ——— had made a 'low offer' for my two books. I asked her what low meant; she told me, and I whooped with joy, for I lived very cheaply in those days, and what she considered 'not nearly enough' was to me a windfall, in that it allowed me to quit my job at the bookstore.

After that I wasted no time in sharing my good fortune – rather boastfully, I am afraid – with those among my friends whom I thought it would either please or distress: to wit, Liza (whom I knew would tell Eli); Carey (whom I knew would tell Flint); Sara (whom I knew would tell Marge); and finally Anka, through whom I hoped the news would be quickly spread not only to Edith, but to those amorphous others whose views she represented, and who had rejected all but one of the stories in the collection. My hope was that, upon discovering that a major publisher had disagreed with their assessment of my stories (not to mention the half-finished novel), Flint and these others would be compelled to wonder whether they had made a mistake in dismissing me. And yet behind that hope there also sounded a vague echo of self-recrimination, the voice of Flint repeating the words 'ready to pounce on a sure thing,' as well as the nagging suspicion that in the end his opinion counted more than that of a publisher whose interests were essentially commercial.

The other person I told was Ricky, who alone among these acquaintances greeted the news with unalloyed delight, and even insisted on taking me out to dinner to celebrate. I balked – after all, I was the one who had just made some money, whereas he had only his income from the shoe store with which to support himself, help out (I suspected) his family, and pay his tuition. Nonetheless he was adamant. He would take me to Windows on the World, he said, on top of the World Trade Center.

The next night, more than a hundred stories up, Ricky ordered a bottle of champagne. To mark the occasion, he had put on a special outfit: a rayon jacket that shimmered from green to brown, depending on the light, and a melon-colored shirt, open at the throat to show off the gold chain that seemed to draw luminescence from his chest as pearls are said to derive their glow from the heat of a woman's skin. He had bought me another present – a silver-plated bookmark, from Tiffany's, inscribed to 'M.B. from E.A.M.F.J.' – and though I thanked him profusely, and even felt myself on the verge of tears, my embarrassment must have shown through: I, who was so unused to receiving presents, had so far bought him nothing.

The champagne arrived. 'To you,' he toasted, lifting his glass. 'And to me. I've got good news too.'

'Really? What?'

'I didn't want to say anything until it was official, but I've been cast as Mitch in *Streetcar*. Not an official drama department production or anything – just something some kids are doing on their own. We've got to keep it under wraps because we can't afford to pay the rights. Still, I'm happy.'

'Congratulations, Rick,' I said, simultaneously marveling at this innocence that allowed him to equate our successes, and feeling my vanity wounded that he did not acknowledge the superiority of mine. (For this latter reaction – so unworthy of you, Ricky – I now apologize with all my heart.) Meanwhile he was studying the menu with an enthusiasm that touched me even as it irked me; for like his correlation of our victories, like his clothes, like the cologne in which he doused himself, his appetite for the sort of tasteless, fat-drenched dishes in which the restaurant specialized simply proved the width of the gulf that separated us. I really was more cultured than he was, I saw, which was why his pretensions annoyed me. And yet if this was true (and I couldn't pretend otherwise) it was only because one more generation separated me from my immigrant grandfather's shtetl than separated Ricky from the island life, at once pastoral and primitive, into which his own parents, five decades earlier, had been born.

The dinner progressed slowly. Because Ricky could sense my anxiety, which made me grasp for topics, he didn't talk much. He ordered a second bottle of champagne. *You drink too much*, I found myself thinking, not so much because his drinking in and of itself distressed me, or even came as a surprise to me, but because already I was looking for excuses to end our affair. For just as in college I had imagined that the person with whom I was destined to spend my life, when I met him, would instantly set off the Geiger counter in my heart, so now I subscribed to the even more bankrupt (yet convenient) theory that compatibility is merely a matter of shared predilections, and that only with someone who matches seven out of ten requirements on a checklist could one make a happy life. 'Nondrinker,' as it happened, was one of my ten requirements, as was 'good taste in clothes, food, etc.' Ricky did not make the grade on either count, and that evening I resolved, despite his kindness, to break with him.

It was shortly after this dinner that Liza, having finished up her residency at Yaddo, at last returned to New York, where she reclaimed her old apartment after a two-year sublet. This basement studio – a cave – was located three blocks away from Eli's sixth-floor walk-up. Indeed, Liza told me, Eli's apartment got so bright in the mornings that he kept sunglasses by the side of the bed; hers, on the other hand, was so dark that she had to have the lights on even on the sunniest of afternoons.

Almost as soon as she had settled in she told me that she wanted to fix me up on the long-promised (and long-postponed) blind date with Eli, her own romance with Jessica, with whom she had just spent a 'blissful' month at Yaddo, having reached a sufficient pitch of intensity (or so I surmised) to cause her to reconsider the pledge that she and Eli, though never in so many words, had implicitly made to each other, and according to which neither would ever allow a love affair to take precedence over their own, less definable bond. This meant that for the moment at least, it was in her interest for Eli to fall in love, since such a turn of events would both preclude any possibility of jealousy on his part, and allow the four of us (for some reason this prospect delighted her) to double-date.

But I, like Liza, am jumping ahead of things. At the moment I still haven't met Eli, though I have spoken to him – once – on the phone. Having been given his number by Liza, who assured me that he had seen my picture, thought me 'cute,' and was definitely 'looking,' I called him up one afternoon to make a date. To my surprise a woman answered. 'May I speak to Eli?' I asked.

'This is he,' the woman said, her voice suddenly going gruff – for Eli, it turned out, though a baritone, had a voice like Lotte Lenya's over the phone, which meant that whenever he received a call from someone selling newspaper subscriptions or trying to convince him to vote for a particular candidate for the city council, it was always as 'Mrs Aronson' (or later 'Mrs Bauman') that he was greeted.

Not wanting to embarrass him, I glossed over my mistake, which in any case I had no reason to think he'd noticed. 'This is Martin Bauman,' I said. 'Liza's friend.'

'Oh, Martin Bauman. I've been wondering when you'd call.'

We talked for a few minutes. Eli told me that he lived on Elizabeth Street, near Little Italy, only a few minutes from my apartment by taxi. Accordingly I suggested we have dinner together some evening. 'Great,' he said, 'why not tonight?' – which surprised me only in that I had expected him to say (as New Yorkers so often do) 'Let me check my book . . . Yes, I'm free a week from Wednesday.' This urban habit of planning everything ahead, I have always believed, endures chiefly because it provides such an easy means of proving to other people how much busier and fuller one's life is than theirs. Liza indulged in it all the time, as did I, sometimes even going so far as to pretend to have dates on nights when none existed simply in order not to be thought 'out of the swim.' Eli's impulsiveness, on the contrary, suggested either that, like Ricky, he was unequal to tactics, or that in his eagerness to meet me he was perfectly willing to cancel another date. Either likelihood pleased me, and having nothing to do myself that night, I accepted his proposal in the spirit of spontaneity with which it had been made.

A few hours later, just as I was about to walk out the door, the telephone rang. Thinking it might be Eli, I hurried to pick it up.

It was Ricky. 'What are you doing?' he asked. 'Because I'm standing at a pay phone on your corner, feeling lustful.'

I lied. I told him an old friend of mine was back in town, and that I had to have dinner with her.

'Hey, no problem,' Ricky said. 'Tell you what, I'll call you tomorrow.'

'I'm sorry,' I added, and in trying to embellish my lie, no doubt only succeeded in calling attention to it. 'It's just that this friend of mine, I haven't seen her in months, and she's one of the only people I can really *talk* to, you know what I mean?'

'What am Í, chopped liver?' asked Ricky. 'Just kidding. Toodles. Big kiss.'

He hung up. Having taken stock of my appearance, I rode the elevator down to the lobby. Through the doors I checked to make sure Ricky wasn't still standing on the corner. Fortunately he was gone, probably to the subway. The thought of him alone in those dreary catacombs made me wistful for a moment, even made me wonder if, in betraying him, I was making a great mistake. And yet at this point I was well beyond imagining a life with Ricky. So I strolled southeast, toward Little Italy. At the address Eli had given me a modest stone building rose up, its fire escapes festooned with climbing roses, ivy, wisteria: lower Manhattan's answer to the hanging gardens of Babylon. I rang. 'Yes?' Eli's voice intoned through the intercom.

'It's Martin.'

He let me in. *Well, here goes*, I remember thinking, *my life*, for even then, somehow, I knew that Eli and I would go far together. Finally on the sixth floor, winded from the climb, I knocked on his door. 'Hello,' he said, opening it, 'I'm Eli.'

Hello, I'm Eli. How strange – especially from the perspective of so much time wasted and distance traversed – to contemplate the innocuous, even tedious words with which most marriages, by necessity, must begin! Accepting his proffered hand, I stepped into the apartment. He did not look anything like what I'd expected. In fact he never looked the same from one minute to the next. He was shape-shifting, mercurial. If you'd shown a stranger six photographs of him, taken on different days, probably the stranger would have sworn they were of six different people. A few years later, crossing back to West Berlin from East Berlin (the wall had not yet fallen), Eli was nearly arrested because he looked so unlike his passport picture. Nor did his tendency to worry his appearance – for example, to regrow his beard one month, then shave it off the next – do much to lend to his countenance that quality of permanence, of singularity, in which it was so lacking. Indeed, all I could have said about him – this man whom I even doubted I would recognize were I to see him on the street the following morning – was that he was about six feet tall, that he had a full head of thick, Semitic hair, and that he wore glasses. (Even here, however, there was variation, for he had several pairs among which he moved as casually as Ricky among his names.) Like Barb Mendenhall, Eli's eyes were deep and liquid, though of indefinite coloration: green-gold one day, blue, or even pale gray, the next. Finally, because he was wearing only running shorts and a T-shirt – a common enough outfit for him, and also one by means of which, I suspected, he hoped to make a good impression on me, for he was as proud of his body as he was ashamed of his face, which he thought ugly – I could tell that he had a well-formed, hairless (or did he shave?) weightlifter's chest.

We sat together on his futon sofa bed, behind which a massive wall of books spread out – comfortingly disordered, and featuring amid the masses of Wildeiana a small press paperback titled *Anal Pleasure and Health*, prominently displayed, for there was a touch of the provocateur in Eli. All told, his one room – a literal garret, with a high ceiling on which brown water stains bloomed, and a row of clattery windows that looked onto the street – had an aspect at once more intelligible and coherent than his own. A worn Oriental carpet covered the floor, which was of battered wood, splintering in places. Against the far wall, next to the surprisingly tiny desk at which, presumably, he wrote his novels that were not 'natural,' there stood an immense loft bed, installed to take advantage of the apartment's height. The walls were decorated with framed posters depicting Fra Angelico frescoes.

I relaxed instantly, and only in part thanks to the glass of white wine Eli had poured for me (and which, for once, I actually drank). There was something so comfortingly bohemian about that room, something so ordinary – *my* ordinary – about sitting there, talking lazily, as on so many nights I'd talked lazily with my friends in the room Jim Sterling and I had shared at the university, that in its beneficent atmosphere everything I'd found foreign and unfamiliar in Ricky slowly separated itself from him and stood out in relief. These were his attributes, which he might have offered as marks of identity, had he been the Renaissance nobleman in the Bronzino portrait to whom I had likened him. As for Eli, in his company a voice, perhaps his own, seemed to whisper, 'You are home': home in this room as musty as the used book-stores I'd once scoured with my brother in San Francisco, home amid these smells of wood and glue and paper, and of the lavender spilling its buds through an open window onto the corner of the futon, and the traffic that made the windows shiver, and the fresh rain. For Eli's apartment was, if not that very brownstone in which I'd dreamed of reposing side by side with Carey Finch in leather chairs, at least a place in which I could read. 'I'm a little drunk,' I said, as, leaning back against the bookshelf, I let my head droop against his shoulder.

'That's okay,' he answered. Nor did he flinch. I think he felt at home with me too.

That night we ate dinner at a restaurant the mad owner of which made only soup (but fifty-six varieties), before returning to his apartment, where he showed me pictures of himself as a little boy, and of his family. In one he was an eight-year-old in a football uniform. He did not have to tell me he hated football. I knew. I'd hated it too. Now I see that more than Eli himself, it was our common heritage – the fact I did not have to explain to him who Denton Welch was, just as he did not have to explain to me what a *kreplach* was – by which, that evening, I felt myself so seduced. And yet at the time I could not have made such subtle distinctions. I put too much trust in my emotions, which told me that I was happy, to bother parsing their grammar. More like Ricky than I realized, I simply felt.

Not that Eli and I came from exactly the same world; on the contrary, he had grown up in the realm of high finance. His father (whose name, like mine, was Martin, or Marty) worked in Great Neck, where his own father had founded a small brokerage firm; his mother, Harriet, was a housewife. *Marty*, *Harriet*, I repeated to myself, knowing that I would need to memorize these names, for they belonged to people who were going to be my in-laws; and then there were *Nadine* and *Sandra*, the sisters; Nadine's husband, *Brian*, a thug and (worse still) a 'goy'; and their children, *Abigail* and *Jonah*, over whose religious upbringing Harriet was currently engaged in warfare with her in-laws. At present, Eli told me, she was incensed because 'that woman,' after making promises to the contrary, had snuck Jonah off one Sunday morning and had him baptized. At Harriet's insistence, however, the boy had also been circumcised. There had been a *bris* – another word the meaning of which I would have had to explain to Ricky, who for all his chopped liver really knew nothing about Jewish life.

After a while Eli and I stopped talking. Switching off the lamp, he lit some candles, then removed my glasses (thinking of Joey, I couldn't help but flinch a little when he did it), and kissed me. His lips tasted like lip balm. In the absence of corrective lenses the candle flames seemed to multiply, until they were a choir of dancing genii from the Arabian nights, or the edging, at once hallucinatory and precise, of some Persian carpet. Yet this time the unexpected scream, that voice from nowhere that shouted 'Give me the fucking money!' – I could not hear it.

We undressed each other – to my relief, I found, he wore underwear – then climbed up into his loft bed, which was unmade, draped randomly with blankets from his childhood, old quilts he'd picked up at rummage sales, a down comforter through the seams of which tiny feathers now and then wafted. Climbing on top of him, I dug my fingers (on one of which, I realized distantly, I still wore Ricky's ring) into his chest. His penis was sleek, cigarillo-sized, with a scrotum that receded as tidily as a Murphy bed when he became aroused. At the tip the skin tautened where during his own *bris* an overeager rabbi, handling the knife for the first time, had cut too close. Mine, by comparison, was avid and clumsy: a slobbering dog.

For about an hour we had sex of a sort, albeit not very successfully; and yet this did not trouble me at the time, for my old fantasies of submission at the hands of a stern uncle were remote from Eli's loft. Anyway, the thing I wanted here was not sex at all, so much as that intimate cuddling that precedes or follows sex, and of which I recalled hearing jealously that Lars had partaken with his graduate student. Nor was there any question (as there had been with Ricky) of where I would spend the night: it went without saying.

As we lay there together, Eli's phone rang twice. First, through the answering machine, his mother spoke – something about a bar mitzvah gift she was going to buy on his behalf – then Liza, laughingly asking, 'Where *are* you? Call me as soon as you can! I can't wait to hear all about your *hot date*': words which, because they were not meant for my ears, made me laugh, and sent a subversive thrill down my spine.

Then Eli blew out the candle he'd carried up to the loft with him, put his arms around me, and whispered, 'Good night, Martin Bauman.' His body, as Liza had promised, curled around mine. He slept quietly, easily, his breath sweet in my ear, while I listened to the clattering of the old windows, the loud, almost gooselike shrieks of the street cleaners. And to my surprise – for I knew I was supposed to be happy – I found myself missing my own empty bed, as well as all those beds in which every night of my life I'd gone to sleep alone, and in the mornings woken up alone: a nostalgia that seemed to evaporate even as I breathed it in, like that early-winter snow that melts to raindrops the instant it touches the earth.

The next morning we got up early and strolled together to a coffee shop on Sheridan Square. It was unseasonably warm out; shirtless, dressed in running shorts and a black leather jacket that showed off to advantage the chest that was his best feature, Eli might have been a Village clone from the seventies, had the glasses he'd chosen, battered gold-rims with tape on the hinges, not paid such homage to his nineties fetish: John Addington Symonds, then, from the neck up, Tom of Finland from the neck down. He held my hand as we walked. Blushing, I kept looking over my shoulder to see if anyone was staring at us. No one was. In that part of New York two men holding hands was normal. Then at the coffee shop the sight of some uniformed policemen smoking and eating omelettes puzzled me – 'I thought policemen weren't supposed to go to restaurants on duty,' I said to Eli – until I saw that their badges read LAPD, not NYPD, and that both of them had tiny gold earrings in their right ears. Eli laughed; pressed his knee into my crotch. We ate eggs and toast without bacon – Eli was a vegetarian, while I feared offending the Jew in him with my gluttony for pork – and had the first of a thousand conversations about Liza. To my surprise, he spoke of his great friend both with malice and a formidable lack of discretion. For instance, when I asked him to describe the famous Jessica, whom I had never met, he told me that she was in her late thirties, an avid runner, and had been living for the last twenty years with Peggy, to whom she was, for all intents and purposes, married. 'Which means Liza's the other woman,' he concluded. 'And she can't stand it.'

'Liza didn't tell me that.'

'Of course not. She's ashamed of it.'

And did Liza love Jessica? I asked next. Was she, in his view, *really* a lesbian?

'To answer that question, all you have to do is take a walk with her. A handsome man and a beautiful woman walk by. Quick: which one does Liza stare at?'

I inquired how he and Liza had met. He told me that in college, in a seminar on Colonial American Literature, they had become friends because they felt so isolated from the other students, all preppy types in monogrammed sweaters. At that time both of them had roommates they loathed, so the next semester they moved off campus together into a tiny apartment. There was only one bed. Though they never had sex, they 'experimented' sometimes – not a problem for Eli, who according to the Kinsey scale was probably twenty percent heterosexual anyway. ('We were stoned at the time,' he added. 'We were usually stoned at the time.') During those years he also nursed Liza through any number of emotional crises, most of them revolving around her sexual indecision, as a consequence of which she was forever volleying between men and women. 'She's terribly selfish that way,' he explained. 'When she has a problem, she expects everyone else to drop whatever they're doing and run to help her. But when someone else has a problem, she just sort of yawns or turns on the television.'

Eli's other grievance against Liza had to do with her 'arrogance,' as a consequence of which she had no qualms about mentioning herself and Oscar Wilde in the same breath. This had became especially problematic during their senior year in college, when Eli was still struggling to get his stories into undergraduate literary magazines, and Liza had just sold her first novel. 'Don't get me wrong, I wasn't jealous,' he said. 'I loved her novel. Only she had this way of forgetting that I was a writer too. For instance, whenever she introduced me to anyone – her new editor, say – it was always as "my friend Eli," never "my friend Eli, who also happens to be a talented young writer." Even today it rankles me. Like, just before Christmas, there was this big party for Sam Stallings – you know, that guy who wrote *Rodeo Nights*? Well, Liza's mother (a nightmare, but that's another story) invited her to come and told her to bring a writer friend with her. So what does she do? She runs over to my apartment and says, "Who should I invite? Who should I invite?" as if it hadn't even occurred to her who was sitting there next to her. Your name was on the short list, incidentally.'

'It was?' I said, pretending surprise, not wanting to admit that in the end it had been I whom Liza had chosen.

After we finished breakfast, we walked to A Different Light, the gay bookstore, where Eli showed me a story of his in an anthology edited by Henry Deane. The story was called 'Ineptitude' and described a clumsy attempt on the part of two teenage boys – cousins – to fuck in a shed in the narrator's backyard. Eager to read it, I both bought the anthology and made a show, in front of the salesclerk, of asking for Eli's autograph, then walked him back to his apartment, where at the door, in full view of passersby, he kissed me on the mouth. Embarrassed – especially when an old woman strolled by with her dog – I pulled away. He stared at the ground.

'Well, it's been wonderful meeting you, Martin,' he said, and in a gesture of mock machismo, punched my arm.

'I hope you don't think I'm a prude, or that I'm ashamed,' I said falteringly. 'It's not that, it's just – I've never been very comfortable with public displays of affection. PDAs, my friend Kendall calls them.' I laughed stupidly.

'Don't worry.'

'I wouldn't want you to think—'

'I don't think anything. Good-bye.' He held out his hand.

'And what are your plans today?' I threw in, for now that he seemed annoyed with me, I could not bear the prospect of being parted from him.

'Oh, I don't know. Probably I'll write, call Liza back, go to the gym. Then tonight I teach.'

'Really? I didn't know you taught. Where do you teach?'

He named a technical school in Brooklyn, on the urban campus of which, two nights a week, he instructed a group of black and Hispanic secretaries in basic composition. Of this class and its students I would hear much in the coming weeks; for the moment, however, it was merely a source of anguish, a prior obligation by means of which he could achieve the swift breach with me that I felt certain, as a consequence of my rude response to his kiss, he now wanted to make.

At last it became clear that he was not going to invite me back up, and said good-bye. Returning to my apartment, I gazed at the pristine bed, which seemed to stare back at me rebukingly, like a mother whose very silence makes it far more obvious that she has been up all night worrying herself to death over her child's waywardness than could any words. Next I checked my answering machine, on which, unlike Eli's, I had not a single message. Then I switched on my computer, only to discover that I could hardly muster the concentration to finish a sentence, much less the chapter of *The Terrorist* on which I was at work. So I read Eli's story, which I liked, even though the exalted language he used when describing sex left me rather cold. I watched television. I also watched the phone, which did not ring until about five that afternoon.

'Hey big guy, what's going on?' Ricky asked when I picked it up.

I stiffened. In the wake of my night with Eli, I had almost entirely forgotten about Ricky. Nonetheless a sense of duty to this man who had been so decent now compelled me to suggest that we meet at a coffee bar near my apartment. I had something I wanted to talk to him about, I said.

'Fine, right,' Ricky answered, 'only wouldn't it be easier for me to come by your place?'

'No, I'd rather we talk at the coffee bar,' I stammered. Then – fearful that I might be causing him pain (though of course this would be unavoidable once we sat down) – I added for stupid comfort, 'I've been cooped up all day. I'd like to stretch my legs.'

'Hey, no problem. So when do you want to meet?'

'Is half an hour okay?'

'Be there or be square,' Ricky said. 'Only I may be late. I have to get across town.'

I said that was fine, that I would wait for him, and after brushing my teeth, left immediately for the coffee bar. He was already there when I walked in, an untouched slice of apple cake crumbling in front of him.

'I lied,' he said. 'I wasn't across town. I was across the street from your building.'

I sat down. During the walk from my apartment I'd been rehearsing what I was going to say, and now I launched into a monologue the very scale of which (not to mention its rhetorical excesses) Ricky must have found, to say the least, bewildering. I told him that the night before I had met the person with whom, I felt certain, I was destined to spend my life; that in light of this wholly unexpected (and unplanned) eventuality, we could obviously not go on 'seeing' each other as we had (though of course I hoped we would remain friends, eat lunches and dinners together, etc.); that I would always recall fondly the time we had spent together; that he was a wonderful person and must not think any of this had anything to do with him per se, for it did not; that, finally, I hoped he would forgive me.

To all of this Ricky listened raptly, his eyes wide, his lips curved into a smile different from the one with which he had greeted me, more like the smile I myself had often affected when, as a child, my mother had shared with me some piece of bad news (the death of a relation, for example), and I had found myself barely able to contain my laughter.

At length I shut up. He was quiet.

'Well?' I asked – as if he owed me a response.

He put his hands together and rested his chin on them. 'Actually, I've got to tell you,' he said, 'from your tone of voice on the phone, I was expecting something like this.'

'Really?'

'So I guess last night you weren't having dinner with an old friend after all, were you?'

'No.'

'I didn't think so – not even last night.'

Then he sighed once – loudly – and with that disarming naturalness that had marked, when we were together, his experience of pleasure, began to weep, noisily, indiscreetly, tears reddening his eyes and making tracks on his cheeks, for he was as artless in sorrow as in joy. I gave him my napkin. 'I'm sorry, man,' he said, noticing that the waitress and some of the other customers were staring at us, 'I'm just – it's just very emotional for me, that's all. I mean, I'm happy for you. I really hope you've found what you're looking for. And I'll always treasure these months we've had together, I'll always treasure these memories. I mean that.'

'Thank you. Do you want some water?'

He shook his head. He had stopped crying. 'I'm ready to talk now,' he said, and then for about twenty minutes, as if I owed it to him to listen (which I suppose I did), he spoke of what he called his 'happiest moments' with me – the greatest of these, according to him (and this surprised me) being our dinner at Windows on the World, the mere recollection of which, he said, would be enough, even forty years from now, to bring a smile to his face. Flustered by his outpourings of affection, I played, under the table, with the glass ring he had given me, and which the night before, with Eli, I had neglected to take off. Yet Ricky did not ask for it back, nor did I feel prepared to return it to him.

At last the bill arrived – Ricky would not be dissuaded from paying it – and we headed out together onto Greenwich Avenue. During our talk the sun had gone down. Standing between a pair of tailored yews, their needles bedecked with tiny lights that seemed to lend to our farewell a holiday atmosphere of nostalgia, regret, and glamour, we spoke of the weather, the imminence of winter, the inescapability of age. It was windy out. I pulled my collar tighter around my throat. 'I hope you don't mind if we don't prolong this,' Ricky said, affecting an actorish voice I had never heard him use before.

'No, of course not,' I answered.

'Okay, good. Well, good-bye.'

Turning away from me, he left. For a few moments I watched him moving into the dark, a lonely figure, head bent and shoulders clenched against the wind. I saw him only once more, a few years later, when on an equally windy night we quite literally bumped into each other on East End Avenue. Still handsome if a bit heavier (but weren't we all?) he told me that he had given up acting and was now a computer programmer; that he lived in a small apartment on 94th Street; that he had a boyfriend, Liam, who sang in the Met choir.

'And you?' he asked, as people always will on such occasions, before adding, a little sardonically, I thought, 'Still living with that great love of your life?'

I said that I was. I did not tell him that I was also more unhappy than I'd ever thought it possible to be. Checking his watch, he made a show of being surprised by the hour, explained apologetically that he had not realized what time it was; he was late to meet Liam for a movie; he hoped we'd run into each other again. Then he waved and was gone. In such ways, even at great distances from the wounding moment, revenge can be exacted. Nor did I bother wondering, as I might have once, whether with this man with whom I shared nothing I might have made less of a botch of things than I had with Eli, with whom I shared everything. For Eli was waiting for me, and I had to go; in an Indian restaurant eighty blocks downtown from this corner onto which I had just emerged after having hurried sex with a man named Lewis, a man who had picked me up an hour earlier at a porno bookstore, Eli, who hated to be kept waiting, was waiting, no doubt drumming his fingers against the table. I hailed a taxi, and tried to think up a convincing lie.

That night, when I got back to my apartment, I found a message on my answering machine. 'I'm just back from class,' Eli said, 'and I've been thinking about you. All day, as a matter of fact. Call me. Bye.'

I sat down at my desk. The message, which might have surprised me a few hours earlier (when I assumed Eli must hate me), did not now; indeed, at that instant it seemed natural that he should feel fondness toward me, because Ricky did, and who was to say that affection, like a sort of pollen, can't be carried on the breeze along sidewalks, even all the way to Elizabeth Street, where it might blow through Eli's open window and onto his futon?

I phoned him back. 'Are you coming over?' he asked, as if it were the most ordinary thing in the world. And I said that I was, that I would be there in twenty minutes. Before I left, though, I took the cassette out of the answering machine and stored it away in my desk drawer, as if it were a love letter I should someday nostalgically savor, and then, into the same desk drawer, because I didn't want to wear it anymore, but like my mother's deviled-egg plate I also couldn't bring myself to part with it, I put Ricky's ring.

9

Trial Marriage

THERE IS A joke – not a very good one – that I remember hearing a lot in those years, the mid-eighties. 'So this lesbian is having a drink with her straight friend,' the joke goes, 'and she says that the next day she and her lover are celebrating their fifth anniversary. "Well, I've been meaning to ask you," the friend says, "when you people talk about your anniversary, do you mean the anniversary of the day you met? Of the first time you slept together? Of the day you moved in together?" And the lesbian says, "Yes."'

Much can be deduced, from this joke, about the speed with which Eli and I, in the weeks following our long-postponed meeting, moved from blind date to what he was calling, even on the second night, 'trial marriage.' Honorary lesbians, as Liza put it, beginning on the evening that we had dinner at the restaurant with fifty-six kinds of soup, neither of us slept alone for a year. Instead we spent every night together, usually at his apartment. This was my choice. Unlike me, Eli knew how to make a place feel like a home.

Nor were we apart much during the day; only when he went to the gym, or his yoga class, or choir practice – activities to which I would have also gladly accompanied him had not some scruple about making a nuisance of myself checked my enthusiasm.

Some afternoons I brought my computer over to his garret, where I set it up on the dining table and wrote while he wrote, deriving comfort from the parallel clatter of his own computer even as (though he told me this only much later, and in anger) the comparative speed and recklessness with which I worked affronted that part of him that valued caution, steadiness, what he saw as a nineteenth-century literary prudence. On the evenings when he taught I accompanied him to his school (which, occupying three floors of a tired office building in downtown Brooklyn, hardly conformed to any previous notion I held of a school), then waited in the cafeteria until he'd finished. Yet even this was not enough for me. Indeed, in my need to gorge myself on intimacy with Eli, I would have been happy never to let him go, to hold onto him even while he was lecturing his students, even while he was sitting on the toilet. Now it was I who, when we went out together, grabbed *his* hand tightly, or slid my arm protectively around his shoulder, no matter who was looking.

To justify our impulsiveness in leaping so recklessly from first date into a condition closely resembling if not strictly adhering to the definition of matrimony, we often pretended to have known each other much longer than we had. For example, to my father's query 'When did you meet this guy?' (asked when I called to tell him I'd fallen in love and hoped to bring my new boyfriend home for Christmas), I answered, 'Six months ago.' In fact, it had been six days, yet so gravid with possibility had those six days seemed to me that I did not feel I was lying, only translating a rare experience into the language of ordinary human intercourse – just as, when considering the life of a dog, we must remember that one of his years equals seven of ours.

As for Liza, she greeted the news that Eli and I were 'together' with unqualified delight. Only a few days earlier Jessica had at last secured from her lover, Peggy, permission to move out of the apartment they shared and sublet a studio, which meant that now, in New York as at Yaddo, Liza could sleep with Jessica whenever she wanted. This unexpected change in circumstances unleashed a new intrepidity in her. Abandoning, for the moment, her waffling ways, she gave herself over fully to lesbianism, of which she spoke, for the first time in her life, without grief or worry. She even went so far as to throw out her skirts and to start wearing only a single earring in her left ear, though both of her ears were pierced; gestures which, though today they may not sound terribly subversive, counted for Liza – in whose war with her mother clothes were the primary ammunition – as the gravest insurgencies.

Our days took on a comfortable quality of routine, which was surprising only in that Eli and I had known each other, at this point, for all of two weeks. Youth, I now believe, is rather like one of those vacations during which your sense of time itself is foreshortened, so that the couple with whom you've started chatting only that morning at breakfast, and in whose company you've made an exhaustive survey of the Vatican Museum, eaten lunch, and climbed the Spanish Steps, you feel by evening that you've known far too long, since childhood. In the same way, within a matter of days, breakfast at the diner where I'd noticed the policemen in the LAPD uniforms had become, for Liza and me, a 'ritual,' for Eli, whose personality was more corrosive, a 'habit.' There, over an egg-white omelette, Liza would describe – sparing no detail – the transports and ecstasies to which Jessica had brought her the night before. By contrast, Eli and I would have usually just passed an evening more in keeping with the conventions of retirement than of youth. This was mostly a matter of choice; we shared a deep longing for domestic peace, one which our sexual discordance (which seemed to get worse the more we labored to repair it) only underscored. Or perhaps I should say that for me it was a matter of choice. In hindsight, I suspect that Eli suffered more deeply from this incompatibility, in part because he expected more from sex than I did, in part because fantasy – that reservoir from which I could draw at will – simply did not satisfy him; like Ricky, he preferred 'the real thing,' which was why Liza's accounts of multiple orgasms on Jessica's futon provoked in him such unexpected irritation and impatience.

To give but one example – and here the reader who prefers to be spared, as my mother might have put it, 'the gory details' is advised to skip to the next paragraph – one night not long after we met, when we were in bed, Eli asked me to insert one of my fingers into his anus. Though I had never before been called upon to perform this particular *manoeuvre*, I agreed; oiling up my index finger, I thrust it in clumsily. Eli yelped. 'Jesus, Martin, do you always have to be such a klutz?' he cried, only to check his vexation upon noticing how crestfallen I looked.

Then, as a patient mother might explain to her child why he must not poke her in the eye, Eli said, 'You just have to learn to be gentle, sweetheart. Because when you do that, remember, you're touching the most intimate part of me' – words which, in their utter unsexiness, brought to mind the man at Boy Bar through whose mouth Mr Mooney had ventriloquized the terrible phrase 'window dresser.' I almost laughed. Yet Eli, I saw, was bristling with an almost rabbinical fervor that would become, over time, the most implacable of the many impediments to our happiness. The trouble was that whereas my own erotic satisfaction, as I have said, required the presence of certain situational props, and Ricky took to lovemaking as naturally as certain prodigies, when first seated at the piano, seek out euphony, Eli considered sex a sublime, even sacred business in which childish delight played little part, and fetishism none. Pleasure, for him, was not even its purpose; its purpose was to redress the many injustices he felt he had suffered, beginning with his father's remoteness and continuing on to his rejection by Princeton, his inability to publish the three novels he'd already written, the failure of the theatrical production of *Daphnis and Chloe* (with incidental music by himself) that he had staged in college, etc., etc. To compensate for what he had endured, Eli needed a lover in whose eyes he could see his own face reflected as an object of desire, which made me in certain ways exactly the wrong person for him to have taken up with. And just as my remoteness made Ricky sad, it made Eli angry.

However, I see that I have once again divagated from the subject at hand, which is the way Liza, Eli, and I passed our days in those days. To wit: having finished our breakfast at the coffee shop (by now it was usually around eleven), we would take a stroll through the neighborhood, perhaps stopping off to browse at one of the local bookstores, of which our favorite was Three Lives. Here Liza would pick up and throw down shiny new novels as casually as Sylvia Fowler samples perfume in *The Women*. 'I heard Avon's put in a hundred-thousand dollar paperback floor for this one,' she might say – she had close friends at every publishing house, with whom she consulted daily – 'only they really regret it. It's supposed to be a bomb.' (She was referring, as it happened, to Julia Baylor's first effort, hot off the press.) Or, 'Oh look, here's another Stanley Flint book. You can tell because the jacket copy's incomprehensible.'

I looked – it was the book of stories by the young woman

who designed headstones – while Eli, for whom these book-store visits served chiefly as a reminder of the fact that unlike Liza and me, he himself had been unable to publish any of his novels, turned away and with a gesture of repudiation took up a dog grooming manual. To his frustration, however, Liza hardly noticed. At last she put down the story collection, the acknowledgments to which she had been skimming assiduously, and without buying anything – 'why buy?' she argued, 'when we know people everywhere, we can get everything free?' – led us out of the store. At this point she returned to her apartment to work, while Eli either went to the gym or, if it was Saturday, to his yoga class.

He and I next met up in his studio after lunch. If I hadn't brought over my computer, while he toiled away on his novel I would examine his books. Only *Anal Pleasure and Health* proved to be a disappointment, with its pruriently sincere illustrations and advice on how to maintain the proper balance of intestinal fauna through laxatives. Much more interesting to me (and less unctuous) was a battered old volume that he had picked up at a yard sale, containing reproductions of homosexually themed art through the ages, and titled, for reasons at which I could not guess, *L'Amour Bleu*. By an accident of casual alphabetization it was shelved next to *Bloodroot Sisters*, an anthology of 'dykewomyn poetry' that I remembered my sister having also owned. (Indeed, I see now that if I took pleasure in exploring Eli's library, it was in part because it reminded me so much of my parents', an eclectic collection into the equally vague alphabetization of which, as we all went off to college and they reclaimed our rooms for various new uses, my father had gradually incorporated many of our own books, with amusing results: *Liberace Cooks* rubbed shoulders with C. S. Lewis's *Surprised by Joy*, *The House* with *Managerial Psychology*, *Naked Came the Stranger* with *The Order of Things*.)

About the novel on which Eli was at work I knew very little, except that it included (as Chapter Two) his story 'Ineptitude,' which I'd read in Henry Deane's anthology. Perhaps as a consequence of Liza's habitual laxness in responding to the pages he sometimes showed her, he refused categorically to share it with me, no matter how loudly I pleaded. Nor was writing, I soon learned, the only art in which he dallied: he was also a painter who had on his trip to France completed some bold watercolors, a poet who had once won a prize for a sestina, a baritone, a violinist, and lastly a composer, in which capacity he had been working for the past five years on an unfinished string trio ('basically Mozartian and unfashionable'), which his mother hoped to persuade the Beaux Arts Trio to perform. (She was friendly with a cousin of the cellist.)

That Eli could spread himself so thin impressed me at first, given that like Liza, I could do nothing *but* write; I had no other talents. And yet I am no longer so sure that a multiplicity of gifts is any great advantage to an artist. Certainly in Eli's case his refusal to settle down and devote himself exclusively to one pursuit – which he manifested, those afternoons, by jumping restlessly from his desk to his violin, and then from his violin to his easel – lent to all his efforts a distinct odor of (what else to call it?) dilettantism. Though Oscar Wilde was his hero, it was one of those minor figures who lurked on the fringes of the twenties, publishing dozens of forgettable books on all manner of subject (someone like Sacheverall Sitwell), that he most closely resembled. Rarely did he write (or paint, or compose, or play, for that matter) with anything like the concentrated, even agonized vehemence that marked Liza's own periods of intensest work, those days on which she would sit bent over her typewriter for hours at a time, in a contorted posture from which Eli was always trying to discourage her by buying her special stools or orthopedic back pillows, for he feared (quite rightly) that the upshot of such self-torture would be scoliosis. He, on the other hand, had perfect posture: indeed, it was perhaps this very lack of manic devotion by dint of which his back had been spared to which Liza referred when she said that he wasn't a 'natural' writer.

Yet there was another reason for Eli's artistic promiscuity, one which Liza, possibly from a sense of misplaced delicacy, never mentioned. It was this: unlike her, he had wealthy parents who were always happy to write him thousand-dollar checks, which meant that he could afford, as she could not, to put off that inevitable moment when an artist must start thinking of his work as a job. My own situation was more ambiguous, my parents, though by no means poor, lacking altogether that rooting in the financial sector by virtue of which Eli's mother and father seemed always to have ready cash on hand (not to mention their willingness to dispense it). So far I'd met his mother only once, at the bottom of his stairwell on Elizabeth Street, where she'd stopped to leave him a check (what else?) before rushing off to a New York Philharmonic concert. Our encounter, which lasted all of a minute, had that strangely artificial air that seems always to environ introductions the prearranged nature of which both parties have agreed tacitly to ignore. Thus, though the meeting was supposed to be 'accidental,' we had both dressed to make a good impression, she in heavy pearls and a fur coat, I in a Harris tweed jacket and the same wide-wale corduroy pants that Edith had admired. I remember that her skin was flushed from the cold. Shaking my hand, she expressed her hope that I would join the family in a few weeks for its annual Chanukah party. 'What I love about the Jewish holidays,' she said, 'is that they celebrate freedom.' For Eli had already informed her of my own family's habit of putting out both a menorah *and* a Christmas tree in order to profit from two opportunities to receive presents: a practice of which Harriet, as devout as any reform Jew can be, disapproved strenuously. (I think that at this point her eagerness to inculcate in me a new spirit of Jewish pride far outweighed any anxiety she might have felt about my being her son's homosexual lover, given that her older daughter had married a Catholic and her younger daughter was now threatening to marry a Seventh Day Adventist; though I might be a member of one tribe, I had at least the advantage of also being a member of another.)

In any event, Eli's work and my reading usually kept us busy, those afternoons, until five or so, at which point Liza would invariably telephone and ask us what we were doing, in the same tone of voice that a bored child adopts when she has just woken up from a nap and – seeing that the sky is cloudy – calls up some friend to inquire laconically if he or she would like to play. Not that this pose of indolence effaced her more serious purpose: for Liza, in those days, without necessarily even being conscious of the aspiration, was trying to create in her apartment what would have been called, at a different time and in a different city, a 'salon.' This was the real reason she never agreed to come over to Eli's studio, or (heaven forbid) mine. Like Madame Verdurin, she felt safer when the 'little clan' of which we were the principal members was safely assembled under her own roof. Nor, in truth, did I mind going over to Liza's those afternoons, for I loved the walk to her building, which took us along a succession of tree-lined side-walks on which the streetlamps, when they came on, made the changing leaves look as if they were pressed from gold. Hand in hand, Eli and I would stride down Second Avenue, some-times stopping at a newsstand, where I'd buy the current issue of the magazine, or a chocolate bar; or Eli, at a health food store he liked, would get for himself and Liza some speci-mens of what he called 'health food junk food' – carob chip cookies, 'fruit 'n' fiber' muffins sweetened with apple juice, taro chips.

Then we'd ring her buzzer; she would let us into her dark little cave, the narrow windows of which gave onto the back of an untidy garden with a dogwood tree and a decrepit fountain from which a dolphin dribbled brackish water. In contrast to Eli's apartment, the decoration of which revealed his instinct for recognizing, in inanimate things, a reflection of himself, Liza's furniture had a curiously affectless quality. In front of the window a sofa in striped cotton exchanged dumb glances with a wood-veneered coffee table. The desk, of white laminate, came from the Door Store. The loft bed was an exact copy of Eli's, crafted by the same team of lesbian carpenters. As for the red-brick walls, they were hung with posters of paintings by Monet, Degas, and Frida Kahlo – posters Liza had purchased framed – as well as a portrait of her that Jessica had just completed, and out of which she stared daringly, almost reproachfully, shirt open to reveal breasts so red, they might have been scarred by burning.

What gave Liza's apartment its special charm, however – indeed, it was the major reason she had rented it – was the corner fireplace in which Eli, on those cool afternoons, was always trying to fuss up a little blaze, using as kindling some sticks he'd bought from a vendor at the Union Square Market. Mostly these efforts failed, and we would resort to one of the Duraflame logs that Liza was always sending me to the corner supermarket to buy along with chocolate-covered raisins, if she was stoned and had the munchies. Not that I minded. Youngest child that I was, I liked doing errands. On such afternoons we were sometimes alone, though more often Liza also had over one or two of what Eli called her 'minions,' those friends in whom her wit inspired adoration, and whose number included Janet Klass, Ethan (the boy with whom she liked to watch *Jeopardy!* over the telephone), and, especially on weekends, a whole flock of girls who worked in publishing, and on whom Liza relied for gossip and free books. Most of these girls, so far as I could tell, were called Amy.

Here is a typical day: it is a cold Thursday in November, and Eli and I – intertwined as usual – are lying with Liza on her loft bed. Below, on the sofa, sit Ethan and one of the Amys, an assistant editor at Avon (it was from her that Liza had gotten the intelligence on Julia Baylor) who as a consequence of a similar but far more consequential indiscretion has just been fired. Now, in her distress, she has been spending most of her time trailing after Liza, never talking much, yet at the same time not really getting in the way, in which regard she resembles also in behavior one of those innocuous yet pleasant lapdogs, a toy poodle, or bichon frisé – that her physiognomy (she was small, round, with frizzy apricot hair that she tended to wear teased up in a topknot) brings to mind.

As for Ethan, he is pallid and lean, with the sort of toneless, drooping body that skinny men who spend all of their time at desks seem fated to develop. The year before, he and Eli had had a disastrous affair; how this bad business concluded I have no idea, though I do know that Eli, even though he maintains in Ethan's presence a posture of unrelenting civility, cannot seem to control, when Ethan isn't around, his desire to insult him. When Ethan isn't there Eli refers to him as 'the Bellows,' because of the way that his stomach, when he sits down naked, partitions itself into five distinct pleats. He complains about Ethan's maniacal fastidiousness, as evidenced, among other things, by his socks, which he keeps arranged according to the color spectrum, and the fact that in his apartment he maintains a fish tank in which there are displayed all the typical decorative amenities of fish tanks – plastic diver, buried treasure, anchor, lurid pink gravel – yet no fish; not a single fish. To Eli such an incongruous artifact is the ultimate sign of moral frigidity, of a disdain for life in all its messy glory; and yet in my view (though I would never dare say this to Eli) all that the fish tank implies is the depth of loneliness into which a soul can devolve once the very prospect of human intercourse – from which experience (particularly with Eli) has taught Ethan to expect only grief – has begun to pall. For in fact (though again, I would never admit this to Eli) I quite like Ethan, who never fails to amuse me with his cleverness, and who possesses without question the most blazing intellect of anyone in the room. (He really is, for instance, a brilliant pianist, in comparison with whom Eli, when he takes out his violin, seems merely an amateur.)

But to return to the past tense: on the Thursday afternoon of which I am writing, and which I have chosen not only because it was representative, but because it presaged the first real crisis in my relationship with Eli, the five of us were, as I said, sitting around Liza's apartment, and we were stoned – or I should say, everyone but Ethan, who had allergies and never smoked. In my case, even though a scruple from childhood still forbade me from taking so much as a puff from a joint or water pipe, I had managed, by inhaling the fumes that escaped whenever the forbidden object was not in someone else's mouth, to become intoxicated without actually being implicated. Already, this afternoon, we had eaten the health food snacks Eli had bought, listened to Liza chat on the phone with her mother for twenty minutes, and played a game of her invention in which, having been shown the cover and the title of a book, you had to make up its first sentence. These amusements had been concluded, however, and now, as rain started to beat on the roof, we had fallen into one of those surreal chats that marijuana smoking so often seems to induce. While on Liza's face-sized television, on *Wheel of Fortune*, Vanna White revealed the next-to-last letter of a word Ethan had already barked out three minutes earlier, Liza showed Eli her left foot, the big toenail of which – having become afflicted with a fungus – her doctor had only that morning had to remove.

'Will it grow back?' I asked her.

She shook her head. 'No,' she answered mournfully. 'Once it's gone, it's gone. And that really . . . I mean, the human frame really *is* fearfully made, isn't it?'

'Liza, it's only a nail,' Eli interjected pragmatically.

Liza, having become lost in the minute examination of her toe, appeared not to have heard him. 'The doctor says I should scrub it with Bon Ami once a week to keep it smooth. Isn't that disgusting?'

'At least you've still got your toe. Remember Charlie Eccleston, who only had half the fingers on his left hand? That is, half of each finger,' he specified for my benefit. 'Frostbite, dear.'

'It all makes me think of my grandmother,' said Liza. 'I remember that whenever I came to visit her in the city, and we passed a beggar on the street, she'd say – I don't know why, because it had nothing to do with Confucius – she'd put on this fake Chinese voice, and say, "Confucius say, I cried because I met a man who had no shoes, and then I met a man who had no feet." The point of which, I suppose, was that because for every person we encountered who was badly off, there was someone else who was worse off, we didn't need to give anything to the beggar. But it never made sense. I mean, not to have shoes – that's economics, isn't it? That's poverty. Whereas not to have feet – well, for all we knew the man who had no feet was rich, he could have been *born* without feet. Or lost them in a water-skiing accident. I ask you, why should I have felt more sorry for him than for the poor shoeless beggar?'

'Liza, you're so funny!' Amy interjected, clapping her hands together (and this was the only comment she made on the subject worth repeating).

I tried to interpolate, here, an anecdote of my own, about a girl I'd known in high school who never wore shoes and had written a poem called 'Summer Is a Stillborn Child,' but Liza ignored me.

'I mean, if no one took the trouble to give the poor beggar a pair of shoes, he'd probably step on a rusty nail, or get frostbite, like poor Charlie Eccleston, and then he wouldn't have any feet or any shoes, would he?'

'More fundamentally than that, if you don't have feet, you don't need shoes,' added Eli, who was inclined to a metaphysical view of things.

Leaning against her brick wall, Liza took another drag from the joint. Clearly the toenail had been forgotten. And yet I could see her mind racing: already she was planning a story, already, in her mind, all the stick figures in this little fable – the grandmother, the shoeless beggar, the footless millionaire – were taking on heft and detail.

Often, on these afternoons – as in Proust, on Madame Verdurin's Wednesdays, Morel might play his violin, or Russian dancers might perform an excerpt from *Scheherazade* – Liza would read aloud to us from the novel on which she was at work. This was the chief difference between her and her Parisian counterparts: she liked to perform as much as to host. Her novel, as she had explained it to me, was about a young woman trying to come to terms with her lesbian longings. Although I hadn't read any of it, I'd already heard her recite several chapters, in the strangely incantatory, even bardic tone – utterly unlike her ordinary light contralto – that she adopted on such occasions, as if to lend to her prose an atmosphere of gravity and pathos.

This afternoon, she prefaced her reading by announcing that she had decided to go back on her earlier resolution (which she had told me about after Sam Stallings's party) to change the novel's point of view from first person to third person; for though this resolution, she said, had been arrived at as a consequence of a genuinely artistic impulse (the desire to 'open up the narrative' so that it could include the perspective of Joseph, the boyfriend whom the heroine, Lydia, ultimately leaves for another girl), in the end it had only led her up a blind alley, which was why she was now resolved to tackle the story afresh from Lydia's point of view. This announcement delighted Eli, who had from the beginning attributed the decision to Sada's nefarious influence, which he saw it as his duty to oppose. 'Oh Liza, that's wonderful,' he cried, letting go of me, and kissing her. 'Believe me, it'll be a great novel now.'

Though Liza may have liked praise more than any human being I have ever met, she became curiously reticent, even shy when actually receiving it. 'Really? Do you think so?' she asked, her cheeks, already crimson where Eli had kissed her, flushing a little.

'Oh, yes,' he answered emphatically.

Tumbling down the loft ladder – nearly tripping on the bottom rung – Liza picked up a sheaf of manuscript pages and started to read. In the chapter she chose, Lydia describes her initiation into the pleasures of Sapphic love at the hands of Gin, who has 'a tongue like a darting flame.' Lydia's voice is comic. Liza's, on the contrary, resembled that of a cantor; its rhythms, though melodic, bore no relation to those of the story, which she seemed not so much to be reciting as channeling. Like a catatonic, she rocked. Eli squeezed my hand tighter at the best lines. As for Amy, on her small canine face she wore an expression of raptness, almost of ecstasy, as if she wanted to convey to Liza the degree to which – despite her much avowed heterosexuality – this seduction scene was really turning her on. Indeed, when Liza finished the chapter, it was Amy who jumped to her feet first. 'It's great!' she chimed. 'It's engaging! And more than that, it's *hot*!'

Liza blushed. 'You really liked it? You're not making it up?'

'Of course not,' Amy said.

'It was terrific,' Ethan echoed. 'Some of the best writing you've done.'

'I loved it,' Eli affirmed.

'I'm really grateful to you all for listening,' Liza concluded modestly. 'But now the thing that's worrying me – because of my decision to go back to first person – is whether *The Island of Misfit Toys* is really the right title, whether it strikes the proper chord.'

'I don't see why it shouldn't,' I said.

'Were you thinking of another title?'

'Not really. I mean, I do have another title in mind – but then again it's a title I've been wanting to use for years, and never found the right story for, and it really doesn't have any bearing on this one: *Under the Weather*.'

'That's nice,' said Eli.

'Maybe there's someplace where you could incorporate the idea behind the title into the text,' suggested Amy, 'such as – well, for example, does Lydia at any point get the flu?'

'I like titles that have two meanings,' I said, 'one literal and the other suggestive.'

'Maybe I could insert something,' Liza mused, 'you know, some passage in which Lydia thinks about the implications of the phrase "under the weather."'

'What about *The Quick-Change Artist*?' suggested Eli, referring to a title that he himself had proposed – and that Liza had rejected – months earlier.

She ignored him.

'What about *A History of Hands*?' I proffered, a title I had derived from a line she had just read.

A History of Hands, however, Liza didn't like either. 'It's too poeticky,' she complained, suppressing a yawn, for she was growing bored with the topic of titles. 'No, in the end I suppose I'll probably stick to *The Island of Misfit Toys*,' she said conclusively, then, turning to the little television (which, though muted for the reading, had been left on), shouted, 'Oh, who is Grandma Moses?' For in the interval *Wheel of Fortune* had segued into *Jeopardy!*, which meant that it was past seven. 'The time!' Liza suddenly cried, like the White Rabbit, 'I'll be late to meet Jessica!' And, leaping to her feet, she started the water running in her tiny bathtub. Ethan and Amy got up and put on their coats, as did Eli, for though normally Liza liked us to stay a little longer than the others, tonight was one of his teaching nights, and he was in a rush.

'Good-bye, dear one,' he said, kissing her on the cheek.

'Good-bye,' she answered vaguely, too caught up in her ablutions (not to mention her abstracted eagerness to see Jessica) even to be aware, in any real way, that he was leaving. 'Typical Liza,' he complained when we were out on the street. 'The minute there's the possibility of pussy, she's off and running.'

We returned to his apartment, where he put on what he called his 'teaching suit,' then took the subway and together to his Brooklyn campus. As usual Eli had entreated me not to bother accompanying him, which was very nice but finally pointless. In my eagerness to share every aspect of his life I no longer enjoyed being alone; indeed, whenever I returned to that high-rise apartment in which I now lived only nominally, I became instantly disoriented. Just as in childhood, when I had sometimes suspected that nothing except my perception was real, that when my back was turned all the facets of the world except those I was momentarily experiencing folded into one another, like the panels of a fan, so an opposite anxiety would seize me, and I would worry lest in the absence of Eli's responses and reactions – which seemed alone to vouchsafe my existence – I should discover that I had no identity at all.

Of course, by giving in to this fear I also made it real: by grabbing and holding on to Eli, as once kings had kidnapped and held on to those Venetian glassmakers who possessed the secret recipe for mirrors, I ceded to him the power to corroborate my very reality. In this way the thing I feared losing through sex – that kernel of selfhood, which I imagined might slip away as inexorably as my mother's diamond down the bathtub drain – I ended up losing through love.

So we went to school, where I waited for him in the cafeteria, drinking Diet Coke and watching as behind the steam table a cook in a dirty apron halfheartedly rotated the hamburgers and hot dogs in their moat of grease. Eli's class lasted an hour; then the door clicked open, and a low burble of voices sounded, within which I could easily distinguish his curious, cracking baritone. The sound of the door was my signal to leap up and run to where he stood amid the throng of his admiring pupils, at which point we would ride down in the elevator, cozily ensconced amid the chatter of women, the smells of perfume and wool coats. 'Good-bye, Mr Aronson!' the students would cry happily on the street. 'See you next week!' And, parting from us, they would disappear in a thousand different directions, after which we would head into the subway, Eli telling me everything that had gone on that night, how Maria Hernández had explained worriedly that she had 'comma splice' (as if 'comma splice' were some medical condition, to be corrected by surgery) and Evensha Hopkins – a Brooklyn girl and his favorite – had offered a brilliant response to last week's exercise.

'Listen to this. I gave them the old "point of view" assignment – you know, "tell the same story from two points of view" – and this is what she turned in.'

Two Points of View
by Evensha Hopkins

Point of View One:
The other day my friend Josie's boyfriend beat her up
so bad she ended up in the hospital. When we went to
see her, her eyes were swollen. She could hardly open
them. It was very sad.

Point of View Two:
Speaking of this same Josie, I happen to know that the
week before her boyfriend beat her up she beat him up
twice as bad. He wasn't a creep. He was just evening
the score.

'Isn't that amazing?' asked Eli. 'I mean, with this exercise,
usually it's just, "My daughter, she's such a brat," "My
mother, she's such a cow."' He smiled. 'It's the miracle of
teaching women like this – if you can only tap into it, they've
got so much to tell!'

'You're a good teacher,' I said, which he was – better than
Liza, who had a bad habit of lecturing too much; better than
I; better, perhaps, even than Stanley Flint. 'So what would you
call the two points of view?'

'I don't know. The naive and the informed?' But by
now the train had arrived at his station. We got out. In his
apartment the little red light on the answering machine was
blinking. 'Five messages!' Eli said. 'But how could I have
gotten five messages? I've only been away a couple of
hours.'

Sitting at his desk, he began to play the messages back.
The first was from Liza. 'Eli, where are you?' she implored,
'I've got to talk to you. Please, please call me as soon as you
get back. I'm at home. Bye.'

Eli stopped the machine for an instant. 'What's she doing at home?' he asked. 'She's supposed to be with Jessica.'

He played the second message. 'Eli, where *are* you? It's me. Please, if you're screening calls, pick up. It's urgent . . . Oh well, I guess you're still teaching . . . Well, call me as soon as you get back.'

Third message: 'Why aren't you back? I need to talk to you!' (This last sentence was delivered almost as a rebuke.)

Fourth message: 'I need to talk to you. Call me.'

Fifth message: a dial tone.

Without a word Eli picked up the phone and punched out Liza's number. It was busy. I ordered Chinese food to be delivered. 'Why don't you eat dinner and call her afterwards?' I suggested when it arrived.

'I guess you're right,' Eli agreed, and sat down with me at his little table. Even as he ate, however, he kept looking over his shoulder at the telephone, getting up, and trying her number again.

Finally I threw my fork down dramatically. 'I don't see why you're even bothering to pretend to have dinner with me,' I said, 'when obviously you'd rather be at the telephone dialing Liza's number obsessively, over and over.'

'I'm sorry,' Eli said, 'I know it's not very polite . . . it's just, that tone in her voice . . .'

'But if she's so desperate to talk to you, why is the line always busy?'

'Probably she's talking to someone else. That's how Liza is, when she's suffering, she has to talk. She'd even talk to the lady at the Korean grocers if there was no one else around. My suspicion,' he added, 'is that she had a fight with Jessica.'

'So?'

'Well, in that case I'm the only person who can help her.' He smiled. 'I'm her best friend . . . You don't understand, you never have, you haven't known us long enough.'

Again he walked to the phone and dialed. This time she answered. 'Liza,' he said.

Getting up from the table, I started packing the leftover food and putting it into the refrigerator. From Eli's expression, from the way he repeated the words 'It's okay, it's okay' into the receiver, in the tranquilizing tone of the policeman trying to talk the suicide off the ledge, I was able to deduce without difficulty what Liza must have been saying. Nor did the possibility that she and Jessica might have broken up in any way make me feel sorry for her; instead it made me worried for myself.

Finally Eli hung up. 'What's wrong?' I asked from the refrigerator.

He was already reaching for his coat. 'Jessica's gone back to Peggy,' he said hurriedly. From atop the desk he picked up his watch and wallet, then searched for his keys, which were next to the answering machine. 'I've got to go. I'm sorry.'

'But why?'

'Because she asked me to.'

'But can't you go in the morning?' I pleaded, suddenly grasping the reality – more terrible, now that it was imminent, than it had ever been in theory – that Eli was actually intending to leave me. 'I mean, you haven't even finished dinner.'

'I know.' He took my face in his hands. 'And you're sweet to worry. But this is an emergency. Liza's hysterical.'

'But she's got other friends, you said so yourself. God knows she was on the phone with *them* long enough.'

'They don't count. It's me she wants.'

'But you count for me too.'

'I've got to run. I'm sorry, Martin, I'll call you as soon as I can, within the hour. Stay here if you want.'

'Eli—'

Kissing me hurriedly, he left. Through the open door I gaped after him. 'Do you want me to come with you?' I shouted down the stairwell, in the depths of which I could hear footsteps echoing.

'Better if you stay here,' a distant voice called, a voice that hardly sounded like Eli's at all.

Then a door slammed. He was gone.

I stepped back inside. It was the first time I'd ever been alone in Eli's apartment. Now, in his absence, all that furniture that spoke so eloquently of him – of his fondnesses, his predilections, even his occasional descents into bad taste – seemed to be laughing at me, it was poignant and hostile at the same time, like a cat that, missing its owner, urinates in the shoes of the friend who has volunteered to take care of it in his absence. Noticing a pair of dirty socks that Eli had dropped idly by the dresser, I picked them up. When we were together I never dared clean up after him, in case he should interpret my efforts as an interfering, if motherly, reprimand. Tonight, however, in my need for some activity with which to fill the void his sudden departure had created, I decided that if I cleaned the entire apartment, which was in a sorry state, perhaps when he got back, Eli would be grateful. So I washed all the dishes that over the last few days had collected in the sink. I made the bed. I put away *L'Amour Bleu* and plumped the futon, which was starting to droop off its wooden frame. Finally I swept the floor, and would even have vacuumed Eli's threadbare carpet had I not feared that the noise of the vacuum cleaner might drown out the ringing of the phone.

Then – cleaned out, as it were – I sat down and looked at the clock. Only twenty minutes had passed since Eli's departure – twenty minutes! But it had seemed an eternity. The more sensible part of me knew that the best course of action would be simply to sit tight, watch television or read until he called, which he'd promised to do within the hour. And yet in such situations it is rare that only one voice speaks up within the mind. Indeed, at that moment, even as the first voice (the voice of reason) was urging patience, a second voice, both louder and more militant, had entered the fray, insisting that patience was pointless and that the time had come to act, if not for Eli's sake, then for my own. For no matter how bitterly he might inveigh, in her absence, against Liza's arrogance and selfishness, nonetheless it was obvious that she still exercised a formidable hold over him. And from this hold it was my duty to wrest him free, in order to prove to him that unlike Liza – who looked upon him merely as a convenience, a crutch to throw aside until the moment when, finding herself suddenly bereft of Jessica's 'tongue like a darting flame,' she telephoned in outrage to demand the return of her property – I really loved him.

Impatience, needless to say, won out; picking up the phone, I dialed Liza's number. To my surprise she picked up after only one ring. 'It's Martin,' I said.

'Oh, hi, Martin,' she answered, her voice surprisingly cheerful.

'Are you all right?'

'I suppose so, considering. Did Eli tell you what happened?'

'Only a little.'

'It was horrible. This evening I went over to Jessica's assuming, you know, that we were going to spend the night together just like any other. And I had no reason to expect otherwise. I mean, we'd talked on the phone this morning, and she'd said that she was going to make this wonderful salmon teriyaki that I love for dinner. Do you eat Japanese food, by the way? I've just found the most fantastic sushi place on Greenwich Avenue, we've got to try it. Anyway, when I got there, she had her fists clenched and tears in her eyes, and before I even had the chance to say hello, she said to me, "I'm going back to Peggy."'

'But why?'

'Who knows? She wouldn't even tell me. And now the thing is, I'm just in shock, which is probably why I'm babbling about Japanese restaurants. I mean, I trusted her, Martin. I really put my faith in Jessica. Not that I assumed our relationship was going to last forever – I didn't – and yet at the same time I always took it for granted that at least, if it ended, it would end gracefully, and we'd part as friends. Instead of which this sudden about-face. And on top of that her refusal even to explain. She just wanted me out of there. I was back on the street five minutes after I arrived.'

'I'm so sorry.'

'Thanks. Eli's here now. He's trying to put me back together, like Humpty-Dumpty. Do you want to talk to him?'

'If you wouldn't mind.'

'One second.' And putting her hand over the receiver, she muttered something to Eli, who laughed.

'Hello, love of my life and fire of my loins,' he said, taking the receiver from her. (As I imagined it, they were lying in her loft bed, naked for all I knew.)

'Are you okay?'

'Fine. What are you up to?'

'Not much.' I drew in my breath. 'I was just wondering when you were planning to come home.'

'Oh, but . . . hold on. What?' Again, the sound of laughter. 'Sorry, sorry. Actually, I thought I'd spend the night here with Liza, if you don't mind. She'd rather not be alone.'

'Are you stoned?'

'A little.'

'But I do mind.'

Eli breathed heavily. 'Oh, honey, don't worry. Tell you what, why don't you stay at my apartment, how does that sound? And then at dawn I'll wake you with a kiss.'

'But why should you stay there? I mean, it's not like she'd do the same for you.'

'Martin—'

'Just today you were complaining about her, about how she takes so much more than she gives, about how as soon as there's pussy—'

'But that's not the point.'

'It is. I give you so much more, and you're perfectly willing to shaft me—'

'I'm not shafting you.'

'You know as well as I do we've never spent a night apart.'

'Yes, but this is hardly an ordinary situation. Liza needs me.'

'And I don't?'

'Martin, for God's sake, it's one night!'

I let out a loud groan. 'Eli?' I heard Liza call questioningly.

'If you don't come back,' I said, appalled and thrilled by my own brazenness, 'it's over between us.'

'Oh, Jesus—'

'I mean it.'

Eli emitted a strangled noise. 'Why are you doing this to me?' he asked. Then, when I didn't answer: 'We'll talk about this when I get back.'

With a violence that made me jump, he hung up.

Pushing the tiny buttons on top of the phone, I called him back. The line was busy.

I sat down at his desk. What I was feeling, at that moment, was a paradoxical blend of exultation and cowardice – just as, many years later, having smashed a bottle of expensive wine against a tiled floor, I would stare down at the shards of glass, the hurried rivulets of wine, and find myself at once emboldened (by the discovery in myself of a genuine capacity for action) and horrified (by the realization that one action can lead, on the part of another person, to a reaction). For though I understood, in the wake of my conversation with Eli, that on one level I had succeeded – I had browbeaten him into coming home – I also saw that by so doing I might have incurred a wrath of which the frigid, even ominous tone of his voice when he had uttered those last words – 'We'll talk about it when I get back' – was only the faintest echo; and to this presumed threat I reacted as a dog does when, having gone one step too far in testing his owner's patience, he suddenly abandons aggression and rolls over onto his back, as if to say, I acknowledge your superiority; I acquiesce to punishment; and yet at the same time, by exhibiting such remorsefulness, I hope that I can also dim your wrath.

Taking off my clothes, I climbed up into Eli's loft. Never before had I been alone in this bed, and remembering the many nights I had spent here with Eli – nights during which I had derived, from his proximity, not only bodily warmth but a sensation of security and well-being – I found myself craving more viscerally than ever that presence the permanent forfeiture of which, because I had protested its cessation for a single night, I might now have guaranteed for the rest of my life. For I feared that by challenging Eli in this way I had startled a swarm of furies in their hive, from whence they would fly at me, recriminations and counterrecriminations, as pernicious as the colony of red ants that once, when I was very small, I had made the mistake of disturbing, and which had attacked me. Screaming, I'd run to my mother and sister, who had torn off my clothes, thrown me into a tub filled with cold water. Only now neither my mother nor my sister, even if they'd been here, could have helped me. Only Eli could help me. And given the circumstances, what right did I have to ask him for help?

I decided then that when he got back and ordered me out (as I was sure he would), I would simply refuse to leave; I would cling tight to the sheets of his bed; even if he tried to drag me down the ladder, force my clothes onto my body, pull me toward the door, I would hold on to him, as I'd learned once to do in a lifesaving class, not letting go until we reached shallow water.

It was now nearly midnight. Exhausted, I felt myself, despite my valiant efforts to remain awake, lapsing into an uneasy sleep, in the course of which old memories assailed me. I thought of the bus stop at which I had been taunted to the point of tears, of the science class during which Dwight Rohmer had dropped my notebook into a vat of cow eyeballs. And though I could not deny that in these remote and scarring episodes there lay the origins of certain bad adult habits – for example, in my fight with Dwight Rohmer the habit (demonstrated only this evening) of exploding when angry, then withdrawing as soon as my explosion had provoked a response, or in my running away from the taunting boys the habit of assuming that any challenge I made to another person's authority, no matter how legitimate, would be met not merely with resistance, but banishment – neither could I pretend that my woefulness made these episodes in any way interesting. For the sources of our pain are often appallingly banal, which is why their recitation can elicit irritation in a listener, rather than the sympathy we hoped to find. So your father was cold, the world says, so the other boys teased you . . . so what? It doesn't make you special. It only makes you ordinary. Yet it is the knowledge of our ordinariness that, once acquired, proves to be the most painful, and the most instructive, of all.

Thus it was from tiresome and repetitive musings, a vicious circle of recollection and self-pity, that Eli's keys in the lock, an hour later, pulled me awake. 'I'm sorry,' I called out automatically upon hearing them, and in so doing set the tone for the rest of our relationship. For though I didn't know it, Eli had taken my threats seriously, and come home prepared to submit to them. That 'I'm sorry,' issued with such bathos, clued him in to the truth, which was that my conduct over the phone, far from instinct with potency, had been merely histrionics. My fear, in other words, was a self-fulfilling prophecy, alerting Eli as to exactly which weak spots he might exploit.

I sat up in bed. 'Eli, I'm sorry,' I repeated. He did not answer. In the quiet I heard his keys crashing against the top of the desk, the unbuckling of his belt.

'I made a terrible mistake. I tried to call you back, but the line was busy. I wanted to tell you—'

'Well, here I am. Are you satisfied? You've got me right where you want me, back in your clutches.'

'But that's what I wanted to tell you. I was wrong to ask you to come back. I wanted to tell you to stay at Liza's after all. In fact, why don't you go back there now?'

'It's too late.'

'No it isn't.'

'Of course it is, after I left her there crying—'

'Eli—'

'Weeping, begging me to stay.'

'Oh God, I feel so guilty! It's all my fault.'

He went into the bathroom. From the loft I listened to him peeing, brushing his teeth, spitting toothpaste foam into the water. Then the door opened; the ladder rungs sighed as he climbed up into the loft. *Well, at least he's not sleeping on the sofa*, I observed privately, as I felt his body, with a gratifying thunk, fall next to mine.

I reached for him.

'Don't touch me,' he said.

'But, Eli—'

'Don't you dare touch me. You've got what you asked for. I'm here. Now don't you dare ask for one more thing.'

'But you're not being fair!'

'And you were?'

'Listen! It wasn't just that I wanted you here. It was for your own good. Because it makes me furious the way Liza treats you, the way she acts like you ought to be available

whenever she wants you, twenty-four hours a day, no matter
what else you might be doing—'

'That's my business.'

'All she has to do is say jump, and you—'

'Will you shut up? Will you please just shut up and let me
get some sleep?'

I shut up. He breathed.

'Jump,' I added after a few seconds.

'You always have to have the last word, don't you?'

'I'm sorry. But I could never get to sleep if I thought you
thought I was trying to drag you back here only because I—'

'Look, what do you want? Do you want me to leave?'

'No, of course not.'

'Then be quiet.' He rolled away from me.

'I'll never get to sleep,' I said.

'Is that my fault?'

'I wish we could solve this before—'

'It's going to take a lot longer than that.'

Reaching under the mattress, then, he took two foam
rubber plugs from a box he kept there and stuffed them into
his ears. Within a few minutes he was snoring.

I had lied. I would fall asleep – I knew I would – both
because I was exhausted and because, despite my protesta-
tions, the mere presence of Eli's body next to mine was a
consolation. For once he fell asleep, I knew, I could touch
him without his even realizing it, I could flout his orders, I
could pretend that it was an ordinary night. Nor had the
militant voice, despite the mortifications it had witnessed,
been completely silenced in me; on the contrary, it was rel-
ishing its victory, if not over Eli, then over Liza, whose hand,
by dragging him back, I had at least forced. No one else had
ever done that. To Liza, I knew, I had proven myself once and
for all an adversary not to be taken lightly. Yet even as I
cherished this victory, I also recognized that it counted for

little, because it proved only that I could be a bigger bully than she was. What remained to be seen (but to this question my dubiousness, auguring a future of struggle, served almost as the answer) was whether I could also be a bigger bully than Eli.

10

Sleeping Arrangements

NOT TWENTY-FOUR HOURS later, the three of us were friends again (youth is like that), eating dinner together at the Japanese restaurant on Greenwich Avenue of which Liza had spoken over the phone. This time there was no question as to where Eli would spend the night, Liza having realized, to her sorrow and annoyance, that I had no intention of ceding him willingly to her; nor could much advantage be gained from starting a war with me that she would very likely lose. Much wiser, she must have reasoned, to lie low, at least for the time being. After all it was hardly in her interest to lose both of us. Though she loved Eli, it must not be forgotten that she also liked me. Nor was she above professional considerations, and what was the point of risking a friendship that in the future might be helpful to her in her career?

Nevertheless, after we'd finished our sushi and were standing on the corner of Greenwich and Seventh avenues, preparing to say our good-byes, almost in spite of herself Liza let a look of indignity cloud her eyes, as if my impudence in staking such a claim on attentions to which heretofore she had held an exclusive deed was simply intolerable. Just as quickly the look dissipated – Liza was more self-controlled than she let on – and, bidding us farewell, she headed bravely back toward that tiny apartment (the very nexus of her abandonment) in which she would sleep, no doubt, with the telephone cradled in her arms.

As for Eli, as soon as she was gone he slipped his hand through my arm and squeezed it. His rage of the night before had passed entirely, leaving in its wake a greater tenderness, as if the storm clouds of our fight had irrigated the landscape they had also battered, making it more verdant if less tidy. Now I suspect that he was actually rather grateful to me for standing up to Liza. After all, to be the object of a rivalry cannot – especially for one who craves attention as much as Eli did – be entirely displeasing. Nor can I help but wonder to what degree he himself might have fostered those feelings of antagonism that ended up so thoroughly corroding my friendship with Liza – feelings by which he claimed to be repulsed, but which, when you thought about it, belonged more to his combative nature than to either of ours. For Eli, though he advertised himself as a paragon of gentleness, a sort of emotional Pillsbury Doughboy, could also be a dragon. When driving, for example, he had no qualms – if, say, another driver pulled out ahead of him in traffic – about opening his window and letting fly a torrent of abuse so scathing that nine times out of ten the offending idiot would race away in terror, fearful lest Eli should in his 'road rage' pull out a shotgun and blow his head off. His sisters were the same away. Their amazing streams of invective – 'part and parcel of growing up on Long Island,' Eli said – bore little semblance to human speech. Instead they were inarticulate spewings of fury, punctuated by incessant, even Tourretic repetitions of the word 'fuck.'

More than once I saw him reduce unlikely enemies, who had made the mistake of picking fights with him, to tears or silence, for if my way of coping with childhood cruelties was to flee, his response to a history of similar persecutions was to retaliate, as it were, retroactively, by enacting upon unwitting strangers the vengeance he wished he could have taken on the bullies of his adolescence. There was a story Eli liked to tell about a girl in his neighborhood who had teased him at the bus stop, making fun of his hair, his clothes, even his name; one afternoon, taking as a cue a phrase he'd heard an older cousin use, he had preempted her harassment by shouting, 'Shut up, you flat-chested, dog-faced bitch' – an epithet in response to which the girl, utterly stunned, had burst into a fit of weeping and run off.

Such a rejoinder, alas, was typical of Eli, whose reprisals were often out of proportion to the injury that had provoked them. Indeed, even the very generosity and sweetness that marked his general behavior could become an occasion for rancor, as on the evening when, in the midst of giving Liza a back rub, he had suddenly removed his oiled hands, stood up, and started complaining about the fact that in six years she'd never once given *him* a back rub, that all she did was take, that all anyone did was take, and that he was sick of being a servant to other people's pleasures – a diatribe to which Liza, still semiconscious in the wake of one of his superb and anesthetizing massages, hardly knew how to respond. For it was never his way to protest each grievance as it occurred, and thereby dilute his anger in the ordinary tides of human intercourse; instead he would compile, over the years, a list of these grievances, never mentioning them, yet mulling them over in secret, masking them with an almost wincingly immoderate courtesy, until the moment came when he would unleash upon his tormentor a deluge of righteous indignation so immense and so indisputable that in its drenching aftermath the victim would be unable even to muster words. Dumbfounded, he or she would limp away, and never attempt communication with Eli again. And because he was too proud ever to make a first step toward reconciliation, he would never attempt communication, either. Thus within only a few years of our meeting, he had severed all relations with his father, he had severed all relations with Liza, and eventually, he would sever all relations with me.

The truth was, in those earliest months of our acquaintance Eli and I were like one of those antique couples forced by their families into arranged marriages, and therefore compelled to learn about each other only within the claustrophobic parameters of conjugal intimacy, from which there is little opportunity of escape – the only difference in our case being that we ourselves had done the arranging, instinctively, as soon as we had recognized in each other a shared longing for the domestic stability of which the television shows of our childhood had been a parody, instilling in us a paradoxical blend of appetite and distrust. Such a dream of cozy coupledom, moreover, besotted me to such a degree that soon I began to view every sign Eli gave of his individuality, his peculiarity, in essence, his humanity, as an intrusion upon the stage set I had constructed around him, and to which he himself, though essential as a prop, was irrelevant as a person. For I was as consumed by the wish to live out my fantasy as those ersatz officers we'd seen at the coffee shop on Sheridan Square had been driven by the need to act out theirs. Thus (to return to the evening after our fight), upon getting back from dinner with Liza, and seeing that it was almost eleven, I had insisted that we immediately climb together into Eli's loft bed, snuggle up among the blankets, and watch the double bill of *I Love Lucy* reruns that always came on at that hour: a ritual I had, for some reason, often dreamed of sharing with a lover, and in which Eli, so far, had been happy to indulge me. And yet tonight he kept interrupting the sublime sensations of warmth and security that this program – the very nexus of childhood comfort – called up in me, with unwelcome brushings and rubbings, or worse, pullings and grabbings, most often of my hand, which he was always putting on his penis, as if he wanted me to avert my attention from Lucy and do something to it. Finally, irritated by his refusal to take a hint (after all, I was not without my own streak of belligerence) I turned to him, and said, 'Will you quit it? I'm trying to watch.'

'Sorry,' Eli said hotly. Letting go of my hand, he climbed down from the loft, switched on his computer.

'What are you doing?'

'Working.'

'But what about *I Love Lucy*?'

'I don't even like Lucy,' clever Eli answered. 'You're the one who's crazy about Lucy. You watch.'

'But you have to watch! It's not the same alone.'

'For Christ's sake, Martin, will you give me a break? I don't interrupt you when you're doing your work. Is mine less valid?'

'You've spoiled everything.'

'*I've* spoiled everything!'

Such rapprochements, alas, were typical of our intercourse. Eli's attempts to excite me I rebuffed because they embarrassed me and seemed ill-timed, yet what must have hurt him even more than my mania for ritual was the obliviousness, even the callousness, with which I greeted what were to him gestures of the gravest sincerity. Indeed, so consumed was I by my own perspective that even my worry lest Eli should leave me amounted merely to the projection of self-involvement onto a larger canvas, neatly sidestepping as it did the more delicate question of what he himself might be needing (and not getting).

My erotic history, as it happened, had in no way prepared

me for someone like him, just as his had in no way prepared him for someone like me. His (compared to mine) was both intricate and thorny, and included among its major players Ethan, Gerald Wexler's twin brother, a yoga teacher who ate raw onions for a snack, a girl named Zoë whom he had dated in high school, and a British medical student (also a girl) with whom Liza had also had a long affair. Men and women both, in roughly equal numbers, for on a purely physical level Eli claimed actually to prefer sex with women – an avowal that puzzled me less because it seemed incompatible with his calling himself 'gay' than because for me the very idea of sex on a 'purely physical level' seemed so incomprehensible. It was in this regard, as he later reminded me rather cruelly, that I differed from everyone else with whom he had ever been involved.

Curiously enough, however, the natural hostility that sex tended to stir up in both of us did not stop us, at least at first, from having it all the time: much more, probably, than we would have if we'd been less ill-matched. The reasons for this were twofold. First, we felt it incumbent upon ourselves to endow the 'great love' we were always parading in front of other people with the weight, the experiential ballast, of which sexual passion is supposed to be the measure. Second, from ideological motives, we were determined to prove – if not to these others than at least to ourselves – that contrary to popular opinion gay men could enjoy guilt-free sex in the context of a 'healthy' relationship, as opposed to only cheap and impersonal sex in a bathhouse or in one of the dreaded 'back rooms,' which I envisioned always as entryways to hell. Such practices as these appalled us. With a sort of automatic contempt we mocked (and rigorously defied) that shopworn convention according to which homosexual men must be either 'tops' or 'bottoms,' just as we looked down our noses at the 'clones' in their lumberjack shirts and mustaches whom we sometimes passed on the street in Eli's neighborhood, and who were to us less human beings than emblems of a degraded era, one that it was the duty of our own generation to surpass.

Young people, in their arrogance, are thus able to diminish the experience of their elders without even attempting to grasp its complexity. Yet what made this snobbery even more pernicious was the fact that despite my many avowals to the contrary, I was secretly attracted to this antiquated social order of tops and bottoms, just as I often found myself secretly drawn to the clones Eli and I would run into when, say, we had gotten up early in the morning and were taking a walk along the river, and they were stumbling home from the piers whereon they had just enjoyed a night of licentious abandon that had left their hair mussed, their skin pallid, their clothes smelling of amyl nitrate and cigarettes. After the clones I stared with an envy that I draped in the vestments of disgust, a sleight of hand that Eli must have seen right through, just as he must have seen through the excuses I made whenever he asked me to fuck him. For he knew as well as I did that despite the tedious lectures I was always giving on 'internalized homophobia' – as a consequence of which, I argued, homosexuals felt obliged to take on the roles of 'male' and 'female,' rather than formulate their own democracy – I myself was (as Roy Beckett would later put it) a natural-born piece of ass. Or perhaps I should say a 'natural-born piece of ass' *of the mind,* attracted more to the idea of being fucked than the reality, which frightened me.

What was this thing about fucking? I often wondered. Was it because of its procreative function that for homosexuals as well as heterosexuals, penetration was so often viewed as the ne plus ultra of intimacy, in comparison with which what might be called the ancillary sex acts – masturbation, frottage, sucking and licking – were merely nostalgic adolescent diversions? Certainly this was Eli's view. If he took pleasure in those varieties of sex that come under the heading of 'foreplay,' it was in the same way that I took pleasure in *I Love Lucy* reruns. Fucking, on the other hand, was to him an adult taste, like the taste for raw oysters and strong cheeses – it was, as the Italians say, 'important' – which was probably why I shied from it, confirming Eli's suspicion that I lived in a state of arrested development, a chronic adolescent whose weirdly goofy demeanor would seem less and less becoming the older I grew.

I must also add here (though with no great pride) that throughout this period of frequent, ill-timed, and unsatisfying sex – and despite the mounting evidence that anal intercourse provided the most efficient avenue for HIV infection – Eli and I never once used condoms. I'm not sure why this was. Perhaps we were simply unwilling, in the face of grim statistics, to suspend, as it were, our belief, and accept the disease as an actuality in response to which we would have to disown many of our most basic tenets. Or perhaps, given our youth, we could not yet fathom the possibility (the truth) that an illness so far associated almost exclusively with 'them,' the older generation, might also be a threat to us. Or perhaps we had simply not yet grasped the full horror of mortality, of which neither of us had had much experience. Indeed, I remember – and today the memory makes my blood run cold – lying in Eli's loft bed one rainy afternoon, reading a newspaper article that speculated on 'routes of AIDS transmission,' and thinking, well, if we both get it, if he gives it to me, or I give it to him, it won't be so bad: we can just lie here in the loft together like sick children, watching cartoons. The appalling facts were still so remote from me that I could actually romanticize them that way. Nor did the arguments on which the gay left was then wasting its breath – arguments that in essence attempted to justify sexual consumerism by recasting AIDS in the terminology of a class struggle, in which 'they' were using the disease to try to suppress 'our' hard-won freedom – do anything to dispel this voluntary blindness, which only an instinctive skepticism could have cured. For instance, I remember once receiving a phone call from Liza, who was in a panic because she had just read an article advising all lesbians to use 'dental dams' when engaging in cunnilingus. 'But Jessica and I never used dental dams!' she told me. 'Do you think I should have? I'm so worried! Because once – I'm embarrassed to say it – she was menstruating, only we didn't realize it until after I'd started to . . .'

To allay her anxieties, I reminded her that at the moment there were only five (but previously there had been one) documented cases of female-to-female AIDS transmission – which did not stop her, for months, from feeling her glands ritualistically, neurotically, and at the most unlikely moments: in restaurants, say, or at literary parties, where in the midst of a conversation with Billie Eberhart and Sam Stallings about Penguin's purchase of Dutton, her fingers, as if of their own volition, would suddenly fly to her neck. Eli was the same. We all were. 'Swollen glands' became for us a sort of shorthand for AIDS, about which, in truth, we knew next to nothing, except that swollen glands were supposed to augur its onset. For about two years we palpated our glands obsessively, worrying over every unusual bulge or distention we might encounter, the subsequent abatement of which would seem to us cause for celebration, because it meant that we were not, after all, dying.

It was around this time as well – though curiously this development did nothing either to dispel or accentuate my AIDS anxieties – that I came down with a case of venereal warts: clusters of them, like tiny heads of that wonderful Roman broccoli, sprouting inside and around the opening of the anus, as well as in that nether region just south of the anus that Kendall Philips (always a wit) referred to as the 'taint' – 'because it ain't this and it ain't that,' he said. At another moment in my life such an event (probably a legacy of my affair with Ricky) would have anguished and humiliated me. Now, however, I was able to view it less as a grim portent for the future than as the residue – mercifully insignificant when compared to other possibilities – of a period in my life that had come to a decisive end.

Accordingly, and with Eli's forbearance, I made an appointment to see a dermatologist in whom I felt fairly certain I could confide my embarrassing condition, because he advertised in the *New York Native*, a gay paper. This dermatologist, Dr Spengler, was not, as it turned out, gay himself. On the contrary, he was married with three children, a handsome Jew from New Jersey a decade older than I, and possessed of that amazingly supple, flat, characterless skin – unblemished by so much as a freckle – that seems to be the hallmark of his profession. I don't think he had any particular opinion, positive or negative, on the question of homosexuality; what had motivated him, rather, to advertise in the *New York Native* was simply that mercantile instinct by means of which his grandfather (like Eli's) had managed to rise from the poverty of Hester Street to the affluence of Saddle River. (By a similar stroke of intuition, numerous West Village Indian and Pakistani newsstand owners were at that time starting not only to sell, but to specialize in the sale of, gay pornographic videos, with which they soon filled their windows, and in the selection of which a complete lack of personal interest did not forestall them from offering unsolicited and cheerful advice: 'Oh yes, sir, I'd recommend *The Bigger the Better,* very popular this week, I've sold twenty copies!')

As I recall, the treatment of the warts required six or seven successive visits to Dr Spengler, visits during which, while I lay on his examining table in my jacket, sweater, shirt and T-shirt (elegant clothes seemed necessary as a way of asserting my personal dignity), my lower half denuded, my legs in the air, holding my balls in my right hand so that they might not interfere with his nimble laborings, he would discourse enthusiastically about the bluegrass camp in the Adirondacks at which he sojourned annually, and where he would play the banjo 'morning, noon, and night,' while at the same time probing what Eli would have called 'the most intimate part of me' with an alarming instrument at which I preferred not to look. The treatment involved liquid nitrogen and when it was over, when at last I was liberated of the tiny heads of broccoli, he sent me off with a smile and a pat on the back, as if I were a pupil who had just passed a final exam and to whom his professor feels obliged to offer words of advice: 'Remember, they can recur, but if they do, don't worry. That's what a dermatologist is for.'

As for Liza, her fear of AIDS was taking a different form, becoming entangled with that old uncertainty about her lesbianism to which, in the wake of Jessica's flight, she had instantly rebounded, just as she had rebounded to her old dependency on Eli. Such a reversal disheartened him, for he had supposed himself, through Jessica, to have won a decisive victory in the battle he was forever waging against her mother. Now, however, she was reverting to old habits. Once more, she wore two earrings. She even spoke about rewriting her novel yet again, reinstating the third person.

Worse, to her many arguments against lesbianism she now added the risk of AIDS – perversely, we thought, given that (as I constantly reminded her) the risk was extremely low for lesbians. At this point she would always revert to dental dams. Dental dams – and her failure to employ them – became her bailiwick. At a drugstore she bought some, and the three of us tried to figure out how they worked – a comical effort, for she could not get one over her tongue without gagging. Yet when I reminded her that by having unprotected sex with men she was taking a far greater risk than she ever could have with Jessica, she brushed me off, now that she was looking for reasons to be straight rather than vice versa.

From Janet Klass, meanwhile, we learned that Philip Crenshaw – dark-eyed, spidery Philip Crenshaw, whose tales of the Mineshaft had been the peephole (or should I say the glory hole?) through which I had caught my first horrified glimpse of gay New York – had AIDS, and was dying, the first person I actually knew to be taken ill. This news sent a shudder of terror not only through me, but through Liza and Eli. Suddenly our hysterical worry over swollen glands revealed itself for the gratuitous pantomime that it was. Then dread, which is stultifying, stopped us cold. Liza even forgot about dental dams – but only briefly. For just as the trespass of an alien presence into the bloodstream is enough to trigger the immune system (at least when one does not have AIDS), so after the initial period of numbness that comes in the wake of terrible news, the mechanism by which we are able to rationalize, to distort, to edit painful truths and make them bearable, switches on. We reminded ourselves that Philip had been – how else to put it? – a whore. He had not lived, as Eli and I did, in monogamous 'bliss.' Instead he was – and for using this word, several years later, I would be chided by my fellows in ACT UP, who considered it overly judgmental – promiscuous; from the clones, only a distance in years, not attitudes, separated him. Yet even as we tried, by such justifications, to sequester not only Philip's illness, but his death (which came a few months later), the news had shaken us to the marrow. We wanted to make sense of it. We tried to make sense of it. The trouble was, it made no sense at all.

The clones – those men whose postures and costumes I disdained without ever bothering to interrogate them – became our scapegoat, the convenient target at which we could volley all the unintelligible terror that AIDS started up in us. It shames me, today, to recall how casually I badmouthed them. Even my tendency to refer to them as 'clones' (as if they were less than human) was, I see now, part of a failed effort to smother the desire they sparked in me. For in those days the Village was still full of them, AIDS having only just begun its bloody pogrom. If I'd ever bothered to get to know any of the clones, then perhaps my manufactured disillusion would have given way to a more real (and thus humane) disillusion; I would have discovered that in sharp contrast to the image I sustained of them (and that they themselves promulgated) as sexual rebels, radicals, outlaws, they were by and large rather middle-class white individuals, accountants and shopkeepers, who would have had more in common with Eli's parents than with Eli. What they constituted was a gay bourgeoisie, the members of which, in addition to being aficionados of ball stretchers, handkerchief codes, and the like, were also expert cooks, serious collectors of antiques, authorities on home decoration, as well as – though this was less known – baseball fans, devotees of fly-fishing, and observers of the stock market. In short, they differed from their suburban cousins only in the outer emblems that marked their trust in conventions: instead of station wagons, motorcycles; instead of tea parties, tearooms; instead of the synagogue, the country club, and the 'no-tel motel,' the cowboy bar, the back room, and the bathhouse.

It was around this time as well that Stanley Flint came gamboling back into my life. Previously, when I'd lived across the street from him, I'd hardly ever seen him except in the Hudson-Terrier offices. Now, however, we seemed to run into each other all the time: at parties, on the subway, once, even, in Dr Spengler's waiting room (Flint, it turned out, was seeing him for the treatment of a skin cancer). 'Young man, you never applied to my class!' he scolded when I walked in. 'I'm offended!' Then he broke into a smile I found far more off-putting than any expression of offense. 'Sit down, sit down.' He patted the vinyl sofa. 'How much more pleasant to have a chat with you than gaze wearily at a year-old issue of *People*!'

As at his office so many months ago, I sat. 'You're right, I didn't apply,' I admitted. 'I'm sorry. I suppose I was just so tired of being a writing student.'

'But you'll always be a writing student! Indeed, the minute you stop thinking of yourself as a writing student, you might as well stop thinking of yourself as a writer. And accolades provide no immunization against failure.' He placed a fatherly hand on my knee. 'Take my word for it, Bauman, every time you pick up a pen, you court disaster. Even the great Leonard Trask can fuck up. The pages he sent me last week – vile! I told him so. Let's hope he listens to reason and doesn't let his reputation go to his head.'

'And how's *your* novel proceeding?' I asked, to yank the conversation away from teaching.

He shrugged. 'Not as well as before I sold it. Selling it – that was the mistake. Because now there's a deadline, and little threatening notes, and phone calls I have to return. In effect, I've been seduced into the position of a dependent, which is something that a writer must never become. What we really need' – he leaned closer – 'is the establishment of a system whereby writers are paid an annual salary and given the freedom to do whatever they want. Imagine that, a paycheck every two weeks, health benefits, the whole package – just what *they* get to publish, only we'd get it to write! But of course (and I speak from experience) it would be impossible. How would you implement it? Also, they like having us in their clutches. They want us hungry, sniffing at the haunches of the marketplace, because that way they can turn a quicker profit.'

I thought of mentioning the fact that in his dual role as editor and writer, Flint stood on both sides of this divide, then decided against it. 'Ah, it was better back in the age of disinterested patronage!' he went on. 'Unfortunately, we're living in an age of institutional patronage, and the problem with institutions is that in the end they're always going to try to get you to do what's best for *them*.'

'Yes, but if you have to work at a job all day to make money,' I averred, 'how are you ever going to find the time to write?'

'Ah, now that *is* the sticking point, isn't it? Literature – I'm sorry to say it – belongs to a far less democratic age than ours, when there were servants and the lower orders and only people of means even had time to *think* about writing. Today, it's true, some of us can make a living at it. But look what you give up in exchange! You become a slave to a publishing house or a university, and once they know you've got mortgage payments to make, Bauman, you might as well hand over your balls on a plate right then and there.' He put an arm around my shoulder. 'If you want to know what I think, the only people who *really* ought to be writing these days are these rich Park Avenue ladies with stockbroker husbands, not because they're necessarily any more talented than the rest of us, but because they're the only ones who can afford to take the time. For we're long past the years when Leonard Woolf did the typesetting at the Hogarth Press. There are no more Hudsons at Hudson. Instead, I fear, we've entered into the corporate dark ages, with the conglomerate taking the role of the church. And frankly, I fear that literature might just not survive.'

'But it always has! Even during the Dark Ages!'

'Ah, so you think that art is immortal! It isn't. Books, pianos, paintings – all can be burned. The spirit can be starved, yes, all the way to death. Nothing endures without some degree of sustenance. And what's worse, once the state's wiped out art, there are plenty around who will be perfectly willing to collaborate in the dissemination of that sort of substitute, fake art that to be perfectly frank most people prefer to the real thing . . . I know, I know, you think I sound like an old man. And yet with the fatal sun, and poison in the air, and skin cancer' – he pointed to the small bandage on his cheek – 'how can I keep saying that what one writes matters? That's my dilemma. Even if they earn money, books won't save my daughter from radiation.'

After that the receptionist called his name. Flint stood. 'Well, must run,' he said, smiling as casually as if we had just concluded a thirty-second discussion of the weather. 'Be well, Bauman.'

'You too,' I echoed, my voice trailing off (I still didn't know what to call him) as, picking up his cane, he made his way toward Dr Spengler's door.

This encounter, not surprisingly, had a profounder effect on me than Flint probably intended it to. Indeed, riding the subway back to Eli's that morning, I couldn't help but replay his pronouncements in my head. The death of literature, he'd said . . . such a far cry, this doomsday paean, from my own modest experience of publishing, which so far had been both gentle and pleasant. For instance, I had in my shoulder bag (I had just that morning received them in the mail) the bound galleys of *The Deviled-Egg Plate*. Thumbing through the pages in the subway, I was stunned by how much more authority my words radiated, now that they were printed in beautiful Bodoni Book (a helpful note at the end of the galleys gave the typeface's history) instead of the familiar Helvetica of my computer. Or was my enjoyment of this private pleasure, as Flint had suggested, merely evidence of the degree to which I had effectively renounced my integrity? I couldn't be sure. Nor could I be sure whether to take at face value his outlandish assertion that only those who had independent means should become writers. After all, Eli had means, and rather than reveling in the freedom that his parents' money had bought him, he lived in a chronic squall of anxiety, irritation, and impatience. To Eli exterior validation – not cash – was the longed-for thing, which meant that when, in my thoughtless excitement, I interrupted his writing to show him my bound galleys that afternoon, his insistent enthusiasm could not disguise the crisis of doubt into which I had just thrust him: no matter how loudly he *kvelled*, there was heartbreak and hopelessness in his voice.

Much better, I decided after that, to confine my excitement to my own apartment, to make from there the long phone calls to Liza during which she filled me in on all the latest publishing gossip, to field from there the many party invitations I was receiving. For somehow my name was now on what Manhattanites call the A-list, and I was getting invitations all the time. Usually my date was Liza, who was looking for a boyfriend, and hoped to find one at one of these parties. She didn't, of course; under such circumstances you never do. Instead it is usually only when you have just happily settled into matrimony that someone alarmingly attractive suddenly takes an interest in you – as happened in my case when at one party Roy Beckett, who had previously refused to give me so much as the time of day, suddenly started flirting with me. Liza, on the other hand, could not seem to attract a man to save her life – a failure that, because she had always enjoyed such a superabundance of suitors, both depressed and appalled her. 'You'll never go wanting,' Eli had told her once, which was true. The dry spell through which I was escorting her was exceptional, and would last only until spring – none of which stopped her (self-confidence being that fragile) from dissolving into a heap of self-loathing and bewilderment at the end of each party, broken pieces out of which, in Eli's absence (for the same reasons that he hated bookstores, he refused ever to go to publishing parties) I would attempt to reconstruct the old Liza, usually by suggesting that if she wasn't succeeding with men, it might be because, in her heart of hearts, she didn't want to. Liza, however, disagreed. She was no longer interested in being a lesbian, she said. She was over lesbianism.

Sometimes, in her company, I wondered what it was, this category, this idea of the lesbian, that Liza alternately fled and embraced with such avidity. In college the answer, like most answers, had seemed clearer: lesbians, I'd thought then, were either girls like Tammy Lake who lusted viscerally after other girls, or girls like Erica for whom lesbianism was mostly an offshoot of feminism, or fashionable girls like Schuyler who disdained heterosexuality as being simply too boring and conventional for them to bother with. Liza, on the other hand, had only the vaguest conception of feminism, while her attraction to men – though by no means commensurate with what she felt for girls – was nonetheless potent enough to keep the ball of her destiny suspended, as it were, in midair. Even the word 'lesbian' – the utterance of which, at certain moments, sent a frisson of excitement down her spine – could at times make her bristle. And why *this* word? I would ask myself, so quaintly antiquated, with its musty smell of Victorian England, of Sappho, of Amazonian brutalities as imagined in the fusty depths of a Maida Vale bed-sit? Why not instead *tribade*, popular in continental Europe during the nineteenth century and derived from *tribology*, 'the science of the mechanisms of friction, lubrication, and wear of interacting surfaces that are in relative motion'? Thus in Proust, Dr Cottard warns the narrator not to tolerate Albertine's habit of dancing with her friend Andrée, because, as he observes with medical authority, 'It's not sufficiently known that women derive most excitement through their breasts. And theirs, as you see, are touching completely.' Certainly Liza spoke on occasion about the beauty of women's breasts, especially Jessica's. Yet she had also said to me once, at the height of her affair with Jessica, 'I must say, I *do* miss the thrust,' in that glib tone of someone who is perfectly content to have made a superfluous sacrifice.

Perhaps it really was simpler for men, I sometimes reflected; a matter, as Liza had once joked, of which pictures one liked to jerk off to – except that neither Eli nor Ricky liked to jerk off to pictures at all, while Eli claimed to enjoy sex with women more. (This didn't stop him from declaring himself, with genuine militancy, to be 'gay,' and later 'queer.') No, in the end all I could conclude was that the fault lay with categorization itself, that crude and elementary tool the inadequacy of which becomes more evident the deeper one probes. For homosexuality is a discipline the advanced study of which necessitates, as it were, its own transcendence, which is why all its serious students finally dispense with terminology altogether, and focus their attentions solely on the particulars of human lives.

But to return to Liza: just as, in Eli's view, my own reluctance to engage in penetrative sex signaled a larger reluctance – a refusal to go gently into adulthood – so Liza, whose retreat from lesbianism, in the wake of Jessica's departure, had been both panicked and swift, clearly placed this grown-up pleasure at a great remove from that cult of childhood she had taken such pains, both in her writing and her life, to foster. Only Jessica, it seemed, had ever been able to lure her away from *Jeopardy!* Eli, for all his disparagement, was a willing member of her cult, as was I. Those afternoons at Liza's studio were for me a logical extension of the summer Sundays I had spent with Jim Sterling in his parents' apartment. Nor did our habit of reverencing the gratifications of our youth prove an exception to the rule that all private indulgences have their equivalent in public life. For instance, at the literary parties to which Liza and I went together, we were able to discern that our habit of standing awkwardly by the hors d'oeuvres table, instead of drawing bemused and piteous glances as it once had, was now winning us admirers. Seasoned veterans like Billie and Henry Deane seemed to view our lack of refinement as a refreshing indication of vigor. Behaving almost like a couple, like a pair of adorable and clever child geniuses, we charmed them all, Liza with her wit, I with my fecklessness: even when we showed up in jeans and T-shirts at parties where everyone else was in black tie, no one seemed to mind, just as the cousin of Jacqueline Onassis next to whom I found myself seated, one evening, at a benefit dinner at the New York Public Library, did not seem to mind when – bereft of any education in table manners – I drank out of her water glass.

No doubt her tolerance, which hinted at larger movements in the fashion world, was part of the glorification of youthful achievement taking hold at the time, chiefly as a result of the fact that so many young people – to quote Kendall, who, we must remember, worked for *House and Garden* – were earning 'scads of yummy Wall Street money to spend on upholstery fabrics.' My own gains, by comparison, were, like Liza's, chiefly in prestige. All at once, for instance, we were being sought after as book reviewers, in which capacity we were asked to review not only first novels by my peers, but 'big books' by writers whose very presence at a party, only a year earlier, would have been enough to start my heart racing. Even film people started taking an interest in us: that year Liza sold the rights to *Midnight Snacks*, while I found myself fielding, through Billie, a score of inquiries from producers, most of whom, she assured me, had not even read my stories (which had in any case not yet been published), only the early reviews that had appeared in *Publishers Weekly* and *Kirkus*.

That some of these producers had managed as well to get hold of the just-completed (and not yet edited) manuscript of *The Terrorist* at first stunned me, until Billie explained that it was a common practice for editorial assistants – in exchange for much-needed cash – to supply Hollywood agents with photocopies of unfinished novels on the sly. No doubt while I'd been working at Hudson, Carey had been doing it; Sara had been doing it; they had all been doing it.

At the time, it rather went to my head. No city in the world is more provincial than New York, nor is any realm of the arts more provincial than that of literature, nor is any community more provincial than the one composed of writers who hobnob with editors, and are to some degree homosexual. And yet these were the only milieus in which anyone knew who I was. To the establishment, literary people and homosexuals are equally suspect if not interchangeable populations, to be regarded with ambivalence at best, contempt at worst. Yet from the parties to which we went the establishment could not have seemed more distant, just as to Kendall the housewife in Smyrna, Georgia, who buys a copy of *House and Garden* at the grocery store because she's thinking of redoing her dining room, and upon whose dissatisfaction with her chairs a magazine like *House and Garden* depends in order to keep up its circulation – to Kendall she did not exist. Instead what existed, all that existed, was New York: decorators and fabric houses and the competition, above all, the competition, *Architectural Digest, House Beautiful, Elle Decor.* For New York has always been the 'secondary city' of which George Steiner writes, in which puff pieces, analyses, interviews proliferate, nearly suffocating those primary works from which they leech sustenance. And not only secondary but tertiary: there were magazines (I read all of them) that existed solely to review books that existed themselves solely to critique other books; there was even a journal devoted exclusively to the review of reviews, so New

York was in its way also a quaternary city. Nor were those of us who aspired to the writing of fiction unimplicated in this frenzy, for we all wrote reviews in addition to reading them (which would be a little like, in the music world, Martha Argerich reviewing a recital by Alfred Brendel), and were forever reporting to each other the 'buzz,' or, as they called it in Hollywood, the 'coverage' on new novels (especially those by our contemporaries), gossip picked up from the Amys about authors we'd never met and books we'd never read, though we received free copies of them. In high school and college I'd dreamed of a day when I could afford to buy any hardback book I chose; now I got sent hardbacks by the dozen, and didn't pay a dime. And though I professed – we all did – to write only for the sake of art, the truth is that like Billie at Sam Stallings's party, I had my ear cocked to the *Zeitgeist*, inventing even as I sat at my computer the interviews and the reviews and the *Publishers Weekly* articles that I hoped my book of stories would occasion, as if these counterfeit documents might serve as a guide by which my imagination could find its way.

None of this was particularly fun: obsessions rarely are. Instead, standing together at those parties, Liza and Amy and I would profess how much we 'absolutely hated' this sort of thing – a declaration to which any stranger would have sensibly responded, 'Well, why did you come?' And our answer to this question, if only we'd had the wherewithal to formulate it, would have been that this squabbly, small-town society which for all its aspirations to worldliness finally resembled, more than anything else, one of those cottage Devon villages of which E. F. Benson wrote, had taken us in. It had become home for us, a place we felt we belonged.

I remember standing alone at one of those parties – or perhaps I was not alone, perhaps I was flirting with Roy (and wondering if I'd made a mistake to fall in love with Eli), or listening to Kendall hold forth on the vulgarity of the host's curtain pelmets, or chatting about his impending move to Madrid with Henry Deane, with whom I had become friendly . . . in any case, I was standing at one of these parties when I noticed Liza, only a few feet away, huddled in anxious conference with a new friend of hers, the tulip-shaped, peroxide-blond Violet Partridge, several of whose stories Edith Atkinson had bought for the magazine. And though I could pick up only fragments of their dialogue – 'hundred-thousand-dollar advance,' I heard, and 'front-page review,' and 'Shirley MacLaine wants to play the mother' – their very posture (hunched and scoliotic), Liza's ear tugging, the anguished way she was pulling a tissue through her fist, like a rabbit out of a hat, were enough to tell me that the conversation had nothing to do with pleasure, and everything to do with that need to stay informed that compelled us both, every week, to hurry out and buy the *New York Times Book Review*, *Time*, *Newsweek*, *Publishers Weekly*, *Entertainment Weekly*, and *New York Review of Books* (not to mention the magazine) the minute these publications hit the stands, not so much to read them as to winnow from them (an operation we could perform in record time) those bits of innuendo by means of which we were able to sustain the illusion of being up to date. For hindsight was to us less frightening than foresight, and therefore we both breathed more easily when, as Liza put it, we felt that we were 'on top of things' – a revealing phrase, suggestive of waves, the scrambling of the drowned, the terror of going under.

It may have been at this party too (tellingly, I cannot remember in whose honor it was being thrown) that, while talking with Liza, Billie, and my new editor, three women who seemed to gather around me a veritable cloak of maternal protection, I noticed Marge Preston, whom I hadn't seen in a year, ascending the stairs with Baylor. According to Liza,

Marge was in serious trouble at the moment, her efforts to revive Hudson's fading glory (of which Stanley Flint's hiring had been the most vivid example) having so far come to naught, at least from a financial perspective. Indeed, according to the sibilations of the buzz, the powers that be at Terrier and its amorphous parent company were now pressuring Marge to fire Flint or risk being fired herself; for though he had brought the company a certain prestige, he had also failed to generate the bestsellers she had promised.

That she had arrived at the party with Baylor surprised us, since of course Baylor herself – on whom Marge had banked, quite literally, to justify Flint's hiring – was the major source of this disappointment, her own novel, despite favorable reviews, having sold only a few thousand of the fifty thousand copies printed. To make matters worse, Baylor's agent had been shrewd enough to secure for her, well before the novel had come out, an advance of five hundred thousand dollars for her second book, which put her in the peculiar position (though in literary New York, where reputation and income rarely correspond, perhaps this position is not all that peculiar) of being substantially richer than most of her better-known and more highly regarded contemporaries.

And yet if either she or Marge was losing sleep over this predicament, their expressions, as they stepped through the door, did not reveal it. On the contrary, both looked flushed and happy. Marge, who had lost weight since I'd last seen her, appeared younger and more robust than when she'd fired me. As for Baylor, sleek and natty in a black jacket and trousers that belied their own expensiveness ('Armani,' whispered Kendall, who had wandered over to join our conversation, 'cost at least two thousand bucks'), with her elegantly short hair and pearl earrings she presented an even greater contrast than at our lunch to that studious girl with the braids upon whom I had stumbled in Stanley Flint's seminar room. Indeed, she wore the relaxed expression of someone for whom such environments are utterly without threat because she has been born into them.

Our little groups, in the way of parties, now collided. Smiling, Marge greeted Billie, to whom certain professional liabilities made her beholden. 'And how's Stanley doing?' Billie asked her.

'Well, as it happens, he's just signed on this fabulous new novel by a young black writer from Indiana,' Marge said, 'only now everyone's complaining that it's unethical because the kid was one of his private students. But I don't think it's unethical at all! After all, Stanley Flint's students, generally speaking, make up the body from which all of tomorrow's great writers, the Hemingways and Woolfs of the future, are going to be drawn, don't you think? Just look at the examples we have in front of us. Julia Baylor and Martin Bauman, both former students of Stanley Flint, both rising literary stars . . .'

Baylor turned away. I blushed. Liza coughed.

'I was thrilled to hear about his selling his novel,' she said. 'Have you read it yet?'

'Alas no. No one has. He won't show it to anybody, not even his closest friends, apparently he doesn't even want galleys sent out. Typical Stanley to be so secretive, he's even made the people at Knopf swear not to breathe a word about the plot until he's finished his revisions. Excuse me, story. I know Stanley hates the word "plot."'

'Tell him congratulations from me,' I threw in.

'Of course. And as for you, Martin' – I turned from her gaze as from the sun – 'what an honor it is for me to hold the distinction of having once given the sack, given the heave-ho, to a young man whom I guarantee, within a very few months, is going to be a major player, not just Martin Bauman but *the* Martin Bauman.' She pinched my cheek. 'But I'm sure you forgive me, don't you, dear? You realize it was for your own good. I've always had a sixth sense about these things. And who knows? If I hadn't fired you, today you might still be reading slush at Hudson, instead of standing here, client of Billie and author of Trish.' (Trish was my editor.)

'Well,' I said, uncertain as to how I was supposed to greet this peculiar testimonial.

'By the way, Sara asked me to send you her regards. You know she's been promoted. She's an editor now.'

'Oh, I'm delighted.'

'And Carey – it's tragic, really – you know he's been out of the office for the last few weeks, he hasn't been well. Somewhere along the line he managed to pick up a bad case of hepatitis. And then today he called me and said that he's planning to quit. Apparently he wants to go to graduate school.'

'Who's Carey?' asked Liza.

'A friend of mine,' I said. 'Stanley Flint's assistant.'

Henry Deane – always a fixture at these parties (but then again, so was I) – now approached us, dragging in his wake an extremely tall, distinguished-looking man in his fifties, with a luxuriant gray beard, stooped shoulders, and bushy eyebrows. 'Oh, hello, Michael,' he said to me, for he could never seem to get my name right. 'Michael, have you met my friend and former lover, Seamus Holt?'

'No, I haven't,' I said, 'though of course I've seen his plays.' (This was a lie.)

'Michael Bauman, Seamus Holt. Oh, and Seamus, you know Billie Eberhart, and Marge, of course – and everyone knows Kendall. And tell me, Michael, who are these charming young ladies?'

Trish, Julia, and Liza were introduced first to Henry, then to Seamus, who, having hurled at them a series of rudimentary hellos, turned to me and glowered. 'Young man, I've got a bone to pick with you,' he said. 'You've written such a wonderful collection of stories, which proves you've got a real talent, and in the whole book, in all two hundred and sixteen pages, not a single word, not a single fucking word about AIDS. It's outrageous. Don't you realize that by shirking your duty, by failing to bring this horrible crime to the attention of our brothers and sisters, you're collaborating with the enemy? You're adding to the silence in which we're all going to die, die, die?'

'Oh, Seamus, please,' said Henry. 'I have to apologize for him, Michael,' he added. 'You see, he has this insane idea that AIDS is the result of germ warfare by the government or some such thing.'

'Misrepresenting me as usual,' said Seamus. 'What I said was—'

'Or that AIDS started because of experiments on monkeys in Africa, I don't know, he changes his conspiracy theories more often than he changes his socks.'

By now the women, as if instinctively, had crept away from us and into another conversation. 'So when's moving day, Henry?' asked Kendall.

'The fourteenth. You may have heard that I'm moving to Madrid for a year,' Henry said to me. 'Certain people' – he indicated Seamus – 'insist I'm doing it to run away from AIDS, but I ask you, how can anyone escape AIDS? If you've got it, you've got it. Though I've got to admit it'll be a relief not having to visit any more friends in hospitals. Last week I was at Bellevue every afternoon. I've got six friends in the same ward. Six! The nurses all know me by now.'

'Really? Is it really that bad?' asked Kendall.

'Horrible. One ex-lover of mine, he's been in intensive care a week now. Some weird pneumonia. And when *his* lover checked him in they wouldn't let him go into the emergency room because he wasn't "next of kin."'

'Well, there you have it,' said Seamus, 'that's exactly the sort of thing a young man like you, a young gay writer with potential, owes it to the rest of us to write about. Instead of which – I'm sorry – in your stories, it's just all this coming-out shit, and what's my mother going to think, and crap like that.'

'I'm not sure it's fair to dictate to a writer what he ought or ought not to write,' I said bravely.

'Exactly! Good for you!' Henry patted me on the back. 'You see, Seamus, Michael here is obviously a serious artist, not some hack propagandist like you.'

'And have you been writing about AIDS, Seamus?' Kendall asked.

'I'm working on something. That's only the half of it, though. We're trying to start an organization to cope with all this – because, you see, it's much worse than anyone's letting on. Much, much worse.' He stepped closer. 'I mean, look at all these goddamn faggots. Half the men in this room must be faggots, and half of those are probably carrying the virus, and do they care? Are they doing anything about it? Are they using condoms? By the way, I hope all of you, especially you young people, but you too, Henry, are using condoms, because if you're not you're signing your own death warrants. And in Henry's case, I promise, he's signing other people's death warrants.'

'You know what Gore said to me the other day?' interjected Henry. 'He said if AIDS is really spread by butt-fucking, then every woman in Italy would have AIDS. Ha!'

Liza had now rejoined our little circle. 'Excuse me for butting in,' she said, 'but I couldn't help but overhear you talking about condoms, and I wanted to ask . . .'

'Yes, you too, young lady,' said Seamus, 'make sure that when your boyfriend fucks you with that huge *membrum virile* of his, he puts on a sleeve. No glove, no love.'

'No, not that,' Liza persisted. 'Actually what I wanted to ask was what your feeling was about dental dams for lesbians.'

'Oh, lesbians. Pooh! Lesbians don't get AIDS. It's a waste of breath.'

'But how can you know that, Seamus?' asked Kendall, whose deft faculty for posing questions that were challenging enough to keep the conversation interesting but not so challenging as to generate serious worry had made him in recent years a much sought-after guest at Park Avenue dinner parties. 'I mean, given all the surprises we've had lately, who's to say that AIDS won't turn out to be a scourge for lesbians too?'

'Well, scourge is a strong word,' Liza threw in, blanching a little.

'I'm not saying it's *going* to be a scourge,' Kendall continued, 'I'm just pointing out that the evidence isn't in yet.'

'But there's documentary evidence,' said Henry. 'Like I said, I've got half a dozen gay male friends in Bellevue with AIDS right now. On the other hand, I don't know a single lesbian who's got it.'

'You don't know a single lesbian,' Seamus said. 'But that's not the point. The point is, penetrative sex, semen up the asshole, mucus membranes, that's where the danger lies, not in one girl tonguing, excuse me, another one's clit.'

'God, that Seamus Holt is just horrible!' Liza said a few minutes later, when we were standing in line at the bar. 'Really a maniac! That's why Marge didn't want to talk to him, you know. Apparently the other night, at a dinner party, he threw a drink in the face of one of the trustees of Mount Sinai, because he said the hospital wasn't spending enough on AIDS research. Can you believe that? Diet Coke, please. I mean, I don't want to diminish what he's saying,' she went on, taking her drink, 'but you've got to admit, he goes over the top. My mother says he's always been that way, that AIDS has just given him the soapbox he's needed. So I guess I shouldn't be too upset. But that's not what I wanted to talk to you about.' She had pulled me, I noticed, into as remote a corner as the party had to offer. 'What I wanted to ask you about – in confidence, of course – is your friend Julia. Please don't hate me, but I have to know. Is she in any way, at all . . .'

'A lesbian?'

'Ssh!'

'I don't think so. Why?'

'Because all evening I've had this impression, this very strong impression . . . you know . . . that she's been, well, *looking* at me.'

'And what if she has been?'

'I don't know! I'm so confused! Do you think she's pretty? I do. Only she smokes so much, it would be like kissing an ashtray . . . And anyway, the last thing I need right now is to get involved with another woman. And even if I did, you know, approach her or something, what if it turned out I was misreading her? That would be so humiliating.'

Liza's monologue – so maddeningly familiar – had already started to vex me. Suddenly impatient, I suppressed the urge to pick her up by the shoulders, to shake her, to throw a drink in *her* face – anything but be pulled back into that vortex of egoism and uncertainty in which she was always spinning. For Liza's greatest problem, I now saw clearly, was not her sexuality at all, but rather that stubborn resistance to self-examination – common in writers, who for all the fluency with which they pry into the pathologies of others become like children when any degree of self-analysis is required – that led her to crave so desperately the calming pat on the head by means of which 'society' (personified by her mother) indicates its approval of our decision to toe the line and respect convention. I wished that for once she would think deeply about this conflict that rumbled at the core of her being, instead of electing merely to fixate yet again on Nora Foy, whose specter she was now, for the umpteenth time, evoking: 'I'm so afraid of ending up like Nora,' she was saying, 'old and alone and living with all those cats! And the Gertrude Stein and Alice B. Toklas dolls on the bed!' Yet Liza's view of Nora, I could safely say, had nothing to do with Nora's view of herself, or even with what might be called the general view of Nora. Instead, her preoccupations, which the willingness of her friends to discuss her problems with her *ad nauseam* only aggravated, had brought into being a second Nora, a clone or doppelgänger, who nonetheless managed to live in harmony, at least in Liza's mind, with that Nora of whom, at other moments, she spoke in such adulatory terms, either as the mentor who had encouraged her in her writing from an early age, or as the second mother in whose house (a different house, which seemed to have nothing to do with the cat-littered wreck in which the doppelgänger ruled) Liza was not only welcome, but had actually lived for long periods, including the summer over the course of which she had finished *Midnight Snacks*.

By now the party was reaching that climactic moment – so common at gatherings advertised as 'Cocktails, 6–8' – when the decision of one guest (in this case Billie) to say good-bye and fetch her coat provokes everyone else, in a sort of frenzy, to follow suit. This meant that over the course of five minutes our host's living room, with its curtain pelmets of which Kendall had been so critical, had almost totally emptied out, the mass of humanity that defined the party having been convulsed in a sort of unified seizure to the coat check, where in the sudden and enormous queue its members gazed at their watches, as if they had all just remembered dinner parties for which they were late. Fearful of overstaying our welcome, Liza and I left too, though happily the fact that we'd brought no coats allowed us to bypass the nervous queue. Liza was still talking about Nora

Foy; in fact, she was talking about Nora Foy so continuously, and with such unceasing agitation, that I couldn't help but wonder whether she might not be trying – in contrast to her usual routine of simply riding the rat's wheel of her obsessions until the effort had exhausted her – to wrench the conversation toward this particular topic for some specific reason, with the same clangorous infelicity that marked, in her writing, certain transitions between one paragraph and the next.

Out on the street, she asked if I wanted to have dinner with her. I said yes and suggested we call Eli and invite him to join us.

'Actually, let's not,' she said. 'Instead let's just go out to dinner the two of us, shall we? After all, it's been ages since we did that. Not since before you and Eli got together.'

'Well, all right, if you like,' I answered, as crossing the street, we walked into a local Chinese restaurant. 'Only if you don't mind I think I'll phone him and tell him what we're doing, so he won't worry.'

'Fine.' Sitting down, she picked up her menu. I went to the pay phone. As it happened Eli wasn't home, and I could only leave him a message.

'Did you reach him?' she asked when I got back.

I shook my head.

'Where's he been today, anyway? When I called him earlier I kept getting his machine.'

'He's with his mother. This afternoon he had to take her to a doctor's appointment.'

'Ah, the hideous Harriet.' Liza giggled. 'Have you met her yet?'

'Briefly. I didn't think she was so hideous.'

'I don't mean physically. I mean . . . well, let's just say I find her a little hard to take. And I don't think there's anything wrong with my telling you that, especially since Eli makes no bones about hating my mother's guts.'

'I'd say that's a bit exaggerated, Liza.'

'Really? I don't. Anyway, it's not that I don't like Harriet – it's just that I find the way she treats Eli, the way she's always treated him, a little sickening. She's done him a lot of damage, in my opinion.'

'How so?'

'By coddling him too much. By encouraging him in every one of his little artistic pursuits – which is fine, except that she's completely oblivious to questions of talent. She's an ignoramus, culturally speaking. All that matters to her is that he's Eli Aronson, as if that automatically makes him a genius at everything he tries. And the result is that Eli has this really inflated sense of his own abilities, as well as of his mother's power, all of which makes him in the end miserable and resentful, especially toward me, because I've had so much more success than he has. The story of what happened when he didn't get into Princeton is typical.'

'I haven't heard that story.'

'You haven't?' Liza quieted. 'That's funny. Because goodness knows he's told it to all sorts of other people. It's not like it's a secret.' She paused, arranged her hands on her lap. 'Shall *I* tell you?'

Though I had the distinct feeling that I was being led into a trap, that by agreeing to listen to the story I would be tacitly entering into a conspiracy with Liza against Eli, nevertheless I let my curiosity get the best of me. 'Go ahead,' I said.

'Well, you do know that all his life Eli's mother wanted him to go to Princeton, right? And that when he didn't get in it was, like, a major tragedy in the family.'

As it happened I did not know this, though I recalled an afternoon not long ago when, lying in Eli's loft, I'd read aloud to him a line from Renata Adler's *Speedboat* that I'd thought funny – a reference to a girl 'who cried all the time because she hadn't been accepted at Smith' – only he hadn't laughed.

'Well, when he didn't get in, Harriet got this insane idea into her head that it was all because of Zoë.'

'Zoë?'

'His high school girlfriend.'

'Oh yes, of course.'

'Because Zoë's father was the local alumni interviewer for Princeton, which meant naturally that Zoë herself, being a legacy, was going to go to Princeton. Anyway, Harriet decided that if her son, her magnificent Eli, hadn't gotten into Princeton, there was only one explanation, and that was that Zoë's mother had put pressure on Zoë's father to keep him out, probably because she didn't approve of their relationship. So Harriet called the admissions office and demanded to speak to the director, and when she got him, she put up this huge fuss, she protested his rejection, demanded an investigation of Zoë's parents, in short, made a complete fool of herself. After that he was so ashamed he wouldn't even go to his own graduation.'

'How terrible!'

'But that's not the worst of it.' Liza leaned closer. 'You know that when we were at school, Eli put on this production of *Daphnis and Chloe*? Typical Eli, really, staging something like that. Anyway – he doesn't know this, and you mustn't ever tell him I told you, you have to promise me – one afternoon just before the first performance, Harriet called me up and told me that she'd just heard from Eli, and that he was all mopey because no one was planning to throw a cast party. And since she knew he was too proud to give the party himself, or accept the money from her to give one, she wanted to give *me* some money to organize a cast party, only I wasn't under any circumstances to tell Eli that it came from her. Eli was supposed to think that all the people in the cast, who really couldn't have cared less, had chipped in.' She sighed, as one might at the pathetic spectacle of an overclipped poodle.

'And really, that was just Harriet to a tee, always believing that her little boy was something special and that when the world didn't do its part to celebrate him, it was her job to step in and rectify things. Only I think in the end it was Eli she hurt, by making him assume that somehow he was entitled to a certain degree of success, to Princeton, to a cast party – the production, needless to say, was the kind that put your teeth on edge – even if he hadn't earned it. What she ended up doing was teaching him that when he failed, it was only because of other people's prejudices and ignorance. And that's what bothers me about his novels, if I'm going to be totally honest – the sense that he hasn't really given them his all, that he still thinks he ought to get accolades just because he's his mother's son. But he's not seven years old anymore, and what we're talking about isn't some synagogue Purim pageant. And then you see, the worst part of it is that if anyone does say anything against his work, he can just apply what his mother taught him and turn on that person. Believe me, I've been down that road with him.' She narrowed her eyes. 'I suspect you've been down it too.'

In fact I had, though I wasn't about to admit this, for I felt it was my duty to defend Eli.

'Actually, no,' I said. 'Actually, I'd say I have a different outlook on him from yours.'

'Oh come on, Martin. I know you love Eli. I love him too. Still, all you have to do is read his writing in order to realize—'

'But I've read his new novel,' I lied, 'and I think it's brilliant.'

Liza raised her eyebrows. 'Really?'

'Of course.'

'Well, if that's true, it must mean he's had a big growth spurt recently,' she said, 'because I've got to tell you, his first three, they were pretty mediocre.'

'Not this one. In fact, once he's finished his revisions, I'm planning to show it to Billie.'

Now Liza looked not only surprised, but genuinely amazed. 'Seriously? You're going to give your agent Eli's novel?'

'Well, why not?'

'But aren't you afraid . . . I mean, if she doesn't like it, wouldn't it put you in an awkward position? Make her think, you know, less of you for having liked it yourself?'

'Of course not. Anyway, even if Billie doesn't like it – which I really can't imagine – it hardly matters. She's not the only agent in the world.'

'Oh, I know, it's just . . . you know, I've been down *this* road with Eli too. A couple of years ago I showed his novel to my agent – well, not to my agent himself, but to his assistant, who happened to be a friend of both of ours. And when she said she didn't think she could sell it, Eli took it really personally. I felt like I had to mediate between them.'

'I doubt that will happen in this case,' I said, 'since Eli's never met Billie.'

'No, I guess not.' Our food arrived. 'You know, I think that's really generous of you, Martin,' Liza said, 'to help Eli that way. I'm sure he'll be very grateful. You've clearly been good for him, and I'm really glad that the two of you have found such happiness together. I mean that.' And, staring at the food in bewilderment, as if she were as confused by the dishes she had ordered as by her failure to win me over to her viewpoint, she began to eat.

Afterward, I shared with Eli an edited account of our conversation. 'Yet the one thing that puzzles me,' I concluded, 'is why she began by talking about Nora Foy in this very determined way, then dropped the subject.'

'Oh, that must have been because of the trip next weekend,' he answered casually.

'What trip?'

'Didn't she tell you? It figures she didn't. You see, every year around this time Nora goes away for a weekend to visit some friends in Bucks County, and we have this tradition, Liza and I, of house-sitting for her and taking care of the dogs.'

'But I thought she had cats.'

'Nora doesn't have any cats! She's got two fox terriers, Charlus and Pimperl – Charlus after Proust, Pimperl after Mozart's terrier. Anyway, we were talking about it yesterday, and Liza asked if I was planning to invite you along. And I said that yes, of course I was. She didn't answer, but I could tell she was annoyed.'

'Why?'

'Because when it comes to these rituals, these things that she and I have been doing together for a million years, she's very . . . protective. Even if I couldn't go with her because of a real emergency, even if my mother were at death's door, she'd be furious. And what makes it even more tiresome is that when we're there it's always the same thing: the first night we eat dinner at the Quiet Clam, where Liza orders the grilled scallops. Then we go home and get stoned and play Scrabble – not that I like Scrabble. I hate Scrabble. And I always lose, because Liza's so bloodthirsty. Still, it has to be Scrabble. And then the next morning we have breakfast at this little place at the golf course where Liza always has the cheese omelette – and then, and then . . . Always the same! She's trapped by habit. Her whole life, when you think about it, is a repetition compulsion.'

'So you're not looking forward to the trip.'

'Oh no, on the contrary, I can't wait. I love this trip. That's why I want you to come along.'

'Me?'

'Yes. To shake Liza out of her complacency. And also to prove to her that my having fallen in love with you is a good thing, a boon to our friendship. And also' – here he kissed me on the nose – 'because I'd be lonesome without you.'

I frowned. 'But if she doesn't want me to go—'

'She's going to have to accept it whether she likes it or not,' Eli said, getting up and walking into the bathroom, 'since the only alternative is her going alone.'

'Yes, but Eli, if Nora's her friend—'

'Oh, but she's my friend too,' Eli interrupted. And from the sink he launched into a complicated story about how on a certain occasion, years earlier, he had gone out to Nora's house without Liza, to help her repaint her living room, and become intimate, over the course of a weekend, not only with Nora but Hilda, with whom Nora had been living for the last fifty years. Hilda, who had left both her husband and her job as a high school librarian for Nora, had no profession. Instead she devoted herself entirely to the organization and maintenance of the Nora Foy archive, which took up the entire attic of their house in East Hampton, and in which every document that could reasonably be considered relevant to Nora's career – even shopping lists and the little scraps of paper on which Nora jotted down messages to herself – was now, thanks to Hilda's industry and affection, stored and catalogued.

'And where's Hilda now?' I asked, for until today I had heard nothing of her.

'Oh, she died. She had Alzheimer's.' By now Eli, his face wet from washing, had emerged from the bathroom. 'So you see, Liza's in no position to tell me what to do where Nora's concerned.' He patted me on the cheek. Clearly it pleased him as much to have a weapon against Liza as it pleased Liza to have a weapon against him. Yet in all this fractiousness, where did I fit in? No doubt Eli's wish to bring me along was sincere; still, I couldn't help but recognize in it a desire to hurt Liza. Nor had she been entirely truthful, I suspected, when she'd insisted that she wished the best for Eli and me, for if she did, then why had she tried so hard at dinner to make him look ridiculous?

It is always disturbing to recognize the capacity for malice in friends whom we are used to viewing as generous and kind; yet such an acknowledgment is less essential if we wish to cut the friendship off with impunity than if we intend to carry it on. And this was especially true in the case of Liza, whose aggression owed less to retaliatory anger than to that very quality of oblivious self-interest that made her at once such a companionable friend and such an unreliable ally. Thus (to give but one example) it was not until Eli threw it in her face many years later that she even realized how badly she'd hurt him by asking for his advice on whom to take to Sam Stallings's party. Instead, that salvo, like most of her salvos, was friendly fire; it was a stray bullet slipping through a chink in the battlements, as opposed to one of those hydrogen bombs that Eli sometimes detonated. And though I cannot blame him for feeling the need to defend himself against Liza (and later me), since to stretch the war metaphor a bit further, we were both such loose cannons, neither can I pretend that his inclination toward vengefulness made my sleep easy. True, lack of intention does not excuse the perpetrator of a cruelty any more than a blind corner excuses the driver who hits a child; and yet, if asked with which one you would more likely trust your life, the terrorist or the hit-and-run driver, which would you choose?

It was all very sad. Indeed, in hindsight I realize that the best thing I could have done that weekend would have been to make myself scarce, to invent some excuse for not coming along, and thereby give Liza the opportunity to end that part of her life with dignity. After all, only a year later I would be jumping at opportunities to spend weekends alone in the city, for by then I would have started having affairs. At the time, though, all I wanted – and at any cost – was to stay with Eli. This was the real reason I accepted his invitation, not, as I told myself, to show spousal loyalty, or to defend him against Liza's belittlements.

So we all went together, in Eli's mother's station wagon, which he had borrowed for the trip. Because Liza and I had neither seen nor spoken to each other since the dinner at the Chinese restaurant, I worried that she might be sullen or short with me. Instead, when we met that morning, she greeted me with a cheerfulness that made me wonder whether Eli might have been exaggerating her disgruntlement. In fact, I would have willingly chucked all my negative expectations for the weekend out the window had Liza not, almost as soon as he got into the driver's seat, preempted any discussion of which of us would ride in the front by claiming, with a sort of pro-prietary cheek, the seat next to Eli's for herself. Annoyed but reluctant to provoke a rupture, I said nothing, only climbed into the back, where I fumed like the child to whose place I'd been relegated. Meanwhile Liza had put on a cassette tape, the cast recording of an early Sondheim musical I did not know, with which she and Eli sang along all the way to Manorville: yet another tradition from which lack of infor-mation excluded me. Was this her new strategy? I found myself wondering as we pulled into Grace's for Cokes. That is, simply to ignore my presence for the duration of the week-end, as if I were a third fox terrier that some neighbor had asked them to care for? If so, it made me no more happy than did Eli's refusal to heed the loud and simmering silence I'd been trying to radiate all through the drive. Indeed, when Liza went to the bathroom, giving us our first moment alone together, he did not even ask how I was. Instead he just said, 'Having fun?'

I shrugged. 'I don't know any of those songs,' I said.

'Poor Martin. I'm sorry, I forgot you might be feeling left

out in the back seat. Tell you what, when we get back in, we'll teach them to you.'

I was not, however, about to give up so easily, and taking advantage of Liza's absence, I hurried to the car and claimed her place in the front. 'I hope you don't mind,' I said when she came out a few minutes later, 'you know I've got long legs. I was starting to feel cramped back there.'

'No, it's fine,' Liza responded listlessly, and got into the back. We resumed the drive. Once again Eli put on the cassette; then, when Liza did not start singing, he took it out again.

By now we were passing through that long stretch of car dealerships, pool companies, and traders in marble and tile that precedes the actual villages of eastern Long Island, and that gives way, soon enough, to the old shingled houses, the dimly lit restaurants in which Nora and her literary cronies were reputed to get drunk together, the hardware stores and thrift shops and 'candy kitchens' that distinguished that lovely part of the world, for this was in the days before investment bankers and movie directors had begun colonizing the Hamptons, the days before Pets Painted with Love had become yet another Ralph Lauren Country Store, and the villages still retained a touch of antiquated charm. Because it was late fall, sodden leaves clogged the gutters. In front yards, on green, green lawns, raked-up piles of them waited to be carted off. Then Eli made a left turn, drove down a few narrow streets (on one of them some black children were playing stickball), and stopped the car. We got out. In contrast to most of its neighbors, Nora's house was an old and sagging harridan, with brown shutters and a weedy front garden. Through the mayhem a few tea roses thrust out their decadent heads. On the stoop, the bricks of which also had weeds growing between them, Eli fit the key into the lock and fiddled for a minute, while behind the door a sound of snuffling and whining started up, those barks and scrapings that signify the almost uncontrollable vehemence of canine ardor.

Then he shoved the door open, and they were all over us, two terriers who, with their bearded muzzles, their black and white coats spattered with tan, would have resembled exactly the mascot of my former employer had they only been well groomed, instead of, like the garden itself, walking thickets of fur from the depths of which, at any number of points (for they were constantly in motion), here an eye popped out, there a black nose, a pink tongue. They jumped us; they pawed us; they squealed and licked our ears. Never in the world, it seemed, had there been gratitude to equal theirs, never had there lived, anywhere in God's green kingdom, creatures so ecstatic, so avid with love.

We stepped inside. 'Poor Nora,' Liza said with a loud sigh, and led us through the living room, past a pair of sofas draped in dirty beige sheets, along floorboards scratched by generations of dogs' nails and never resanded. In the kitchen the faucet dripped, the wooden breakfast table was coated with a layer of grime you could draw pictures in with your finger (and Liza did). How she loved this place! She loved the bedrooms, both the spare one with its framed lace and the other, larger, in which, on a sagging bed with a white spread, the famous Gertrude Stein and Alice B. Toklas dolls – grandmotherly Raggedy Anns – reclined. Here the windows were curtained in a blue Chinese *toile de Jouy* on which a happy mustachioed fellow in pointy shoes and a jester's cap swung on a cord suspended between two branches of a tree. On one of the branches, through a trick of perspective, a pair of elaborately plumed birds his own size had built a nest big enough for him to sleep in, along with three tidy eggs. 'When I lived here one winter I used to stare at this fabric for hours,' Liza said. 'I used to make up stories set in that little world. You wouldn't walk here; you'd skip. You'd frolic and sport.'

'You'd cavort,' Eli said.

'You'd bobble.'

'You'd frisk.'

Then we fed the dogs, and once they were sated, went ourselves to feed at the famous Quiet Clam – Liza, as promised, ordered scallops – where we wondered why Nora had given them such pretentious names. 'Frankly, I think it's show-offy,' she said. 'And Nora's not the only one. For instance, Seymour Kleinberg, did you know that he calls his pugs Isabel and Caspar, after *The Portrait of a Lady*?'

'I had a music teacher in high school who named all his cats after opera heroines,' Eli said. 'Tosca, Aida, Musetta, Doretta.'

'My friend Kendall Philips,' I offered, 'was in Southampton last summer, on the beach, when he heard a couple chasing after their Dalmatian puppy, and calling "Doghampton, Doghampton, bad dog!"'

I smiled. Liza and Eli smiled back – a bit condescendingly, I thought.

'And what's wrong,' Eli asked, 'with giving dogs and cats ordinary dog and cat names – you know, like Frisky or Skipper?'

'Our dog was called Lulu,' Liza said wistfully.

'We had a cat called Daisy.'

'And yet by the same token certain names are almost too normal, so much so that they sound ludicrous when applied to a pet. For instance, Susan. Can you imagine meeting a cat called Susan?'

'How about Margaret?'

'And yet the funniest name of all for an animal – I'm sorry, but it's got to be' – Liza covered her mouth with her hands – 'is Martin. Martin!' She guffawed. 'Can you imagine it, Eli? "Martin, here, boy! Good Martin!"'

'Darn,' Eli said, 'Martin peed on the rug!'

'Ha-ha,' I said neutrally – and made no fuss; after all the last thing I wanted was to be accused of being a spoilsport. And yet the words rankled. Once again, I was the outsider, the interloper. It seemed to be my fate.

By the time we got back to Nora's that evening, the dogs had once again entered into a state of ecstatic loneliness. Having first jumped on us and licked our ears, when we bent down, to make sure we were ourselves, they headed out into the backyard to pee and dig and do all the other things that for dogs amount to serious business.

'Have you got the joints?' Liza asked Eli, who nodded.

'Good. I'll get out the Scrabble set.'

Bending down, she set to digging in her suitcase. Eli yawned theatrically.

'Actually, Liza,' he said, winking at me but for her, 'I'm pretty bushed tonight. Couldn't we save Scrabble for tomorrow?'

She gaped up at him. 'You mean you don't want to *play*?'

'Not right now.'

'And what about you, Martin?'

I turned to Eli. In fact I would have been happy to play, only his look told me to pretend otherwise.

'I'm pretty tired myself,' I said.

Liza stood up. 'Well, I guess that's that, then,' she remarked, crossing her arms over her chest. 'Since I can't play alone, I suppose there's no choice but to hit the proverbial hay.'

'The land of dreamy-dreams,' Eli echoed.

'Still, we could at least get stoned—'

'But what's the point, when we're going to bed?'

'Oh, I see,' Liza said huffily, and forced a smile. 'Okay, if that's how you want it, that's how it'll have to be.'

'Yup.'

'Well, pleasant dreams.'

'Pleasant dreams,' Eli repeated pleasantly. Yet he did not move. None of us moved. Liza, still standing by her suitcase, fingered the bag with the Scrabble letters in it.

The dogs scratched at the door; Eli let them in.

'Well, well, well,' he said once he had both terriers inside.

'What is it?' I asked.

'I'm afraid that we're on the horns of a dilemma.'

'Why? Which dilemma?'

'That tired old dilemma,' Eli said, sitting down on a sandy armchair, 'of sleeping arrangements.'

'Sleeping arrangements! But why should there be a problem?'

'You tell us, Martin,' Liza said. 'Where would you like to sleep tonight? Or perhaps I should ask, with whom would you like to sleep tonight?'

'Well, with Eli, of course . . . I mean, doesn't that make sense?'

'And where?'

'In the room with the double bed. Where else?'

'So in other words, you two'll take the big bed and the big room, and I'll sleep in the little bed in the little room. Is that right?'

'Liza, stop this this second,' Eli suddenly barked. 'You're being ridiculous.'

Falling onto the couch, Liza buried her head in her hands and began to weep. Alarmed, the dogs ran to her. They licked her ears. They tried to lick her eyes.

'I don't understand,' I said – though I did. 'Why is this such a big deal?'

'It's a big deal, Martin, because for the five years that Liza and I have been coming here we've always slept together in the big bed. And now she doesn't want to give that up. She doesn't want anything to change, ever, if it involves me.'

'But when you've come here before, you've always been

alone, it's always been just the two of you. Doesn't that make a difference?'

'Of course it does. It's a new situation – a permanent one.'

Liza wept more loudly. Standing, Eli took a box of tissues from the mantel, then sat next to her. 'Oh, come on,' he said, putting his arm around her shoulder, 'there's no reason to blow this all out of proportion. I mean, think of it this way: how's it any different from when we're in New York?'

'But we're not in New York! We're at Nora's. And so I don't see why just because the two of you are fucking, it means I should get left out in the cold – literally.'

'But whether you like it or not, Martin is my lover.'

'And so you have to sleep every night of your life with him?'

'But the thing you never seem to realize, Liza, is that if the tables were turned, if it were you and Jessica instead of me and Martin, you'd take it for granted that you two would sleep together and never even think about what I wanted.'

'But that's my point! I'd never have invited Jessica! I'd never have been that insensitive. I'm sorry, Martin,' she continued, dabbing at her eyes, 'but I've got to tell the truth. I'm really angry that you're here. I'm angry at you for coming, and I'm angry at Eli for asking you, and I'm angry at myself because I see now that introducing you two was the biggest mistake I ever made in my life.'

'Oh, so my happiness is a mistake? My future is a mistake?'

'For me, yes.'

Eli stood. 'You never think of anyone but yourself, do you?' he shouted, loudly enough so that the dogs ceased, for a moment, their endless task of comfort. Alarmed, she looked up, looked into his eyes, before spiraling away from him.

Then there was a silence. Their backs turned to each other, tensely poised in this stand-off that neither arbitration nor argument would resolve, Eli and Liza stared at anything: the bookshelves, the dogs, the half-open door to the kitchen. How they loathed each other at that moment! And yet what struck me even more viscerally than the depth of their enmity was the strength of the love from which it had grown, and without which it would have desiccated into indifference. For it was as if Liza's words had burned away a layer of cant in which their friendship had been swathed, revealing its fundamental, polarized elements, circling each other endlessly: pain and love, love and pain.

No one else was there to help. Even the dogs looked at me pleadingly, as if they recognized the limited potency of their tongues.

And so I got up. Very tentatively, I approached Liza, who was hunched in a corner of the sofa. I put a hand on her warm shoulder. 'Look, how about this?' I suggested. 'The bed in Nora's room is pretty big. What if all three of us sleep there . . . together?'

She laughed.

'That way we'll all get what we want. Both of us will get Eli, you won't have to sleep alone, I won't have to sleep alone. Plus it'll be fun in its own right. Like a slumber party. What do you say?'

She rubbed her nose. 'I don't know . . . Eli?'

He shrugged.

'And what's the alternative?'

Again, silence. 'I suppose,' Eli said, 'the alternative is that we don't sleep.'

'I see your point,' Liza conceded, laughing a little – which relieved me. 'Well, okay . . . I guess.'

So we headed upstairs, to Nora's bathroom, where like children we brushed our teeth together; we took turns peeing. While Liza put on her nightgown, Eli and I gingerly moved the Gertrude Stein and Alice B. Toklas dolls onto the dresser, turned down the spread, took off our pants and shirts and climbed into the bed. 'Brr, it's cold,' I said, switching off the reading lamp and burrowing into his chest.

Liza climbed in last, on his right – it went without saying that he would sleep in the middle – then switched off the other light. 'Good night, Eli,' she said.

'Good night, Liza.'

'Good night, Martin.'

'Good night, Eli. Good night, Liza.'

'Good night, John Boy.' She giggled. Another silence fell, which only the mattress, sighing whenever one of us turned over, interrupted. Clinging to my corner of the sheet, I felt the bed curve under me like the earth itself; I felt Eli's hand take mine. And far away, on the other side of this continent, was he touching Liza too? Was she touching him? For once I didn't care. What mattered was that I was here, in the moment, in this bed, with these people who loved each other, and whom I loved. These were interesting times for me, they were exciting times – and someday they might even be pleasant times to remember.

11

I'm Not Here

OF MY MOTHER'S DEATH, which occurred late that summer, I shall say little here. I have already made too much of it in fiction, milked it too much for sentiment and dread. Such episodes ought to be recounted only in the spare nudity of their experiencing. Yet how could I have done that when her death broke every rule I'd been taught in writing classes? To wit, it told what it should have showed; the dialogue was hackneyed; the descriptions were banal; none of the principals was likable; its author put himself in a position of moral superiority to his characters . . .

What I'm trying to say here (but it's painful) is that for the sake of pats on the head, good reviews, and fan mail (as well as to satisfy a clause in my contract that promised me an extra ten thousand dollars for every week the book I wrote about my mother spent on the *Times* bestseller list, which it never made), I spruced up her death like a corpse before an open-casket funeral, in the process committing several sins of omission and at least one bold-faced lie: in the book I place my protagonist at his mother's bedside at the moment of her death. Yet in fact, during those last hours, I was nowhere near her hospital room. Instead I was hiding with Eli at my sister's house, eating pot brownies and watching a video of Pepe Le Pew cartoons: over and over the cat, on whose back circumstance had painted a slender white stripe, scrambled out of the passionate skunk's arms; over and over the skunk declared undying *amour*. What kept me away wasn't fear so much as a youngest child's pouty indignation that my brother and sister should have gotten her for ten more years than I had. Well, I would show them, I decided. I would make them all sorry. But I only made myself sorry.

I suppose someday I shall forgive myself for not being with my mother when she died. I suppose I shall even forgive myself for not sticking around long enough to be with my father when he scattered her ashes over the bay. But I shall never forgive myself for the ease with which, in that novel I wrote about her death, I inserted myself into both these solemn scenes – as if my absence were merely the sort of plot inconsistency it is the duty of fiction to correct. (Stanley Flint, of course, would have seen right through such a lie: he could smell the inauthentic a mile away. And yet by that time I had long since stopped showing Flint my work, not, as I told myself, because I didn't trust him, but because I feared he might catch me out in my mendacity.)

That spring my story collection, *The Deviled-Egg Plate*, had been published to what that tiresome if useful reference work, *Contemporary Authors*, called 'favorable-to-mixed reviews' – a locution more suggestive of weather reports than literary criticism. I quote:

Helen Shipley of the ——— *Gazette* lauded Bauman for his 'fluency and grace,' while Joann Finkelstein of the *Reporter* praised the 'crystal-clear lucidity' of his prose and the 'human warmth emanating from the characters, all of whom really fizzle.'

On the other hand, Seamus Holt complained in *Queer Times* that Bauman's 'wan, watered-down portrayal of gay life' amounted to 'the worst kind of assimilationist nonsense,' while J. J. Frakes of the —— —— *Tribune-Sentinel* objected to Bauman's 'obsession with homosexuality – is nobody straight?!' Of one of the stories he observed: 'If this were about Jim and Polly instead of Jim and Paul, who'd give a darn?'

Kendall Philips, who read all reviews of everything, even in the most obscure newspapers, called me to commiserate. 'Opinions are like assholes,' he asseverated. 'Everybody has one.' Yet despite the cavils of gay activists and right-wing mavens alike, the story collection did well (for a story collection) – that is to say, it made it into paperback, got nominated for a prize, and even landed me a leading role in an article published that summer in *Broadway* magazine that would prove to be both the making and unmaking of my career. This article, which was titled 'Invasion of the Prestige Snatchers: The *Nouvelle Vague* of Young Writers and Where It Hangs Out,' featured two photographs – one of me, Liza, and Eli playing Scrabble and drinking tea in front of her fireplace (my big head threw Eli's into shadow), the other of Sam Stallings, Violet Partridge (to whom Liza, you may recall, was cozying up in the last chapter), and someone called Bart Donovan, who wrote mostly about cocaine, shooting pool in a louche Bowery bar. 'It's like they're our evil twins,' Liza giggled when the early copies arrived, 'the bad kids to our good kids.' Yet oddly enough, while the good kids in this little drama were gay Jews, the bad kids (with the possible exception of Bart Donovan) were straight WASPs. *They* didn't wear sweaters their mothers had knitted. Instead Sam had ex-wives, while Violet (better known as 'Vio') had once earned her living dancing naked in a vat of Jell-O. In the end it was their *vague*; they were the ones who surfed it. As for us, we simply clung to the edges of the crest until it broke.

Our position was ambiguous, sometimes uncomfortable; in our own minds at least, we were always the scholarship kids, the wallflowers at the tailgate. Thus I remember arriving with Liza at one of those parties that *Vanity Fair* was forever throwing for itself. Ahead of us in line stood Jay McInerney with his girlfriend of the moment, a model who had become famous after a lunatic had attacked her with a razor. As they neared the gauntlet of paparazzi, a hundred flashes erupted. 'How stupid,' I said to Liza, yet was unable to hide my chagrin when upon our own entrance the photographers reloaded their film.

Even more distressing to me were those occasions on which I found myself the object of an attention that seemed to me misplaced, or in some way warped. For example, in Milan once with Eli to promote the Italian translation of my stories, I attended along with Sam Stallings a party honoring 'the new generation of American writers,' the host for which was a famous clothes designer. Here, though wearing a pink-and-white-striped jacket purchased for twenty dollars at a Seventh Avenue knockoff shop, I was compelled by the regiment of fashion photographers present to dance before their cameras with a former Italian starlet of the fifties, now boozy and hoarse-voiced. No doubt the artificial intimacy into which we were thrust embarrassed the actress as much as my jacket did; nonetheless, being a veteran of such publicity stunts, she played along gamely, whispering in my ear what appeared to be endearments but were actually arch instructions not to clutch so tightly at her crimson tulle dress. Afterward, at the end of half a dozen interviews with regional papers in which I was asked, 'Can you tell us at which clubs you and the other members of the Brat Pack drink together like the Lost Generation in Paris?' a journalist with purple hair stuck a microphone in my face, and said, 'What is death to you, in two words?'

'This interview,' I would have answered, had I been clever.

Later that night Eli and I had a fight. We only had one fight in those years, but we had it over and over. It went like this: first some ineptitude or insensitivity on my part would enrage him. In retaliation he would be cruel. In response to his cruelty I would bristle, lash out, then, as my own anger burned off, retreat into a posture of remorse and supplication that was in fact aggressive, because it demanded instant forgiveness as the ransom for leaving him alone. Soon our fight would take on a life of its own, its origins would be forgotten, it would adapt to the same invariable and sorry trajectory, with me banging furiously at a door Eli had locked. And though, every time, he proved himself to be the more skilled and cruel antagonist, keen to my weak points, which he gauged expertly, who's to say whether in my own frantic flailing I didn't hurt him just as much? Probably I did. Still, anger was a condition of his life in a way that it had never been of mine. For he had a tornado in him. Far from earth, the little house of his soul flew about in churning winds. A few years earlier he'd read Alice Miller's *The Drama of the Gifted Child*, and it had set him off for life, authorizing his rage, which was both relentless and lacerating. Now, every time we argued, the drama began again. Outside the window his father, like Miss Gulch, rode by on a broomstick. Liza failed to invite him to a party. Rejection letters flapped in the furious air.

The problem wasn't anything so simple as jealousy, or that things were going badly for him; on the contrary, despite Liza's naysaying, Billie Eberhart had just sold his novel to an eminently respectable publisher. And yet even this good news

did not make him happy, because, as he was always reminding me, though ———— had just bought his novel, my
publisher (which he considered more prestigious) had turned
it down. 'Which, when you think about it, is like getting
rejected by Princeton all over again,' he added.

I should have realized, then, that what I was dealing with in
Eli was something far less remediable than lack of reputation;
he could have won the Nobel Prize in literature, and still
found a way to view his victory as somehow trumped up, fal-
lacious, without meaning. Nor were matters made easier
when mutual friends, to his face, dismissed his career as
merely a subdivision of mine. Not only to newspaper subscription salesmen was he 'Mrs Bauman'; instead at that time
it must have seemed that every phone call, every letter, every
dinner invitation he received concealed a secret motive. Out of
the blue, old friends from whom he hadn't heard in years
would call, apparently just to say hello, really to see if,
through him, they could get me to do some favor for them.
Fellow homosexuals, whom you would have thought more
sensitive, asked him outrageous questions – 'So why are you
really with Martin, Eli? For your career?' Others praised his
'selflessness' in giving up so much 'to help Martin write . . .
how hard it must be for you, Eli!'

No doubt the zenith (or perhaps I should say the nadir) of
this period was an Author's Guild panel titled 'What's the
Matter with Kids Today? Young Writers Speak Out' that
took place in the auditorium of the same Brooklyn school at
which Eli had once taught. The other participants were Julia
Baylor, Violet Partridge, and an elegant woman named Lise
Schiffrin who had just published an equally elegant collection
of short stories, *I'm Not Here*. Neither Liza nor Eli were in
the audience. In Liza's case, this was because she was out of
town, having been invited (it was the sort of invitation only
Liza ever seemed to receive) to take part in a 'youth think

tank' sponsored by a manufacturer of video games; at the moment she was sitting poolside with six other 'geniuses' (one of them, Ben Pollack, the man she would eventually marry) at a Ritz-Carlton in southern California. As for Eli, because we had had a fight earlier that day, at the last minute he'd refused to come with me. Instead, he said, he was going to stay home and do some of his own work for a change.

Lise Schiffrin was a startling figure. Her eyes, which were immense and dark, suggested the staring panic of certain marsupials, while her long, magnificently erect torso made me think of those exotic water birds whose feathers turn pink from eating shrimp. All told she provided a welcome contrast to Vio, whom I had come to distrust in recent months, in large part due to her duplicitous habit of simultaneously reviling the literary establishment for its 'elitism' – her supposed exclusion from the corridors of power owing, she argued, to her roots in the rural south, where her (very good) novel was set – and exploiting that establishment for all it was worth. Thus every Christmas for the past five years she was rumored to have mailed to about three dozen famous novelists giftwrapped packages of homemade divinity – a present by means of which she must have hoped to drum into the consciousness of these eminences at least the rhythm of her name, so that when the bound galleys of her novel arrived in their mailboxes, instead of throwing them aside along with all the other bound galleys they received, they would take note of them, recall the association of the name Violet Partridge with the sugared delectability of the divinity (enough to make their mouths, like those of Pavlov's dogs, water), and read the book. And this strategy, moreover, appeared to have worked, for the back of Vio's novel boasted no less than fourteen blurbs, penned by (among others) Sam Stallings, Leonard Trask, Nora Foy, Henry Deane, *and* Stanley Flint.

Such a tactic put Vio in the opposite camp from Lise, who

suffered from that allergy to professionalism that distinguishes a certain kind of very dedicated and very innocent artist. She was, in the most dangerous sense of the word, a purist, which was why, when the panel began, and from each of us the aggressive moderator extracted an opening statement, she could express only her bewilderment at being asked to take part in the first place, after all, she pointed out, even though she had just published her first book, she was not, in any ordinary sense of the word, *young* – she was forty-four – thereby giving voice to a bafflement similar to the one I had experienced a few years earlier when Jim Sterling had taken me to see a musical review in which all the songs were based on poems written by the elderly; the trouble was, of the dozen cast members, few looked to be more than fifty, with the result that when a vigorous black woman strode onto the stage and belted out the showstopper 'I Am Not Old!' we could only agree with her.

What a welcome presence Lise was on that panel, especially during the question-and-answer session, when Vio – in response to the question, 'Do you make a living from your writing?' – first claimed that her work earned her only enough money 'to pay the rent' (when everyone knew she had just sold the film rights to her novel for half a million dollars), then went on to excoriate the 'meritocracy' by which she felt herself to have been, as a consequence of her origins, excluded (yet at that moment she was weighing teaching offers from no less than three universities)! Lise, on the other hand, when asked what her plans were for the future, simply gazed at the audience with those wide eyes of hers, and said, 'What are my plans? Very simple. *Write, write, write.*'

Afterward we were taken to the cafeteria and sat down at four card tables piled with copies of our books. A long line – at least fifty people – had already gathered in front of Vio's table, where she was now signing away and chatting with the

professional suavity of a talk-show host. Julia's line was
slightly shorter, and consisted mostly of current or former
students of Stanley Flint. Mine was limited to about a dozen
young queers, some with female accomplices in tow. As for
Lise, though she was without question the most gifted writer
present that evening, not a single person waited at her table.
Instead she sat alone before thirty copies of *I'm Not Here*,
clearly wishing she weren't, so that I longed to get rid of my
own admirers if for no other reason than to claim my rightful
place as one of hers.

'And who is this book for?'

'Erika, with a K.'

To Erika. All best wishes, Martin Bauman.

'Hello. And who is this book for?'

'Could you make it out to Jamie and Stuart – with a U – on
their anniversary?'

'But what if you split up? Who'll keep the book?' They
didn't laugh. 'Just kidding.' *To Jamie and Stuart. Happy
Anniversary! Martin Bauman.*

'Hello. And who is this for?'

'Roy.'

I looked up. Before me stood Roy Beckett. 'Howdy,
stranger,' he said.

'Roy,' I answered. And smiled. Though I hadn't seen him
since Christmas, since that party during which we had flirted
and Liza had discussed dental dams with Seamus Holt, in the
intervening months his face, I had to admit, had stayed with
me, a vision to be called up and mused over not while Eli and
I were fighting, but rather in the exhausted aftermath of our
fights, when fatigue itself had brokered a kind of peace
between us. For with his lustrous, clean-shaven cheeks, Roy
was in many ways the very antithesis of Eli, whose face
seemed every day to become more rabbinical, more darkly
scowling, as if through it the agony of history were revealing

itself. Roy, by contrast, was squeaky-clean, smelling of limes. Tonight he wore a gray suit, pressed white shirt, Hermès tie, the usual Manhattan uniform, and a far cry from Eli's tiny running shorts, his underpants pinkened by contact with something red, the jeans he had owned since high school.

I told Roy how much I appreciated his coming to hear me – something none of my other friends had done – which made him laugh. 'Do you think I'd miss one of your rare public appearances?' he asked. 'Not a chance. And now, if you wouldn't mind . . .' And he pressed a copy of my own book toward me, back cover facing out, so that his hands seemed to be caressing my cheeks. Opening it, I wrote, *To Roy Beckett, whose arrivals into my life, though rare, always bring pleasure. Yours, Martin Bauman.* Then I handed it back to him. He opened the book. 'You should've been a doctor,' he said, examining my signature, 'I can hardly read your writing. So listen, what are you doing now?'

I balked. 'There's supposed to be a dinner . . .'

'With those women? Forget it. Come have a drink with me instead.'

'But I—'

'You'll have more fun with me, I promise.'

He winked – which decided me – and after I'd agreed to go, went to wait for me near the back of the room. Finishing up my signatures, I bid Lise good-bye, glancing over my shoulders, as we talked, to make sure that Roy hadn't left. And what a different place this cafeteria seemed tonight from all those evenings on which I had sat here alone, waiting for Eli to finish up with his class! Back then I could have imagined no greater happiness than to roost amid the smells of hamburger grease and salad dressing, listening through traffic for the sound of Eli's voice, the moment when the door would open and he and Comma Splice and Evensha Hopkins, in a riot of laughter, would tumble out . . . Afterward, on the way back to his apartment, we might stop for dinner at the restaurant that served fifty-six varieties of soup. No more, though. Now rancor had contaminated the waters of our domesticity; the soup, cooked with the bones of contention, was sour.

Roy, on the other hand, seemed to me the embodiment of freshness that evening, and not only because he cultivated such a straight-from-the shower affect (and smell); also because, in his urbanity and carriage, the smoothness of his suit and of his words, he was, once again, the very opposite of Eli: a professional, with his own co-op, an MBA from Stanford, furniture he had bought (as opposed to inheriting it from his mother's basement). Beautiful civilities embraced him, the same ones that Eli, in his irascibility, so consciously and high-handedly flouted. For as I was discovering, the quirky charm of his studio (and Liza's) could pall quickly. Those little rooms that in winter had seemed so cozy became stale with the arrival of warm weather. My infatuation with Roy (and consequent disillusionment with Eli) initiated a long period during which I was forever shuttling between two worlds, which charmed and repulsed in equal measure: the first, of which Eli was the exemplar, aggressively private, and governed by the creed of personal relations; the second both more cosmopolitan and less commodious, with its grand pooh-bahs and guest lists, that world that the French call – imparting to the word both a lacquer of glamour and the slightest patina of contempt – 'society.'

Roy, of course, never used this word. He had grown up poor, in a Philadelphia ghetto, which might have explained (oddly enough) the ease with which he now made his way in the corridors of blue-chip office buildings and blueblooded apartment buildings. Though Baptist and black, he was nonetheless more of a WASP than any WASP could be, just as T. S. Eliot was the consummate Englishman. Thus he did all his shopping at Paul Stuart (never Brooks Brothers), had his eye on a house in Newport, and kept a copy of Paul Fussell's *Class* by his bedside. In subsequent months, when our affair really got going, I would find myself being dragged along by him to any number of AmFAR benefits, evenings that were in their way far more brain-numbing than the intimate, Amy-filled, pot-infused gatherings Liza had once convened, yet at which I might at the very least meet a Rockefeller, or hear anecdotes about the latest White House dinner, or catch the eye of the waiter as he spooned new potatoes onto my heated plate . . . But I have jumped ahead, as is my habit, too far, too fast. I have to rein myself in, and bring us back to the evening of the panel, on which Roy took me out not, as I half expected, to one of the trendy restaurants where, after work, he sometimes ate a plate of quail and truffle risotto at the bar (these we would frequent later), but rather to a rooftop cock-tail lounge on Second Avenue, very forties, all buttoned red plush and high-hipped waitresses. From our table we could see the Roosevelt Island tramway, above the lit cables of which a surprisingly voluptuous moon rose, gray-blue, veined with canals the color of Roy's eyes.

'I'm glad you came,' he said, winking at me again so that I blushed.

'I am too,' I admitted.

Then we drank Manhattans (what else?), and he told me everything he'd liked about my book. I didn't listen. Quite inconveniently, I thought, Eli had intruded upon our intimacy: Eli who, despite all the forces conspiring to evict him – alcohol, jazz piano, the soft but insistent pressure of Roy's voice – was nonetheless superimposing himself upon the scene as indelibly as the reflection of a passing waitress on the view outside the window. Alone in his studio, dressed in one of the peculiar outfits he favored while working – a Tyrolean sweater, say, and no pants – he puttered about, tuned his violin, brewed some herbal tea. And all the while he hadn't a clue that forty blocks uptown, my knee pressed into Roy's, I was betraying him. That was the thing that got me – not Eli's suffering, but his innocence – which was why I resolved to lie when I got home, to tell him I'd gone out with Julia and Lise Schiffrin. This was my first adultery, though it preceded by months the first time I had sex with someone else.

After a while Roy stopped talking about my book; instead he just gazed at me. Across the narrow table I studied his face. Because I was a little drunk, I said, 'It's not often you meet someone with black hair and blue eyes.'

'It's not often you meet someone with black skin and blue eyes. And you, Martin Bauman, you've got blue eyes too, though your hair isn't black. More mouse's back – Nice Jewish Boy brown.'

'Oh that's right, you like—' I quieted, not sure whether it would be kosher for me to mention what Kendall had told me months ago, that Roy was a yarmulke queen. Yet if this was the case, shouldn't he be warned that he was making a mistake in choosing me, who'd never gone to Hebrew school, much less been *bar*-mitzvahed? Eli would have been more up his fetishistic alley, I suspected, though somehow I couldn't quite imagine Roy and Eli getting along.

That was the closest we came that night to admitting any mutual attraction. Though more banter followed, soon Eli – or more specifically, my worry that Eli would be irritated if I got back late – propelled me to make excuses, tell Roy good-bye, and hurry home. As we parted, he slid his business card into my hand. 'Don't forget to call,' he said, and I told him I wouldn't. What I didn't know was that something was about to happen that would lead to the postponement of that call – and everything it implied – for more than a year.

Eli became a different man during the weeks that led up to my mother's death, both kinder and less contentious, as if the very gravity of the situation had revived the caregiver in him and sent the combatant into retreat. Gone, suddenly, were the great tempests of resentment to which I had become acclimated; instead, in Seattle, where we were sleeping on my sister's pullout couch, he took it upon himself to supervise the grocery shopping and the management of the household. He picked up my nephew every afternoon at day care. In the hospital waiting room, where the rest of us were more or less living, he always made sure there was plenty of water and fruit juice around – and not only for us, but for those loved ones of other dying people with whom we were obliged to share that starkly intimate space.

One morning (I made much of the episode in my novel, which whitewashed our relationship as much as it did my own cowardice) he even excoriated a nurse who, upon noticing us hugging in a corner, had asked us to please 'stop making such a spectacle' of ourselves. Eli – employing to someone's actual benefit, for once, that flair for invective that he had honed over years of insults – had flayed the poor woman so pitilessly that in the end she'd had no choice but to limp back to her station, as voided of spirit as the girl he had called, many years earlier, a flat-chested, dog-faced bitch.

This attitude of protectiveness (coupled with a rerouting of hostilities in other directions from my own – that of the nurse, for example) only intensified when we got back to New York; here, too, instead of returning to his old habits of bellicosity, he treated me with an almost excessive tenderness, as if I were an injured creature whose very survival depended upon gentle handling. Nor did I fail to take advantage of this change in his demeanor, which was entirely to my benefit. For now, whenever I did something inept or insensitive, Eli, instead of snapping at me, choked back his vexation. He watched *I Love Lucy* in bed with me every night. He even got me a dog, an eight-week-old fox terrier called Maisie (via Nora Foy), simply because I had mentioned one day, apropos of nothing, that I wanted to have one. And when, in my simple grievousness, I begged him to take me to stay for a few days with his family – after all, though she wasn't *my* mother, at least Harriet was *a* mother; nor was I above, at that moment, accepting a substitute for the irreplaceable thing I had just lost – he always agreed, even if it meant postponing a yoga lesson, or missing out on a choir rehearsal, or having to cancel a long-planned dinner with Liza.

I remember vividly his parents' house on Long Island, to which we traveled by train, or if circumstances permitted – if, for instance, Harriet had come into town to take in a concert – by station wagon. It was situated on a wide, sidewalkless thoroughfare that linked the interstate to the village, and that was called, funnily enough, Park Avenue. A vast ornamental lawn, incised in summer with stripes where the power mower had pushed back the grass like the nap of a carpet, separated traffic from the house, which was Colonial, huge and yellow; indeed, somehow it seemed *too* huge for its inhabitants, who stole about nervously in their own corridors, heated only the principal rooms in winter, and never sat in the living room with its bow windows and silk curtains, its gleaming Steinway, its damask couches. There was a reason for this. Until he was eight, Eli told me, his family had lived in a different house, more modest, and filled with homely, practical furniture from a department store in Westbury. But then his father, deciding that a grander residence was needed to match his grand sense of himself, had moved them out of their comfortingly crowded little neighborhood and into this haughty quasi mansion with its cargo of lowboys and ottomans, flirtatious little footstools and claw-footed coffee tables, which Harriet kept scrupulously clean, yet refused to use. Instead she sat only in the little room off the front hall to which the few items she had been able to salvage from the old house – a consolingly rumpled sofa, two BarcaLoungers, and a battered cherry cabinet – had long since, like poor but dependent cousins, been relegated.

Sometimes, at my insistence, we stayed on Park Avenue for days at a time. Because they were not my own, the rooms comforted me. Everywhere there were emblems of grief – for instance, the Stair-a-Lator that climbed up the staircase to the second floor and that had been installed the year that Eli's grandmother had come to die in an upstairs bedroom – yet because it was not my grief, I could regard these emblems with indifference, just as I could listen with indifference to the acrimonious arguments Eli sometimes had with his mother, or the music he alone played on the grand piano, or the mutterings of Marty as he tried to fix (and only broke further) the antiquated VCR. (Though one of the first to come on the market, and state-of-the-art at the time of its purchase, it was now a dinosaur.)

Of my own mother, meanwhile, I tried to think as little as possible. The last time I'd seen her healthy had been that summer in Florida, where she and my father had gone to visit one of his sisters. 'If anyone ever tells you growing old is a tragedy,' she'd said to me, 'don't listen to them. Believe me, growing old is wonderful. You *know* so much.'

I dreamed about her all the time. In one dream (I had it in the guest room on Park Avenue) I received a notice in the mail that at a certain hour, at Aquatic Park in San Francisco, shadowy authorities would be making her 'available' for fifteen minutes. In this dream I rushed to make the appointment, fighting traffic the whole way, then found her waiting near where the old Italians play *bocci*, dressed in a tartan plaid skirt fastened with a safety pin. All ravages smoothed, gazing out at the fanned red ribs of the Golden Gate Bridge, she put her arm around me and pointed to that monument to inescapability, the island of Alcatraz. 'Look, Martin,' she said, as if I were still a child whose attention she had to captivate. 'Look, honey. Isn't the world an interesting place?'

Sometimes, during those somber days on Park Avenue, I also thought of Roy. Since returning from Seattle I'd neither called nor heard from him. Even so, his hands caressing the outline of my photograph stayed with me; their imagined touch, which only the book jacket had felt, intimated possibilities of joy, freedom from warfare and sorrow, tranquillity, and at the same moment stimulation, because (of course) such a life was remote from this world; reality had not yet smudged it with dirty fingers. And then Roy, too, would intrude upon my dreams, often in the company of my mother, with whom he walked peacefully on the rocks that front the Pacific near Port Angeles, and where once (it seemed eons ago) I had gone with her to see the sea elephants. Me, I was alone, in the distance, as always, watching.

I did not go home. This was mostly to avoid my father, who in his perfectly reasonable eagerness to get on with his life was making all sorts of changes to the house of which I disapproved. Gone, for instance, was the hydromassage tub that had previously been the Hole; in its place a new bathroom, all chrome and glass, had risen. Where previously the floors had been covered by shag carpeting, new parquet was being laid. He'd even painted the shingles gray, and gotten rid of the bed in which he and my mother had slept, replacing it with a low mahogany platform, a pallet of foam as minimal and sleek as the life for which, in his sorrow, he was preparing himself: all changes that in my view, at least, amounted to acts of desecration, for it seemed to me then that it was his duty to maintain the house as it had always been, as a sort of shrine to his dead wife's spirit at which her children and grandchildren, whenever they chose, could pay homage. Contrary to conventional wisdom, it is usually the old who want to go forward, while the young cling heedlessly to the past.

Much of my time I spent with Harriet. A kind and intelligent woman, she had worried eyes and blond hair for which she had once been famous, but which today she kept short and to the point. Like many daughters of the Depression – like my own mother – she was too well trained in the art of self-denial to think much of her own pleasure. Thus when they were alone, she and Marty never drank wine, rarely went to restaurants, ate plenty of healthful unsalted fish. Let one of her children telephone to announce an imminent visit, however, and the spaghetti to be dressed with a jar of tomato sauce warmed in the microwave would give way to briskets of beef, noodle kugel, chocolate chip cookies. The comfort I took in her home, I see now, must have touched her maternal vanity, yet more to the point was the fact that my presence there, though questionable in its outward semblances – what etiquette guide, after all, explains how to introduce your son's homosexual lover at the synagogue? – had the side benefit of bringing her elusive, much-loved, first-born Elijah back into the fold. Harriet's gratitude to me meant that there was little she would not have done to ease my sorrow, few whims of mine she would not have indulged, if only to guarantee that I would keep bringing Eli back.

Yet she drew the line at Christmas. This was a chronic sore spot between us, my fondness for elves and mistletoe and all the other accoutrements of a holiday that for her would forever be summed up by the girls who in her childhood had pushed her off the jungle gym, chanting, 'You killed Christ! You killed Christ!' Thus when she saw the little tree that Eli – at my behest – had set up and decorated in his apartment, her response was to weep. 'Don't you know the lights are suppose to represent the drops of Christ's blood?' she cried. I didn't know – further evidence of my family's laxness and ignorance. If she'd had her way, Harriet would have used Christmas as an opportunity to inculcate in me, at last, some knowledge of my own religious heritage. Instead I kept putting in for a tree. I begged for a tree. 'You can call it a Chanukah bush if you want,' I reasoned.

'But it's not our faith.'

Finally, as a concession, she agreed to roast a turkey, so long as it could be accompanied by something decidedly un-Christmasy. (We settled on lasagna.) Most of the morning she and Marty devoted to back taxes; then around five we sat down at the kitchen table. Only the four of us were there. While we ate Marty watched C-Span on the little television. Eventually Harriet got up to clean the kitchen, and I went to call my father, who was spending the holiday at the beach house of some friends. 'Happy holidays,' I said to him glumly, as in the background music played, ice clinked in glasses.

'Happy! Ha!' my father answered. 'I'm about to cry.'

On New Year's Day, Eli and I went back to New York; once reinstalled in his apartment I spent most of my time in the loft bed, watching television, just as at his parents' I had spent most of my time riding the Stair-a-Lator up and down, up and down. Such behavior, needless to say, worried Eli. Eager to remedy the situation, he made it clear that he would be available at any hour, to satisfy any little desire I might have; indeed, all I had to do was mention, in the most off-the-cuff manner, some casual yen – for an ice cream sundae, say, or the video of a favorite movie – and he would be on the phone or out the door to satisfy it. Still, I got no happier. Because I so rarely left it, the apartment took on a stuffy smell that frustrated the athlete in him; after all, spring was coming; he needed fresh air, grass on which to stretch his limbs. Finally one warm morning he threw open all the windows, admitting a breeze big drafts of which he gulped like water. I stayed in bed. 'I'm going to take Maisie to the park,' he announced loudly, perhaps in the hope that I might volunteer to join them. But I didn't.

'Too bad we don't live closer to the park,' I said, 'or you wouldn't have to take the subway.'

'Would you like that? Would you like to live closer to the park?'

'Sure, I guess.'

A few days later a dentist's appointment compelled me, for the first time in weeks, to leave the apartment. When I got back, Eli had vacuumed, taken the sheets to the laundry, even made the bed – no mean feat, when the bed is ten feet off the ground. 'I have a surprise for you,' he said and, sitting me down, announced that he had just sublet his studio for a year to an NYU undergraduate, renting in its stead the uptown apartment of a friend of his, a composer called Glenn Schaefer who was about to leave for a sabbatical in Florence. Ostensibly the purpose of this rather troublesome and complex removal was to fulfill my wish that we live closer to Central Park, the healing properties of which Eli advocated mightily, not only for us, but also for Maisie, who could run free there as she never could in the East Village. Also, we would have more space: a one-bedroom instead of two studios. Also, if I followed his lead and sublet my own apartment, we could try out, as we never had before, the experiment of actually living together.

To work of the details, Eli and I went to have dinner with Glenn at his apartment. Comparatively speaking, he was a new friend of Eli's; that is to say, they had met only a few months before, during the intermission of a Met performance of *Aida*, where in the men's room Glenn had tried to pick him up – unsuccessfully, as it turned out, though they became great pals anyway. More recently, Eli had shared with Glenn the unfinished string trio on which he had been working for so many years, and to which, in the wake of Glenn's suggestions, he had recently returned with renewed zeal. As a composer, Glenn was notorious for his 'Nonet in F-sharp

Minor Never to Be Played,' a postmodernist conundrum that had earned him ridicule from the *New York Times*, as well as veneration from the music students who now flocked to his composition seminar at Rutgers.

What Eli saw in him I was never able to fathom. In his early forties, troglodytic and muscular, with an unmown blond face and heavy-lidded eyes, he suffered from terrible halitosis, as well as that more typical New York malady, a sort of halitosis of the mind, the victims of which feel compelled to share with you, from the word go, all the most scurrilous details of their lives. Thus at dinner, in response to an innocent inquiry on my part as to why he liked Florence so much, he had led me to a bookshelf filled with thirty years' worth of sketch-pads, pulled out '1984,' and, handing it to me, said, 'Turn to page seventeen.' I did. A hirsute youth, wearing only white boxer shorts, sat open-legged on a Dante chair. 'His name's Pierluigi,' Glenn said rapturously, 'and he plays double bass in the Orchestra della Toscana. Straight of course, but I've had him. If you go to Florence, you could have him too.'

He returned to the kitchen, where Eli was supervising the final stages of a chicken tetrazzini – chicken tetrazzini being, as it happened, Glenn's gastronomic calling card. This left me alone in the sunken living room with his boyfriend of the moment, an underfed Russian émigré called Ivan, in his early twenties, whom Glenn liked to tease by instructing to repeat what he referred to as 'that sentence.'

'But vy?' Ivan would protest. 'Vy you vant me to sya this stupid thing?'

'Come on. Please.'

Ivan would huff. 'All right, all right. "Ve must get rid of moose and squirrel." But vy is this funny? Vy?'

Poor Ivan, this evening, appeared desolate, no doubt because in a few days his lover of the last several months would be departing for Tuscany, for umbrella pines and *ribollita* and a hundred Pierluigis. Slumped on a sofa from the brocade covers of which dust rose in mushroom clouds, he gazed out the window at windows. Traffic noise roared up. Me, I was too busy studying the apartment to take much notice of him. It was a very weird place. Table lamps and wall sconces with red shades threw an opium-dennish light against the walls, which were painted black; photographs mottled them, many of famous people, including an actor I recognized naked against a cream-colored screen. His penis, though flaccid, hung halfway to his knee.

'Oh, that,' Glenn said when I asked him about it. 'A little treasure of mine. Avedon took it – on the condition that it never be shown publicly.'

'Then how did you get it?'

'I used to have a friend who worked in his dark room. Sometimes he'd sneak me a print . . .' He shook his head sorrowfully. 'Dead now. My friend, as well as the actor.'

'It's beautiful.'

'Isn't it?' Glenn leaned closer. 'I only wish *all* Russians . . .' And indicating poor Ivan, he sighed loudly, so that I caught a whiff of his sour-sweet, mulchy breath.

After that the famous chicken tetrazzini was served. Because he talked so much, Glenn ended up eating very little, whereas Ivan ate huge quantities of food very slowly, like Klothilde, the poor relation in Thomas Mann's *Buddenbrooks*. Neither he nor I took much of a role in the conversation, which centered on the vilifications a pair of opera singers were reputed to hurl at each other during rehearsals: much more up Eli's alley than mine, that topic. Also, I was far too busy trying to figure out how on earth I was going to live in such an unlikely place to pay much attention to what was being said. Around the sunken bowl of the living room, a collection of human and animal skulls, *memento mori* and shrunken heads, was ranged. This wasn't so bad – such objects could easily be stowed in a closet – and yet could the same be said for the vast découpage of snapshots with which Glenn had covered one entire wall of the bedroom, a farrago of faces and bodies I didn't know, arranged with such intricate (and intimate) care that once undone, I suspected, it could never be reconstructed? It was to this mesh of Glenn's history – what Eli called his 'little black wall' – that we would wake every morning during the months we lived there. While we dressed, strangers' faces scrutinized our nakedness. In the night they infiltrated our dreams.

The next week I sublet my apartment to Julia Baylor, who had just broken up with her boyfriend. Then, dog and computers in tow, we moved uptown. Earlier, Glenn had encouraged Eli and me to take advantage of his collection of CDs and videos, especially the pornographic ones, which, he'd hinted, were a far cry from the usual West Hollywood fare. Our curiosity piqued, we put one in the VCR the first night. It turned out to be a medley of Glenn's favorite scenes from various commercial productions, spliced together to provide a sort of route map to his orgasms. Indeed, at the end of the tape a clip for which he must have felt a special fondness, in which a burly man in his forties plunges a dildo into a blond boy's upturned ass, was repeated over and over, as if a needle had gotten stuck on a record.

On another tape, the usual porn gave way, after a few minutes, to footage of a naked Ivan sitting cross-legged on Glenn's bed with another youth. This boy was even skinnier than Ivan was, and had terrible pimples on his back. While off screen Glenn's voice issued orders, the pair sifted through a cardboard box filled with whips, buttplugs, and vibrators, eventually laying hands on a sort of two-ended dildo which reminded me of the pushmi-pullyu in *Doctor Dolittle*. 'Okay, Ivan,' Glenn's voice instructed from the distance, 'now take the lube and grease up Ignat's butt.'

At this point Eli switched off the tape. 'Most shocking,' he said. 'Maisie is scandalized. I'm putting her to bed.'

Carrying the dog under his arm like a purse, he disappeared through the bedroom door. 'I'll be there in a minute,' I called after him. Instead of following, however, I turned the video back on. What excited me about it was less the fact of Ivan's presence – he wasn't at all my type – as the knowledge that only a few nights before, in this very room, he and I had eaten dinner together, conversed, exchanged bored glances across the table. This was the intoxication of the real, and I was experiencing it for the first time: that moment when the line between what is imagined and what is smelled, touched, tasted, suddenly blurs. Wasn't the sofa on which he and Ignat were currently engaging in such a fascinatingly rarefied act of fornication the very one on which I, pants around my ankles, now sat? True, it was distasteful to think that from across an ocean – by proxy, as it were – Glenn was seducing me as, despite his bad breath he had presumably seduced Ivan, Ignat, and the double bassist from Florence. Yet unlike Eli, I submitted willingly to his remote control. I did not go into the bedroom. I stayed, and I watched.

Living in that apartment, I later told Roy, was a bit like being trapped in one of Glenn's videos, in the endless loop of his tics and compulsions. From every wall, every cornice and doorknob, he bore down, the whole corrosive mess of him, squeezing the breath out of me as no doubt, heaving over him, he must have squeezed the breath out of poor scrawny Ivan. And though at night, it was true, the living room took on a certain sheen of metropolitan glamour, the lamps with their fringed scarlet shades glowed languidly, the light of passing taxis, bouncing upward, made a pleasing show against the mullioned windows (so that I understood, for a moment, how easy it would be to succumb to Glenn's strategic caresses), by daybreak his almost fungal presence – immanent in the books on his shelves and the suits in his closet – would have reasserted itself, as heavy as the smell of old beer and cigarettes in a nightclub from which the last partygoer, at five in the morning, has just departed.

It was during the weeks immediately following our move uptown that I became accident-prone. Walking one afternoon down Broadway, a movie marquee across the way having caught my eye, I tripped over the curb, twisted my ankle, and landed nose down on the pavement. Blood poured out, strangers screamed, though in the end it turned out merely to be a surface wound; no bones broken. Then a few days later, driving Harriet's station wagon through the Midtown Tunnel, my eyes blackened as if I had been beaten (and one of the ironies of my accidents was that they always left me looking beaten, so that many people began to suspect Eli of assaulting me), I nearly rear-ended a Hampton Jitney on its way to Montauk. Eli cursed my spaciness, almost got angry, then controlled himself. How on earth could I be so careless? he asked. Did I have a death wish? I hotly denied it. Even so, balancing atop a precarious ladder in Glenn's apartment a week or so later, I stretched too far to adjust a book and crashed to the ground, bruising my hip so that it turned a purplish black. As it happened I was alone at the time, which was fortunate: I couldn't have borne Eli's reproachments. Dragging myself to the sofa, my ankle still aching from when I'd hit my nose, I wondered if perhaps he was right. And yet I didn't *think* I wanted to die. If anything, I had a life wish, not a death wish. I was teasing fate to prove my invincibility.

The truth was that in the wake of my mother's death, I was having to confront for the first time the very phenomenon of mortality from which her illness, curiously enough, had always protected me. This, I think, is why I was constantly walking into lampposts or slipping on the ice all that winter:

to test my own immunity, to establish that what had happened to her (not to mention what had happened to Philip Crenshaw) would never happen to me. For everywhere I turned, it seemed, someone was dying. Lars, after a swift illness – five days! – was dead. So was Eve Schlossberg's brother. So, for that matter, was Theodoric Vere Swanson III, the first boy I'd ever slept with. That I knew none of them well, curiously enough, only added to the sense of bewilderment that the news of their deaths called up in me. For it seemed that there should have been everywhere vigorous young men, most of whom one hardly knew, running up and down city streets, chatting and eating and looking for just the right dining table for their apartments; instead of which, mysteriously, there were not.

These were dark days – literally. A blanketing of gray, the color of the iron curtain, as I envisioned it in childhood, descended over the city and would not lift. It was thick, miasmal. Dusk came at five or so, bringing a bit of relief in that it cloaked, for a time, the straitjacket of the sky. Then in the morning we would look for the tiniest breach in the clouds, and not find it. There was little reason to go out. The air was wet and chilly, and in the neighborhood shops everybody had a cold.

I was trying to write about Joey, about being robbed, albeit not very successfully. The problem was that in those days I clung to the notion that any misfortune could be redeemed through its own recounting; and while it is true that the cooking down of experience into something at once more beautiful and less inchoate than itself can be a cathartic process, clarifying as well as purgative, such transformative episodes are both rare and costly, requiring a degree of self-knowledge I did not then possess; what was really a subtle and complex negotiation between fate and art I misconstrued as the crudest kind of barter, in some cases a literal barter, as if by earning more money from the story I wrote about Joey than he had stolen from me, I could not only compensate for, but somehow profit from his attack.

In the wake of my accident, I left the apartment less and less frequently. Most of the time I stayed in Glenn's bedroom, trying to write or – no, not reading but *re*-reading those books that I could trust to provide a sedative effect, a sort of literary Valium: Wodehouse's Jeeves and Wooster stories, the more cheerful of Barbara Pym's tales of provincial English life, the Mapp and Lucia series by E. F. Benson, the filmed version of which my mother, by dying, had just missed. Or I watched television, old Warner Brothers cartoons I'd already seen a hundred times and that I hope will continue to be repeated, every afternoon, for eternity. The frenetic interactions of Tweety and Sylvester, Tom and Jerry – from which a scrim of glass protected me – lent to those days the same hushed air of convalescence that had marked the afternoons when I'd been kept home from school with a cold, and over which, in recollection at least, a subtle rain is always falling. For memory has its own weather; even today, in my mind, a cloud cover hangs over our months in Glenn's apartment, making it difficult to distinguish, in all that cold, wet, concentrated gray, the real source of my unhappiness, with which a hundred mirages furiously competed. No matter that I told myself and others I was fine, 'resting,' recuperating; the truth is, I had entered into what clinicians term an 'acute vegetative depression,' albeit one that refused to recognize its own face in the mirror. And such a state, like a warm bath in a cold room, is easier to drop into than to climb out of. Left to my own devices, I got fat; my breath became sour. Eli was horrified, but checked himself from saying anything, lest my lethargy should be some necessary step in the grieving process that it would be lethal for him to interrupt.

As is often the case, my sorrow coincided, for him, with a

period of great happiness and productivity. If Glenn's apartment brought out the worst in me, coaxed into bloom some germ of sordidness I carried within myself, it had the opposite effect on him. Most afternoons he disappeared for hours, with Maisie, into the park; they ran and played fetch, and fell in with a neighborhood clique, incipient militants whose shared resentment of the leash laws had inspired them to revolutionary tactics. These new friends of his were always engaging in little acts of civil disobedience, such as letting their dogs off the leash all at once in the presence of a patrolman, who would then be hard-pressed to issue summonses. Afterward, Eli would burst back into the apartment, sweaty and exuberant from his exploits, which he would share with me even as he shimmied out of his clothes, switched on the shower. Laconic on the bed, I would pretend to listen; aim the remote control toward the television; watch passively as game shows, talk shows, soap operas sped by illegibly, stations seen from a moving train. What we were engaging in was an unspoken battle of wills, his enthusiasm versus my lassitude, which always won out. Finally, discouraged by my silence, he too would lapse into silence, lie down next to me, and start reading, or else go out again, as if to protest my dissolution, the irritating and obvious fact that the things he had hoped would make me happy, and for the sake of which he had moved us uptown, were making me miserable.

He had a point. I was not cooperating with his efforts to rouse me. For instance, whenever he invited me to go with him to the opera, or to a concert at Carnegie Hall, I always said no, claiming that classical music bored me. (Yet later, with someone else, such music would become a mainstay of my life.) Whenever he entreated me to accompany him and Maisie on one of their park frolics, I begged off. (Yet later, with another dog, I would spend whole days there.) What rankled him even more than my refusals, moreover, was probably the suspicion that they owed less to any real difference in our temperaments than to an unwillingness on my part to join in, and thus enhance, his pleasure, as he had enhanced mine, say, every time he'd sat through an episode of *I Love Lucy* with me. For it was obvious that I was blaming on circumstance a disaffection to which, from blindness or selfishness, I would nonetheless not fess up. What was less obvious was the source of this disaffection. Clearly it was nothing so simple as a conflict in tastes – his for Joan Sutherland versus mine for Joni Mitchell – because such decorative kinks affection, in the long run, always smooths out. Nor was it the erotic threat of another, of Roy, for instance, against whose clean-cut positivity, even if he'd been around at that dark moment, I would have had to shield my eyes. Nor was it resentment at any mistreatment I believed myself to have suffered at Eli's hands, for by then I had come to accept my own partial responsibility for our warfare. No, what I was feeling was something far more unreasoned than that, something more akin to the base antipathy that provokes one dog, without explanation, to growl at another. There is no pretty way to say this. I wanted to love Eli, I tried valiantly to love him, indeed, on some primitive level I probably did love him; but I didn't like him.

There, I've said it. I didn't like him. Very likely he didn't like me, either. That he loved me I am fairly certain, in that heedless, indiscriminate way of siblings whom history has bound together, yet who within an hour of reuniting are at each other's throats. And yet – the vast history of family life to the contrary – this is never a very good basis for conjugal union. You have to like each other as well as love each other, else the thousand irritating little details that make up the human spirit will drive you to rage – as, for instance, Eli's habit of shucking off his clothes like a snake shedding his skin, which in someone else I might have found charming, drove me to grind my teeth, ball my hands into fists. Why?

Because it was Eli. Nor was he indifferent to my aversion, which no doubt bruised his ego. And how unjust it must have seemed to him – yet another example of his fatedness – that at the very moment of his own fledgling happiness, I should be militating against our marital happiness! Still, there it was. He held back from expressing his frustration, while I remained immovably perched atop the slide of my destiny, too frightened to go down yet too proud to admit defeat.

My social life dwindled to nearly nothing. A few weeks earlier, a critic had published a diatribe against what he called the 'scourge' of minimalism, thus initiating a media backlash against the 'brat pack.' Around the same time Sam Stallings's second novel came out to what could only be called barbarous reviews, at which point the party invitations dried up. This was just as well: I was hardly in the mood to see people. Instead, when I got bored or lonely, I talked over the phone with Liza, from whom the combination of our move uptown and her new infatuation with Ben Pollack had distanced Eli of late. No longer did she convene her old 'afternoons' with Ethan, Janet, and the Amys; instead, she told me, she preferred to spend her days and nights alone with Ben, with whom she insisted that she had fallen irretrievably in love – a declaration that Eli and I, quite naturally, took with a grain of salt; after all, throughout their long history, hadn't she claimed on other occasions to have fallen hopelessly in love with men, only to give them up as soon as some pretty girl caught her attention? In our experience, Liza's lesbianism was such an endemic fact of her character, even of her *physiology*, as to render moot any debate over sexual confusion. Yet now she was insisting not only that she loved Ben, but that she loved him in spite of a conscious decision she had made to commit herself unwaveringly to lesbianism – a decision, moreover, of which he was fully aware, and on which she had no intention of reneging.

'But, Liza,' I said in frustration, 'isn't that like being a little bit pregnant?' In response to which she shot back that in her view to reject someone you loved just because he was a man was as dishonest as to reject someone you loved just because she was a woman. Prejudice went both ways, she insisted; existed on both sides of the erotic divide.

Eli, for selfish reasons, would not be persuaded. Since the weekend at Nora Foy's, he had been enjoying a rare equilibrium in his relationship with Liza, who appeared finally to have realized that she could no longer take their friendship for granted. For a long while she had been at his beck and call, free when he wanted her and undemanding when he didn't; but then Ben had come along and, as is so often the case when someone has a new lover, suddenly she didn't seem to need Eli anymore. Nor did his insistence that this didn't bother him, that on the contrary, her sudden lack of availability came as a relief, sparing him from having to take part in the 'cult of her crises,' keep him from needing to express, whenever her name came up, his disappointment at her 'cowardice,' not to mention his conviction that by choosing Ben, she was merely buckling under to convention and trying to get back at Eli for what she saw as the shoddy way he had sometimes treated her. Meeting Ben might have made things easier for Eli, by giving a human face to her treachery; only Eli didn't want to meet Ben. To him Ben wasn't a person so much as a figurehead, allegorical snout thrust forward from the prow of that vast and totemic cruiser, heterosexuality. He and Liza talked for hours on the phone, they argued and hung up on each other and called each other back again, she tried ceaselessly to persuade him of her sincerity while he tried ceaselessly to dissuade her from her 'betrayal.' Neither succeeded in convincing the other of anything. They had reached an impasse – not so much between conflicting ideologies, as between his old-fashioned belief that sexual identity was a fixed boundary, the violation of which amounted to a kind of treason, and her contrary pleas for a more supple definition of the erotic self.

Things only got worse after that. At the dinner that Eli and I, after much nagging from Liza, finally agreed to go to with her and Ben, Eli hardly spoke at all. Ben seemed a likable enough fellow – handsome in his way, and obviously intelligent, though timid, which was hardly surprising, given the slight, almost lewd, almost flirtatious, and in any case inquisitional smile that Eli, in his silence, kept casting toward him. To compensate for Eli's refusal to open his mouth, I talked as much as I could, too much, in the end: I became, once again, the babbling youngest child who had so bored my brother and sister. Liza joined in: we filled the air with banter. Yet the dinner, despite our valiant efforts to salvage it, was a failure. Indeed, as Eli and I walked home afterward, he could only shake his head, interspersing sighs of disbelief with the occasional remark about how Liza had been dressed. 'Did you notice she's growing her hair long again?' 'Did you notice she's wearing two earrings again?' 'Did you see she's carrying a purse?'

'But Eli, she's always carried a purse.'

'Yes, but not like *that*. This time, walking away with him, that purse swinging from her arm, she might have been Sada.'

'She wasn't wearing a skirt.'

'She will be next time.'

Alas, there was no next time. That evening, closing himself up with Maisie in Glenn's bedroom, Eli called Liza on the telephone for the last time. For almost four hours they yelled at each other. Because I had the television in the living room switched on, I heard almost nothing of their fight. Nor, in truth, did I want to: I could guess in advance its import. Whenever Eli's voice grew loud enough to penetrate the closed door, I turned the volume up higher. I remember that I was watching the porno channel on New York cable, the Voyeur Vision lady, whom men called for five dollars a minute to witness her live responses to their live lust.

'Voyeur Vision lady, I want to be your slave!'

'Yeah? You want to be my slave? Then get down on your knees and lick the television!'

After a while I must have fallen asleep, for when I opened my eyes again, instead of the Voyeur Vision lady, I found myself looking at Eli. He was smiling in that curiously lurid way he had smiled at Ben.

'Hey,' he said.

'Hi,' I said, and stretched. 'What time is it?'

'Three.'

'Have you been on the phone all this time?'

He nodded.

'What happened?'

'It's over.' He repeated his smile. 'Liza and me.'

I sat up. 'Oh, Eli . . .'

'But it's okay, Martin! In fact I'm glad. Because it's been on the way for months, hasn't it, when you think about it? And some relationships – this is what I told Liza – you just out-grow. They're too fixed in their own time, they won't mature, which means that to sustain them you also have to sustain the conditions that nurture them – and that would really be impossible, wouldn't it, because Liza and I, we're not college kids anymore, and if we pretended we were until we were old and gray – well, that wouldn't be very attractive, would it?'

'Still, she's your best friend.'

'Correction. You're my best friend.' He kissed me. 'And now, just think' (sitting next to me on the brocade sofa, he put his arm around my shoulder) 'we're finally free in a way we never have been. I mean, we don't have to worry about Liza being competitive, or making demands, or insisting we all sleep in the same bed. Or her phone calls. Or all those tired rituals, that weekend at Nora's, the afternoons.' He glanced at me guardedly, a little sadly. 'Not that I'm suggesting that *you* should feel under any pressure to change your relationship with her – I mean, after all, your friendship with her is completely independent of mine. For instance, she'd love for *you* to come to the wedding—'

'What wedding?'

'But didn't I tell you? That's what started the fight in the first place. She and Ben are getting married.'

'But they've just met!'

'I know, I know. Needless to say *I* won't be going. I can't give this sort of thing my seal of approval. You're another matter, though. *You* could go.'

'Are you kidding? Without you? Not a chance.' I rubbed my tired temples. 'Oh, it seems so sad, Liza actually carrying through on all those old threats. I wonder if she'll regret it, if someday she'll wake up and think, What the hell have I done?'

'But she insists she's still a lesbian. That's what's so strange. She says she'll even keep writing about it – only she won't act on it.' Eli sighed. 'Well, I'd better take Maisie out. She's about to burst.'

'Want me to come?'

He looked surprised. 'That's nice of you, Martin, only . . . no thanks. I need to think. Anyway, it's late.'

'Okay.'

He left then. Stepping into the bathroom, looking at myself in the big mirror, I tried to reconcile my reaction to the news of this rupture – a genuine feeling of remorse, not only for myself, but for Liza and Eli too – with what I knew would be the more fitting response of a loyal lover (not to mention the response most likely to gratify Eli), a combination of shock and relief. For as I tried to remind myself, only a year ago, in the days when Liza had seemed such a threat to me, it was exactly this sort of rift that I had hoped for. Only now, in the mirror, I was no longer the boy whom Roy Beckett had taken out for a postpanel Manhattan; instead, with my puffy eyes and unkempt hair, I looked more like Glenn than myself, as if his spirit, the spirit of his apartment, were possessing me.

Bankruptcy! Only now does it strike me that this chapter, the hardest in the book to write and the longest in gestation, is Chapter Eleven. Oh, why did I refuse so adamantly (when it would have helped) to name what was rising in my bones that night, and had been rising steadily since the hour of my mother's death – as cold as the ache of a twisted ankle, an echo of which you know (and isn't this the first sign that youth is over?) you'll be feeling for the rest of your life: the penetrating chill of loss?

A few weeks after that, on the spur of the moment, Eli and I cashed in our frequent-flyer miles and went to Italy. What inspired us to make this trip, I think, was the delusion – so common to couples in trouble – that a change of scenery will automatically revive the inner scenery, freshening a tired love; and yet to believe this is to ignore the hermetic nature of marriage, which little outside itself can touch. At first, it was true, the shock of new sights and sounds perked us up a bit. Indeed, in Venice we were almost happy, tripping along the elevated boards that crisscross San Marco during *acqua alta*, when floodwaters turn the piazza into a wading pool. Yet it did not last. Instead this sensation of new possibilities, not only in the world but in ourselves, dissipated as we made our way down the peninsula. By Bologna I was depressed again, Eli frustrated, as always, at his inability to make me feel better. Then we tried the next desperate measure couples take under such circumstances: we invited someone else in to liven things up, in this case Glenn, whom Eli called from the train station in Florence. Yet as it turned out, Glenn was leaving that night for Paris. We had time only to drink a coffee with him, after which he graciously offered us his apartment on Via dei Neri to sleep in before departing himself for a new romance and some concerts of the Ensemble Intercomperain.

That afternoon, walking with Eli through the Piazza della Signoria, amid the spring traffic of tourists and pigeons I noticed a tall, hunched, familiar-looking woman posed earnestly before the statue of Perseus. 'My God,' I said, 'I think that's Lise Schiffrin.' And stepping nearer to where this woman, Blue Guide in hand, was peering at the streaked bronze musculature of the sculpture, I saw that I was right: she was, unmistakably, Lise Schiffrin. 'Hello,' I said, and she turned. It took her a second to register who I was, but once she did she smiled winningly, so that I could see the flecks of lipstick on her teeth. She was wearing a soft black leather coat, very expensive, and a lot of jewelry.

'Martin,' she said, offering me one of her long hands to shake, at which point I introduced her to Eli. 'Oh, what a pleasure to meet you,' she told him, then, turning to me, asked, 'By the way, how's that very good-looking friend of yours – you know, the one you stood us up for after the panel?'

Eli blinked. 'Oh, Roy,' I said. 'He's fine, thanks. Listen, would you like to have a coffee? If you're free, that is – we don't want to interrupt your day. It's just such a surprise and a pleasure, running into you—'

'No, I'd love to,' Lise said. 'We'll go to Rivoire.' And, taking Eli's arm, she led us across the piazza to a big café from the tables of which, in nice weather, you could admire the fake David and the Palazzo Vecchio.

'Clearly you know Florence better than we do,' Eli said, sitting down.

'Oh, I try to come a couple of times a year. I've got a friend here, perhaps you know her . . .' (She named a hugely famous show designer.)

'Well, of course, by reputation,' I said.

'Oh, you should really meet her. She's quite wonderful. Well!' And, smiling, she opened her enormous eyes to the fullest possible extent. 'So how long has it been since that historic panel? More than a year! Is it possible?'

'I'm afraid it wasn't the most stimulating evening.'

'Decidedly not. In fact, if it hadn't been for you, Martin, it would have been a complete washout. He really saved the day,' she added for the benefit of Eli, who was busy trying to signal a waiter. 'Poor Julia and I hardly knew what to say, while that awful what's-her-name – Violet Hummingbird or whatever—'

'Wasn't she terrible?'

'I'll tell you, in all my years in New York – and though I haven't been a writer for very long, I've traveled in other fairly, shall we say, or at least I used to think so, cosmopolitan circles – I've never met such an operator.'

Eli was now lifting his arm into the air, snapping his fingers at the waiter, who elected to ignore him. 'I can't believe this,' he said. 'Such rudeness. And probably only because we're foreigners.'

'Oh, it's not that,' Lise assured him. 'The waiters here are always rude. It's their mandate. You shouldn't take it personally. So that friend of yours, the good-looking one,' she continued to me, 'what's he—'

Eli was on his feet. '*Signore*,' he shouted in his opera Italian, '*per favore, siamo aspettando.*'

'One moment, please,' the waiter shouted back, 'stay calm, please.'

'No, I won't stay calm. You've served four groups that arrived *after* we did, and—'

The waiter made a gesture, at which point Eli let fly an

English obscenity that silenced Lise, and that the waiter must have understood, for suddenly he abandoned the old woman he was serving and marched over to our table in high dudgeon. Cheeks bulging, he and Eli stood eye to eye, nose to nose, and screamed.

'This is absurd. Just because we are Americans—'

'*Ma non,* it is not that you are American, it is that you are vulgar and ugly. You do not behave this way in my café—'

'And you do not behave this way to a paying customer who has come in good faith and expects to be—'

'Eli, please,' I interjected. 'It's not worth—'

'Shut up.'

'Please leave,' the waiter ordered.

'Perhaps we'd better go,' said Lise, standing.

'Eli,' I repeated, 'I really don't think this is worth—'

'Oh, this is wonderful,' Eli said, 'thank you very much, Martin, for being such a support to me when I'm trying to defend myself. Excuse me, Lise, there's no need for you to leave, you haven't been asked to. It's been a pleasure meeting you, but I can't bear this anymore. I can't bear any of it anymore.'

Then he yanked his jacket off the back of his chair and went. I stood. 'Eli,' I called, as he ran toward Via Calzaiuoli, turned a corner onto one of the little side streets, and was lost.

I sat down again. People were looking. Lise, her purse on the table, was busily redoing her eye makeup.

'I'm sorry,' I said, laughing slightly. 'I'm afraid that sometimes Eli gets a little – hot under the collar, shall we say.'

'Oh, don't worry,' she answered placidly; then, arching her face toward mine, she added, 'Listen, if you want to go after him—'

'No, no. What's the point? I wouldn't find him. And anyway, I hardly want to seem to be giving the green light to this kind of behavior. Or to miss an opportunity to spend some time with you . . .'

'That's so sweet of you,' she said, trying to suppress – or so it seemed to me – the look of bottomless pity filling her eyes. 'It must be . . . difficult for you.'

'Yes,' I affirmed, in the tone of someone making a long-withheld confession. 'Yes, it is.' At which point the waiter, at long last, came to take our orders.

An hour or so later, a little drunk from too many Campari and sodas, I returned to Glenn's apartment on Via dei Neri. Eli wasn't back yet, which was a relief: I didn't feel up to talking to him. Instead I opened a program from a concert given the week before by the Orchestra della Toscana that I had noticed loitering on top of the piano. Looking in the back, I scanned the names of the double bassists until I came to 'Pierluigi Pellegrini.' A phone book in the kitchen provided his address – Via Ghibellina, just around the corner – and telephone number, which I dialed.

'*Pronto?*' a youthful voice answered after one ring.

Then I explained that I was a friend of Glenn's from New York, that I was staying at his apartment while he was in Paris, and that he had suggested I given him a call. To my surprise Pierluigi immediately invited me to tea at his apartment. 'But when? Now?' I asked.

'Why not?'

Why not indeed? 'Great,' I said. 'I'll be over in a few minutes.' And, hurrying out of the apartment – making sure, first, that Eli wasn't approaching from either direction on Via dei Neri – I walked briskly through the oncoming twilight to Via Ghibellina, where Pierluigi greeted me at the door to his flat, offered me Fanta because he had no tea, sat me down on his sofa, asked me if I did not agree that Glenn was the best and most loyal of friends, not to mention a genius, and pointed out a pair of Dante chairs he had inherited from his grandmother. 'Why, I recognize that chair,' I said. 'It's in Glenn's drawing of you . . .'

'You mean the drawing where I'm only wearing my boxer?' I nodded. 'I hope you don't mind that he showed it to me.'

'Oh, no. I'm proud of my body.' He sat next to me. 'I am so grateful to Glenn that he sent you to me,' he went on, putting his big, warm hands on my cheeks and pulling my face toward his crotch; nor did I object to the celerity, the lack of ceremony, with which he performed this maneuver. For it was what I had come for, I knew, so I did exactly what was expected of me, and not only by Pierluigi, but by Glenn, by Eli, most crucially, by myself. Letting go of all prudishness, I stripped him to his shorts. I posed him in the Dante chair. And then, for twenty minutes or so on a cold spring Florentine afternoon, I 'had' him.

12

King Fag

I BECAME A slut. It was the natural next step, this fall into the slipstream, this immersion in tongues and sensation where once there had been only ideas and screens. Now, instead of asking Eli to take me along when he went to visit his parents on weekends, I'd beg off his invitations, so that I could stay in New York and devote myself to sex. Nor was it difficult, even when he was with me, to deceive him, for we hardly spent any time together anymore. If I'd found out he'd been having an affair I would have been glad, for the simple reason that an adultery on his part would have lifted the onus from mine. (To such a low point had our great, our exemplary love sunk that I no longer thought in terms of ideals. I thought in terms of what I could get away with.)

Otherwise, when questioned, I lied. I said I had a date to eat kosher Chinese food with Sara Rosenzweig, or to see a movie with Kendall, when really I was planning to go to a safe sex club an advertisement for which I'd read in the back of the *New York Native*, a place where the customers were one another's pornography, and 'lifeguards' wearing pink arm-bands patrolled the premises to make sure no penis ever entered illegally into a mouth or anus. For we were at a transitional moment in the scurrilous history of the AIDS epidemic. Activism – the glory years of ACT UP – remained for the future. At the same time those early days of panic and uncertainty, when total abstinence was urged as the only sure-fire method for avoiding infection – these, at least, were well behind us. No longer did fear of disease corrode every act of intimacy. Instead it was generally accepted that so long as one adhered rigorously to the rules of 'safe sex,' HIV transmission could be dodged. Yet what *were* those rules? There lay the problem. For on procedural matters – which were, finally, the *heart* of the matter – none of the experts seemed to be in agreement; thus in Germany posters in gay bars advised oral sex as a safe alternative to fucking, even as in New York similar posters were asserting that oral sex could be just as risky as anal sex, even if the person whose penis you had taken in your (I thought anxiously of Pierluigi) mouth did not ejaculate. (Did this mean that what was dangerous in New York was safe in Düsseldorf?) Likewise, while the authorities were united, at least, on the point that condoms provided an effective means of blocking the virus, how many of us knew, back then, that the ones made out of lambskin (which later, naively, Roy and I used twice) gave no protection whatsoever? How many of us knew, for that matter, that Vaseline could cause a latex condom to erode? Confronted with such ambiguities, some people – most of them older than I – elected to give up sex altogether, on the theory that once you'd become inured to the licentious abandon of the 'old days,' such a cramped approximation as safe sex, which was to sucking and fucking what a dietetic hard candy is to chocolate mousse, was simply beside the point.

More optimistic souls took on the role of cheerleaders for

masturbation, of which a Gay Men's Health Crisis brochure declared: 'Not only is jerking off with a buddy risk-free and fun, it's *hot*!' Music to my ears! For though such a promotion might represent to the new celibates merely a futile and annoying attempt to make the unpalatable palatable – 'It'll never work,' Gerald Wexler argued, 'people would always rather have *real* sex' – to me the prohibition had the odd effect of giving the green light to the acts I liked best. (Everything was ideological in those days; masturbation, according to post-Stonewall and pre-AIDS thinking, was not only childish but oppressive, a reminder of the closet and its privations.) In retrospect, I don't know whether the patronage of safe sex that marked those years brought to the fore in me a strain of adolescent eroticism that social pressures had heretofore suppressed, or whether, in a subconscious response to the newfound intertwining of eros with disease, I had *constructed* a desire to suit the limitations with which I was faced. Perhaps it doesn't matter. What is important is that those of us who had hang-ups stayed alive. (We were not the majority, though. Indeed, even at the safe sex club I couldn't help but notice the rapacity with which, when the 'lifeguard' was looking the other way, certain of my fellows would bolt down for a quick suck, as if what really excited them was not sex itself but the contravention of authority.)

Much later, I had a funny conversation about those clubs with the husband of a friend of mine, a man who could not fathom why I should find it arousing to be in a room where seventy-five men were masturbating all at once. 'Well,' I countered, 'wouldn't you find it arousing to be in a room where seventy-five *women* were masturbating all at once?' – a scenario the appeal of which, he had to confess, made more sense to him, albeit purely on the level of fantasy: 'Women wouldn't put up with it,' he insisted, which was probably true. Yet with women *or* men, he went on, wouldn't the room get boring after a while? I had to admit that it did; indeed, by my third or fourth visit to the safe sex club its allure had already begun to pall, much as tea grows weaker with every soak of the bag. I hated it when someone I knew waved or smiled at me, or a foolish voice called out of the mists, 'Excuse me, but aren't you Martin Bauman? I loved your stories' – words I shooed away like flies. For at that moment Martin Bauman was the last person I wanted to be; indeed, I wanted to forget him, the baggage – of which there was more every year – that he lugged around with him, and that made the footloose shamblings of his early youth seem so improbable.

Homosexual men are adepts at the banalization of the subversive. And this is in large part, I think, because we are men – no, worse than that, men besotted by masculinity, whose libidos no woman's touch will ever temper. Proust may have been right when he implied that the 'invert' is at heart a woman. Nonetheless there is much in him that is essentially and fatally male: habits of competition, relentlessness, denial, dissimulation. In fact it may be that when heterosexual men (including the friend mentioned earlier) balk not only at the effeminacy of queens, but at their lack of self-discipline, what they are really protesting is the degree to which we hold up a mirror to their own appetite, which perhaps only the influence of women keeps in check. (By the same token, if critics responded with ire to a theorist's recent suggestion that male masturbation is in essence a homosexual act, it may have been less because the idea itself was outrageous than because in every man's masculine self-regard the seed of homosexuality lies dormant.)

Around this time – summer returned, bringing with it a vague melancholic longing for sand and heat (and in my case, for that peculiar alternative to sand and heat, the arctic chill of the Sterlings' apartment) – I received the following fan letter, sent care of my publisher. 'Dear Martin Bauman,' it read:

> Though I'm not in the habit of writing to authors, your book of stories, *The Deviled-Egg Plate*, moved and delighted me so much that I felt I had to acknowledge the pleasure. Thank you! I look forward to reading the novel promised on the dust jacket.
>
> I am a member of a twelve-step group for sexually compulsive men that meets every Monday evening in Room 407 of the Gay and Lesbian Community Center, which is located on West 13th Street. I have the feeling that you would benefit from joining us. Remember, sexual compulsiveness is an illness, and one that can be treated with therapy. Help is nigh!
>
> Yours sincerely,
> Norman J. Parenti

My first reaction to this letter was to wonder whether, or when, I'd slept with its author – was he hot? Would I want to do it again? For so swiftly had I moved from a point where I could count the men I'd had sex with on one hand, to one in which it was impossible to keep track of their number, much less their names, that the possibility of my having done something with 'Norman J. Parenti' I took not only as a given, but despite the distinct thrust of his communication, as an opportunity.

My second reaction – to which the first contributed as much as the letter itself – was indignation. How dare this stranger write me such a letter, I found myself thinking, a letter as unwelcome as it was impudent, and nervy enough to hint that just because I had a healthy attitude toward things libidinous, there was somehow something wrong with me? There was nothing wrong with me! On the contrary, if anyone had anything wrong with him, it was 'Norman J. Parenti' with his faddish faith in twelve-step groups. (Here intellectual snobbery provided the perfect excuse not only for unreasoned disdain, but for closing the door on the question of why, if the letter was so silly, it had so upset me.) For in urging me to join his little group, what was Norman J. Parenti doing but dressing in the simpering language of self-help the very equation of pleasure with evil against which the men and women who had *founded* the Gay and Lesbian Community Center had struggled? Now that I no longer see myself as being 'above' the language of psychotherapy, I'm willing to admit my own sexual compulsiveness. Back then, however, to take such a letter seriously would have been to sanction a process of self-examination the stresses of which I refused, because they would have required me to do violence to my own illusions.

In July, advance reviews began to appear both for *The Terrorist* and for Eli's first novel, *History Lessons*, which were scheduled to come out within a few weeks of each other. They were not good; indeed, in the case of *The Terrorist*, the review in *Publishers Weekly* was so bad as to merit mention at the front of the magazine, where, amid other bulleted news items (including the announcement of Stanley Flint's imminent resignation from Hudson-Terrier), I read the following: 'Coming on the heels of his promising story collection, *The Deviled-Egg Plate*, Martin Bauman's first novel, *The Terrorist*, is a major disappointment.' Thank you, *PW*! To make matters worse, though the reviews for *History Lessons* were marginally more positive, Eli concluded from the rather nasty fuss that *PW* had kicked up that as in the past I had eclipsed him with the spectacle of my success, I was now going to eclipse him with the spectacle of my failure. 'I mean, with all that, who's even going to *notice* my book?' he complained. 'It's Mrs Bauman all over again.' His projected bitterness started us fighting, only more nastily than before, since beneath the surface of our discord lay the unspoken fact of my chronic infidelity.

What boded worse for either of us than each other, however, was a third publication set to coincide with ours: that of Stanley Flint's eight-hundred-page opus, *The Writing Teacher*. According to the buzz, this novel was going to be 'the publishing event of the season': '100,000-copy first printing,' I read at the bottom of the *PW* review (which was boxed and starred), '16-city author tour, major ad/promo.' And all this for Stanley Flint, who despite his demonstrable genius as a teacher and editor was as a writer, at least to judge from those few stories I'd read in college (as well as in his own estimation), utterly forgettable! Why him? I found myself asking. Had greatness touched him at midlife, as it had Proust? Perhaps. For if *PW* was to be believed, then *The Writing Teacher* was not merely 'the literary *tour de force* of the decade,' not merely 'a powerfully moving meditation on art, commerce, and sin,' not merely 'a fascinating postmodernist conundrum, an interrogation of the self and of the border territory between fact and fiction,' but 'one of those rare and original works of art that announces, almost from the outset, its destiny: this one will last.' Well! At the very least, I hoped, Flint's projected success might give Eli and me reason to band together in the irony of our comparative puniness. Yet when I shared the review with him, and laughed over the fact that in the case of my own novel only *fifteen* thousand copies were being printed, and a book tour planned to encompass a mere *eight* cities, he reminded me tartly that he wasn't being sent on any book tour at all.

Eager for news, I called Sara Rosenzweig, from whom I learned that Flint had left Hudson not, as was generally assumed, in order to devote himself entirely to the writer's life, but because the powers that be there had finally had enough of him. For not only had none of the novels and story collections he'd signed up during his tenure done well, some of them had done so badly that both the company and its shadowy parent had felt the repercussions. Nor did he hold much truck with the principle (so often trumpeted by publishing people) that best-selling junk 'pays' for serious books, as in his view the segregation of the 'commercial' from the 'serious' only led to the shortchanging of literature, which makes its profit in the long run: all this the nefarious doing, he was convinced, of the marketing people who had infiltrated the industry of late, and for whom he reserved his most passionate contempt. After all, it was they who were responsible for the sort of idiotic jacket copy then proliferating – 'If you liked *The Joy Luck Club* and you thrilled to *Watership Down*, you'll love *Cats of the Chinese Temple*' – and by which he was almost physically wounded; it was they who were forever rejecting the covers he proposed (severely elegant, all type) in favor of cheesy photographs, half-naked women, or flowers muted by a smear of Vaseline; it was they who were urging the new editors to spend hundreds of thousands of dollars on tacky novels about unhappy housewives being seduced by itinerant strangers – 'jack-off books for middle-aged women,' he called them – merely because one novel of this ilk had done well, and no one had any originality anymore. 'The bean counters are taking over,' he told Carey and me. 'Mark my words, this sort of thing will lead to the demise of books. Why, soon the writer won't matter at all, the book will be merely the occasion for a pretty jacket surrounding blank pages.' The memos of the bean counters, always ineptly written, pained him as much as Lopez's affidavit had. More and more he had to walk every day against the wind, and the effort left him mired in contradiction.

Each week, Sara told me, he grew less jovial. What enraged him was not merely the spectacle of 'unmitigated crap' coming out under Hudson's noble imprimatur, but also the acquisition of books the supposed seriousness of which disguised, in his view, a rancid or hollow core. Thus when a Hudson author he loathed ('a split infinitive in the opening sentence!' he complained; like my mother, Flint was a grammatical puritan) won the Pulitzer Prize, he wrote an editorial for the *New York Times* disavowing all prizes, and even went so far as to withdraw *The Writing Teacher* from consideration for the National Book Award, for which it had just been nominated. (*Before* publication!) With Marge Preston he argued fiercely over her plan to promote Julia Baylor's second novel as a potential bestseller, claiming that to do so would be to 'rape a nun.' Naysayers muttered that this resistance really stemmed from fear lest one of his 'darlings,' as a result of good publicity, should end up more famous than he was; Flint insisted that it was only the demeaning of literature to which he objected. And in Baylor's case, alas, history proved him right, for Marge's effort – far from succeeding – only resulted in a media backlash over the half-million-dollar advance that left her in the unenviable position of not being able to attract, for years, any publisher at all: not only was she hype, she was failed hype, and as such classified untouchable. For her mentor this was the last straw. Convinced that the advance itself had been responsible for his darling's ruin, he now declared himself opposed, on principle, to *all* advances. 'Writers should only get royalties,' he averred, and to prove the point, returned the advance for his own novel. Later, when Henry Deane submitted *his* new book to Hudson, Flint offered an advance of a dollar. Henry's agent laughed in his face, the powers that be were not amused, and he 'resigned.'

Yet even as 'the industry' was stripping Flint of his editorial crown, it was preparing the throne he would occupy as a writer. True, his refusal to lower his standards, the implicit challenge he posed to the conventional wisdom, had won him no friends in boardrooms; nonetheless these same qualities, when touted as the creative harvest of an author rather than the troublesome credo of an editor, would form the touch-stone of his formidable reputation. For if the *PW* review was to be believed, then the virtuosic set piece of *The Writing Teacher* consisted of an extended and corrosive send-up of the very industry that – as if in blind ignorance of its own con-demnation – was now preparing to pull out all the stops on the novel's behalf: an irony of which the most vivid example (one in which, no doubt, he himself took wicked pleasure) was the rousing conclusion to the summary of *The Writing Teacher* offered as part of the press packet accompanying the bound galleys: 'A savage indictment of the fashionable and timely, a vigorous defense of the immortal and timeless – in short, a novel for today!'

It was all very weird and upsetting, a coincidence in the light of which I found it hard to forget that Flint had not only loathed what he'd seen of *The Terrorist*, but had effec-tively told me to chuck it in the bin. Now, as he read my miserable *PW* review, was he gloating? He was in his way a prophet (how ironic that this word is a homonym for 'profit'!), and what had his final warning been to me, so many years ago, but that I showed every likelihood of degenerating into a hack, a sellout, a pouncer on the first available sure thing? He, on the other hand, all his life, had gone his own way, and now he was being blessed with the very laudation I had craved.

Meanwhile the success/failure indicators for my own book were proving to be at best inauspicious. That summer my name had appeared – along with those of Cher, Arnold Schwarzenegger and the South of France – on *Broadway* magazine's annual 'Out' list. ('Bungee jumping' topped the 'in' list, with Stanley Flint running seventh. No other writers were mentioned.) This oughtn't to have surprised me: indeed, it seemed somehow inevitable that the 'brat pack' of which I was an unwilling member should now be finding itself the object of ridicule rather than adulation, a downward spiral other evidence for which included the execrable reviews that had greeted both Sam Stallings's and Violet Partridge's second novels and an astoundingly vindictive article in *Harper's* in which a novelist I admired greatly, himself an open homosexual (so I could not file his attack under the convenient excuse of homophobia), had decried the 'ossified prose' of 'trendy but forgettable' writers like myself before declaring himself an 'unapologetic maximalist.' As for Stanley Flint, that same week he appeared on the cover of *New York* magazine. He was opening the fall reading series at the 92nd Street Y. Perhaps I would have had an easier time contending with all the noise that was being made about him if I'd actually read his book: the known, after all, is never as scary as the guessed at, in addition to which great literature has an uncanny ability to get under your skin and thereby annihilate (or perhaps I should say cure) jealousy. From fear lest *The Writing Teacher* should make my own efforts seem sophomoric, however, I avoided the novel until one afternoon in late June when Henry Deane – just back from Madrid and so happy with his life abroad that he planned to extend it – called me up rather out of the blue at Glenn's apartment. Given the cavalier treatment he'd received at Flint's hands, he was the last person I would have expected to say anything good about him. Instead he turned out to be full of praise for *The Writing Teacher*, which he was reviewing for the *New York Times Book Review*. 'Like it! I tell you, I'm *shivering* from it,' he said. 'The depth of engagement, the pleasure, the sheer beauty! There's been nothing to match it since Cheever.'

'Really,' I observed dully.

'Of course it can't have been easy for *you*,' he went on.

'What?'

'What Flint said. Not exactly kind. I know *I* would have been upset if someone had written that about me. Still, it's my most fervent belief, Martin, that when one writer tries to get revenge on another just because he doesn't like the way he comes off in his book, then freedom of expression goes down the tubes. You not only hurt the other person, you hurt yourself. You hurt literature.' He paused dramatically.

'But, Henry,' I said in perplexity, 'I don't know what you're talking about. I haven't read Flint's novel yet.'

'You haven't read it!' There was a sudden intake of breath. 'Oh dear, but I just assumed . . . well, but it's really nothing, only a few pages, a dozen pages at most.'

'What's nothing?'

'The part about you. Or I took it for granted that it was you. I could be wrong, of course, it could be someone else . . . just a student of the narrator's, a young homosexual he's convinced is in love with him. The Flint figure – he's never named – basically gets embarrassed, which was how I felt when a girl I was teaching fell in love with me a few years back . . . Of course Seamus hates it. He hates everything these days that isn't about AIDS. He hated your stories. Oh, and I should probably warn you, he's going to review *The Terrorist*, and he hates that even more.'

At that moment the call-waiting clicked. Putting Henry off, I pushed down the buttons on top of the phone. It was Billie. 'I feel I ought to warn you . . . ,' she began.

'I know. Have you read it?'

'Not yet. Only heard through the grapevine. Of course he'll probably deny it's you.'

'Get me the galleys as quickly as you can,' I ordered, then, switching back to Henry, told him I couldn't talk any longer: the dog needed to be walked.

An hour later the galleys of *The Writing Teacher* arrived by bicycle messenger. Eli was out, which was lucky: my hurried thumbing through Flint's eight hundred pages – a process at which I had become, like Liza, an adept – wasn't one I wanted him to witness. Yet as it turned out Flint's portrayal of the student, 'Simon,' which I located within a matter of minutes, upset me less than I'd feared it would, for the simple reason that no depiction of me, no matter how offensive, could have possibly matched the scenarios I'd dreamed into being during the hour I'd spent waiting for the messenger to show up. In other words, because Flint did not write that Simon was ugly, or that he scratched his balls in class, or that he mooned at his teacher in some effeminate and unseemly way, I was actually able to experience, as I put the galleys down, a sensation of relief that at least the unflattering portrayal Flint *did* offer wasn't worse. Indeed, so precise was his skewering of the starstruck and lovestruck Simon (Martin was more starstruck if less lovestruck) that as I came away from it I found myself charged with emotion, a combination of humbled surprise at the degree to which he had gotten me exactly right, and a con- noisseur's gratitude for the spectacle of a well-made thing. Nor did it matter that in certain crucial ways Simon did not conform remotely to his more ragged and self-contradictory model: what was important was that he conformed to himself, he was real and vivid to me in a way that I myself would never be. And this meant that when, in an incisive scene near the end of the novel, the Flint character steps out of his apartment building and observes Simon staring at him from across the street, his somewhat anxious reaction, his worry that Simon may turn out to be a stalker, makes perfect sense: Simon, in this regard, is a different person from Martin, whose real presence on that corner, you may recall, had more to do with the coincidence of proximity than with love. On this point, from sheer pride, I would have liked to correct Flint, though probably my correction would have been to him not of the slightest literary interest. As a novelist he viewed fact as merely one of many ingredients to throw into the stew, along with invention, hearsay, books, history, the news. Henry was right: there was no point in being offended by what Flint had written, especially when you considered that in my own book I had done to others exactly what Flint had done to me.

Most notably, our neighbors the Kellers, from whose story *The Terrorist* both derived and in crucial ways departed, had somehow gotten hold of a set of bound galleys and were none too happy about it. Indeed, so distraught had Mrs Keller become upon finishing the book that she had burst into my father's kitchen in tears, complained that thanks to his 'insensitive son' the wound that was their daughter's trial was about to be reopened, and even inveighed against my dead mother, whom she accused of having betrayed her confidence by sharing with me every secret that Mrs Keller had shared with her; otherwise, she asked, how on earth could I have known enough to write the novel in the first place? Yet in fact, as I explained to my father, if I had gotten the Kellers so 'right,' it was mostly as a result of guesswork, not any blabbing on my mother's part. 'All right,' he answered. 'Fine. Only that isn't going to make it any easier for me having to live next door to them.'

'Dad, it's fiction—'

'I know it's fiction. That's the trouble. The only thing that upsets them more than the stuff you got right is the stuff you made up.'

'But that's the whole point of fiction, isn't it?'

It was no use. I couldn't persuade him that the freedom to make a promiscuous hash of things was one upon which the imagination depends, while he couldn't wake me up to the truth that because of my book, people were suffering. He was suffering. Later on, at his urging, I did write an apologetic letter to Mrs Keller, in which I mentioned jokingly that I had been a 'victim' of Stanley Flint in the same way that she had been a 'victim' of me. A week later her reply arrived, in a pale blue envelope. I never opened it. I stuffed it into the inside pocket of a suitcase, which later, either at O'Hare Airport or between Chicago and Pittsburgh, disappeared. Perhaps someday it will turn up again, though I rather hope not.

Near the end of July, Eli and I packed Maisie, our clothes, and our computers into his mother's station wagon and went to spend a month at Nora Foy's house in East Hampton. Nora herself had accepted a residency at Yaddo and needed someone to take care of her dogs. So that we should have an opportunity to learn the house's foibles before commencing our stay, she suggested that we come out the day before she was due to leave. When we pulled into the driveway she was waiting on the front porch, along with Charlus and Pimperl, who leapt from their mistress's feet to yelp and sniff at Maisie almost the instant I opened the car door.

The briskness with which Nora strode over to greet us surprised me; at Sam Stallings's party, after all, she'd barely been able to pull herself out of her chair. Now, however, as a result of recent hip replacement surgery, she got around as well as any of the hardy widows one encountered on winter Sundays in East Hampton, feeding the ducks or taking great treks on the beach. Nor did anything in her appearance give away what distinguished her from those old ladies with their cropped white hair and benign faces. And this was entirely to the point, for as Eli had told me, even at that late date Nora remained hopelessly and rather needlessly closeted – an odd pretense, given that most of her readers accepted her lesbianism not merely as a given but a prerequisite of her work.

Even so, in a little autobiographical sketch she had recently composed, she had been never once mentioned Hilda by name, referring instead only to a mysterious and genderless 'companion.' 'Poor thing, she acts as if no one knows,' Eli had said in the car. 'But everyone knows.'

Still, he loved her: this was obvious from his grin when we arrived, the eagerness with which he jumped out of the car and swept her up into his arms, making her squeal. There was really something so heterosexual about Eli! He charmed women far more than men. 'And this is Martin,' he said to Nora, as if my existence, my role in his life, was something they had already discussed at great length.

'Martin,' she repeated, clearly not remembering that we had already met, 'what a pleasure.' And held out her arms. 'May I kiss you?'

I colored. 'Of course,' I said, moving my cheek toward her lips, which brushed dryly against them. Eli beamed. The pride he sometimes exhibited in my company – as if I were a prize he'd won by throwing balls through a hoop at a sideshow – both embarrassed and pained me. Also, why was it only when we were with other people that he expressed any gladness to have me as his partner? When we were alone everything I said seemed to vex him.

By now Nora had left my side and was grappling with Maisie, trying to hold her still long enough to examine her bite. 'You haven't trained her well,' she muttered to Eli. 'Oh, she's got a gay tail!'

Eli laughed. 'A gay tail? What does that mean?'

'It curls upward.' Nora let Maisie go. 'Still, you never intended her to be a show dog,' she added, brushing off her skirt as she made for the house. 'Well! I'll bet you'd like some coffee after your long drive, wouldn't you?'

'Nora's like my grandmother,' Eli said, leading me into the kitchen. 'She doesn't only drink coffee after dinner, she drinks coffee *with* dinner.'

'Oh, and Eli, take note: if the water in the tap runs rusty, pay it no mind. It'll clear after a few seconds. I know, I know,

I need to have the place replumbed. And a new roof before this one collapses!' She rubbed her hip. 'Well, someday . . . Say, Martin, can't you get one of your Hollywood friends to make a movie out of my new book, or one of your publishing friends to bring some of my old ones back into print, or . . . No, I guess not. I guess I'll just have to write a bestseller while I'm at Yaddo. Or maybe I could put on the cover, "Author needs new roof!"' We laughed. 'After all,' she added cryptically, 'not all of us get huge advances like you and your friend Julia Baylor.'

'But I didn't—'

She clapped her hands together. 'Well, shall we take a tour of the house?'

'Let's go,' Eli said.

Then she led us through spaces we already knew: the living room and the dining room, and the room with the twin beds, and the room with the Gertrude Stein and Alice B. Toklas dolls, with its curtains of Chinese toile. Next she showed us her study, where Eli intended to set up his computer, and a little spare room next door, once Hilda's sewing room, where it was my hope to start work on a novel about my mother's death. ('Dying mothers and whacking off, whacking off and dying mothers,' Seamus Holt had written of me. 'Can this boy speak of nothing else?')

Finally we followed Nora up a steep little staircase to the attic, which was kept locked, and into which neither of us had previously even stepped. The door required some fiddling before she could get it to budge; when it did, it revealed a long, low mansard, its clean geometries accented by rows of putty-colored metal shelving. Everything here was tidy and sparse: the manuscripts, the notebooks, even the frayed and yellowed letters and lists folded neatly in their dusty plastic sleeves. As for the books – and every book Nora had ever written was here, in every conceivable edition, from Japanese to Finnish to Icelandic – affixed to their spines were little labels bearing call numbers, Dewey decimal, written out in Hilda's neat librarian's hand. 'She couldn't stomach the demise of the Dewey decimal system,' Nora said. 'Clung to it to the bitter end.' Pulling a small chair out from under a child-sized desk, she sat down. 'Oh, I really can't keep up with all of this since Hilda died! Why just look over there!' And she pointed to a hasty pile of scraps and books, everything that had come in since Hilda had given up her guardianship, still waiting to be catalogued. 'You know I've never been a very organized person,' she said to me – which I thought strange given that I hardly knew her. 'Left to my own devices I'd live in a chaos. But Hilda – this was her calling. And now I feel I owe it to her to maintain what she began, which is why I've finally agreed to accept Yale's offer and sell them the whole kit and caboodle. Do you think it's all right, Eli? Do you think she'd mind?'

'Of course not,' Eli answered soothingly, rubbing his friend's shoulders.

She sighed. 'Thank you. I don't get touched much any-more, except by doctors. Anyway, they've just upped the offer to fifty thousand. And I could do with the money right now, I must say. The hip replacement – I thought Medicaid would pay for everything. But it turns out it only pays for part of everything! Ow!' She grimaced; Eli had pummeled too hard. 'I'll tell you, I expected old age to be a lot of things, I expected it to be boring and painful and frustrating. What I never expected was for it to be so damned expensive. People really live too long,' she concluded, as she had at Sam's party, then stood again and led us back down the narrow staircase.

That night Nora slept in her own guest room, giving us the room with the double bed. She was leaving early in the morning, and we made sure to be up in time to see her off. As it turned out, however, not only had she risen before we had, she'd made us breakfast: an old-fashioned American breakfast, eggs and pancakes and sausages. 'People live too long,' she repeated from the stove, where she was pouring batter onto a none-too-clean cast-iron griddle. 'You remember that nice boy who used to run the bookstore, Eli? I'm sure you met him. Well, he has to give it up. He can't earn enough off the shop to afford living out here – and his family's been in East Hampton for two hundred years!' She made a noise of disgust. 'And to think that when I bought this place it went for twelve thousand dollars, which at the time seemed like a fortune! But now my friend Pat, who's in real estate, she says I could sell it in a second for half a million just because it's south of the Highway. And I just might. Who knows? The town's not what it used to be, what with all those junky stores on Newtown Lane, the T-shirt shops and the Christmas-all-year shops and the Ralph what's-his-name – isn't he really Lipschitz? It reminds me of Revere Beach when I was a kid. Like one of those gimcrack little amusement park towns on the Atlantic. You never would have expected that here. Here we had Jackson Pollock.' She poured out the last of the batter. 'Still, the last thing I want is to turn into one of those miserable old fools who devote their lives to being bulwarks against change, like Hilda with her Dewey decimal obsession. "Bulwarks against change." Do you like that, Eli?' He nodded. 'Write it down for me, will you?'

'Sure thing,' Eli said, pulling a pad from his pocket, and leaving me to marvel once again at the strange ways writers adopt in each other's company.

Later that morning, after we had safely planted Nora on the Hampton Jitney, we took Maisie for a walk through the town. Newtown Lane was, as Nora had promised, a curious mishmash of rubbish both expensive and cheap. Fly-by-night branches of New York boutiques elbowed the hardware store, while across the street a sentry of overpriced little antiques stores, their windows replete with painted New England dressers and Royal Crown Derby, flanked a pallid pizzeria; with the first fall leaves, we knew, their owners would close up shop, follow the rich and the warmth down south, to Palm Beach, where they maintained their winter headquarters.

As in New York, over the next few days we fell quickly into familiar habits, which was exactly what we'd hoped to avoid in the country. In the mornings we'd work, then eat lunch at an ersatz tearoom over which portraits of Queen Elizabeth and Prince Philip presided, before riding down to the gay beach on a pair of rusty bicycles that Eli had dug out of Nora's garage. I liked the gay beach, where sociable lesbians read mystery novels amid the tanned and oily bodybuilders. Compared to theirs, our towels were threadbare, our umbrella – like the bicycle, dug out of Nora's garage – ill-tempered and prone to collapse. Still, we had fun. While Eli played with the dog, I took long strolls along the shore on the pretense of wanting to 'think something out' and inevitably ended up in a zone of dunes and beach grass, lunar valleys where men lounged naked amid signs warning against Lyme disease. (Everywhere, it seemed, sex and disease were wed.)

Sometimes, when Eli was in New York for an opera, or to see his mother, I'd go to the beach at night. When I took off my shoes, the sand squished up between my toes, not burning as at noon but cool like the other side of a pillow. Often a fog reduced the other men scattered among the dunes to murky bulbs of shadow from which, as I approached, a figure might disjoin itself, veer toward me, then disappear into the tenebrous distance. I'd move on. And though we might meet again, that stranger and I, though he might even grope my chest and stomach like a blind man before a statue – not for pleasure, but simply to get a rough idea of what I felt like, whether I was muscly or soft, hairy or smooth – only rarely would we graduate to the next step, fingers fumbling with belts, the untangling of a penis already moist with the residue of some earlier encounter. Then the game would begin, that familiar and tiresome game; over and over you would bring each other to the point of orgasm and then back away, like children daring each other to jump into a cold pool – 'you first'; 'no, you first' – until it became clear that neither was willing to go first, at which point you would bid each other a resigned farewell, zip up your pants, and walk hurriedly away.

Once, on that beach, on a particularly foggy night, an alluring shadow beckoned me into the dunes, only to reveal itself to belong to Henry Deane. Both of us laughed from embarrassment. 'I think it's probably best if we don't mention to anyone our having running into each other this way,' he said as we made our way back to the parking lot.

'No, of course not,' I agreed. 'And what are you doing here, if you don't mind my asking?'

'Visiting Seamus. He's got a place in Springs. He's been coming out for years.' We had reached the tarmac. A car trained its brights on us, so that we had to squint. Trapped, for a few seconds, in the scrutiny of our nameless assessor, Henry smiled and waved, at which point the driver gunned his engines and fled in a fury.

'The thing is, Seamus would never approve of my coming to the beach at night,' Henry went on. 'He's very puritanical about such matters. Jesus, staying there's like being in a nunnery! Fortunately he's in New York this evening. And what about your Eli? Also in town?'

I nodded.

'Ah well, when the cat's away the mice will play. And there must be honor among mice.'

'Of course.'

'Much more pleasant, this beach, than some bar. The other

night, for instance, you'll never guess who picked me up here – that fellow brat-packer of yours, what's his name, the one they're always comparing to Bret Easton Ellis.'

'Bart Donovan.'

'Right. I didn't even know he was gay – he says he isn't, he dates girls, too – only in his spare time he has a thing for older gentleman like me. Anyway, he invited me back to his place. At first I was worried, he looked so innocent, with these big eyes like a basset hound's, but then when we got there he opened up a suitcase and there were all these dildos. But I mean, *huge* dildos! And he wanted me to fuck them with him – him with them, sorry – from smallest to largest, leading up to the biggest of all, which was this horrifying thing, I don't even know what to call it, in the shape of an arm and fist. It might have been the scale model for some Trotskyite monument! A real paean in the ass, if you get my drift. Ha!'

'And did you do it?'

'Of course! I didn't want to disappoint the boy.'

'And?'

'Well, just as he promised, they all went straight in. No trouble at all! He didn't even need poppers. So afterward, being naturally curious, I asked him how he managed it, and he just shrugged, and said, "Mind over matter, dude." Although of course I couldn't help but wonder, if he needed *that* at twenty-whatever, what he was going to need when he got to be my age.' Henry leaned closer. 'Don't mention any of this to Seamus. If he finds out he'll probably start calling up Bart and railing at him to come out of the closet, and guess who'll get blamed? Moi! Oh, and by the way, how's that nice dyke friend of yours? Lisa?'

'Liza. Getting married, actually.'

'Really! I've never been to a lesbian wedding, though I've heard—'

'She's marrying a man.'

'Oh. And are you going?'

I shook my head. In fact, the question of whether to attend Liza's wedding had in recent days become a source of contention between Eli and me, chiefly as a result of her having sent us two separate invitations, which he took as a hostile gesture: 'As if a gay couple doesn't deserve to be treated like any other couple,' he complained. It went without saying that Eli himself was planning to decline. And yet in contrast to earlier days, I thought I could hear beneath his anger a suppressed choke of regret, that for the sake of mere disapproval he was sacrificing the most enduring friendship of his life. Clearly it was pride, or mostly pride, that kept him from surrendering his posture of defiance. As for me, though I felt less strongly about the matter, the last thing I wanted was to provoke him. As it stood we were fighting far too much about things that I wasn't conscious of doing for me to dare any deliberate provocation.

So we decided not to go, though at Harriet's urging we sent a present. At first Eli wanted to send knives. 'What's wrong with knives?' he asked when I objected. 'A nice set of knives makes for a good, practical gift.'

'But she might take it negatively. The sharpness and all.'

He sighed loudly; scratched his head. 'You may be right. Well, to hell with it, then, I'll call Fortunoff's and have a blender delivered. If you don't think *that's* too aggressive.'

'No, no.'

'I think a blender's the perfect choice,' he continued, picking up the phone. 'You know, because it carries no connotation of malice in its own right, and yet it's so *impersonal* . . . I'm sure she'll get the message.'

A week later a thank you note arrived, addressed, this time, to both of us, and bearing not Liza's but Ben's address. 'Dear Eli and Martin,' it read:

Your lovely gift arrived yesterday, and we are thrilled!
Already we've whipped up a gazpacho and a round of
piña coladas. Thank you so much! We will remember
you with every pesto!

Yours,

Liza and Ben

'Piña coladas!' Eli cried after he read the letter. 'Can you
imagine Liza drinking a piña colada?' He shook his head.
'And when I think of the letters she *used* to write me!' he
added, his voice lilting with a pathos from which I failed to
derive a single useful clue as to the degree to which sorrow
might underlie his anger with me.

We were not settling in. In Nora's house, away from newspapers and telephone calls, we had hoped to find a silence in
which we could once again hear our own voices; instead New
York – and specifically those aspects of New York with which
we found it so difficult to cope – appeared, with a sort of
canine loyalty, to have followed us out. Thus, not only were
we always running into Marge Preston, in shorts and T-shirt,
at the grocery store, but we were also always getting invitations – from Billie, from both our editors, even from Sam
Stallings, who had rented a place in Amagansett – to cocktail
parties. Worse, it seemed we could not leave the house without running into someone one of us knew – for instance,
Donald Schindler, whom we encountered one evening in line
at the movies, part of a crowd gazing bemusedly at a talking
car, its lights flashing. ('Stand back,' it declared. 'Do not
approach.') Yet another of those over-monied Wall Street whiz
kids whose increasingly loud presence Nora so lamented, he
immediately asked us to a barbecue at a place he had taken
with 'some people from Smith Barney.' The address was in the
Northwest Woods, in a zone of cheaply built plywood spec

houses the enormous rent for which ten or twelve remote acquaintances would divvy up, and where in a weird recapitulation of college days these men and women who lived normally in expensive if small apartments, and shared their beds only with lovers, would have to 'bunk' in the same room with two or three virtual strangers. Eli and I, on the other hand, had the run of Nora's vast if dilapidated manse, for which we paid nothing, though under normal circumstances it would have commanded a hefty price. In the mornings we lounged plaintively in the weedy back garden; in the evenings (and against our better judgment) we went to parties from which Eli, as a consequence of being written off one too many times as 'Mrs Bauman,' tended to emerge sullen or wrathful.

One night, at a dinner hosted by Henry's agent (she turned out to be the fat lady from Sam Stallings's launch), we ran into Seamus. With his tall, stooped figure, grizzled beard, and bushy eyebrows, he might have been some rabid Puritanical minister, a gay Roger Chillingworth. 'Nora Foy!' he cried when we told him where we were staying. 'That ridiculous cow, why doesn't she come out?' (I felt the swoosh of heads turning.) 'It infuriates me,' he went on, 'when these people everyone knows perfectly well are queer refuse to fess up, especially at a moment of crisis. Why sometimes I'm tempted to drag her out myself, kicking and—'

'Now, Seamus, temper, temper,' interrupted Henry, who was with him.

'But isn't it a question of generations?' Eli put in timidly. 'I mean, Nora's older than we are. Perhaps for her—'

'Generations, schmenerations, courage is courage and cowardice is cowardice.'

Kendall – always present at such functions – now arrived to change the subject, as was his role. I worried that from then on Seamus might hate me even more than he hated my books, and was surprised, the next morning, to get a call from him.

It seemed that the afternoon before, the Fundamentalist Christian owner of a café on Main Street, Delicious Delights, had fired his lesbian employee, claiming that she had kissed her lover on the lips at work. Now Seamus was putting together a picket in front of the shop of the sort that in New York he had already organized several times with great success, albeit on a larger scale and to protest larger injustices.

Dutifully, then, Eli and I drove over to Delicious Delights, where along with Henry and about a dozen other embarrassed-looking friends of Seamus's, including Henry's agent in dark sunglasses and a straw hat, we marched dolefully back and forth for an hour or so, muttering at Seamus's urging, 'Hey-hey, ho-ho, homophobia's got to go,' while the smirking owner of the café videotaped us, and the lesbian whose firing had incited the fracas gave an interview to a youthful reporter from the *East Hampton Star*. I remember thinking how much less self-conscious I would have felt if I had been (as indeed I would soon be) one of thousands storming city hall in Manhattan, our defiance emboldened by the protective embrace of so many comrades. Instead the fired lesbian sounded demented as she gibbered to the reporter, and when Donald Schindler arrived with some of his Smith Barney pals for a prebeach cappuccino, a gust of shame ran through me. 'What's going on?' he asked. I explained. 'Well, then, I guess I won't go in,' he said, watching regretfully as his Wall Street confreres, slick boys and girls who did not share his historical association with queers, ignored him and me and strode blithely across the picket line.

Later – thirsty in the heat – I noticed Henry standing a little apart from the rest of the crowd, drinking a Coke. 'Where did you get it?' I asked.

'At Delicious Delights,' he whispered. 'Don't tell Seamus, I snuck in while he was taking a whiz' – which was just like Henry. The fact that he was in many ways much more of a literary man than his friend justified, at least to my mind, his comparative lack of scruples, in which I took a giddy pleasure. For I admired the rebel in him, and recognized even then that Seamus, for all his troublemaking, in the end possessed the far less radical soul.

The European grandeur of Henry's writing, combined with his penchant for outrageous frankness, meant that he made many of his colleagues jealous, most notably an elderly, irascible author – like Henry, an expatriate – who had until recently enjoyed the distinction of being the only 'mainstream' American novelist to live openly as a homosexual. A few weeks earlier, at a dinner party, Kendall had found himself seated next to this gentleman, who had spent the bulk of the meal railing against Henry, his words becoming more vituperative the more he drank, until in his stupor he reached for the wine and picked up a bottle of olive oil by mistake. Stunned and fascinated, Kendall watched the old man fill his glass, take a gulp, and splutter olive oil all over his shirt and tie. 'You did that on purpose!' he cried while a servant mopped him. 'You didn't warn me! You all want me to die so you can elect Henry Deane king fag!'

As for Seamus, perhaps *because* he was less of a literary man than Henry, he had a bigger heart; you knew that you could count on him for help if you got into trouble. Seamus had mysterious reserves of money, and had been slaving for the last dozen years on a Great Work reputed to be already seven thousand pages long, the manuscript he carted back and forth in boxes every time he made his weekday trundle from Manhattan duplex to Springs beach house. Yet more than as a writer it was as a muckraker that he was becoming famous, a deliverer of fire and brimstone speeches to which people didn't want to listen but listened anyway. Few could as yet smell the incipience of ACT UP in the air, of those days when rubber-gloved policemen would hoist protesters from the pavement of Manhattan streets, and wizened veterans of Stonewall would instruct boys fresh out of Harvard in the proper way to position their wrists so that the plastic garbage ties the cops used to bind them would not cut any veins. Those who did, though, looked to Seamus as a hero. Others flocked to his speeches for the sheer masochistic thrill of them, as some of my sister's friends had once flocked to a certain Chinese restaurant in San Francisco simply for the pleasure of being bullied and insulted by its waiter, Edsel Ford Fong. And yet I am remiss if I suggest that Seamus's diatribes were gratuitous, or purely sadistic. On the contrary, his anger was as genuine as it was defensible: he was furious at the mayor of New York for failing to prioritize AIDS; furious at the FDA for its slowness in approving new drugs; furious at the smugly apathetic gay men who paraded obliviously up and down the East Hampton beach in Calvin Klein swimsuits even as their brethren lay dying in understaffed hospitals. Their anomie – which revealed itself even under the flattering light of ballrooms, at five-hundred dollar a plate AMFAR benefits of the sort to which Roy would later take me – stood out for Seamus as the greatest sin of all, evidence not only of callousness but collaborationism. For in those years no one wanted to take what he had to say seriously, even at the five-hundred-dollar-a-plate dinners, where, thunderous before a mob of perfectly coifed, elegantly employed young men, he would thrust out his finger like a demonic preacher, and scream, 'In five years half of you in this room are going to be dead. In five years *half* of you in this room are going to be *dead*. In five years *half* of you in this room are going to be *dead, dead, dead*.' And though afterward, over cigars, everyone would make a joke of his pronouncements, or try to soften the edges of his rantings by recasting them as a purely intellectual strategy, 'an attention-getting tactic, and possibly an effective one,' nonetheless the disquiet he had generated was palpable. In the end, of course, history did prove him wrong, though not in the way his enemies would have predicted: five years later, not half, but three-quarters of the men in that room were dead, for no matter how extreme Seamus's vision might have been, the virus's was more so.

AIDS was the fashionable charity in East Hampton that summer: few weekends passed without some expensive benefit, usually held outdoors, in moonlight or sunlight, at a lavish beachfront mansion or in a prizewinning rose garden. The chief purpose of these galas, so far as I could tell, was to provide the overmonied denizens of the region with a tax-deductible means of expiating their altruistic impulses without actually having to touch or talk to the diseases 'victims.' The entertainments on offer ranged from wine tastings to lectures on botany to performances of 'The Art of the Fugue' by a string quartet, as well as, at one comparatively lowbrow affair (the tickets went for only seventy-five dollars a head), a performance by a theater troupe all the members of which had AIDS. Unfortunately, at the last minute the troupe had had to cancel because too many of the actors were sick, which left the event's organizer, the pastor at a local Episcopalian church, in the unenviable position of having to come up with an alternative amusement on less than twenty-four hours' notice. His idea was to pull together a group reading by local writers, in which he asked me to take part.

Of course I agreed. Eli was reading Dickens in Nora's living room when the call came.

'Who was that?' he asked when I hung up.

'That nice minister we met on the beach,' I said, and told him about the reading.

Eli put down his book. 'I don't suppose I should be surprised that he didn't even *think* of inviting me,' he said.

'Oh, Eli, I'm sorry—'

'Or that it didn't occur to you to suggest that he might invite me.'

'I'll tell you what, why don't I call him back right now?'

'Don't bother.'

'But it's easy—'

'You just don't get it, do you?' He threw down his book. 'Jesus, don't you see? It only counts if *you* think of it. You make Liza look like Mother Teresa.'

'Okay, I'll prove it to you,' I said, picking up the phone. 'Here, I'm going to call—'

'I told you no.'

I started dialing.

'Hang up that phone!'

'No, I'm going to—'

'I said hang up that phone!'

He stormed toward me. For a few embarrassing seconds we tussled with the receiver, until Eli pulled the jack out of the wall. 'Jesus!' I cried. But he had slammed out the door, into the yard. 'Oh, why couldn't I have just *asked*?' I lamented, for in those days I was forever announcing my better intentions, in the vague hope of winning praise or forgiveness.

Even so, as soon as he was out of earshot, I plugged the phone back into the wall and called the pastor, who said he would be happy to invite Eli; indeed, the only reason he hadn't done so in the first place, he explained, was that he hadn't known Eli was a writer.

Hanging up, I hurried outside. 'Eli,' I called, 'I just talked to Reverend Davis, and it's okay. He'd love for you to read.'

'I wouldn't give him the satisfaction,' Eli answered tartly. But in the end, ambition – or perhaps a sense of duty – overcame his pride, and he agreed to participate. The event was to take place in Southampton, at the oddly un-South American mansion of an Argentinean lady who happened to be one of the pastor's parishioners. Inside, the furniture was mostly

Shaker, the decor Early American: quilts, frayed flags, evil-looking handmade dolls. A waiter in white gloves led us through the living room to the back garden, where the hostess stood greeting her guests. She had on a curiously countrified dress, a sort of milkmaid's dress, very much at odds with her heavy black hair and Castilian accent. Meanwhile young men in uniforms were arranging plastic chairs in half-moons around a makeshift amphitheater and putting a photocopied program on each seat.

The waiter led us up onto the stage, where the pastor was chatting with those of the readers who had already arrived. Seamus was among them. Waving wildly, he hurried from his seat to greet us. 'God, I can't tell you what a relief it is to see some *sisters*,' he cried. 'Amazing that at an AIDS benefit there should be so few homos – or perhaps they're all too busy running around on that beach looking for a piece of dick!' He shook his head in disgust. 'And how have you boys been getting along since we turned Main Street on its head?'

'Fine,' Eli said curtly.

'Martin, writing the great American gay novel I fully expect from you? I keep telling him,' he added to Eli, 'that he has it in him to write it, if only he'd get over his obsession with stupid little picayune domestic details. I mean, whacking off in bed, for God's sake – did Tolstoy write about whacking off in bed? Did Shakespeare?'

'Still, Seamus,' I averred, 'times have changed. And wasn't the whole point of the sixties that it freed up the discourse on sex—'

'Sex, yes, fine – sex as an expression of love, as a metaphor for the nobility of our people . . . but whacking off, and phone sex, and stealing straight boys' underwear, that's hardly the image we want to project, don't you agree?' (Eli nodded vigorously.)

The pastor now approached us. 'So glad you could come,' he said, offering his hand. 'And have you met Mrs González?'

'Not yet.'

'Carmencita's an angel to host the event for us,' he went on, smiling in that bland, rehearsed manner I recognized from outings with Kendall. 'And now come and meet your fellow readers. Let me see – oh, we're still waiting for Gloria. She's never on time!' I smiled. Introductions were tendered. All of the other readers were women, poets and murder mystery writers. One of them I recognized as the lover of the fired lesbian from *Delicious Delights*; it turned out she was the author of a hugely popular series of detective novels for teenage girls. 'Pleased to meet you,' I said.

'Likewise,' she answered gruffly. 'By the way, Seamus, Lorella's found an attorney. He's talking big bucks. Millions.'

'Good idea. Get the bastard for every cent he's got! Gay people have got to fight the power.'

At last Gloria, who was never on time, arrived. Gathering us around him, the pastor gave a familiar little speech about the necessity of sticking to the ten-minute time limit. Speed was of the essence, he warned, fixing his gaze on Seamus, because Mrs González needed everyone out by six in order to prepare for a dinner party.

'Oh, no problem,' I said.

'I'd rather only read for *two* minutes!' barked Lorella's lover. But Seamus said nothing.

Though only half the seats were taken, Mrs González signaled us that it was time to begin. Gloria read first, followed by Eli, then me. After that it was Seamus's turn. Unlike the rest of us, he hadn't brought along a book or pages from a manuscript, which I suppose we should have taken as a warning sign. Instead he walked to the podium and began to talk extemporaneously. His voice was low at first, hardly audible, as he spoke of the four former lovers he had just visited in the same ward at Bellevue, the grim conditions of the hospital, his five hundred friends who were dead. Five hundred! This was a figure he threw out routinely, and that people tended to dismiss as yet another example of his hyperbolic style, though in fact it represented, if anything, an understatement: all that was questionable was his definition of friendship. For time would soon diminish the shock value of that number, as the list of the dead grew longer, and people built up antibodies against such bardic invective. 'It abashes me,' he intoned, 'when our paper of record will not report justly or adequately on the gravest crisis since the Holocaust. It abashes me when my gay brothers refuse to recognize that by fucking without rubbers they are collaborating in their own extermination.' (At the word 'rubbers,' a flinch of discomfiture rippled through the audience.) 'It abashes me when even you people, yes, even you well-intentioned, liberal-minded straight people, sit by and imagine it will never happen to you, never *your* sons, never *your* husbands. But mark my words. *It will.*' In the distance a dog barked. The pastor checked his watch. 'I tell you,' he went on, 'in that squalid city you all avoid four months out of the year, on the stinking streets of Manhattan and Brooklyn, I'm seeing miracles. I'm seeing men who barely have the strength to get out of bed in the morning dragging themselves to city hall to protest the callous greed of our disgusting mayor. I'm seeing people for whom it takes everything they have to fight the virus finding somewhere the extra bit of energy to battle greedy pharmaceutical companies, and an inept and compassionless national bureaucracy, and a hard-hearted medical establishment! And not only for their own sakes, but for your sakes, the sakes of your thankless sons and husbands! You stupid, stupid, careless people, don't you see we're *dying*? In the city we're fucking *dying*, in *agony*? And all the while you sit out here on your asses and do *nothing*!'

He was quiet. In the distance the dog was still barking.

Anxiously we watched as he took a cloth from his pocket, wiped his glasses, looked out at the audience, and, seeing its members braced with worry, stepped back. 'Oh, why bother?' he muttered, then reclaimed his seat.

There was a silence then. For twenty seconds or so it stretched out, until just at the point when it seemed about to implode, a lone set of hands started clapping. I looked to see whose they were – it was Eli – and hearing him, joined in. The pastor clapped next. Then Mrs González clapped, and then the other writers, and then, very gradually, the members of the audience started clapping too, as if what had been holding them back was not outrage so much as some insecurity as to what would be the proper response to such an onslaught Protocol thus absorbed the sermon, robbing it of its power to sting.

Afterward, during the reception, Seamus was timid. He hid in a corner of the garden with a plate of petits fours. 'What did you think of my speech?' he asked when I joined him. 'Did I go too far? Do they hate me?' His voice had verged into a whine of innuendo, as if by pleading his own immaturity he might avoid some punishment – a slap on the rear, or being sent to bed without his supper.

Such vacillations, as I would soon learn, were typical of him. Publicly ferocious, in private he could reveal unsuspected caches of vulnerability, which was why, though he pined for love, and was constantly plying Eli and me with requests to introduce him to eligible men, whenever he actually found himself in the presence of someone on whom he had a crush he would be reduced to a stutter of anxiety: the great orator, to whom words came so easily at a podium, could not find his voice when faced with the object of his affection. He also detested being alone, and was therefore forever summoning me to his house, either for dinners with ill-tempered friends, or to listen to a chapter of his novel, or to excoriate me for what he perceived as the great inadequacy of my own work: my refusal to write what he called the 'big gay book, the gay *War and Peace*, the gay *Crime and Punishment.*' (Seamus was partial to the Russians.) For he admired epic scale and superlatives and monumentality, whereas I – love child of the magazine and Stanley Flint – believed in concision, leanness, getting the maximum effect out of the minimum number of words. Muriel Spark and Raymond Carver were my heroes, and further back, the Forster of *Where Angels Fear to Tread*, the Ford Madox Ford of *The Good Soldier*. (But not *Parade's End*, heavens no!) I didn't believe books could ever change the world, whereas Seamus believed that if they didn't they weren't worth writing. This was why it vexed him that I'd as yet written nothing about AIDS. 'I mean, how can you *not* write about it,' he'd ask, 'when it's to your generation what Vietnam was to mine?'

'I have to wait for the right story,' I'd answer. 'Remember what Grace Paley says, there has to be a long time between knowing and telling—'

'But we don't have a long time – not anymore!'

'And anyway,' I persisted (for I had ceased to be so afraid of him), 'once you start dictating to writers what they can and can't write, you're robbing them of their most essential freedom. What you end up with isn't literature, it's propaganda.'

'Oh, pooh! Writers are no different than anyone else. We all have social obligations.'

'My only obligation is to myself, to write the very best I can,' I retorted. For I was every day more in agreement with Flint that when one set out to satisfy other people's requirements, the result would be mediocrity. Only by listening for that strange little voice, the one that spoke at the least likely moments (and from the most improbable places), could one hope to produce something that would last.

Once, when Seamus called that summer, it was to tell us

that we needed to go and get HIV tests immediately. 'But why?' I asked. After all, until recently he had been urging gay men *not* to have HIV tests.

'I just got off the phone with Fauci,' Seamus answered. 'He's convinced me – absolutely *convinced* me – that this new drug, AZT, is the ticket. And not only for people who are already sick: also if you're positive but asymptomatic, he says, it'll keep the virus at reasonable levels. The report will hit the papers later this year – he let me in on the results early, he said, because as you're probably aware there's every probability I'm HIV-positive. And so I want to get the word out, trumpet the news: *get the test.*'

This phone call, needless to say, upset me considerably. After all, until now Seamus's antitesting stance, his conviction that the test represented only a veiled effort on the part of the government to establish an HIV 'blacklist,' had given Eli and me the perfect excuse not to subject ourselves to what we both looked upon as an intimidating and gruesome ordeal. Though Eli's fear, moreover, had at least a real world basis, deriving as it did from the knowledge that unlike me he actually had, on several occasions, been fucked without a condom, my own anxiety, despite its more hypothetical origins, was no less intense. For I had gone through too many weeks of awaiting, with my mother, the results of biopsies, ever to want to subject myself to that anguish again.

'What is it?' Eli asked as I put down the phone.

I told him. He mulled over the news for a moment, then said, 'Well, I suppose it's inevitable. I'll call and make appointments—'

'No!'

'Why not?'

'Because I don't want to have the test.'

'But, Martin, you said it yourself, given your history you've got nothing to worry about.'

'Exactly. So why should I need to be tested?'

'For the reassurance of knowing.'

'Yes, and what if I turn out to be positive? What reassurance is that going to be?'

'But you won't turn out to be positive – unless you've been lying to me.' His eyes narrowed. 'Have you been lying to me?'

'Of course not. I just – I mean, you know, there's always the chance that you might have a microscopic cut on your finger or something—'

'You sound like Liza.'

'And then, if you find out you're positive, there's nothing you can do, and your life is basically ruined.'

'But I thought you said Seamus's whole point was that there is something you can do. AZT.'

'Oh, they say that *now*,' I responded prophetically. 'Only who's to say that in two years they won't find out that taking all that AZT only makes things worse?'

So we argued. Every day I found a fresh reason to persuade Eli not to make the doctor's appointment. I wanted to finish my new novel first, I said – my new novel, of which I had so far produced a total of ten pages. As for Eli, whenever I went into his study, I couldn't help but notice that the glowing green diodes on his computer always spelled out the words 'Chapter One' – nothing else.

Sometimes, when Seamus called, it was because he was lonely. 'I'm all by myself,' he said one Sunday, near the very end of our stay. 'I've been writing the whole day, I haven't talked to a living soul in hours, I need company.'

As it happened, that morning at the Amagansett Farmer's Market, Eli and I had received a spontaneous invitation from his former boyfriend Derek Wexler (twin brother of Gerald) to an afternoon party – 'nothing big,' Derek had insisted, 'just a few boys, a little get-together' – so we suggested that Seamus meet us there.

'Fabulous,' he answered. 'Perhaps I'll find the great love of my life.' (This was always his hope.) 'What's the address?'

I told him. 'Sagg Road!' he remarked admiringly. 'So is your friend handsome and eligible, in addition to being rich?'

'I'm not sure if he's single. He's in arbitrage.'

'How old?'

'A few years older than me.'

'Mmm, I'll have to doll up. See you soon.' He put down the phone. We ourselves did not doll up; indeed, almost as a point of honor, we wore our usual ratty jeans to Derek's house, which managed to be very swanky without breaking the rules of a rigorously minimalism aesthetic: the sort of house in which the rooms are referred to as 'volumes.' In the living volume – essentially a shingled cube – the blond parquet floor stretched blazingly toward windows framing a great swath of dune and ocean. Mapplethorpe prints hung over Mies van der Rohe chairs in the dining volume – all a far cry from Mrs González's mansion with its samplers and sorting tables.

We went outside, into the back garden. Around the crisply geometrical pool a dozen shellacked young men in Speedos had been languidly arranged. 'They might as well be wearing price tags,' Eli whispered, as he cast his gaze over the little clot of guests gathered near the bar. 'Oh, there's Derek. Derek!' He waved. Derek detached himself.

'Eli, Martin, so glad you could come,' he said as he approached us. Unlike most of his guests, he was fully dressed, in an old-fashioned morning suit and cravat. Like Gerald (they were fraternal twins), he had black hair and blue, benighted eyes, yet his skin was smoother than that of his brother; indeed, it had that rubbery cast, that alarming angularity that I would later come to associate with face-lift victims. 'As you can see this is nothing formal,' he continued, pressing Eli's bicep as he took in our attire, 'just a little spontaneous get-together with friends.'

A waiter interrupted, bearing a tray of champagne flutes, which made me wonder what Derek's more formal parties were like.

We walked to the bar. Not far from us, on the lawn, stood three movie moguls of great repute and wealth, men whose names routinely appeared on annual lists of America's richest citizens. Dimly I recalled Seamus having flayed them alive in *Queer Times* a few months back, calling them the 'troika of death,' or something on that order, because they had neither contributed enough money to AIDS groups nor helped to bring any of 'our stories' to the big screen. I nudged Eli. 'Oh dear,' he said.

'What's the matter?' asked Derek.

'I'm afraid we may have unintentionally committed a bit of a gaffe,' Eli said. 'You see, when you said "a few boys," I didn't think—' Vaguely he indicated the lawn. 'What I mean is, we've invited Seamus Holt to meet us here.'

Derek blanched. 'Oh my God! You've got to stop him!'

'But how?'

'Head him off at the pass! Go! Go! Hurry!' He pushed us toward the driveway. No doubt the velocity of his transformation from suave host to deranged harridan would have amused us if we hadn't been its cause. 'But how could we have known?' I asked Eli.

We got into Nora's battered station wagon. 'Which route do you think he'd take?'

'I assume the highway.'

Eli turned the key in the ignition. 'Do you even know what kind of car he drives?'

'Something Japanese. It's blue. Don't worry, I'll recognize it.' We turned onto Sagaponack Main Street. Nothing passed us, however. Nor was any car remotely resembling Seamus's to be seen at the traffic light on the Montauk Highway.

'Maybe he decided not to come,' Eli said hopefully.

'Let's drive to his house and see,' I suggested. But when we got there, no blue car – no car of any color – was to be found.

Very haltingly, then, and terrified lest we should find bloodshed when we got there, we made our way back to the party, where that blue car for which we had searched in vain, the sighting of which anywhere else would have eased our racing hearts, sat snugly parked outside Derek's sleek accretion of cubes. Eli switched off the engine. Almost lightheadedly we walked to the front door, which was open, crossed, once again, the exacting living room, and stepped into the garden. On the deck, price-tagged boys frolicked sluggishly. Some had taken off their Speedos. A few had jumped into the pool, where they were throwing a red ball back and forth.

We looked for Derek. He was nowhere to be seen. We looked for Seamus. Far away from us, near the dunes, he stood by himself, holding a beer, gazing out at the ocean. He seemed a very lonely figure, remote and elderly, especially when compared to his coevals, the 'troika of death,' all of whom, no doubt, worked out with personal trainers, and spent an hour each morning at a tanning salon. Currently they were collected near the bar, enmeshed by a protective suite of admirers. Someone appeared to be telling a joke; in a few seconds I heard the laughter that is often the secret weapon of those best trained in social warfare.

Then Derek, from the kitchen door, made a summoning gesture with his fingertips.

We followed. 'I'm sorry,' I said once we were inside.

'He must have taken a shortcut,' Eli added.

'Oh, it's all right, think nothing of it,' answered Derek, who had apparently had a belt of something in the interval. 'So far nothing's happened. Still, it might be a good idea if . . . you know . . .' He indicated Seamus with his elbow.

We understood. Patting Eli on the arm again, Derek went to talk with the 'troika,' one member of which smiled at us as we strolled out toward Seamus. In his 'dolled-up' outfit – purple shirt, tie-dyed bow tie – he looked both uncomfortable and disappointed.

'Sorry about this,' Eli said. 'We had no idea—'

'When he invited us all he said was "a few boys,"' I threw in.

'Oh, pshaw!' Seamus swatted the air. 'Anyway it's not your fault. It's just that I was thinking . . .' He grinned. 'Well, I suppose this is the price one pays for speaking one's mind. Anyway, I should skedaddle. Or should I say scuttle? Scuttle's more appropriate. Thanks for thinking of me. You were kind . . .' His voice trailed off. 'The thing is, I was absolutely convinced I was going to meet the great love of my life this afternoon, isn't that ridiculous? And who knows? He might even be here.'

'I doubt it, in this crowd.'

Seamus, apparently consoled by this suggestion, kissed us both on the cheek, and left. Having seen him out, Eli and I made our way back to the bar. It was our intention to apologize one last time to Derek, then get the hell out of there; before we had a chance, though, a voice from the direction of the pool called Eli's name. We turned. A giant of a fellow in running shorts and singlet, glib and thick-lipped and rudely handsome, was ambling toward us. 'Eli, what a surprise,' he said, and then he was kissing him, while I breathed in the strongly masculine scent radiating from under his arms. His name, I soon learned, was Jonathan Horowitz; he and Eli had gone to college together; he was an in-house lawyer at Disney. 'And what have you been doing all these years?' he asked Eli, throwing a brotherly arm around his shoulder. 'Have you been here all summer? Why haven't we seen each other? Oh, and how's Liza? Man, when I got that invitation to her wedding, I nearly slung a clot. I always thought she was a dyke.'

'She is,' Eli said, laughing, and for a few minutes, in that rushed, catching-up way of classmates, they chatted about reunions and jobs, friends they had shared, teachers who had died. It seemed that Jonathan was renting a house in Watermill for the season, sharing it with his boyfriend, a wonderful fellow, we had to meet him. 'Roy, come here!' he called. 'I want to introduce an old pal of mine.'

Roy turned. I couldn't help but smile. He had changed little in the year since I'd last seen him; indeed, in his pressed khakis and white polo shirt, he might merely have been the vacation version of that well-heeled gentleman about town, that paper doll, who not so long ago had carried me out of a dreary cafeteria and into a New York utterly remote from the one in which Eli and I tarried . . . Yes, there was something that seemed always fresh-minted about Roy; even when he was drunk or exhausted, he gave off an air of mercantile newness and possibility. If Eli was the ancient teddy bear whose rips and stains endow him with an ever-increasing pathos, Roy was the shiny toy robot each child feels he will die if he doesn't get for Christmas. His smile was bright, too bright: I wanted to squint against it, and bask in it too. 'Martin!' he called, bypassing Eli, whom Jonathan Horowitz was holding out to him like a fisherman with his catch, 'I can't believe it's you!' And taking my hand, he embraced me lightly, guyishly, but also with tenderness, filling my nostrils with a scent of limes that shook the past awake as brutally as smelling salts shoved under the nose of a fainting victim.

'Oh, you know each other?' Jonathan asked.

Roy nodded. 'And you must be Eli,' he went on, letting me go. 'What a pleasure finally to meet you. I'm Roy Beckett, by the way – Martin's biggest fan.'

He winked. Eli regarded him with clinical dispassion. Later I wondered whether, with the grasping memory of the jealous spouse, he had been holding onto Roy's name ever since that topsy-turvy afternoon in Florence when Lise Schiffrin had asked me about 'my handsome friend': Roy, roy-alty, king of hearts. The name itself roy-led the dark waters of his dreams withs its ad-royt-ness. For even the shape it imposed upon the lips was enough to give me away: the shape of a kiss.

We stood, then, the four of us, partners in an uncomfortable little square dance, while under our feet poles of habit and security shifted and the ground gave way. Roy asked about my new book: I told him it was coming out in a few weeks, then added clumsily – as if somehow it might soften the retribution I was expecting – 'Eli's got a novel coming out, too. It's terrific, better than mine.'

'No it's not.'

'Oh really? That's great. I can't wait to read it.' Roy felt in his pockets. 'Say, has anyone got a pen?'

'I do,' said Eli.

Roy was pulling a business card out of his wallet. 'I want to give you guys my number in Watermill,' he continued. 'Thanks' – he took Eli's pen – 'in case you have any free time over the next few days.'

'Roy's taking a week's vacation,' Jonathan explained. 'He doesn't have to drive back to Manhattan tonight like the rest of us poor slobs.'

'Oh, how funny,' Eli said, 'I'm planning to go into New York tomorrow morning myself.' He punched Jonathan lightly on the cheek. 'Well, Jon, at least we won't have to worry about the little women being bored, will we?'

'No, we'll have to worry about them *not* being bored.' They both laughed. Roy gave me his card. A grimace of distaste had crossed his face. Not twenty-four hours later, in his bed, he'd be telling me how much it irritated him when men referred to themselves or each other in the feminine. For now, however, the manful way he reached to shake my hand seemed comment enough. 'Good seeing you, Martin. And Eli – great to meet you.'

'Likewise.'

Then they disappeared, once again, into the party. In their absence, suddenly, Eli and I seemed to have nothing to say to each other.

'Well, ready to go?' I asked him after a minute.

'Whenever you are.'

So we bade our farewells to Derek and climbed into the car. We did not speak at all on the drive home. Almost as soon as we got there, Eli went to let out the dogs. I was just preparing a speech of self-defense, in which I would point out how unreasonable it was of him to resent an infidelity that had never taken place, when he came out of the kitchen. 'There's a message from your father,' he said. 'You'd better listen.'

'Really? What is it?'

I followed him back into the kitchen, where he pressed the play button on the answering machine. 'Hi, Martin,' I heard my father say. 'I'm sorry to be a pest, but I thought I should remind you that today is the anniversary of your mother's death, and if you haven't done so you ought to light a Yahrzeit candle. All's well here. My best to Eli.'

A click. I sat down at the table. 'Had you forgotten?' Eli asked.

I nodded. Stealing up behind me, he rubbed my shoulders, as weeks earlier he had rubbed Nora's. 'Oh, sweetheart,' he said, 'it's okay. The A&P should still be open. We can buy one there.'

'Can we?' Bad Jew that I was, I had no idea how easy (or difficult) it was to buy a Yahrzeit candle; indeed, I had only the vaguest conception of what a Yahrzeit candle was, though dimly I could recall my mother lighting one twice a year, on the anniversaries of her parents' deaths, a glass cup of wax glowing on the ledge behind the kitchen sink.

We drove to the A&P. Because East Hampton still cleared out at the end of every weekend in those years, there were at most half a dozen cars in the parking lot. Inside, only a single checkout lane was open. While Eli stocked up on groceries, I headed for the kosher section, where amid the chilly freezer-burn smell emanating from the ice cream cases I found, just as he had promised, a cache of Yahrzeit candles for $1.99 each. When I picked one up, dust blackened my fingers. Here it was, a thick cup of wax into which some uncaring thumb had pressed an aluminum wick like a sequin. Homely and crude. And not for the first time it startled me, the ease with which Judaism transforms its mystic symbols into common-place, even drab commodities: not only Yahrzeit candles, but the matzoh in its bright red and white boxes, so remote from the Old Testament's 'unleavened bread'; the lumps of gefilte fish in their cloudy juice, in big jars the labels of which listed as ingredients carp and pike, though my father had once told me that gefilte fish combined every fish in the sea. Of course there was no truth to that; the legend spoke more of his fancy than any tradition. Yet it had stayed with me over the years, from Passover to Passover, those dinners at which, being the youngest, I always got to ask the Four Questions . . . And then after dinner, in mimicry of the egg hunts of Easter, we would search the house for the piece of matzoh my father had wrapped in a paper napkin and hidden, pirates avid for the prize, which was not much of a prize really, only a few of those weird jelly candies, shaped like slices of orange and lemon, and of which, along with matzoh and gefilte fish, the A&P kept an ample supply . . . I threw my Yahrzeit candle into the cart and went to find Eli, who was in the fruit section.

After that, we loaded up on apple cider, milk, yogurt, muesli,

Pepperidge Farm cookies, Listerine, and cottage cheese, and got in line. Ahead of us a heavy man with a gray-flecked beard was smoking a cigar. Eli coughed. 'How gross,' he muttered, just loudly enough to be heard.

No response. The man took another puff, exhaled. Eli coughed a second time. Nothing. He jabbed the man in the back.

'Excuse me.'

'Yeah?'

'Would you mind thinking of other people for once and not smoking that disgusting thing in a public place?'

The man, who was taller than Eli by a head, turned and gazed down at him. 'What did you say?' he asked, laughing a little, as if he couldn't quite believe his ears.

People looked. 'Eli—' I whispered.

'I said, why don't you put that thing out? It's gross and self-ish.'

'Yeah, and why don't you shut the fuck up?'

'Yeah, and why don't you stuff that fucking cigar up your goddamned fat ass, asshole? Just get it out of my face.'

'What, you own the fucking store, buddy?'

'It's disgusting—'

'Just answer my question. You own the fucking store?'

'Eli, don't.' I pointed to the Yahrzeit candle.

'Oh great,' he said. 'Great.' Suddenly he was bearing down on me. 'Goddamn it, Martin, sometimes I wonder why I even bother. You won't support me when I try to defend myself. You are so fucked up. This whole thing is so fucked up. Excuse me.' He pushed at my cart. 'Excuse me.' The other people in the line stepped out of the way.

Then he was racing off, jumping the barrier at one of the closed lanes, flying out the automatic doors. Strangers gawked. Shaking his head, the man with the cigar said, 'Goddamn queer.'

I waited. What else could I do? With a curious delicacy the cashier rang up my total. 'That's twenty-two sixty-three, honey,' she said, her voice smug with what sounded like pity as I paid, took my bags, and hurried outside. Eli was already in the car, his brights trained on the supermarket doors. I loaded the groceries in the back and climbed in.

'Eli,' I said.

'Shut up.' Brights still on, he turned onto Newtown Lane. A man crossing the street cursed us. Eli gunned the engine, hurtled to a stop as the light on the corner of Main Street switched to red.

'I'll only say this once. I can't bear you anymore. Tonight I'm going home to my mother and you're not coming with me.'

I started to cry. 'How can you say that when I don't even have a mother?'

'How can you betray me – again? How can I trust you? You won't even stand up for me.' The light turned green, and we swerved around the corner.

'But you were overreacting! You were acting like a lunatic!'

'Oh, so when I defend myself I'm a lunatic? Jesus, just because I'm not a goddamned wimp like you.'

'I'm not a wimp.'

'You'd let anyone walk over you, Billie, Liza, your father.'

'Shut up.'

'Anyway, I should think you'd be glad I'm leaving, it'll give you a chance to fuck around with Roy what's-his-name.'

'I said shut up!'

'What, do you think I'm stupid? Do you think I haven't noticed that when you come back from your "walks" your clothes always smell like smoke? Or the condoms in your wallet.'

'How dare you search my wallet.'

'I can break any rule I want because I don't give a shit anymore.'

By now we were in Nora's driveway. Brakes screeched. Without even taking the key out of the ignition Eli slammed into the house, up the stairs, ignoring the plaintive eagerness of the dogs, who were closed inside the kitchen. 'Eli,' I called. 'Please don't be this way!'

'Go away!' he shouted through his study door.

'Eli, please! I'm not going away until you—'

'Leave me alone!' He was weeping. 'God, can't you ever leave anyone alone?'

'Not until you talk to me! Don't you know how you're hurting me?'

'Oh, so little Martin's hurt! Isn't that a pity! Is that all that matters to you your *own* fucking hurt? Well, fuck you, then, because the world doesn't revolve around your suffering, no matter what your mommy told you.'

'Don't talk about my mother anymore!' And I smashed my fist, hard, into the locked door. He was silent. My wrist throbbing, I backed down the stairs, to where the dogs were trying to nudge their way out of the kitchen. I let them go. They ran to Eli's door. Then I got the groceries from the car and put them away, very carefully, the milk in the refrigerator, the muesli in the pantry; I wiped the countertops; I scrubbed away some bits of food that were stuck to the inside of the sink. No noise . . . Stealing upstairs again I saw that Eli, in his study, had switched off the light, that the dogs were sleeping, all three, outside his door.

I went back downstairs. In the kitchen I lit the Yahrzeit candle and put it on the ledge behind the sink, as I recalled my mother having done; for a moment the flame jerked, as if uncertain whether it wanted to catch, before taking hold. Then I took off my glasses and gazed at it. Shadows flew over the table. In the dark mirror of the window a moon was rising over cabinets, rivulets of hurled light, my own face, which might have been my mother's. How far away she seemed – as far as the moon! Yet somehow she was also there, in that flame that writhed like a gypsy, a fierce little dancing girl, mutely convulsed by pity, pain, and love.

13

Flint's Limp

HARRIET DIDN'T want to go to the Rosh Hashanah service; indeed, if it hadn't been for her grandchildren, who were visiting at the time, she probably would have just stayed home, in the defiant hope of showing, by her very absence, how fiercely she disapproved of the rabbi's conduct. For he was having a rather flagrant affair with the *shiksa* organist, of which everyone in the congregation except his wife was vividly aware. The illicit couple had even been seen kissing, one afternoon, in the back rose garden, in broad daylight, as if they wanted to be caught, as if a wish to incur his own ruin were part and parcel of the midlife crisis through which the rabbi was so obviously suffering.

Still, for the grandchildren's sake, she stifled her pride and went anyway. There was a strong missionary impulse in Harriet; to instill in them (as well as in me) a passion for that religion about which they had been so ill educated, she was willing to put aside even the desire to make a point. So she had her nails done, put on a stoic red dress, and prepared to drive to the synagogue. It was a mild fall morning. Like Eli and his father, I was dressed soberly, in a black suit and pressed white shirt; a stiff little yarmulke was pinned into my hair. Though in my childhood I'd been taken a few times to synagogues, usually for the bar mitzvahs of cousins, until today I'd never been to a Rosh Hashanah service; nor did those modest synagogues of my childhood in any way prepare me for the grandeur of the edifice to which the Aronsons drove me that afternoon: a palatial structure of glass and glimmering steel, designed by a famous architect, and containing within its groomed, grassy confines not merely the temple itself, but a school, a community center, a cemetery, a playground, and a halfway house wherein Russian émigrés, their ransom paid by the members of the congregation, were taught the skills necessary to negotiate American life – all a far cry from the tiny Lower East Side shuls at which our grandfathers had worshipped, and where Sara Rosenzweig's grandfather worshipped still.

That I was there at all was pure compromise, the upshot, like so much else in those weeks, of extended negotiations not only between Eli and me, but between my desire to be free and my fear of losing, along with him, the stability of which his family had become my only source. For I was in the throes, right then, of an affair with Roy Beckett, and he had made it clear early on that if I ever expected to meet *his* family, I was badly mistaken. '*No one* meets them,' he said when I asked him. 'No one.' End of discussion. This affair, which I had not been able to keep from Eli, he had for the last few weeks been enduring 'for the sake of our relationship,' he said – a leniency on his part at once generous and stupid, since in such a situation tolerance, rather than bringing the crisis to a head, only serves to perpetuate it. Every day was a mediation. If I went, say, to a benefit dinner with Roy one night, in exchange I would have to go somewhere with Eli the next – in

this case, to his parents' house for the Rosh Hashanah festivities. And what a contrast Harriet's brisket-smelling kitchen
presented to the sleek apartment at which, the evening before,
I'd gone with Roy to a housewarming party, all men in their
twenties and thirties, good-looking, well paid! In that glossy,
underfurnished living room with its views of the 59th Street
Bridge, under track lighting, we had chatted with a pair of
bankers about the advantages of Dutchess County over the
Hamptons. Every ring of the doorbell brought another bottle
of vodka in a brown paper bag. Someone put the new
Madonna album – *True Blue,* I think – on the stereo.

And then, the next morning, an early train out to Long
Island, where Eli, who had gone the night before, picked me
up at the station; drove me to his parents' house, dressed me
hastily in a borrowed suit and tie. In the kitchen, Harriet was
making noodle kugel, there was everywhere the bustle of holiday preparation, the smell of singed oven mitts. For old time's
sake I rode the Stair-a-Lator up and down, up and down, and
then we all piled into Eli's father's Mercedes and drove to
that lavish synagogue with its pearwood *bimah,* its torah
scrolls behind bulletproof glass. The temple itself was high-
ceilinged, and crowded, as the ceremony began, with perhaps
five hundred celebrants, all nattily dressed, cozily affluent,
the hair of the old women piled high in elaborate coifs, the
youngest boys eager to be outside getting grass stains on the
knees of their suits. Finally the rabbi emerged, in his fine vestments, a robust, bearded man whose face, for some reason,
reminded me of Stanley Flint's. Clearing his throat, he told a
few jokes, then began to sing, in a lovely, full-throated baritone, while above him, in her gallery, the red-haired organist
pushed keys and pedals, and brushed the curls out of her
eyes.

I looked at Harriet. She had her eyes fixed not on the rabbi,
not even on his mistress, but rather on her own nails. And

what was she thinking about? Adulteries – her own or her husband's – or mine? Or was she feeling sorry for the rabbi's wife, or the *shiksa* organist, or me, or Eli? I couldn't guess.

It was now time for the rabbi to blow the *shofar* – that primitive trumpet, forged from a ram's horn, with which the Jewish New Year is ushered in. Around me I heard backs stiffening: after all, this is the crucial moment in any Rosh Hashanah ceremony, the moment of highest drama, in which the moan of history itself must be viscerally sounded. And so the rabbi picked up the *shofar*, blew mightily once, twice, a third time less mightily, then swayed and suddenly crumpled to the floor. Someone screamed. The organist leapt to her feet.

What had happened? Had he been shot? Had the roar of the *shofar* masked the firing of a bullet? No, apparently, for there was no blood. 'Is there a doctor in the house?' a voice cried, almost comically, as if we were in a theater, and then – this being an affluent synagogue in suburban Long Island – twenty doctors descended, swarming like ants around the stricken rabbi. People held their breath. Some of the older congregants prayed in Hebrew, their voices a low mutter of entreaty, directed toward a deity to whose prankishness and ill-temper they had long since learned to accommodate themselves. And then from the swarm one of the doctors called, 'Does anyone have any nitroglycerine?' at which point – this being an affluent synagogue in suburban Long Island – a dozen old and middle-aged men swept down onto the temple floor, calling 'I do! I do!' each eager to be the provider of the magic lozenge that, once slipped under the rabbi's tongue, would bring him back to life.

As for the organist, from her perch I watched her gazing down, eyes wider than ever, presumably trying to edit her anguish down to a level that would appear commensurate with a merely 'professional' connection. In the meantime the assistant rabbi – a girl my age – had been summoned from the auxiliary chamber in which up until that moment she had been leading the children (including Eli's nieces) in a sort of junior version of the service. Now, with the breathless self-assurance of emergency, she ascended to the lectern and swiftly raised her hands into the air. There she stood, the young understudy suddenly given, as a consequence of the elderly star's attack, the opportunity of her life. It was *All About Eve* all over again. 'Let us pray,' she intoned.

One of the doctors stood. 'His heart's beating!' he cried, and applause – the applause of relief – burst forth. Suddenly Harriet, as if in atonement for the vengeful thoughts she had been harboring about the rabbi, burst into a fit of weeping, as paramedics swept through and with agile efficiency lifted him onto a stretcher and carried him away.

'I know,' the assistant rabbi said – no one was listening; she pressed her lips to the microphone – 'I *know* that Rabbi Meyer would have wanted us to bring the ceremony through to its conclusion.'

Quiet then, heads turned. 'And so let us welcome the New Year by sounding the *shofar*.'

Picking the thing up, she blew. Alas, however, she did not have her predecessor's lungs, for instead of a mighty roar there issued forth only a series of shrill bleats. 'Let us pray,' she repeated.

After the ceremony ended, we took a walk through the synagogue's rose garden. 'It seems so sad,' Harriet said, bending down to smell some late buds of Perle d'Or.

'Yes, but it could have been worse,' said Marty. 'If it had happened when he was alone, when there were no doctors around, he could have died.'

'That's not what I meant.' She picked a rose. 'What I meant was – oh, Eli, why do people always make such a hash of their lives?'

'I don't know. Why do they?' He looked at me.

Taking her husband's hand, Harriet turned quickly, and began leading him toward the parking lot.

After lunch – the brisket I'd smelled that morning, and glazed carrots, and sweet potatoes – I asked Eli to drive me to the station. 'I need to be back in the city by six,' I told him.

'But I was hoping you'd stay the night!' he said, paling suddenly, his stalwart confidence suddenly crumbling like dried-out make-up.

'Eli, you know that wasn't part of our agreement.'

'Still, I thought that maybe, once you got here . . . well, that you'd decide you wanted to stay.'

'But I'm going to Stanley Flint's reading!'

'Won't there be other readings?'

'But it's sold out! I've already bought the ticket!' I glanced at my clock. 'Look, if you'd rather, I could call a taxi—'

'No, no, I'll drive you. Come on.' And grabbing a set of keys from a hook over his mother's kitchen desk, he stormed into the garage. I followed. 'What are you getting so upset about?' I asked once we were in the car. 'It's not like I pulled a switcheroo.'

'No, you haven't.'

'In fact, I've stuck to the plan exactly as we mapped it out.'

'And are you going to the reading alone?'

'Yes – though of course I'll probably see people I know there. Julia Baylor, for one, I'm sure will be going.'

'And Roy?'

'I told you, Roy's out of town.'

'Hmm.'

'What, you think I'm lying?'

'I didn't say that.'

'Oh, great. So now I tell you the truth and you assume—'

'There's something I need to talk to you about,' Eli interrupted. 'I've been thinking about it for a long time, and I've decided to get an HIV test next week.'

'Why?'

'I've already made the appointment. And I also think . . . well, let's just say that I think it would be strongly advisable for you to have one too.'

'But, Eli, we've talked about this.' He raced a yellow light; I cranked the window open. 'I mean, you know how I feel . . . God, what is it with you today? It's like, just because I'm leaving, you have to bring up some subject, at the very last minute, that you know is going to upset me, in order to make sure I get on the train miserable.'

Eli sighed loudly. 'Oh, if you could only see beyond your own anxieties for once—'

'But my anxieties are real!'

' – you'd realize that I'm suggesting this for your own good. The fact is, Jonathan wanted me to tell you weeks ago, and I didn't, because I felt it wasn't my place . . . only now I can't help but feel—'

'Jonathan? What Jonathan?'

'Jonathan Horowitz. I never mentioned it to you, but last month I went to a meeting for prospective GMHC buddies – you know, where you go and help out someone who has AIDS – and he was one of the facilitators. He's very unhappy about the way Roy broke off their relationship. Very abruptly. And he asked me to tell you – for your sake – well, that Roy doesn't always practice safe sex, even though he says he does. There. Which is why, in my opinion, you ought to have the test.'

'But that's stupid! Anyway, Roy and I always use condoms.'

'Condoms can break. You know that.'

We arrived at the station. Five minutes remained before the train was supposed to come in. Pulling into a parking space, Eli switched off the ignition.

'I wish you'd consulted me,' I said after a moment, 'before making that appointment.'

'Why? What business is it of yours?'

'Well, Eli, you know very well—'

'What?'

'It's just that in the past we agreed that this was something we'd do, if we did it, together. Unless you're saying you no longer think of us as being together.'

'Do you?'

'Oh God, why do you have to put such pressure on?'

'*I'm* putting pressure on!'

'So what are you saying, that you want to break up?'

'It sounds to me like that's what *you're* saying.'

'No I'm not.'

'And Roy?'

I was silent. 'We've been through this already.'

He put his head against the steering wheel. 'Oh, Christ,' he said. 'I just can't believe it.'

'But I can't help what I feel!'

'If you'd chosen someone worthy of you, Martin, then at least I could have the consolation of not having to fear for your soul – not to mention your life – but Roy Beckett! A black Republican! A *gay* black Republican, for Christ's sake—'

'That's not fair.'

'Or maybe I overestimated you. Maybe people just find their natural level, and yours is lower than I ever believed – hoped.'

'No, it's not.'

'Well, at the very least you can wear that yarmulke when you fuck him.'

I slammed out of the car. In the distance the train, its nose like a basset hound's, was edging against the haze. Then it neared, slowed, stopped. I climbed aboard. Through a dirty window I looked to see if Eli was waiting for me, if he was going to run after me, if he was going to follow me onto the train. For I think I could hear, even then, the seams tearing; I think I knew this was our last opportunity, and that both of us, perhaps to our lasting regret, were going to flee it.

After that I rode to New York, to Penn Station, where I got on the subway and headed uptown. Here I was, living alone in Glenn's apartment, Eli having decided, a few days earlier, to throw out his subletter and move back, with Maisie, to Elizabeth Street. ('So long as you are carrying on with Roy,' he'd written at the time, 'I simply cannot bear to live in a space so emblematic of our failed "marriage"; much better for me to be surrounded by my own possessions, my bed, my books, my futon, my battered pots and pans: in short, things that help me remember the life I had – that I had a life – before I met you.') And how strange, I thought (stepping through the door), that of all the places on earth I might have ended up, it should be here, in the one place I'd always felt least at home, that I should find myself obliged to create, at least for the time being, some semblance of a home. For I hadn't the heart to throw out Baylor as Eli, so much more capricious, had thrown out his NYU student. Instead I'd agreed, reluctantly, to stick it out at Glenn's until he got back from Florence, figuring that in any case I'd spend most of my nights at Roy's. Only tonight Roy was away, in Chicago. In my wallet, scrawled on a corner of the *New York Times*, I had the number of his hotel, which I dialed.

'Roy Beckett,' he answered in his room, as he did at his office.

'It's me,' I said.

'Oh, hi!' (Was he glad to hear from me? His tone of unyielding cheerfulness made it hard to say.)

'How are you?'

'How are *you*?'

'Oh, Roy,' I said. 'God, I wish you were here in New York tonight, and we were planning to go out to dinner together, and to a movie, and then home—'

He drew in his breath. 'Wait, someone's at the door.' A hand over the mouthpiece. Then: 'Sorry, Martin? I've got to dash. Business. I'll call you later, okay?'

'No problem. Bye.'

'Bye.' He hung up. And how stupid of me, I thought (putting down Glenn's black phone), to have used the word 'home,' when Roy had made it so vividly clear that I was never, under any circumstances, to think of his apartment as anything more than a place where I was welcome *as a guest*! Not that he'd ever said as much; he was far too polite to make statements; instead he'd simply never bothered to give me a key, or empty a drawer for me, or clear a few hangers in the closet, though I slept there half the nights of each week. For there were always limits with Roy; his whole life, when you thought about it, was constructed of limits, restraints, shut doors (his parents, whom I was never to meet, his childhood, even his blackness) – so many of them that in his company (dared I admit it) I often found myself missing the impulsiveness, even the recklessness, that had led Eli and me to make our quick leap from blind date to trial marriage. No doubt it had been rash of us – indeed, if we'd been more careful, I knew, I might not have found myself in the dilemma I was in now – yet what fun it had been!

No, I reflected – moving into the bedroom, preparing to dress for Stanley Flint's reading – in the end this weird flat with its red-shaded sconces and homemade videos was probably as much a home to me as any of the many rooms I'd slept in over the years: my studio, and Eli's with its high loft, and Liza's with its little fireplace, its messy books, its face-sized television. At Eli's parents' house, yes, there I'd felt at home; yet now, from Park Avenue, I was banished, as I was effectively banished even from the house where I'd grown up, not because my father had willed it, but because my fear of running into Mrs Keller made me reluctant to go back. My dorm rooms, the ones I'd shared with Jim Sterling and Donald Schindler, had long since passed into other hands, as had the old apartment on West End Avenue where I'd taken Ricky, and befriended Faye. Which left me – where? – exactly here, among Glenn's skulls and brocades, his photo of Nureyev, what Eli so cleverly called his 'little black wall.'

And so it was from a place I would never have guessed I'd have ended up living that I set out, that September evening, by myself, to hear Stanley Flint give his reading at the 92nd Street Y. Uptown I walked, through warm winds and that smell of bread rising from subway grates to which I'd once thrilled, past Korean markets where women in business suits and tennis shoes, pumps in their briefcases, were picking out plums, past paid walkers leading tangles of dogs – five or six together – out toward the park. This was New York, the city in which I had always wanted to live, and where today I did live, after a fashion, along with Liza, and Eli, and Stanley Flint, and all its other denizens. And then I was at the Y, outside of which an eager crowd had already gathered, no doubt drawn by Flint's interview with Bill Moyers (it had aired the night before), or perhaps by Henry Deane's review, which had just come out in the *Times* or perhaps by the fact that *The Writing Teacher* had recently hit the bestseller list at number seven. 'Anybody got a ticket?' I heard a man shout, and pushed past him, just as years before I'd pushed past the journalists trying to get into the TV star's theatrical premiere, just as before that I'd pushed those students whose names, unlike mine, hadn't been 'on the list' to claim my rightful place in Stanley Flint's seminar: all rather fatiguing, this constant pushing past. Still, I handed in my ticket; stepped through a pair of wide doors into that inner sanctum, the auditorium itself, where people milled more quietly. Not far off I noticed Julia Baylor, with whom I rarely socialized these days, though she lived in my apartment. Never comfortable alone, she hurried up to me, slipped a bejeweled arm through mine. 'We'll sit together, is that all right?' she asked.

'Of course.'

'A real gathering of the clan tonight,' Baylor went on – and with her elbow, pointed out the boy with the wire-rimmed spectacles. 'Silvery's here too,' she added. 'You know she's a senior editor at Morrow. And look over there!' It was Mittman, shy in a business suit and tennis shoes, probably with her pumps in her briefcase.

After a few minutes we sat down. Though Baylor was talking, avidly, however, and about any number of things – her new boyfriend, who was French; the allure of Paris; oh, and could I give her any tips on running the dishwasher, because somehow no matter which detergent she used, the glasses always came out spotty? – the crowd funneling into the theater had captivated my attention too thoroughly for me to catch much of what she said. For among the faces flowing past, in addition to our former classmates, I could recognize all sorts of people I knew: several Amys, and Henry Deane's agent, and Janet Klass, looking sleek and scholarly in a beige linen jacket and matching skirt. No Marge though, and no Carey. And most disappointingly, no Liza, though her mother – dressed as always in a tartan skirt, a ruffled blouse – could be spied holding court near the stage, where all the seats had 'Reserved' signs taped to them. And then, to my utter surprise – for she was the last person I would have expected to see here, or for that matter anywhere, ever again – the florid woman who had strode up to me in the Hudson-Terrier lobby and demanded to see the editor, thus precipitating the end of my career as a slush reader, passed through the doors. I smiled. I almost waved. She must not have recognized me, though, for she walked right past us, right down the aisle, and took one of the seats with the 'Reserved' signs taped to them.

Then the lights dimmed, the crowd hushed, Sada and her cronies hurried to their places. A bony little man in a brown suede jacket stepped out onto the stage. 'Hello,' he said, his voice a barely audible stutter, 'my name is Leonard Trask, and it's my pleasure, tonight, to introduce my friend and teacher, Stanley Flint . . .'

Leonard Trask! I looked at Baylor, whose gaze was fixed on his glasses. But it was impossible! I wanted to shout. How could Leonard Trask – whom Flint, we must remember, had discovered when he was still a mineworker in Montana, and who was by all accounts a ferocious figure, of Hemingwayesque proportion – how could this little man, with his mumbly tonalities and his bald spot, be he? Why, he would have looked as out of place drilling in a mine as he did here, on the stage of the 92nd Street Y in New York City, babbling and spitting and expressing his incoherent gratitude to have been given this honor, this privilege, the opportunity to introduce, tonight, a great writer . . . Stanley Flint.

Applause, then. Cane thrust forward, Flint limped onto the stage. His eyes blazed; his beard, glinting in the footlights, looked as if it were studded with mica. 'Good evening,' he said, in his familiar stentorian voice, his classroom voice, and put a copy of *The Writing Teacher* on the lectern. 'Tonight I'm going to read to you – it probably won't surprise you – from my novel *The Writing Teacher*. An early chapter, about youth, which is always a dangerous subject. You may have noticed that I walk with a cane . . . Many people have asked me, over the years, why this is. What happened to my leg. Well, the chapter I'm going to read tonight amounts to an explanation, albeit not necessarily the true one.' A low murmur of laughter. Flint cleared his throat. 'So . . . onward. Chapter Three. The Leg.'

Baylor gasped. 'Oh, I love this part,' she whispered, and pulling a copy of the novel – much dog-eared, stuck through with Post-it Notes – out of her purse, opened it to Chapter Three.

Then Flint began to read, and what he read undid me, not only because it was great, but because it offered a rare glimpse into those muddy depths, the Flintness of Flint, by which as a student I had been so maddened and mystified. In those days, after all, Flint's limp, like every other facet of his character, had been the subject both of speculation and rumor. It was said that a jealous lover had shot him; that during his rodeo days (also unsubstantiated) a horse had thrown him; that it was Hemingway himself, during a barroom brawl precipitated by the young Flint's daring to call the great man 'a phony,' who had administered the crucial blow. And yet, if the story he read tonight was to be believed, then the explanation for his limp was both less alluring and more terrible than anything his idolatrous students could have invented. Put crudely, it was the story of a gregarious child made outcast by his peers. The harder he struggles to gain their approbation, the more coldly they disdain him, until finally, in a bid to win their attention, he becomes a clown. The other children, glad as always for the cheap spectacle of foolishness, egg him on. He willingly mistakes their mockery for appreciation. Then one day, on a dare, he runs in front of a bus as it turns a corner; the bus mows him down; his left leg is crushed, and must be amputated at the knee. ('Oh, the clownish longing,' he read, 'of those who have not been loved for what they are!')

This, then, was the unhappy yet eminently commonplace story of Flint's limp – a story he related, that night, in a voice at once grave and uninflected, and lacking utterly in those oratorical flourishes that had distinguished, say, his readings of Leonard Trask or Nancy Coleridge, back when Baylor and

I were his students. For it seemed that he too had reached the conclusion that certain episodes must be told simply or not at all. The pleasure they provide is that of naked empathy. Indeed, it was only as he put his book down that I remembered the question with which he had been rumored to open his seminars in the old days (though in truth I'd never heard him ask it): would you be willing to sacrifice a limb in order to write a sentence as good as the one that opens *A Portrait of The Artist as a Young Man*?

After the reading ended, in the lobby, Flint sat at a card table and signed copies of *The Writing Teacher*. Acolytes and aspirants – dozens of us – we waited patiently as the line snaked forward. And what would I say to him when I reached its head? Something – but how to phrase it? – about the way that art slices right through all that nonsense . . . no, to say that would be to add to the nonsense, not to art. Much better to strike just the right balance between judiciousness and praise, to indicate in the space of a few words not merely that his reading had moved me, but that I understood *why* it had moved me . . . And then I was there, hovering over him (so much more demeaning, this posture, than that of the supplicant, who kneels) while he gazed up at me, eyes vague, as if he couldn't quite connect my face with my name.

'Martin Bauman,' I said, to help him along.

He smiled – 'Oh, Bauman, of course!' – and shook my hand. 'You'll forgive me, so many of my darlings are here tonight I'm rather overwhelmed. Well, you're looking fine, I must say. And what are you up to these days? I must tell you, in my last weeks there the offices of Hudson-Terrier seemed a sorrier place without your loud and cheerful presence.'

I grinned. How I still longed for his approval!

'Actually, my own novel's about to come out,' I volunteered.

'Is it? Congratulations.'

'To you, too. Not that I've read *The Writing Teacher*' – where had all my fine speeches gone? – 'I've only read the part about me, and I just want to say—'

'About you?'

'Well, about Simon, as you call him. And I just want to say that if you ever saw me standing across the street from your apartment building, it was because I used to live across the street from your apartment building.'

'But why is this relevant?'

'Well, I wouldn't want—'

'Bauman, you disappoint me. Recall what Beethoven said when the violinist complained that his part in a quartet was too difficult.'

'What?'

'"Do you really believe I'm thinking about your miserable fiddle when I write?"'

I laughed, as did several people behind me in the line; as usual Flint's anecdotes, even when offered at my expense, both charmed and amazed me. Then I backed away, leaving him to less compromised admirers. On and on the line wove, full of men and women in whose faces you could see reflected that rare purity of appreciation that comes when a work of art, entirely on its own terms, changes – no, not the world (Seamus, on this point we will always disagree) – but our souls. As for Flint, he shook hands, he sat and signed, tired and faintly embarrassed, the unwitting crafter of the well-crafted thing. Because of the thing – the book – dignified rooms welcomed him, this outpost of culture and civility welcomed him. Yet not far off those voices – the voices of taunting children – could still be heard, just as what had driven him here, like a missing limb, could still be felt: the longing of those who have been hated for what they are to be loved for what they have made.

ARKANSAS

David Leavitt

'David Leavitt's writing has a polish and suavity
which can only enchant. In this collection of three excellent
novellas, he tackles the surprising, painful emergence of
jealousy between carers for an Aids patient, sexual pursuit
among gay and straight Americans in Italy (rendered not with
farcical energy but with honest suffering), and a novelist
selling academic papers for sexual favours (deliciously
funny). Perfect. Leavitt's best book for years'
Mail on Sunday

'A literary triumph'
Independent

'Leavitt is a real writer. He tells stories, creates characters
and turns every human moment he touches, however
mundane, into compelling fiction'
Scott Bradfield, *TLS*

'A must-read book, linking wit and compassion
to laser-sharp descriptions of the minutiae of life'
Marie Claire

'Excellent . . . a pleasure to read'
Spectator

Abacus
0 349 11042 5

THE PAGE TURNER

David Leavitt

At eighteen, Paul Porterfield aspires to play the piano
at the world's great concert halls. So far the closest he has
come has been to turn pages of sheet music for his idol, the
dashing, temperamental Richard Kennington, a former piano
prodigy on the cusp of middle age. Months later Paul
encounters Richard on holiday in Italy. As the innocence
of first love becomes entangled with the quest for a more
enduring happiness, Paul comes to realise that he cannot
be a page turner all his life and that he has to
confront his ambitions.

'Gripping . . . Leavitt has always been an erotic and erudite
writer but in *The Page Turner* his elegance has acquired a
greater emotional depth. Bravo'
Evening Standard

'A beautifully written, elegant story . . . perfect'
Time Out

'Pleasurable, orderly, sophisticated –
and as readable as its punning title signifies'
Independent

'Shrewdly insightful . . . Leavitt's deceptively easy style
covers a lot of ground with seemingly little effort'
Gay Times

Abacus
0 349 10952 4

Now you can order superb titles directly from Abacus

☐	The Page Turner	David Leavitt	£6.99
☐	While England Sleeps	David Leavitt	£7.99
☐	Arkansas	David Leavitt	£6.99
☐	Family Dancing	David Leavitt	£6.99

──────────── ⬭ ABACUS ⬭ ────────────

Please allow for postage and packing: Free UK delivery.
Europe: add 25% of retail price; Rest of World: 45% of retail price.

To order any of the above or any other Abacus titles, please call our
credit card orderline or fill in this coupon and send/fax it to:

Abacus, 250 Western Avenue, London, W3 6XZ, UK.
Fax 020 8324 5678   Telephone 020 8324 5517

☐ I enclose a UK bank cheque made payable to Abacus for £ . . . .
☐ Please charge £ . . . . . . to my Access, Visa, Delta, Switch Card No.

☐☐☐☐☐☐☐☐☐☐☐☐☐☐☐☐☐☐☐

Expiry Date ☐☐☐☐   Switch Issue No. ☐☐

NAME (Block letters please) . . . .

ADDRESS . . . .

. . . .

. . . .

Postcode . . . . Telephone . . . .

Signature . . . .

Please allow 28 days for delivery within the UK. Offer subject to price and availability.
Please do not send any further mailings from companies carefully selected by Abacus ☐